They're Here . . .

Joe paused just inside the open garage door, holding the pump-action shotgun in both hands in front of him against his chest. He peered out into the night. Something was wrong—he could sense it but couldn't put a finger on it. A moment later he realized what it was—*silence*. For the first time since he had moved to the city, Joe couldn't hear *anything*. Besides being the city that never sleeps, New York was also the city that was never *quiet*. There was *always* sound of some kind going on, no matter what time of day or night it was. But now, Joe heard *nothing*. No sirens, no distant music, no hum of traffic, not even the sound of airplanes overheard—all of which were normal, constant background noise in the Big Apple.

It was eerie.

For the first time since this nightmare started, Joe felt an overwhelming sense of despair. He realized just how *bad* things really were. This was not a dream he would awaken from. This was not a disaster, like a fire or a hurricane, that the city and the people would recover from. This was not a terrorist attack that people could fight back against and rally round the flag and the president—go to war and kick some ass and get a sense of vengeance.

No. This was the end of the world.

'VADERS

R. Patrick Gates

PINNACLE BOOKS
Kensington Publishing Corp.
www.Kensingtonbooks.com

PINNACLE BOOKS are published by

Kensington Publishing Corp.
850 Third Avenue
New York, NY 10022

All Kensington titles, imprints, and distributed lines are available at special quantity discounts for bulk purchases for sales promotions, premiums, fund-raising, educational, or institutional use. Special book excerpts or customized printings can also be created to fit specific needs. For details, write or phone the office of the Kensington special sales manager: Kensington Publishing Corp., 850 Third Avenue, New York, NY 10022, attn: Special Sales Department; phone 1-800-221-2647.

ISBN-13: 978-0-7860-1825-3
ISBN-10: 0-7860-1825-9

First printing: July 2007

10 9 8 7 6 5 4 3 2 1

This book is dedicated to "Sissy" who knows what for. . . .
And to my wife . . . just for.

In the beginning ...

The outer rim of the Milky Way galaxy

At the edge of the galaxy, where the most remote stars of the Milky Way face the vast, deep blackness of interstellar space, there is movement where no movement should be. There is light where no light should be—a second's shimmering in the solid darkness. There is a sprinkling of silver, like the scales of a fish caught in a submerged beam of sunlight for a moment, and it is gone. But the blackness of space *moves*. It swirls and roils; it expands like a great black thunderhead that plumes and boils, belching up the inky blackness of deep space ... and something else.

In a silent explosion, a spray of shimmering lights bursts forth from the blackness like a golden sun shower. Spinning and whirling, they form together into a swarm and take on a distinctive pattern—the most common pattern in the universe—*a spiral*.

The spiral revolves and the swarm moves. Traveling near the speed of light, the swarm reaches the outskirts of our solar system. In less than a second, the swarm whirls through the Oort Cloud of comets and on past the nomadic asteroids of the Kuiper Belt. In seconds it streaks past Pluto, Neptune, Uranus, through the rings of Saturn and past massive Jupiter. Over and around Demos and Phoebus, the moons of dusty red Mars, the swarm swirls like a sparkling snake, or a glittering magical river. Ahead lays Earth, a dazzling blue-and-green gem compared to its naked, barren moon, shining golden with reflected sunlight. The swarm pauses and slows. The arms of the spiral tighten like the lens of a camera focusing before it moves on again. Streaking toward the Moon and over it, less than a hundred feet above its cratered surface, the swarm approaches the horizon, where Earth rises beautifully blue and inviting.

The swarm accepts the invitation and descends toward the planet. There is a flash of red as the mass of light breaches the atmosphere, but the flames of atmospheric friction do not hurt it, do not slow it. The swarm falls furiously, passing through clouds thick and thin. Emerging from high cover, it spirals down over the vast planet. Lower and lower it spins, over land now and spreading out. The first arm of the spiral descends over flooded fields of rice. A gray ribbon appears below, a giant winding wall girdling the land like a stone belt.

The swarm rushes toward it. . . .

Day One: Sunday

China. 11:00 p.m.

On the Great Wall, Captain Chin looked at the night sky and thought he was seeing a meteor shower, but it was unlike any he had seen before. Being an amateur astronomer with a decent-size telescope, Chin had witnessed quite a few meteor showers and knew what he was seeing now looked at first like shooting stars, but moved with too much of a discernible *pattern*. To him it looked like a glittering version of a hypnotist's trance-inducing revolving spiral.

"Hey! Look!" he called in Mandarin Chinese to his men standing outside the modern guardhouse on the ancient wall. His best friend and second in command, Lieutenant Lor, immediately ran into the guardhouse and came out with binoculars. He trained them on the sky lights.

"What the hell is that?" Lieutenant Lor asked Captain Chin while he focused and refocused the field glasses.

"I don't know," Chin answered slowly. He could see the dazzling array of lights more clearly now, and noticed that the spiral cloud was made up of individual light orbs of varying size, none larger than a human eyeball, most as small as peas. Captain Chin didn't like it. He didn't know why but seeing the lights brought a tingle of fear to the back of his neck. A moment later, the captain's sense of trepidation increased—the orbs descended faster and were less than fifty feet above him. Only now, he realized, they weren't falling, they were *flying;* like insects in a swarm or birds in a flock.

Two Red Army soldiers came running along the wall to where Captain Chin and Lieutenant Lor stood watching the heavenly display.

Lieutenant Lor called to the two soldiers, asking why they had left their post. As Lor spoke, one of the eyeball-size luminous orbs flew into his open mouth and down his throat.

The lieutenant gagged, coughed, and groaned, struggling for breath. He tried to expectorate the thing in his throat, but reflex took over and he swallowed hard, feeling the orb go down. He took a deep breath, looked at Captain Chin, and laughed nervously.

"Was that some kind of bug?" he asked.

"Are you okay?" Chin asked in return.

"I think so," Lor replied. It was the last thing he would ever say. His head suddenly snapped back with a loud *crack!* and his body jerked—arms and legs stretching out like an opera singer reaching a crescendo. His entire body began to jiggle, then convulse. Several more loud cracking sounds were followed by disgustingly *squishy* sounds emanating from within his body.

Lieutenant Lor began to grow.

He shot up five feet, and his clothes nearly exploded off him. The flesh of his abdomen rippled as if something were crawling just under the skin. It bulged and the ripples spread out from his stomach, reaching every part of his anatomy. He continued his epileptic dance, looking like a marionette on speed. All the while his legs, arms, feet, hands, fingers, facial features, and torso *grew*. He reached ten feet, fifteen, twenty! Every part of his body, except for his sexual organs, expanded proportionately to the size of every other part until Lieutenant Lor no longer existed.

In his place now stood something out of a nightmare.

It was twenty feet tall, bulging with muscles and naked, though lacking any discernible genitalia. Its head was massive, and shaved as Lor's had been. Three stubby, hornlike protrusions jutted from the top of its forehead. The new creature's eyes retained no semblance of their former self; they were now huge and bulging bloodshot from their sockets, the pupils reptilian and leering at Captain Chin. Lor's nose became a great, fleshy blob over a mouth that stretched from ear to ear and was filled with row upon row of daggerlike teeth, each nearly a foot long. His ears were large like a bat's, the tops sprouting whiskers and splitting into three pointed sections that moved constantly, like a cat's tail.

Captain Chin, Lor's lifelong best friend and superior officer, was struck dumb by Lor's rapid transformation. His first thought was that his friend had turned into a gargoyle; he looked just like stone gargoyles Chin had seen in pictures of cathedrals in France and Germany. He stared in disbelief but soon became a convert, paying the greatest price. The thing that had been Lieutenant Lor snatched Captain Chin with both hands, snapped him in two, and shoveled the bloody halves of its former friend's body into its mouth. A chew and a swallow later, the monster grabbed the two soldiers who also had been frozen in deadly disbelief at what they saw. They were ingested quickly.

The swarm of lights moved on. It descended on a nearby village, followed by the raging beast that had been Lieutenant Lor. In the sky over the rest of China, more spiraling swarms descended.

France. 4:20 p.m.

On the Eiffel Tower, Loretta Gleason was out of breath, her back hurt, and her feet were throbbing from a day of shopping and sightseeing, not to mention the trip up the stairs to the top level of this infernal Erector set. Of course, Bebe had insisted they *climb* the tower instead of using the elevators. Still, it was worth it just to see the look of excitement and joy on her daughter Bebe's face.

Yeah! Right!

She smirked at herself, then grew serious, reaching out to

her daughter, who was leaning against the railing at the edge of the observation deck. "Careful, Bebe!" she shouted, the sarcastic attitude immediately gone.

"Look, Mama! Shooting stars! A whole bunch of shooting stars *during the day*!" Bebe pointed excitedly, and Loretta followed her direction but saw only blue sky and high thin clouds.

"I think you're getting *high* up here, honey. I don't see nothin'."

"I don't see *anything*," Bebe corrected, ignoring her mother's pun. "If you *don't* see *nothing* then you must see *something*!"

Loretta's eyes narrowed. "I see a little wiseass who's not going to get to go to the Louvre tomorrow if she doesn't watch her smart mouth." Loretta frowned at her daughter; Bebe was ignoring her. When Loretta used a serious tone of voice, usually Bebe was all attention. Not now; she had returned her gaze to the sky, standing on the bottom bar of the railing and sticking her head through the bars. Loretta was about to *shout* at Bebe (something she *rarely* did; saving it for emergencies such as this), when her eye caught a flurry of twinkling sparks in the Parisian sky.

She looked up—Bebe was right! There was a meteor shower directly overhead. Loretta went to her daughter's side, and both stood transfixed by the sparkling display. Loretta had never seen one before, but even so, she sensed this was not normal. The first compact swarm of sparks suddenly multiplied and spread over the entire city. She looked around; the City of Lights was being deluged with a downpour of lights; only this downpour had *direction*. The bits of light seemed to be *soaring* down from the heavens rather than *falling* like rain or particles from outer space.

Other tourists on the tower's highest observation deck joined Loretta and Bebe at the railing, staring at the approaching array. One of them, an elderly woman, said something in French and turned away, heading for the stairs. Having lived in France now for eleven months because of her husband's job at the U.S. Embassy, Loretta's French was fair and she thought the woman said, "That's no meteor shower!" Loretta watched the woman hurry for the exit before looking back at the sky. The swarm of lights was dissipating, not burning up or disappearing the way meteors would, but separating and spreading out, changing direction like a flock of birds but always headed downward toward the city.

Loretta had the sudden conviction that the elderly French lady was right—this was no meteor shower; this was not something *safe*. The old frog had the right idea in getting off the tower where she and Bebe were openly exposed to the glowing things. She reached for Bebe, noticing that none of the other tourists seemed worried—all were ooh-ing and aah-ing over the aerial light show. An enormously obese blond-haired lady, about as tall as she was wide, became frantic with excitement. She stood at the far end of the platform, clapping her hands and laughing with delight.

"Oh marvelous! The French really go all out, don't they?" the woman asked no one in particular. Her voice twanged with the nasal accent of a fellow American. From the way she dropped her *r*'s Loretta guessed she was from New England.

Something flew by Loretta's face, and she felt a slight wave of heat upon her cheek as it passed. It was one of the orbs; several of the swarm had broken off from the rest of the light cloud and now swirled around Loretta, Bebe, and the other tourists on the Eiffel Tower's topmost observation platform. Loretta reached blindly for Bebe, unable to pull her own gaze from the fat lady trying to snatch orbs from the air as three buzzed around her. She grabbed at the smallest one right in front of her face, missed it, and the luminous particle flew up her nose.

She gasped and her eyes widened, looking directly at Loretta. "Oh my!" she said quite clearly before letting out a horrendous groan. She staggered away from the railing to the back of the platform, her rolls of fat wobbling uncontrollably. In the next thirty seconds, she grew from four-foot-two to seventeen-foot-two. Her expanding flesh tore her clothes to shreds. Her bones could be heard snapping and grinding against squishing muscle and crackling tendons as everything inside her stretched and grew—ripped apart and healed in larger proportions. Her face became the mask of a demon straight from Hell.

The metal supports of the platform groaned under the sudden increase in weight. An almost musical shriek followed as one of those supports separated from the rest of the structure. Startled tourists were thrown to the platform floor as it shifted and dropped beneath their feet. Screams of terror came from three who immediately fell over the side, plummeting to an impact death below.

Loretta was thrown from her feet and would have joined those going over the edge but for the platform railing, which she managed to hang on to, clinging to it for dear life as it swayed precariously over empty air. Realizing the railing was not going to hold for long, she grabbed for the edge of the platform, got it, and miraculously pulled herself up just before the railing broke free from the platform and crashed to the plaza below, taking more tourists with it.

Lying on her stomach, breathing dust and exhaling fear, Loretta looked frantically for Bebe. She screamed when she saw her. The fat lady-now-turned-monster had her. The fat lady monster seemed to be stuck on its side, wedged between the damaged, slanted floor of the platform and the ceiling. Its grotesque left arm was trapped behind its body, but the right one was free and clutching the screaming Bebe. The creature was trying to get the terrified Bebe into its drooling, fanged mouth but couldn't due to the tight jam it was in.

With a massive effort, Loretta clawed her way up the tilted platform and regained her footing.

"No! Let my baby go!" she screamed at the thing. She picked up a loose metal bolt from the broken platform and threw it at the monster attempting to eat her only child.

The bolt struck the thing's stomach just hard enough to distract it and make it aware of Loretta's presence. The fat lady monster regarded Loretta, then Bebe, as if comparison-shopping. It shrugged—Loretta was clearly the better deal—and tossed Bebe, screaming, over the side, before grabbing Loretta instead. With the effort, the creature broke free of being jammed. The platform, and the tower itself, began to crumble. The fat lady monster didn't care; as she fell she devoured Loretta Gleason in four bites.

England. 4:25 p.m.

Jerry Booth stood at the bus stop at Trafalgar Square, crying—openly, loudly, head down, and in public no less—and he didn't care who saw him. He didn't care if he lived or died; the love of his life, his sweet Brenda, had just dumped him. As if losing her wasn't bad enough, she'd just *had* to explain how being with Jerry had made her realize she was a lesbian, and then she'd had the *audacity* to thank him!

If any of his mates found out about this, he'd never live it down.

He wiped his snotty nose on his bare arm and gave a dirty look to a hunched old bird standing nearby at the bus stop who was doing the same to him. Suddenly, something that looked like a small glowing pebble flew into the old lady's ear. Jerry laughed despite his gloom as the old crone leaped into the street and danced with the force of the transformation her flesh was undergoing. Before Jerry could do anything but watch, the hunched old woman had morphed into something not of the world and stood towering over him, still hunched, but no longer a woman. Looking up at the monstrosity, Jerry, an art student, was immediately reminded of the nightmare paintings of Hieronymus Bosch.

It would be his last thought. The hunched old monster snatched Jerry from the bus stop and stuffed him into her mouth a moment before the 4:30 bus smashed into her legs, toppling her. She landed on the bus, crushing it and the screaming Londoners within.

New York City. 11:30 a.m.

"This fuckin' city smells like *ass!*"

Tashira Mendez laughed loudly at her friend Jesenia's comment. Jesenia was always saying funny shit like that.

"You'd know what *ass* smells like, *puta!*" Dona Perez, Tashira's cousin and the oldest of the three, quipped. Tashira laughed even louder at that, surprised Dona had got one over on Jesenia.

"Oh! So it's like *dat*! Huh?" Jesenia blustered, fighting to feign seriousness in the face of Tashira's infectious expression of mirth. "You wanna go? You dis' me, girl, an' I gotta call you out! Le's go. Come on. Right'chere, right now!" Jesenia challenged Dona with her words *and* posture—arms wide apart, hands out, fingers splayed, shoulders hunched—but the smile she couldn't keep from twitching at the corners of her mouth betrayed the threat.

"Yeah, I wanna *go*," Dona said, taking a step forward and getting right in the shorter Jesenia's face. "I wanna go . . . *shopping*!" She smirked. "Ain't that what we came to this *shit*-hole for?" Dona looked at her two friends and wiggled her eyebrows up and down. "Get it? Shit-hole? The city smells like *ass*?"

Tashira cracked up anew and Jesenia grinned and shook her head at Dona. "You ever think about, you know, like, doin' stand-up, or sumpin' like dat?"

Dona gave Jesenia a startled look. "Actually, yeah!" she confessed, about to add how she had just signed up for open-mike night at a club in their neighborhood when Jesenia cut her off.

"Well, *don't*!" Jesenia laughed cruelly, but Tashira saw the sudden hurt in her cousin's eyes and realized Dona had been serious. Before she could think of anything to say, Jesenia turned on her.

"So, *writer*, what' we doin' at Columbus Circle instead'a Midtown at Filene's Basement?"

Tashira smiled and shook her head; she was used to being teased by her two best friends. "I told you guys! I wanna show you the Time-Life building, where I'm gonna be doin' my internship," Tashira said, indicating with a nod of her head the building they stood before. All three looked up at the towering glass skyscraper and simultaneously caught sight of what appeared to be a shower of sparks, not unlike the aftermath of a fireworks display, falling out of the sky like rain.

"Hey, girls!"

The gravelly voice from behind them distracted the trio from the overhead light show and they turned to the speaker. A grizzled, gray-bearded, filthy-faced old man in a clichéd, chin-to-ankle gray trench coat stood on the sidewalk near the curb. With a flourish, he whipped open his coat, revealing his equally filthy and wrinkled old body crowned by an unusually large and dirt-smudged erection for such a thin, wizened old geezer.

"Fuckin' pervert!" Dona cursed, and looked around for a cop, or better yet, something to throw at the old scumbag.

"Gross!" Tashira cried, and turned away, shrieking with laughter.

Jesenia, too, howled with laughter but did not shy away from the old man's exhibition. Instead she turned around, unbuckled her belt, and pushed her jean shorts and black thong underwear down to her knees as she bent over and mooned the creep.

A glowing orb immediately flew up her ass.

With a surprised leap in the air, she went into convulsions and changed. She joined the throng of other New Yorkers in Columbus Circle who were suddenly succumbing to the invading sparks and, like Jesenia, rapidly transforming into ravenous, man-eating monsters.

In shock, Dona and Tashira stood frozen as their friend became a fiend before their eyes. So mesmerizing was Jesenia's transformation, neither girl saw another orb fly into the old exhibitionist's ear, nor saw him transform nearly as rapidly as Jesenia. Just as wrinkly and filthy—but noticeably missing his raging erection—the old man became a twenty-foot gargoyle. Backing away from the now monstrous Jesenia, Tashira and Dona backed right into his clutches. In the blink of an eye he bit Dona in two, gulped her top half down, and shoved the rest of her in after it. Howling with rage, the creature that used to be Jesenia Rodriguez grabbed at Tashira Mendez, clutched tightly in the old man monster's right hand.

A tug-of-war ensued, the result being a compromise of

half for each when Tashira's body separated at the waist in a spray of blood.

11:35 a.m.

Tommy Moua pulled his Yankees cap low over his eyes and sighed. Surrounding him, waiting in line to get tickets for the express elevator to the top of the Empire State Building, and chattering nonstop in Hmoob, the language of the Hmong people of Laos, were his newly immigrated relatives from the old country. Because Tommy was the eldest son, his father had commanded him to show them the sights of New York City. Of course Tommy had protested; he was too cool for that. He had received a backhand to the mouth for his insolence. That was the way of the old country. Every year from third grade, when he first came to America with his family until his graduation this year from high school, Tommy's father had made a point of visiting his teachers and giving them permission to beat his son if he got out of line or didn't do his work properly.

At first ignorant of the ways of his new country and knowing of his father's instructions, Tommy had been scared to death of his teachers. He soon learned that no matter what his father said, his teachers were not going to hit him, *ever*. That was not the way of America—he fell in love with his new country on the day of that realization—but his father, mother, and endless stream of aunts, uncles, and cousins from the old country didn't *get* it. That's why they'd never understand Tommy and never be like him; they'd never be *Americans*.

Suddenly, his relatives' endless chatter changed in tone, became excited. Tommy caught only a few words—they all spoke too fast, and he had willfully forgotten as much of his original language as he could in his fervor to be an American—but it was enough to understand there was something in the sky. Not wanting to look like a "neck craning staring at the gosh golly tall buildings typical" tourist (sure that his hick relatives were marveling over a plane or a helicopter or something equally mundane to a seasoned New Yorker such as Tommy) he didn't look until the tone of their voices changed to fearful.

Ready to laugh at, and explain, whatever it was they were afraid of, Tommy looked up just in time to see, close up, a twinkling little ball of light, about the size of a small ball bearing, hovering just above him. It floated closer. Through its opaque shell, Tommy could see pinpoint flecks of light, swirling within the sphere like fireflies trapped in a round jar, or glowing spores ready to burst from a pod. Like a child reaching for a shiny toy, Tommy tentatively reached for the sparkling object, but it avoided his grasp and flew up his nose.

Tommy Moua looked surprised, then sneezed, and sneezed again. The orb flew from his nose and into the mouth of his aunt Hnu, who stood mouth agape and in shock, staring at the hundreds of flying orbs of light that now were everywhere. In a screaming, bone-wrenching, gut-twisting, muscle-rippling display that was so horrifying it caused Tommy Moua to do a very *un*cool thing and defecate in his pants, Aunt Hnu began her new life in America, the Land of Opportunity, by transforming into a creature from Hell and grabbing *her* nearest opportunity—her nephew, Tommy Moua—and devouring him on the spot.

The rest of her family scattered, screaming and trying to avoid the sudden crop of monsters that had sprung up everywhere in the space of less than a minute. And more were being created every second as the flying orbs chased victims and invaded bodies through any orifice available. Aunt Hnu was about to lumber after her children for the second course when a body hit the pavement hard in front of her, splattering her grotesque new look with blood. She scooped up the pulpy remains and gobbled them down as she looked up for more manna from Heaven. Seeing none forthcoming, she reached up, got a handhold, and, Kong-like, began to climb the Empire State Building.

11:40 a.m.

Joe Burton got out of bed, disappointed in himself for sleeping so late, and headed for the bathroom. During the routinely lengthy relieving of his bladder, he came fully awake and contemplated the day ahead of him.

Knicks–Lakers!

The thought was like a neon marquee in his mind; it sat as a centerpiece to the day around which all other events and activities had to revolve.

Game seven of the World Championship, the series tied 3 games to 3. Everything on the line.

It was a New York basketball fan's wet dream. Though Joe was a relatively recent resident of New York—he'd grown up in New Hampshire as a Boston Celtics fan and had played basketball in high school fantasizing that he was Larry Bird—once he had moved to the Big Apple he had adopted the Knicks as his new team, much to the disappointment of his father, who had also been his high school coach. Joe had quickly become as rabid a Knicks fan as any other lover of basketball in the city. He had been waiting, and wishing, for this matchup since his switch of allegiance and was now euphoric with this culmination. In the past month, Knicks fever in the Big Apple had become rampant, and Joe had been one of the most diseased. Now it was down to one game—win or lose, live or die.

Joe returned to his bedroom and donned his running gear—cutoff jean shorts, a gray V-neck T-shirt, two pairs of white athletic socks, and Nike running shoes. He opened the bedroom window and immediately felt the day's humidity, like a warm wet blanket, try to muscle its way into the air-conditioned apartment. Joe stuck his head out and looked at the sky; despite the heat and humidity, the day was overcast and there was an omen of thunderstorms to come in the darkly bruised purple clouds massing over the ocean to the south. Joe decided he wouldn't need sunglasses or a hat today.

Since his three-room apartment—on the seventh floor of a brownstone on King Street—was little wider than the average supermarket aisle, he had to perform his stretching exercises in the living room's narrow strip of open floor between the couch and the TV stand. He preferred to stretch inside and finish with a high-stepping jog down the seven flights of stairs to King Street. He liked to hit the street full-stride and running all out.

Though traffic was light, Joe wished he had gotten an earlier start; not only would it have been cooler and less humid, the awful *stink* of the city wouldn't have been so bad. Joe had lived in the city for just over four years and had come to the conclusion that it was at its malodorous worst during summertime. The stench was difficult to describe—a mix of exhaust, sewer fumes, garbage left too long curbside, and an underlying sourness that Joe supposed came from all the water surrounding the island city but which he imagined to be the smell of human *sweat*—the city coated in over four hundred years of it deposited since its beginnings.

He found the stink difficult to smell in the winter, but still there. The cold winter air tended to cleanse the city, but it could not dispel the ages-old odor completely. It took the heat of summer to really bring out the full bouquet. Weekend mornings, with less traffic and less exhaust fumes, were the least offensive times as far as air quality went, but Joe still breathed through his mouth as he ran across Varick Street and headed south toward the Hudson River where, if it was high tide, the air would be cleaner, fresher.

Turning right on Greenwich, Joe crossed to Houston and made a left, continuing south toward the river and passing under the St. John's overpass. He caught the light at West Street and was able to sprint across the four-lane intersection without stopping or having to slow down. Reaching the wide running path on the other side that followed the Hudson River west and uptown to the Village if he turned right, and east all the way to Battery Park, past the Port Authority Piers 40 and 26, if he turned left—he chose left, his regular route.

Foot traffic on the path was heavy as it usually was on Sunday mornings. Runners of both sexes—all ages, shapes, and sizes—ran at a wide range of speeds, each intent on secluded thoughts, isolated amid the vast sea of humanity around them; none of them aware of the high sparkling cloud moving rapidly toward them through the sky. With the river so close it was easy for the runners, and large numbers of bicyclists, walkers, Rollerbladers, and skateboarders who also used the path, to not look uptown as they ran. Despite the pollution and the frequent stink of the river, especially at low tide and when the sea breeze was still, it provided a long stretch of picturesque scenes that even the most insensitive and culturally ignorant person couldn't help but appreciate. Just past Pier 40 and the long stone walkway to one of the Port Authority's annex buildings, which reminded Joe of an ancient Egyptian temple sticking out into the Nile River that he'd seen on the History Channel, the riverside became more rustic for a stretch, bringing to Joe's active imagination a sense of decades, even centuries, past. Rows of wood pylons, all that remained of some riverfront warehouse, jutted out of the water, stretching nearly to midstream, haunting the water like forgotten ghosts. As he often did, Joe imagined what kinds of activities, legal and criminal, had gone on in the building that had once stood there. As an aspiring playwright/actor, Joe considered it a creative exercise that might prove fruitful with a sweet story line someday.

To the left, the New York City Parks Project had been renovating and adding interesting summer activities in addition to planting more trees and making the riverfront path more of a garden park. Four new tennis courts had been put in, enclosed in a shiny, fifteen-foot-high chain-link fence. Next to them, a good-size area had been enclosed with an even higher fence that was hung with a large sign designating the place as the New York City Summer Parks Project Trapeze and Acrobatics School (For Boys and Girls—Ages 3 to 16). Joe often slowed as he ran past if there were kids on the high wire, swinging on the trapeze, or just diving from the high platform into the safety net that was always employed. More than once Joe had wished he could be sixteen again to take advantage of what looked to be a blast.

_12:10 p.m._

As Joe Burton paused to watch the children in the Trapeze and Acrobatics School, Corey Aaron was waiting in line to perform an exercise on the high trapeze. He noticed Joe Burton slow down outside the fence and run in place while he watched a kid on the trapeze. Corey didn't know Joe, but he recognized him from previous Sundays; he always slowed his run to watch Corey and the other kids at the trapeze school. If it hadn't been for the look of longing on the guy's face, Corey probably would not have noticed or remembered him. But Corey knew that look, he knew how that look felt; there was a new chopper-style bike from Schwinn that Corey wanted but his parents had denied him, saying there was no safe place in their city neighborhood to ride it without adult supervision.

A sudden loud roar from the tennis courts next door, immediately followed by a tumult of screams and horrific snapping and crunching noises, startled Corey and the other students, as well as the several instructors and many parents standing around watching. Something shiny flew past Corey's face and his eyes followed it, trying to focus on the moving streak of light heading straight for his mother, who was seven months pregnant, and his aunt Helen. Both were walking quickly toward him, worried looks on their faces. Corey's mom opened her mouth to call him, but instead of his name coming out, the flying ball of light went in and disappeared down her throat. His aunt Helen grabbed her sister's arm to help, but before she could do anything, one of the orbs of light flew up her nose.

Aunt Helen's hands flew to her nose as if she'd been punched. Her eyes bulged. She started coughing as the thing slid through her nasal passage and into her throat. She tried to hack up the foreign object as if it were an inhaled insect. She was unsuccessful. Like every other person on the planet who ingested the glowing, soaring orbs from space, Corey's aunt morphed into something alien, monstrous, and hungry for human flesh.

And she had her new monster eyes focused on Corey. "Aunt Helen?" he whimpered.

12:15 p.m.

In less than a blink of an eye the world went crazy.

One moment Joe Burton was jogging in place and watching a cute little redheaded girl bravely swinging upon the high trapeze, the next, the air was filled with little glowing globes like marbles or ball bearings and—as hard as it was to believe—people started changing into gigantic monstrous creatures. One reared its head over the tennis court fence, a pair of bloody human legs, sneakers, and socks still on the feet, sticking out of its mouth, but not for long. It sucked them in like noodles. Numbed by the sheer unreality of what he was seeing, Joe stopped moving, as did most of the other people on the path, and stared in shock at the creature. Suddenly, more people began to change as the sparks of light infected them. Three adults—two male instructors from the trapeze school and a woman spectator—were infected and immediately became huge, cannibalistic monsters, grabbing at the children around them. One of the creatures, formerly an instructor, pushed the other instructor-turned-monster aside as it reached for a meal. The shoved creature smashed through the fence surrounding the trapeze school, knocking it down before falling sideways onto the running path and nearly crushing Joe and several other stupefied runners. With the fence down, the children had an avenue of escape from the beasts preying on them.

One of those who escaped was Corey Aaron. He was frozen to the spot as his aunt Helen, in her new hideous form, came toward him. His survival instincts got him moving, finally, and he fled. He knew, deep down, that *thing*—even though it still superficially resembled his aunt with its long strawberry-blond hair—was not, and would never again be, his loving aunt. She lunged at him, proving her lack of affection for him, but missed as he dodged her and ducked under the high wire–trapeze staging. As he scrambled away from his monster aunt, Corey frantically looked for his mother. He saw her and cried out to her for help, but though she was looking right at him, she didn't answer, didn't seem to see him.

"Mom! Help!" Corey cried again. The creature that had been his aunt tore through the wooden trapeze staging, sending wood and wire cables flying. Corey backed away from her and was about to try and dash past her to his mother when a monster that had been one of the acrobatic instructors just seconds ago scooped his mom up in his huge hands and carried her off. The monster charged through the fence on the other side of the school and headed toward West Street.

"Mom! No!" Corey screamed. Not wanting to, but seeing no choice as his beastly aunt came after him, Corey scrambled over the razed cyclone fence and ran to the guy he had noticed each week watching. The man was just standing there, gaping at the mayhem around him. Without slowing even a half step, Corey ran by the guy, reached out, grabbed his hand, and pulled. The effect was immediate. The man sprang to life as if finger-snapped out of a hypnotic trance. He gripped Corey's hand tightly and ran with him. Behind them, Aunt Helen let out a bellow of rage at her nephew's escape. Enraged, she rampaged through the remnants of the trapeze staging and over the downed fence in pursuit.

12:15:01 p.m.

Thirty feet away, where the city had converted a former boathouse into a public bathroom, Cindy Raposa sat in a stall on the women's side. She sat on the plastic, cigarette-burned toilet seat and very carefully drew heroin from the small, blackened spoon she'd just cooked it in. With the delicacy of a surgeon, careful not to waste a drop, she drew all of it into the syringe, then licked the spoon for good measure. An examination of the proliferation of tracks on her right arm resulted in her looking for a spot on her slightly less punctured left forearm, where the needle had not yet been. She tied off, the end of the rubber tube between her teeth, and shot up. She held her breath, then let it out as she let the tubing fall from her mouth and loosen from her arm. She pulled the needle free and slumped against the side of the stall, nearly sliding off the toilet to the grungy floor.

"Fuck yeah," Cindy said breathily. The sound of many sirens outside—about the *only* sound that could slice through the thick cloud of *stoned* she was in—made her suddenly wary. Though it was doubtful the sirens were coming for her, she knew it wasn't a good idea to stay in one place too long when holding and using, and she had enough various drugs on her besides the heroin that she could be charged with intent to sell. She quietly stuffed her works into her large leather shoulder bag and went out to the row of sinks along the wall.

"Damn!" she swore, seeing there were no mirrors above the sink. The city had learned its lesson and no longer invested in such easily vandalized items as glass public restroom mirrors. She headed for the door, opened it, and was stunned by the sight of a screaming man being plucked from a ten-speed bike and bloodily devoured by something out of a horror movie. Cindy immediately slammed the door and stood with her back against it.

"What the fuck was that dope cut with?" she whispered aloud. "I'm trippin'." Slowly, she turned around, gripped the doorknob, and opened the door just enough to peer out again. A woman dressed in the universal gear of a jogger— sweatsuit, sneakers, headband, and earphones—ran by screaming. She didn't get far. An incredible creature, huge, deformed, and bringing to Cindy's mind vague images of trolls and ogres she'd seen in illustrated fairy tales as a child, grabbed the woman and proceeded to gobble her down in a bloody frenzy that took less than a few seconds.

Cindy slammed the door again and stood retching and trembling, honestly unsure if what she'd just seen was a drug-induced hallucination brought on by bad smack or reality.

The latter thought was *crazy*—it *couldn't* be reality. It *had* to be the juice she'd just shot. *It had to be.*

Never in her many years of being a junkie had horse affected her like this.

This was *wack!*

She closed her eyes, took a deep breath, and told herself to keep cool no matter what she saw when she opened the restroom door again. From the sound of multiple sirens outside growing louder and more numerous by the moment, she didn't want to go freaking out and attract the attention of cops.

She couldn't afford to get busted again.

"Z-Jay will kill me if I get busted again," she muttered worriedly. Her pimp could be vicious—crazy, *nasty* vicious—when pissed off. Steeling herself as best she could, she tried the door a third time—and was instantly bowled over by a man and a young boy. As she crashed to the floor on her back, the man pushed the boy on top of her and swung the restroom door shut as he, too, hit the floor but kept his feet against the bottom of the door. A second later, the top half of the metal door shuddered and bowed inward from the force of something outside pounding against it. The top corner of the door was pushed in far enough for Cindy to see that the *something* pounding on the door was one of her hallucinations.

But the boy on top of her and the guy lying with his feet against the door were real—she was *sure* of *that*, at least. "Please tell me I'm trippin' or dreamin' or *somethin!*" she pleaded with the guy cowering beneath the buckling door.

"I wish you were, sweetheart, but you ain't," the man grunted before scrabbling on his hands and knees away from the shaking door.

"No!" Cindy gasped. "Don't tell me that! I asked you not to tell me that! I said please!" Cindy rebutted, slurring her words as much from *shock* as from the effect of the heroin.

12:22 p.m.

Joe Burton looked at the skinny blonde. Her face was pretty but hard looking; her cheeks were sallow, her eyes distant. She was dressed like a hooker with her short black spandex miniskirt, black fishnet stockings, leather sandals, and red blouse unbuttoned to her navel over a black spandex tank top that emphasized her ample cleavage, and he detected she was less than sober. The kid, who was dressed in khaki shorts and a T-shirt with the logo for the trapeze and acrobatics school on the front, lay half on her legs, half off, looking up at her with the most dazed, confused, and *pathetic* face Joe had ever seen on a kid.

"A monster took my mom!" the kid cried. As if in answer, a deafening roar came from the other side of the door. "Don't let Aunt Helen get me!" he pleaded tearfully.

"What are those things?" the hooker shrieked, looking from the kid to Joe. He pointed at the gaping hole in the top of the door, where a grotesque face peered in, trying to spy a meal to snatch.

"I think that one is the kid's *aunt*!" Joe said, indicating the creature with a nod of his head.

The monster thrust its hand and arm through the aperture in the door, jamming it up to its wrist. It grappled about with its huge fingers and long sharp claws. The stoned hooker screamed and scrambled backward like a frightened crab. The kid quickly rolled off her and did the same.

"We gotta get out of here!" Joe said, ducking just in time to avoid the thing's searching digits.

"One of those things got my mom," the boy cried, tears streaming down his face.

Joe felt bad for the kid, but at the moment, survival was more important than soothing the kid's sorrow. He stood and took the boy's hand and pulled him to the row of porcelain sinks over which were three rectangular windows set just under the ceiling. They were the only other way out of the restroom.

The monster that had been the kid's aunt sounded different suddenly. Her roars were no longer inflected with rage but with pain. Joe realized her arm was stuck in the door and she couldn't pull it free. Her roars took on a pathetic, whimpering note.

Joe leaped onto the sinks and unlatched the middle window. He pushed, but it wouldn't budge. The window frame's hinges were rusted, indicating the portal had not been opened in a long time. Placing both palms on the bottom of the window frame, Joe lunged forward, pushing on the window with everything he had. Powered by adrenaline, panic, and fear, he broke the rust's frozen grip and the window opened with a grating scraping sound.

Joe turned back, reached down, grabbed the kid by the arm, and pulled him up to the window. Joe looked out and was momentarily stunned by the mayhem he saw. The man-eating gargoyle-like monsters were *everywhere*, and more people were being infected and transformed every moment. Over on West Street, which ran along the Hudson and the running path, cars were smashing into each other. Those that avoided collisions with other vehicles ran into buildings and fleeing people being chased by the monsters. The sound of sirens, screams, inhuman roars, and explosions near and distant filled the air. It was riveting and would have kept Joe entranced if not for the hooker behind him screaming for help. He turned and looked. The restroom door, in fact the entire wall containing the door, was bulging inward, ready to collapse. With a loud snarl, the monster that had been a human, caring aunt to the boy pulled her arm free, leaving behind a cloud of scaly flakes of skin.

Joe looked out the window again and down. Just below was a large, square green industrial trash bin. Joe picked up the kid, turned him so his feet went through the window first, then lowered him to the bin, letting the boy slide slowly through his hands until he clutched only the kid's wrists before letting him drop less than a foot to the top of the covered receptacle. He reached back for the hooker but there was no need. At the same moment he turned for her, the wall collapsed and the girl leaped onto the sink and scrambled through the window before the crumbled concrete and dust could settle.

The boy's monster relative was hunched over peering through the mist of rubble, leery of entering the now unsteady building. The roof overhead was bowing and emitting loud groans and creaks.

Joe took advantage of the monster's hesitation and followed the blonde through the window. It was a tight squeeze, but he managed and lowered himself to the bin. He jumped to the blacktop where the blond hooker cowered, staring in shock and awe at the world gone mad. The kid, still on top of the bin, jumped into Joe's arms.

"I can't carry you, kid, you've got to run," Joe said loud enough to be heard over the boy's aunt's furious roaring and the growing cacophony from the world outside. He felt like an instant heel looking at the kid's sad and terrified face, but he knew neither of them would make it if Joe had to carry him. Though shocked and grief stricken—Joe couldn't begin to imagine how the kid must feel—he seemed to understand that Joe was right. He nodded, and Joe put him down.

"We can't stay here," Joe said, dropping to a crouch next to the boy. The girl huddled against the trash bin, looking as though she was trying to make herself as small as possible. Before Joe could say another word, a park security officer came around the corner to Joe's right, but got no farther. A massive hairy arm and clawed hand followed him round the bend and grabbed him before he could take more than a couple of steps. The hulking, fang-toothed monstrosity attached to the arm appeared a moment later. The grinning gargoyle leaned over, lips pursed, as if it were going to kiss the screaming guard. The creature's lips touched the man's face—there was a loud sucking sound—and the man's head disappeared. The monster rolled the head around in its mouth for a moment like a jawbreaker candy before crunching it loudly in its powerful jaws. It jammed the blood-spurting neck of the twitching corpse into its mouth next and sucked it greedily.

"Go!" Joe shouted, pushing the blonde and the kid in the opposite direction of the feasting ghoul. He followed and sprinted past them while searching wildly for help or a place to hide, but everywhere he looked he saw creatures straight out of Hell. West Street was a scene of utter pandemonium, as was Riverfront Park and the running path. Monsters chased people, flying orbs chased people; the monsters caught people and gobbled them down; the orbs, too, caught people, changing their size in order to fly into any exposed and available body orifice and transform individuals into cannibalistic demons.

Twenty yards ahead, amid a smattering of thin, anemic park trees to the left of the running path, a skinny, dark-haired man in his twenties ran like a halfback using the trees like blockers as he tried to escape from several pursuing monsters. Instead of a football, the young man carried a tiny white poodle that yipped and snarled ferociously from within the protection of its master's arms. A moment later, man and dog were separated, done in by a tree root. The man went down, face-first into the gravel; the poodle went up, flipping into the air like a tossed toy, and landed on the elongated nose of another nearby monster. The terrified dog sank its teeth into the strange flesh and locked its jaws. While its master was being devoured from the feet up in four bites, the poodle hung on for dear life despite the now howling monster shaking its head madly. Just as the creature reached for the dog as though it were a feeding mosquito that could be plucked and popped, the monster who had eaten the dog's owner saw the dog and snapped at it. It got the dog in its jaws, along with most of the other monster's face. With a gurgling scream, the suddenly faceless monster staggered back, blood spewing from the gaping wound in its grotesque countenance. It was immediately set upon by a half dozen others of its kind who proceeded to feast on their wounded comrade.

Joe pivoted away from the carnage, but a loud rumble and crash from behind made him glance back. The boathouse restroom had collapsed. The kid's monster aunt came charging over the pile of rubble, intent on finding the boy. Joe glanced at his fellow fugitives; the girl was too intent on fleeing and the boy had not realized his aunt had resumed her pursuit. The boy started to turn around, but Joe sprinted by and pulled him away from the sight of what was chasing after him.

A creature half the size of the others—making Joe think it had been a child a few moments ago—lurched out from behind a wide tree, its stubby, grotesque arms reaching for the blond hooker. She screamed and the child monster fell dead on the grass, blood spurting from a hole in the center of its forehead.

"Come on! I've got you covered!"

Joe turned around. The commanding voice had come from a short, fat cop holding a pistol in one hand and gesturing wildly with his other toward a flashing cruiser parked in the middle of West Street. Its driver side front and rear doors were open. Joe shoved the kid toward the cruiser. The hooker went up quite a few notches in Joe's eyes when she grabbed the boy's arm and pulled him along with her. A horrible scream made Joe turn just in time to see the savior cop set upon by a massive, dark-skinned hairy monster sporting an Afro.

Joe stopped. Instinct made him want to save the policeman *and* run away at the same time until the policeman's severed right arm, gun still clutched in the hand, landed at his feet. Part of his mind registered shock at the bloody limb on the pavement; the rest thought only of survival. The world became a slow, underwater ballet, and every thought he had, every movement he made, seemed to *glide*. Fighting the air, which now felt as thick as gelatin, Joe stooped and *pushed* his hand through the resisting atmosphere and grabbed the gun.

It wouldn't come free of the cop's dismembered limb. Joe tugged and pulled but the dead hand held on and the arm followed. In frustration—the shocked part of his mind registering horror at his actions—he stepped on the wrist and *yanked* on the weapon. The bone in the dead man's wrist snapped, clumps of blood squirted from the severed end of the arm, but the gun still would not come free.

And the monsters were closing in.

The one with the Afro charged Joe, followed closely by the kid's former aunt and another half-size child monster sporting long, luscious blond curls, tiny pink ribbons still intact next to its grotesque batlike ears. Joe picked up the gun, hand and all, and pointed it at the oncoming creatures. He pulled on the cop's index finger still wrapped around the trigger. The first shot winged the Afro monster, catching it in the left elbow and spinning the thing around as it stumbled from the hit. Joe's second shot caught the fiend dead-center in the chest and it fell, skidding on the tar on its knees. The half-pint pursuing monster immediately leaped upon its fallen fellow and bit a sizable chunk out of the Afro monster's Afro. Getting nothing but hair, it let out a roar—a grotesque echo of a child's, "Eww!"—and spluttered, trying to spit the mass of wiry hair from its mouth.

The boy's monstrosity of an aunt was not so easily side-tracked. She came charging on past the row of old black hitching posts that marked the entrance to Hudson River Park and headed straight for Joe. He raised the dead cop's arm, aimed the dead hand, and pulled the cop's finger. The bullet struck the creature in the shoulder but did not slow it. Joe stumbled rapidly backward, pulling the dead cop's trigger finger repeatedly. Monster Aunt was hit in the stomach, twice in the chest, and one each in the throat and face, respectively, before she fell to the curbside barely three feet in front of Joe.

Having reached the cruiser, the boy turned just in time to see Joe murder the thing that used to be his favorite aunt.

12:30 p.m.

"No!" Corey screamed, watching Aunt Helen go down, her head amid a halo of blood that turned her strawberry-blond hair to dark red. Flesh and bone, from where one of the bullets had ripped open a good part of her face from her jaw to her eyes, added to the halo effect. She hit the road wound-first and skipped along a few feet, like a flat rock on the surface of hard black water.

"Aunt Helen!" Corey screamed even as part of him refused to believe *that* could be his aunt. Despite the pain of seeing Aunt Helen killed, even if she was a monster, Corey turned away. He used the short respite from running for his life to look around for his mom. Part of him refused to believe she had been carried off and probably eaten by the monster that had grabbed her. The same part of him expected her to come running to save him at any moment.

The tall runner turned toward Corey, guilt and remorse stamped on his face at having to kill the boy's transformed aunt. The part of Corey's mind that refused to believe that his mother had been eaten and his aunt was now a dead monster was glad to see the guy was okay, but a bigger part, enraged as much as terrified, instantly hated the guy and wanted to kill him for murdering his aunt. Maybe she could have been saved, that part wanted to believe. Maybe she could have been changed back into "Aunt Helen" somehow. Maybe Aunt Helen, in her new form, no matter how horrible and frightening, hadn't *really* wanted to eat him. That line of thought reinforced the hope that maybe his mother was still alive, too, somewhere, somehow.

The runner reached the cruiser, shoved Corey into the backseat with the skinny blond girl, who smelled like she had peed her pants, and slammed the door, nearly catching Corey's foot. He then jumped in the driver's seat and tried to close the door, but a monster with one arm—the other merely a gimpy stump—grabbed the door and ripped it from its hinges. The screech of metal being twisted from metal set Corey's teeth on edge, and his screams went up a notch. The one-armed ghoul flung the door aside and reached back with its only good appendage. The guy in front aimed the cop's arm and pistol at the thing's head but was rewarded with an empty *click*. He flung the gun, arm and all, at the creature, and started the car. The armless monster caught the cop's arm with its single hand and took a bite out of it as though it was a drumstick.

Corey was flung back against the blonde again as the guy stepped on the gas and the vehicle spun out with a screech of accelerating tires and headed up West Street.

12:35 p.m.

Cindy Raposa grunted involuntarily as the kid in the backseat with her was thrown into her midsection by the vehicle's sudden takeoff. The effect of the jolt was the opposite of what it normally would have been; instead of knocking the wind out of her and disrupting her breathing, it slowed it down from a hyperventilating panting to a slightly more calm, and oxygen-supplying, gasp. Along with her breathing, Cindy's mind had raced to the brink of blackout; the collision with the boy slowed her panting thoughts and made her focus on senses other than vision.

Because her eyes were telling her she had gone stark raving *mad*.

Her ears, full of terrible horrifying death screams set to the beat of bones being crunched by huge and deadly sharp mouths, gave her the same message. Her frantic mind refused to accept these two perceptions and latched onto a thought she could believe in: "This is not real. This is a dream." Never mind that she had never had a dream that felt so real. Her frightened little-girl ego maniacally repeated, "This is not real. This is just a dream," over and over again.

Her senses of touch and smell quickly defeated that tactic; feeling the air being pushed from her lungs, touching the boy's soft brown hair, and smelling the urine running down her legs from her wetting herself in terror, she was thrust back into the moment and forced to accept the unbelievable as real.

"What the fuck is going on?" she heard her mouth say, the words sounding more like sobs than language, and coming from someone else.

The car, now racing along West Street, swerved from side to side as the guy driving spun the wheel to avoid monsters and pedestrians alike. The side-to-side motion caused the kid to repeatedly slam into Cindy's stomach until she thought she might toss her cookies.

12:50 p.m.

Joe Burton put the pedal to the metal and cut the wheel hard to avoid a vintage '70s blue Volkswagen Bug whose top had been pried open and its owner turned into a box lunch for an albino monster. The police car spun hard to the right, the back end fishtailing dangerously close to the flip-top Bug before the rear tires caught the road again and the cruiser shot round. Joe maneuvered the car between and around the rampant carnage in the street while trying not to fall out of the doorless cruiser.

Later, Joe would reflect on this moment and remember how *in-the-zone* he had felt. It was like the time he had scored thirty points in a basketball game in high school. Everything he did, every move he made, was without thought or the hindrance of emotion. Running on high-octane adrenaline and panic, his brain had downshifted into *survival instinct* gear.

West Street is one of the widest streets in downtown Manhattan, and Joe was glad of it. He drove like a pro, feet performing an intricate dance between gas and brake, in perfect sync with his hands spinning and jerking the wheel left—past an incredibly fat monster sitting on a city bus, picking the trapped people inside out one by one and swallowing them for dinner—then to the right, around a huge, muscle-bound creature bench-lifting a delivery truck to its mouth and shaking free the screaming driver, which it promptly ate.

The muscle-bound monster flung the truck at the passing cruiser. It hit the pavement with an explosion of sparks and a rending of twisted metal. The girl and the kid in the backseat screamed. Joe looked in the rearview mirror, saw the truck hit on its right side, flip over, smash down on its left side, and flip over again and again as it came crashing after them, closer and closer.

Joe ground the gas pedal into the floor, trying to coax some extra power to stay ahead of the rampaging delivery vehicle. Too late, he returned his eyes to the road. Dead ahead, striding the intersection with Hubert Street, was the biggest of the nightmare creatures Joe had yet seen. From the top of its bald, scale-encrusted head to the tips of its long-taloned toes it had to be nearly thirty feet tall. The thing's face reminded Joe of someone—an ex-girlfriend maybe, the ugliest he'd ever dated. As the beast leaned forward, its eyes gleaming with carnal anticipation, its mouth dropped open, revealing double rows of great white shark teeth, ten times larger, longer, and sharper. A thick rope of slimy mucus dripped from the horror's hanging bottom lip and made a great splash on the road between its legs.

Joe drove the cruiser on through the puddle of spit—it splashed against the windshield in gooey strands—and between the thing's legs. The giant monstrosity bent over and swung its hands to catch the speeding car as it went under him, but missed. It continued to bend, watching upside down between its legs as the cruiser sped off. A moment later, the delivery truck barreled into the back of the monster's head and split its skull open like a dropped melon.

The car careened on, swerving from one side of West Street to the other as though driven by a drunkard. Joe cut the wheel, sending the car over the curb and onto the sidewalk, to avoid a potbellied creature that Joe guessed had been a cop from the tiny NYPD cap it still wore on its massively grotesque head. The capped horror whirled about as the cruiser went by. It lunged at the car. Its outstretched left hand slammed down on the cruiser's trunk, denting it and causing the car to pop a wheelie. The rear windshield shattered and the cruiser's siren suddenly came to life. In the backseat the kid and the blonde screamed and ducked as pieces of glass peppered them. Joe's head slammed into the roof of the car when the front end left the street. His nose punched the steering wheel when the car came back to earth. Blood spurted from both nostrils and sprayed over the wheel, the dashboard, and down the front of his T-shirt as the car rocked back and forth and slowed.

Though dazed, Joe still had enough presence of mind to feel the car suddenly slowing. A quick glimpse in the rearview mirror told him why—the cop monster, now minus its tiny cap, had managed to snag one of its claws on the rear bumper. Joe grabbed the shift lever behind the steering wheel, put it in low gear, and once again stomped on the gas pedal. The car strained forward, the rear tires screaming and smoking from the effort. With a sound like a giant pop-top can being opened, a section of the rear bumper came free of the car, leaving the rest hanging, and the vehicle took off, siren screaming louder than ever.

Joe's head jerked back at the car's sudden acceleration, then forward again, where his nose became reacquainted with the steering wheel, and the nasal blood flowed as if from a faucet. It gushed onto his lap and went down the back of his throat, making him gag and cough. The explosion of pain in his face was the worst Joe had ever experienced. His vision darkened for a moment, giving him the feeling of being suddenly enveloped by a gray mist. He stepped on the brake and the cruiser slowed but couldn't avoid colliding with the rear end of an SUV that had run into a streetlight pole.

1:00 p.m.

In the cruiser's backseat, Corey got up from the floor, where he had been thrown when the car crashed into the SUV. The blonde in the backseat with him looked dazed almost to the point of unconsciousness. Corey leaned forward to check on the guy driving. He banged on the metal screen that separated the backseat from the front. The guy appeared to be out cold.

"Hey! Wake up!" Corey cried, trying to rouse the guy, but received only a groggy grunt for his efforts. He was about to bang on the divider screen again when he heard a loud roar from directly behind. He looked back and saw the cop monster on its knees about twenty yards away. It was getting to its feet, ready to come and pluck him and the blonde from the backseat for a quick snack. Corey frantically banged on the dividing screen again and shouted, "Wake up!" at the driver several times.

Suddenly, the SUV they had slammed into began to rock side to side. From within came a mangled scream followed by an inhuman roar. A moment later, the SUV seemed to explode as its roof was peeled back and the sides of the vehicle bulged violently and its rear doors crashed to the pavement on both sides. From the backseat of the vehicle, a demon

monster erupted, smaller than the cop monster behind the
cruiser but just as hungry. Corey heard screams again from
within the SUV and watched in horror as the smaller monster first pulled a man from the front seat, then a woman,
wolfing both down in a matter of seconds.

Having finished its meal, the gnomish monster's eyes
fixed on the cruiser and the unconscious driver. Kicking the
rear cargo door of the SUV aside, sending it spinning across
the street, where it struck the concrete median with a loud
crash, the smaller monster leaned over the hood of the cruiser,
one taloned paw reaching for the windshield and the guy behind the wheel.

"Wake up! Wake up!" Corey screamed at the driver, who
was slowly stirring. The car rocked suddenly; Corey turned
to see the cop monster behind them leaning on the rear end,
reaching for the blonde on the backseat next to him. Suddenly the cruiser lurched forward and crashed again. The
crash was followed by an explosion so loud it wiped out all
other sounds. It made his ears ring with such volume it hurt.

1:03 p.m.

Joe Burton regained his senses not a moment too soon.
With his head lolling on the steering wheel, the first thing he
saw when he came to was a short-barrel shotgun stuck in a
holster fastened to the inside of the driver's door. The second
thing he saw, lifting his head at the sound of the kid screaming in the backseat, was another of the half-pint imps leaning over the hood of the cruiser, reaching for him.

The windshield was cracked in a hundred places, resembling a spider's web. Realizing the cruiser's engine was still
running, Joe stepped on the gas and rammed the small monster, pinning its legs against the rear bumper of the SUV. The
thing let out a howl of pain. He pulled the shotgun from its
holster, rested it on the steering wheel, and pulled the trigger. The ensuing blast, which blew out the entire windshield,
was deafening and painful as the gun's recoil drove the stock
into Joe's chest. The effect on the creature in front of the car,
though, was worse. Being blasted at such close range, its

face and most of its head disappeared in a mass of blood and torn flesh.

Joe threw the gearshift into reverse and hit the gas without a backward glance. The car shuddered from another impact and the kid in the backseat screamed, "Look out!" Instinctively, Joe slammed on the brakes and looked back just in time to see the cop monster—whose talons had been inches from the blonde's head—knocked to the street on its ass. Before the thing could regain its feet, Joe threw the gear into drive and stomped on the gas pedal again.

"Hold on to something!" Joe cried, spinning the wheel and steering the cruiser around the crashed SUV, but the kid in the backseat was tossed around like an autumn leaf in the wind. With the police car out of reach, the cop creature set upon, and devoured, the remains of the child-monster lying dead against the SUV.

With its hood dented and the damaged front end shuddering, The NYPD cruiser continued along West Street past Leight Street and a construction site where several monsters were devouring hapless construction workers earning some Sunday overtime. Just beyond the construction area a yellow city cab lay on its side, gasoline pouring into the street from its ruptured fuel tank. Not realizing that part of the cruiser's rear bumper was still intact, dragging behind and sending up a shower of sparks as it skipped over the asphalt, Joe drove through the stream of gas. Sparks from the bumper ignited the fuel, creating a burning fuse that ran back to the cab. The crashed vehicle exploded into flame with a loud *whump!*

Ahead, another police cruiser was in motion, swerving through the havoc in the streets. From behind a delivery truck that had smashed into a building on the corner of Vestry Street, a young woman, carrying a swaddled infant in one arm, ran into the street and hailed the cruiser by wildly waving her free arm. The cruiser swerved toward her and, for a moment, Joe thought it was going to stop and save the woman. In a matter of seconds, however, it became clear the other cop car was not going to stop. The woman had as much to fear from the police vehicle as she did from the hungry goblins in the street.

Seeing what was about to happen and frustrated by his inability to do anything about it, Joe hammered on the horn to no avail; he could barely hear it above the siren's blast. The cruiser ahead swerved away from a squat, red-haired creature feasting on a bicyclist—ten-speed and all—and hit the woman with its right front fender. Arms and legs akimbo, the woman rose into the air as if jettisoned from a catapult. Her baby flew from her arms upon impact. It somersaulted sideways and looked like it was going to collide with the side of the building its mother had just come out of, but at the last second a very fat abomination caught the infant as easily as a baseball player fielding a pop fly. The fat brute cradled the infant in its massive paw. The baby looked up at the gargantuan cooing over it and began to cry. A second later, a luminous egg flew into the baby's bawling mouth and the infant underwent an immediate transformation into a demoniacal horror, six feet in length with a wide mouth full of thin needle-like teeth. The deformity that held it no longer found the changeling attractive and dropped it to run after the baby's poor mother, who had landed, sprawled on her back, on the roof of a white Cadillac Deville. Two other hellish creatures got there first, and a fight ensued when the third joined them. The dropped baby monster crawled feebly on all fours along the sidewalk, its ungainly mouth still open and emitting a feral mewling sound as it searched for sustenance.

The police cruiser responsible for the destruction of the mother and baby spun out of control after the hit-and-run and slammed into the concrete meridian dividing the east and west traffic lanes on West Street. The car hit the wall with its left front fender and leaped sideways in the air, its back end swiveling around to strike the divider again with its right side before sliding to a stop.

"Good enough for you!" Joe shouted, horrified and outraged by what the car had done to mother and baby. His vengeful elation was short-lived, though, when he saw two teenagers—neither old enough to drive by the looks of them—get out of the smoking wreck and try to make a run for it.

Within five yards both were caught and quickly devoured by grotesque, inhuman aberrations.

Joe drove by the wreck, keeping his eyes averted from the carnage. "Oh, shit!" he exclaimed.

"What's wrong?" the blonde in the backseat screamed.

Joe didn't have time to answer; dead ahead the road was blocked from the sidewalk on the right to the concrete divider on the left by half a dozen crashed cars. The multicar accident had drawn a horde of the alien creatures, who stood atop and crawled over the wreckage, prying open car roofs to get at the tasty human treats inside. Joe cut the wheel hard to the right, driving up onto the sidewalk at the corner of Vestry Street without stepping on the brakes. The right side of the cruiser scraped against the corner of a building—a large brightly painted blue-and-yellow structure housing the Keystone Moving and Storage Company—causing sparks to fly as metal made contact with stone and the side mirror and door handles, front and back, were ripped off.

1:07 p.m.

Father Ralph Dupont prayed silently and kept a wary lookout from where he lay under one of the Keystone Moving Company's large trucks parked on Vestry Street, just around the corner from West Street. As he prayed, he frantically tried to make sense of the nightmare he had been plunged into. If only it *was* a nightmare. He could wish it to be so, he knew, but that wouldn't make it so. Though he was a man of the cloth, a man of faith, he was also a practical man who had always believed in the old adage: Seeing is believing.

As the leading force in New York City's Catholic Charismatic movement, Father Ralph had made a name for himself both as a healer capable of curing the faithful with a mere laying on of hands and as a debunker of phony miracles. Just a few weeks before the city was invaded by the horrid things he was now hiding from, Father Ralph had been called upon by the diocese to investigate a supposed miracle at Our Lady of the Lilies, a small church in the heart of Little Italy. One of the basement windows of the church had seemingly displayed on it an image of the Virgin Mary that no one could explain. Despite the thronging faithful who gathered outside the church each day to pray to the image, Father Ralph had disproved the miracle with a simple scientific explanation: *condensation.*

The church had recently installed double-pane thermal windows in its basement, but the one displaying the image of the Holy Mother had been put in with a slight undetected crack in the glass under the window's metal frame. Moisture had leaked in, causing the image to appear. Of course, that had done nothing to dissuade the faithful, who cared nothing for science. Finding himself caught in the middle, Father Ralph had tried to placate those who believed the image to be a miracle with an explanation similar to his version of the intelligent design theory, that is, just because the image (like the evolution of man) could be explained scientifically didn't mean it wasn't an act (or design) by God.

The bishop himself had called Father Ralph to congratulate him on his tactful handling of the episode. It had been one of the proudest moments of the priest's life. Now, cowering beneath the moving truck, watching his city possessed by madness and worse, the charismatic priest wondered what the bishop would have to say now. For Father Ralph there was no explanation that he could latch on to and believe to stave off the onset of insanity that he'd been fighting since witnessing the first person—a nice old lady at the little market on the corner of Desbrosses and Greenwich Streets not far from the rectory where he lived—transform into a hellish demon right before his eyes.

"Dear Lord, give me strength," Father Ralph murmured into the asphalt. Repeating the prayer over and over, Father Ralph slid out from beneath the truck. Since hiding there he had been racked with guilt, listening to the sounds of violence and carnage going on around him. For the first time in his clerical life, he had a crisis of faith. Was this an act of God? He automatically thought of the story of Noah and God's promise to the human race that never again would He destroy the earth by flood. Was this then the alternative?

The majority of the people in the world had certainly become wicked and faithless. He also thought about the Book of Revelations; could this be the Second Coming of Christ? Could it be Judgment Day? As a priest, he sorely wanted to believe that, but as a practical man, a man of science, he could not accept it. Having seen the tiny spheres of light pour from the sky, and after seeing what those spheres did to the people they invaded, his scientific side theorized that the orbs were really *eggs*, probably from another planet, and the creatures people transformed into were an alien race. Thus the battle lines were drawn in his mind, and he waged a mental war. The culmination of his inner fight came to this: If this was an act of God, preceding the Second Coming and Judgment Day, then those who became infected and turned into demons were the wicked at heart and deserving of the Lord's punishment.

If, on the other hand, this was a scientific phenomenon constituting an invasion of the earth by an alien race, there had to be some way, scientifically, to fight the aliens and save the planet. Another thought occurred to him—if it *was* Judgment Day, then shouldn't he, as a man of God, be unafraid? Shouldn't he, as God's representative on earth, be able to pass unharmed among the demons from Hell? And, if this had nothing to do with God—except perhaps to disprove His existence—wasn't it Father Ralph's duty as a scientist to try to communicate with the aliens, or at least find some way to fight them?

He was a man of faith first, a man of God, and there was only one simple way to prove the existence of the divine being he believed in.

And this realization brought Father Ralph out of his hiding place.

1:08 p.m.

Joe Burton had cringed at the grating sound of metal against stone as the cruiser clipped the edge of the building housing the moving company. In the backseat, the boy and the blonde had screamed when a shower of sparks flew as the door handle and side mirror were torn free. Joe spun the wheel, maneuvering the car back onto the street, narrowly missing a parked car at the curb. What he saw ahead caused him to slam on the brakes. In the middle of Vestry Street stood a tall priest, eyes closed. He appeared to be praying while holding up a string of rosary beads.

Unbelievably, none of the maleficent beings paid any attention to the holy man. There were three of the abominations on the street going from car to car and building to building, searching for victims to consume, and none of them noticed the priest. The cruiser screeched to a fishtailing stop, and Joe leaned out of the doorless driver's side and shouted to the man.

"Father! Over here! Hurry!"

The priest either ignored Joe's invitation, or couldn't hear it over the wailing of the police cruiser's siren, which caught the attention of the three monsters on the block. As one, they each looked at the cop car. With what Joe could only describe as expressions of joy on their freakish faces, the trio of brutes started for the cruiser. Unbelievably, they still ignored, or did not see, the priest in the road.

"Hey!" Joe tried again, shouting as loud as he could. The man didn't respond. Frantically, Joe scanned the dashboard looking for the siren switch but couldn't find it.

The three monsters came closer.

1:10 p.m.

Father Ralph Dupont was ecstatic. He had conquered fear and proved to himself the existence of God and that this day was indeed the Lord's judgment upon a world and a race that had exceeded the wickedness even of Noah's time. How else could he walk untouched among the hellish demons around him, armed only with his rosary beads and the word of God? It was all the proof he needed that this was the end of the world.

In a state of spiritual bliss such as he had never known, Father Ralph walked amid the inhuman ones, praying ecstatically. Even the jarring siren of a police cruiser and the shouts of its driver could not interrupt his religious fervor.

He ignored the man, certain that he was in God's hands and only God could deliver him to safety. Father Ralph wanted to tell the man that escape was futile and that his only salvation was to get on his knees and beg God's forgiveness, but before he could, one of the flying bits of light appeared in front of him, hovering less than a foot from his face.

Father Ralph said the last line of the Lord's Prayer: "For thine is the kingdom, and the power, and the glory forever," before the hovering orb flew into his mouth. It reminded him of the sacrament of communion. Certain that *his* glowing pod was the Holy Spirit materialized, he whispered, "Body of Christ," swallowed, and added, "Amen."

His metamorphosis was violent and rapid. With an expression of horror and betrayal on his face, Father Ralph began the convulsive dance that marked the beginning of his transformation from human to misshapen colossus. His body became rigid, then relaxed, then rigid again. It repeated this, gaining speed until he was jitterbugging in a mad circle in the middle of the street. His chest heaved and his head jerked back and forth with such violence it was a wonder his neck didn't break. His stomach bulged until it looked as though he had swallowed a watermelon whole. It receded and bulged again, but instead of receding this time the bulge divided into several separate lumps that traveled beneath his flesh to his arms and legs.

Father Ralph grew.

His legs expanded first, splitting his trousers at the thighs, then at the knees and calves. His toes shot through the tips of his black leather wingtips, and the shoes disintegrated in pieces around his swelling feet. His trousers continued to tear under pressure from his expanding anatomy. They split at every seam and more until they flew from his body in rags. His arm muscles bulged to three times their normal size so rapidly that his black frock's sleeves literally exploded from his arms in shreds.

Within thirty seconds, he had grown so large he was naked, his celibate genitalia exposed. His body continued to expand everywhere except between his legs. In contrast his sexual organs shrunk, seemingly sucked up into his bloating anatomy until they disappeared altogether. His fingers and hands refused to be constrained by the rosary beads wrapped around them. They inflated until the strands broke and fell to the ground and still his hands grew. Keeping time with the rest of his multiplying flesh, his facial features and head underwent torturous growth as well. Accompanied by the sound of bones cracking and other wrenching internal noises, Father Ralph's skull took on elephantine proportions. His forehead bulged and gave birth to four devil-like horns. His eyes widened, separated by the massive protuberance of flesh that had seconds before been his aquiline nose. The flesh of his countenance rippled and bulged. The corners of his mouth became a tear, ripping through his cheeks as it spread. Like a teething infant, new teeth—more akin to railroad spikes than dentures—cut his gums in row upon row like a shark's, each one razor sharp, the eyeteeth becoming fangs any vampire would envy. As if heeding a sound inaudible to ordinary human ears, Father Ralph's enlarged to keep pace with the rest of his head. Mimicking the auricles of a bat, they spread out, becoming membranous and capable of catching the faintest of sounds. Their peaks split in three, each part moving independently, the way an animal's ears will move in the direction of sound.

Metamorphosis complete, the repugnant ogre that Father Ralph had become threw back its head and howled with rage and anguish against God for forsaking him.

1:14 p.m.

Hypnotized by the spectacle as much as the kid next to her and the guy in the front seat, Cindy Raposa watched the priest turn into something never before seen on Earth. Still partially in the dopey embrace of her last fix, which heightened her sense of paranoia and fear of being caught and eaten by the creatures that reminded her of pictures of trolls she had seen once in an illustrated edition of *The Hobbit,* she, of the three in the cruiser, broke free first of the mesmerizing vision of the priest shape-shifting. She looked around and realized they were being flanked by the three other demoniacal beasts.

"I think we better get out of here," she said loudly. "Like right *now*!" she added, shouting when the driver didn't immediately respond. The kid next to her was quicker on the uptake. He glanced left, then right, and slammed both hands against the metal screen dividing the front and backseats.

"Get us out of here!" he screamed.

1:15 p.m.

Joe Burton couldn't tear his eyes away from the priest's terrible transformation. It had all the appeal of a car wreck—horrible to look at yet fascinating at the same time. The blonde's words went in one ear and out the other, never registering. Even the kid's banging on the screen couldn't pull him from the sight right away. It wasn't until the boy grabbed the dividing screen, shook it, and screamed did Joe respond.

He looked right—one of the hellish beings was charging like a deranged rhino. He looked left—another of the grotesque titans was charging from the opposite direction. Straight ahead the third one also charged when it saw its meal ticket might be consumed by the other two. Joe hit the gas. The rear tires spun, screeching loud enough to rival the blaring siren while spitting out a cloud of smoke as the tires burned rubber. The rear end fishtailed slightly to the right before the spinning wheels caught. The car took off just as the monsters charging from the sides reached the vehicle, arms and hands thrust out to grab the escaping car. Each missed the cruiser by mere inches but found one another as they collided head-first. The one to the left, having got the worst of it, fell to the ground, its forehead split open and blood gushing from the wound. The one on the right slumped to the street, unconscious.

The sight and smell of the injured monster's fresh blood was enough to distract the being charging from the front away from the cruiser. It galloped past the cop car and fell upon its wounded comrade. Only the brute that had been the priest a moment ago remained in front of them. Joe raised the shotgun barrel, aimed it through the broken windshield at the former priest, but didn't fire. Strangely the monster minister ignored the approaching police car and remained where it was, arms above its head, hands reaching for Heaven, its head back and mouth open wide in what could only be described as a sorrowful howling. To Joe it seemed as though the garish former clergyman was berating God. Instead of blasting the priest monster, Joe steered the car around him and continued speeding up the street.

Without a sideways glance, Joe raced the car through the intersection with Washington Street, nearly crashing into a three-wheeled police motorcycle that looked more like an ice-cream vendor than a police vehicle. A twenty-foot monster gave chase from the intersection, lumbering after them, the pavement cracking beneath its feet with every pounding step. Ahead, Joe could see several pedestrians being pursued by monsters and flying eggs. Thinking the police car was coming to rescue them, they ran frantically toward the approaching cruiser. Joe saw them coming and wanted to stop and help them, but he knew that would mean certain death for all of them, including himself and his passengers.

A young woman ran into the street, her hands up and waving for Joe to stop. Before Joe could respond, a hulking monstrosity pounced, scooped her up, and chomped her body in two, leaving the woman's lower half—her intestines dangling from her severed waist like a string of uncooked sausages—gripped tightly in its brawny mitt. As the enormous thing shoveled the remainder of the woman into its mouth, Joe sped by. With little room to maneuver, the driver's side wheels ran over the creature's left foot, causing Joe and his passengers to be jostled violently. The creature let out a snarling roar of pain, bits of flesh spewing from its bloody maw. It grabbed at its trampled toes, hopping about on one foot until it tripped over a parked car and crashed to the ground, crushing a man trying to escape from another ghoulish predator. The monster giving chase was not pleased at losing its meal and attacked the one who lay upon its dinner. A snarling fight ensued.

1:20 p.m.

The police car reached the end of the block. The driver made a hard skidding left onto Greenwich Street, and Corey was nearly thrown into the blonde's lap again. Only the fact that he had the fingers of both hands entwined in the wire mesh of the dividing screen kept him from falling.

As far as Corey could see in both directions on Greenwich, pandemonium reigned. There were fewer flying pods now, but only because most had already infected people and turned them into things that nightmares are made of. The police cruiser appeared to be the only car still moving on the street. The road was strewn with wrecks of cars that had crashed into each other, into fire hydrants, telephone poles, streetlight poles, and into buildings right and left.

Corey held on tight to the dividing screen as the car swerved back and forth under the driver's control. Corey tried not to look at the scenes of carnage going on all around him but even looking straight ahead was no better.

And it was about to get worse.

1:22 p.m.

Cindy Raposa wanted to see the mayhem on Greenwich Street even less than Corey did. She rode in the backseat slouched down, her knees pulled up to her chest, her arms wrapped around her legs, as close to a fetal position as she could get. She kept her eyes tightly shut and wished she could do the same with her ears. The screams and roars she heard, mingled with the wail of the cruiser's siren, made her cringe and draw deeper into herself until she heard the kid in the backseat with her scream, "Look out!"

He followed the warning with a hard shove to Cindy's left shoulder, and she was forced to open her eyes and look up. One of the glowing, infectious orbs was in the front seat, flitting about the guy driving. His left hand was on the wheel and his right held the shotgun, which he used like a flyswatter, trying to bat the sparkling intruder back through the shattered windshield. The orb dodged his frantic attempts to hit it and suddenly flew straight at the boy, whose face was right up against the dividing screen. Startled, the kid fell back into Cindy's lap. At the same moment, the driver swung the barrel of the shotgun at the thing, hitting it hard, crushing it into the screen. He hit the screen so hard it broke free and tumbled into the backseat, hitting both the kid and Cindy. Though the mesh had scratched his right arm, the boy didn't cry; he was more concerned with locating the orb.

"Where is it?" he cried kicking free of the screen. He pulled his legs and feet onto the seat and looked frantically for the orb.

"I crushed it!" the guy driving cried triumphantly.

A shriek from the kid proved him wrong as the monster-making sphere rose from the floor and made a pass at his head. Moving quickly, the boy dodged it and dived headfirst into the front seat. The ball of light followed.

"Stay down!" the guy driving yelled and brought the shotgun up to shoot the thing. To Cindy's and the driver's surprise it flew right down the barrel. He had only to pull the trigger to send the thing exploding from the car in a hail of buckshot.

"Take that, you fucker!" he yelled.

The sound of the gun in such close quarters was deafening and left Cindy with ringing ears. Every noise she now heard sounded as if she were underwater.

1:26 p.m.

"We've got to find a place to hide!" Joe shouted.

"What?" the blonde in the backseat yelled.

"We've got to find a place to hide!" Joe shouted again.

"What?" the blonde yelled back again.

Joe couldn't blame her; between the ringing in his ears from the gun blast and the wailing from the cruiser's sirens, he could barely hear his own voice. The boy, now in the front seat with him, ducked down and stuck his hand under the middle of the dashboard. A moment later, the siren stopped.

"Way to go!" Joe shouted at the kid. "How'd you know how to do that?"

"My dad's a policeman," the boy replied.

Joe sensed a note of sadness in the kid's voice. He felt for the kid, losing his mother and his aunt and not knowing where his father was or even if he was alive.

"We've got to get off the street and hide," the girl in the backseat shouted.

"No shit, Einstein, I just said that!" He was suddenly distracted as he realized they were passing King Street, where he lived. His apartment was the first place he had thought to hide, but now he saw that the short, narrow street was teeming with monsters attacking the brownstones lining the avenue. They were picking hapless, screaming victims from windows and chowing down on them.

A block farther he spun the wheel to avoid a three-car pileup in the middle of the intersection. Joe steered to the left, turning the corner of West Houston Street within inches of being grabbed by an old, white-haired, grizzled monster. At the corner of the next intersection, where West Houston met Washington, Joe found the hiding place he was looking for—the Big Apple Parking Garage. It was a fortunate discovery, seeing as how the road ahead was impassible due to a bevy of monsters feasting on hapless victims.

1:30 p.m.

Charlie Ebersole woke up in a shitty mood, cramped in the front seat of his tow truck on the rooftop parking level of the Big Apple Parking Garage. It was bad enough that he'd had to come out on a Sunday morning to do a tow job, and that he hadn't had enough money on him—having left his apartment still half-asleep—to get a lousy cup of coffee at Starbucks, he was hungover to boot. A hangover on a Sunday morning wasn't unusual for Charlie, who liked his suds during his Saturday-night dart league at Chubby's Pub on the Lower East Side where he lived, but a hangover of *this* magnitude was.

"It was the goddamned boilermakers," he muttered to himself.

If he had been able to sleep it off, he would have been

fine, but the phone ringing off the hook at 10:30 a.m. hadn't allowed that. Since Charlie hated answering machines, he didn't have one and was forced to pick up when the phone didn't stop ringing. He'd tried begging off due to illness when the call turned out to be his boss wanting him to do the Big Apple tow job, but the other driver for Bean Towing was out of town at his sister's wedding. Even knowing the call meant time and a half, Charlie would have turned it down if he could, but his boss, Harold Bean, was a prick who liked to remind Charlie that tow-truck drivers were a dime a dozen. "Any retard can drive and operate a tow truck," he was fond of saying.

"When am I gonna learn my lesson?" he grunted more than *spoke* the words. The problem was Charlie was not the type to turn down a free drink or back away from a challenge. Charlie burped, tasting the sour mix of beer and whiskey, almost causing him to ralph, and rubbed his protruding beer belly. He got ready to fling his door open if he did puke. Too many times he had upchucked out the window only to have to scrape dried vomit off the door later. Even feeling as sick as he did, Charlie had to smile remembering how he had beaten Bill Straight in a drinking contest by downing ten boilermakers to Bill's seven in the space of three minutes. Of course, after such a win, everyone in the bar, it seemed, had had to buy Charlie a victory drink. Not one to be discourteous or turn down a free drink, Charlie had, of course, accepted each and every one of them until he was so pie-eyed he had barely been able to walk the block and a half from the pub to his apartment.

Feeling his stomach settle a bit and the danger of blowing chunks pass, Charlie took his hand off the door handle and looked again at the car behind him that he was supposed to tow.

"The car's been here three months and the owner's more than three weeks behind on the rent, so it's time to say, 'bye-bye,'" the attendant, a nice enough young Italian-looking guy, had told Charlie.

"Eighteen-kay-t-o-o," Charlie read aloud off the order sheet on the seat next to him and looked at the plate, checking again that it was the right one.

Upon arriving at the top level of the parking garage at 11:15, he had driven his rear end, ramp-loading tow truck around looking for the Honda Civic he'd been instructed to tow. When he found it, he had sized up the job quickly, seeing that if he pulled the front of the truck right up to the guardrail at the edge of the roof overlooking Washington Street he could load the car lickety-split. Seeing as how it was, by then, only 11:30, Charlie had decided to take a little snooze to try to sleep off some of the alcohol he still felt in his system. Besides, there was no use in rushing this one. If he finished the job too soon his time and a half wouldn't amount to much. Chuckling to himself at the thought of screwing his asshole boss for some *real* overtime pay, he had put the truck in position at the edge of the roof to load the car, shut off the engine, and put his feet up on the dashboard.

"That cheap fuck, old man Bean, can kiss my ass," Charlie had muttered as he settled in and closed his eyes. "I'm gonna milk this for as long as I can."

1:31 p.m.

Joe Burton cut the wheel hard right to avoid two cars that had smashed head-on, then cut it to the left again and into the parking garage. The police cruiser hit the speed bump at the entrance with a hard bang of its worn-out shocks. The kid in the seat next to him bounced in the air, nearly going through the now open space where the windshield had been. The girl in the backseat let out a short shriek as she was jostled about, and Joe nearly fell out of the doorless opening beside him. They were all disrupted again when the cruiser hit the bottom of the entrance ramp, where the front end thumped loudly and the bumper scraped against the concrete. Giving the darkened ground level of the parking garage a quick once-over, he saw that there were three rows of parked cars—a short one against the left wall that ran from the entrance to a ramp up to the other levels, a long one in the middle of the garage stretching all the way to the other end of the building, and an equally long one against the right wall. Seeing no monsters or infectious orbs, Joe steered the police car into an empty space between a BMW and a Mercedes in the middle row, almost directly across from the ramp leading to the upper levels of the garage.

"We've got to shut off these flashing lights!" Joe said. The boy next to him pointed to a toggle switch to the left of the steering wheel, and Joe flicked it. The strobing red-and-blue lights died, immersing them in shadows. For several minutes they sat in silence as anguished cries of victims mingled with the terrible sounds of the monstrous creatures devouring them echoed in the cavernous garage. The blonde in the backseat covered her ears with her hands while the boy next to Joe sat up on his knees looking left and right for any sign of danger.

"Hey kid," Joe whispered, "I'm sorry about—" He didn't get to finish.

"Get down!" the boy whispered loudly, pointing toward the entrance. One of the glowing orbs had floated into the garage and was coming their way.

Joe slid down in his seat behind the wheel as the boy ducked and did the same. The girl in the back followed suit but couldn't keep from emitting a constant soft whimper.

"Shhh!" Joe shushed. He raised his head just enough to see. The orb was floating slowly from car to car as if searching each one for victims. It came closer and closer to the police car.

1:39 p.m.

Tiny, four-foot-ten Wendy Tremain had been hiding behind her boyfriend's Jaguar in the Big Apple Garage for she didn't know how long—ever since he had been eaten alive by some kind of murdering, cannibalistic creature the likes of which she never could have imagined even in her worst nightmares. They had been walking down West Houston Street from his apartment to the garage to head uptown for lunch before going to the Garden for the final game in the NBA championship playoffs. Her boyfriend, Conway Bergman, had courtside box seats for the game, courtesy of his boss at Chase Manhattan Bank: a reward for Conway's outstanding work on a recent high-profile account.

After spending all day Saturday and Saturday night together, the weekend had been shaping up to be magical until disaster had struck in the form of a cloud of sparkling flying things that had beset them just as they had reached the Big Apple Parking Garage, where Conway kept his Jag. Wendy had immediately sensed something sinister and ominous in the swarm of firefly-like things, but Conway had been dazzled and fascinated by them—until a deliveryman for the Sunday *New York Times* swallowed one as he got out of his truck nearby. The glowing orb transformed him into a hideous gigantic freak of nature right before their eyes.

Overcome with awe, Conway had realized the danger too late. Wendy, on the other hand, had been slowly moving toward the safety of the parking garage entrance from the first moment the strange fireflies had appeared. She had shouted for Conway to join her and get away from the things, but, like the proverbial cat, curiosity had gotten the best of him. Wendy had watched in abject terror as the former *Times*-delivery-guy-turned-androgynous-carnivore ate Conway in less than a minute. She had been frozen with fear and shock until Conway's blood splattered across her face. The warm liquid on her skin was the catalyst that had got her moving. She fled into the darkened interior of the parking garage.

With no key to unlock Conway's car—he had been holding them in his hand and they were now in the belly of the beast that had eaten him—Wendy had ducked behind the Jaguar parked against the wall near the ramp leading to the upper levels. There she had sat, tears streaming down her face, the knuckles of both hands jammed in her mouth to keep contained the insane scream of anguish that wanted to fly from her lips. Too much in shock to wonder what she was going to do, she blocked out the screams and unearthly roars from the street outside the garage.

Never in her life had Wendy been so frightened, and never

had she been so glad to see a police car as when one, its lights flashing, pulled into the garage. She struggled to stand and found that both her legs had gone to sleep. Awkwardly, she had risen, rubbing the nerves in her legs awake until she was able to run toward the police car. In her haste and joy at being rescued, she was oblivious to the firefly that was methodically floating from car to car less than twelve feet away.

"Help me! Please!" Wendy cried out, running toward the cruiser.

1:42 p.m.

Corey Aaron raised his head just enough to see where the searching orb was and saw the well-dressed, tiny twenty-something redhead running toward the police car at the same moment that she cried out for help. He saw the small glowing round light move quickly toward her.

"Look out!" Corey screamed, grabbing the dashboard with both hands and standing.

Too late the woman saw the orb coming at her. She screamed and tried to duck, but the sphere was too fast for her. It anticipated her move, dipping as she ducked, and flew into her open screaming mouth.

"No!" Corey groaned.

The woman swallowed, coughed. Her eyes, full of despair and fear, locked onto Corey's.

"No! No! No!" Corey cried repeatedly, each negative utterance more emotional than the last until he was sobbing out the words as he watched the small woman succumb to what had invaded her, bringing raw memories of his aunt's transformation and his mother's abduction back like boomeranging sledgehammers. As the woman changed and the last vestiges of her humanness fell away, Corey collapsed on the passenger's seat as if struck.

1:43 p.m.

Joe Burton slid to an upright position behind the wheel when he heard the boy scream. For the umpteenth time that morning he was both enraptured and appalled at the metamorphosis of another human being into a repellent hulk hungry for human flesh. Even knowing that he, the boy, and the blonde in the backseat were in immediate danger from the woman transforming before his eyes, Joe still could not look away or react.

It wasn't until the girl in the back reached over the seat, grabbed his arm, and shook it, screaming, "Get us the fuck out of here!" was the trance broken. Only then, just as the petite young woman finished becoming one of the misshapen hellish beasts, did Joe put the cruiser in gear and floor the gas pedal. Tires spinning, he veered around her and took the only avenue of escape that was open—the ramp to the upper levels of the parking garage.

The redheaded monster, now large enough that the top of her head nearly grazed the concrete ceiling, gave chase.

1:44 p.m.

Cindy Raposa's keening whine erupted into an all-out scream as the car went up the winding ramp, and she saw the newly transformed redheaded monster hunched over and using its hands as well as its feet to scrabble after the cruiser. Its shoulders and back repeatedly scraped against the roof of the ramp, but the thing continued after them. Every few feet it reached with one of its clawed hands toward Cindy. Its sharp talons scraped on the trunk of the cop car as the vehicle kept just enough ahead of it. The sound of the beast's claws scraping on the trunk were one hundred times more piercing and irritating than nails on a blackboard.

"Hurry-hurry-hurry-hurry!" Cindy babbled.

"Faster! Faster!" the kid joined in.

"Take this!" The guy driving offered the pump-action, short-barrel shotgun over the front seat to Cindy with his right hand while steering the car around the curling ramp with his left.

"Shoot it!" he ordered Cindy.

She took one look at the gun and shook her head violently. "I can't!" she cried.

The guy swore under his breath. "Kid, grab the wheel and

just keep it turned all the way to the left like this," he ordered the boy next to him. Looking scared enough to void his bowels, the kid did as he was told. As soon as the boy had the wheel, the guy held the shotgun diagonally in front of his chest and pumped it.

"Get down!" he commanded Cindy as he turned to aim the gun out the rear window.

Cindy dove onto the seat facedown and covered her ears, but the blast from the gun only a foot above her head still proved deafening.

1:45 p.m.

Charlie Ebersole heard sirens—lots of them. He didn't think much of it at first; sirens were common in the city. As he got out of the truck, though, and hit the side lever near the door that put the flat rear bed in the ramp/loading position so that the car could be pulled onto it, screams reached his ears, accompanied by gunshots and the most ungodly bellowing and roaring sounds he had ever heard. His first thought was that lions or tigers had somehow got loose on the streets below, but that made no sense; it was crazy. There were no circuses in town as far as he knew. There were no zoos downtown; the closest one was the Children's Zoo in Central Park. Though he had never been there and didn't know what types of animals were kept, he doubted any of them could have made it the twelve miles or more from the park to downtown.

Charlie was about to have a look over the edge of the roof to see what the hell was going on when something else caught his attention. Rising up over the guardrail surrounding the rooftop level's edge was a glittering little ball. Charlie had never seen anything like it and had to run a hand over his eyes to be sure it wasn't a hangover-induced illusion. His head certainly hurt bad enough that his vision throbbed in time to the pounding pulse in his head.

It was no illusion.

The sparkling object, the size of a pea, was joined by another one roughly the same size. The two hovered in midair, parallel to each other like a pair of tiny disembodied eyeballs. Suddenly a fat pigeon swooped down on the duo, snatching one out of the air as it would an insect. Almost instantly as the bird landed, and eyed the other orb for dessert, it began to change.

Charlie couldn't believe his eyes. The gray-and-white pigeon went into a funny, herky-jerky, spinning dance and its body began to swell. Feathers flew everywhere as the bird twitched and flapped its expanding wings. Its eyeballs bulged from its ballooning head, and the pigeon grew as large as a small dog and kept going. In less than a minute the bird was as big as a German shepherd. In a minute and a half it was as large as a full-grown cow. Its beak swelled to a size large enough to swallow Charlie whole and began sprouting jagged teeth. Beneath its voluminous body, its three-toed feet stretched, quadrupling in size and sharpness until they resembled the tearing talons of a dragon.

As Charlie watched with shock and fascination, the pigeon completed its growth and transformation. By the time it was finished changing, it was as big as a horse with a wingspan of a good twelve feet or more. Its head was three times as large as a basketball and spiked with horny protrusions. Its feathers had morphed into leathery scales. Its talons were as long and deadly sharp as swords. Its bulging eyes were as wide as saucers, and they were looking at Charlie as though he were a tasty, fat worm.

It was too much for Charlie. All the beer, whiskey, peanuts, and potato chips he had devoured during last night's binge churned nauseatingly in his stomach, charged up his throat, and out his mouth, splattering all over the now fully tilted ramp of his tow truck. He tried to back away from the misshapen fowl as he coughed and vomited again. As another flood from his stomach gushed forth, the second little ball of light slipped into his mouth and forced its way down his gagging throat.

Like the pigeon, Charlie now did his own convulsive jig. His head felt as though it were going to explode. He wasn't that far off. With all human thought suddenly expunged

from his mind, Charlie's size multiplied until he was a cor-
pulent demoniacal monster towering over the deformed pigeon. The tables turned, Charlie the monster now hungrily
eyed the big fat scavenger bird as a light rain began to fall.

1:46 p.m.

The shotgun blast had missed. The buckshot struck the
wall, kicking out a cloud of concrete dust. Even so, the thing
that had, moments before, been right on their tail now lagged
behind, seemingly growing tired as it had barely enough
room to move on the ramp. Joe handed the gun to the kid
and retook the wheel.

"Where are you going?" the blonde screeched from the
backseat.

Joe cringed, finding her voice as irritating as a dentist's
drill.

"We'll be trapped on the roof!" she added just as shrilly.

Joe ignored her, but the kid next to him looked worried.
Joe winked at him. "Don't worry, kid. I know what I'm
doing," he lied, but the lie had the desired effect on the kid;
he nodded at Joe. Around one more revolution of the concrete ramp Joe could see daylight. Joe looked in the rearview
mirror. There was no sign of the redheaded monster. A moment later the cruiser emerged onto the rooftop and Joe and
the boy were cooled by the drizzling rain coming through
the opening where the windshield had been. Joe spun the
wheel hard left to avoid the first row of cars near the entrance ramp and came face to face with a giant pigeon so
strange looking Joe almost laughed. But as the thing flapped
its scaly wings, opened its beak lined with menacing teeth,
and let out a roaring *"coo!"* Joe no longer found it humorous.

He slammed on the brakes and brought the squad car to a
skidding stop. As the pigeon charged, Joe tromped on the
gas again. The cruiser sped under the monster bird as it
leaped in the air to pounce on the car. The bird from Hell
missed but immediately spun around and gave chase. Suddenly a Honda crashed across the path of the cruiser. Its li-
cense plate—18K TOO—caught Joe's eye as the car repeatedly

R. Patrick Gates

rolled over, sending broken glass and bits of metal flying in all directions. A former-human-now-a-monster followed the car, leaping out from behind a tow truck that had its ramp up. The misshapen monster had a grotesquely bulging belly. As it crouched to receive them it reminded Joe of a statue of Buddha—only this Buddha had come from Hell, not Nirvana. Joe slammed on the brakes again, causing the car to slide sideways toward the gruesome rotund colossus.

Not waiting for the car to come to a halt, Joe hit the accelerator again and cut the wheel hard left. The wheels spun, sending a thick acrid cloud of burned rubber into the deformity's face, and the cruiser spun completely around until it was heading back toward the winged behemoth. The police car raced under the capacious avian's left wing. Its scales scratched over the hood of the car like a scouring pad. Caught off balance by its prey's sudden change of direction, the pigeon horror nipped awkwardly at the vehicle passing under its wing and managed to hook the edge of the car's roof with its fanged beak. As the police car sped on, the bird monster clamped down and tore the entire roof off the squad car, instantly turning it into a convertible. The burly flying thing tossed the roof aside and continued the chase, its scaly wings flapping furiously. The shorn roof hit the fat manlike monster in the knees, tripping it. The ungainly creature crashed to the rooftop facedown.

"Shut up, for Christ's sake!" Joe shouted at the blonde in the back, who had started screaming the minute she laid eyes on the monster pigeon and had barely paused for a breath since. The blonde did not heed his words. The kid in front with Joe had dived to the floor under the dash when the roof was ripped off, and he remained huddled there, trembling as if it were freezing winter instead of humid summer. The rain fell harder, refreshing Joe, but also making it harder to see. He turned right and headed toward the exit ramp at the opposite end of the roof. Glancing back, he saw the redheaded she-monster emerge from the entrance ramp.

Abruptly, Joe deftly turned the car again. Luckily there were only a dozen or so cars parked on the roof level, giving him plenty of room to maneuver. The car sped around the outer lane of the lot, drawing the freakish fowl after it. Not far behind the bird, the two human monsters had joined the chase. Joe gripped the wheel tightly, mentally urging the battered vehicle on. If he could just stay ahead of the pursuers, he could get back to the ramp they had come up and escape.

Belying Joe's impression of the monsters as mindless eating machines, the one that had tossed a car at them seemed to understand what Joe had planned. It suddenly gave up the chase and cut across the lot to intercept the roofless squad car before it could reach the ramp. Joe saw only one avenue of escape left open to them, and he didn't like it, but it was preferable to being cannibalized or turned into bird feed.

"Stay down, kid!" Joe shouted at the boy huddled and whimpering on the floor under the dashboard. To the still-shrieking blonde in the backseat he commanded: "Hold on to something!"

Joe turned the wheel and pointed the police cruiser dead on at the tilted ramp of the tow truck at the edge of the roof.

1:49 p.m.

Corey Aaron's favorite daydream had always been flying. He loved to imagine himself as a bird, soaring above the city, doing lazy circles in the sky, or sudden dives like a hawk swooping down upon unsuspecting prey. This fantasy was the reason he had begged his mother to let him join the summer trapeze school at Hudson River Park. It was why he loved to watch old World War II stories about pilots. To become the latter was his fervent dream-goal in life. When the guy driving yelled at Corey to stay down, he—like any child—had had to come out from under the dashboard to look. And when he saw what the guy was about to attempt, Corey realized his dream of flying someday was about to come to fruition—only not in the manner he had always imagined.

1:49:15 p.m.

Cindy Raposa shared no such dreams of flying. The only soaring she had ever wanted to do was the kind that came

with a drug high. It didn't dawn on Cindy what the driver
was doing when he yelled at her to hold on to something.
And it wasn't until she wiped the rain from her eyes and saw
they were heading for the ramp behind the tow truck at the
edge of the roof that understanding finally dawned on her.
Hoarse from almost nonstop screaming, Cindy found renewed strength of voice as the car raced toward the ramp and
empty air beyond.

1:49:25 p.m.

Joe Burton didn't like the idea of what he was doing any
more than Cindy Raposa did, but he was out of options. With
two monsters—not to mention the six-hundred-pound pigeon—chasing them, he saw no other escape. The rooftop
parking lot was too small for the police car to keep eluding
the three monstrosities. And with the creatures showing
enough intelligence to block the ramps, it was only a matter
of time before one of them caught the vehicle and made a
three-course meal of Joe and his two companions.

This being his neighborhood, where he ran every day, Joe
knew there was a UPS warehouse across from them on
Washington Street that was several stories shorter than the
nine-story Big Apple Parking Garage. If he could get the
squad car going fast enough, he figured they could make the
jump onto the warehouse's roof. Of course, he knew they
could die trying, but to his way of thinking it was a death
preferable to being eaten alive.

The front wheels hit the tow truck's ramp and he looked
at the speedometer, but it was broken. It showed the car traveling at zero mph. As the rear wheels caught the ramp, he
was certain it was going to collapse and send them crashing
headfirst onto the street below. The ramp held, though, and
the cruiser flew from it into the open air. Time became suddenly crippled and seconds limped by. Though the rain still
fell, the sun came out. Its warmth cascaded over Joe's head
and shoulders. His foot never left the gas pedal and the engine revved in a high-pitched whine as the rear wheels spun
in the air with nothing to grab on to. The car seemed to hang

in midair as if held up by the golden rays of sunshine from above.

Joe hung on to the wheel like a scared kid on a roller-coaster and couldn't help shouting, "Yahoo!" As the car began its descent toward the roof of the UPS warehouse, he glanced in the rearview mirror. The lumbering Goliath-of-a-pigeon was still following, its wings flapping madly in preparation for getting airborne.

At the edge of the roof the ungainly beast leaped.

Its scaly wings furiously beat the air . . . and it immediately dropped like a stone to the street below. Joe looked down just in time to see the grotesque behemoth bird land on a monster that was sitting on top of an ambulance, flattening both into a monster and machine pancake.

"O-o-o-o-h *fuck*!" Joe screamed, looking to the front again as the cruiser started its descent. The edge of the warehouse roof rushed up at him.

We're not going to make it!

He closed his eyes to his impending death and braced himself, hands outstretched and clutching the steering wheel. A moment later, he jolted into the air as the car crashed onto the UPS roof, its rear wheels landing less than an inch from the edge. The car hit nose-first, further damaging the front end, crushing the already smashed headlights, tearing the front bumper free, and crushing the radiator. The hood popped open and ripped free of its hinges. It flipped end over end into the air and went over the roof's edge, falling to the street below. The front tires exploded simultaneously, sounding like twin gunshots, followed by the rear tires doing the same as they hit. Both axles snapped and the trunk lid popped open. The three remaining passenger doors did likewise.

Wedged tightly under the dashboard, the kid was spared the worst of the bone-jarring impact, but the blonde was not so lucky. As the rear end slammed onto the roof, she was tossed into the air. She landed outside the car on her side and rolled to within inches of falling over the edge. Joe had enough presence of mind to take his foot from the gas pedal and slam on the brake, bringing the cruiser to a screeching sideways stop a few feet from the building's large water tank.

1:55 p.m.

Dazed by the impact of the landing, Corey waited a short while before crawling out from under the dash after the car came to a halt. Confounded, he looked around at the rooftop littered with debris from the cruiser. He stared at the long skid marks that stretched from the car back to where the blonde lay near the edge of the roof. His confusion quickly turned to realization when he looked back at the parking garage where the two monsters that had been chasing them stood, bellowing with frustration at having lost their meal ticket.

"Wow," was all Corey could softly say.

"You can say that again," said the guy next to him, who still gripped the steering wheel tightly in both hands. So Corey did.

"Wow!"

The guy relinquished his hold on the wheel and struggled out of the demolished cruiser, which now lay, both axles broken, with its chassis flat against the rooftop. He had trouble standing. Rubber-legged, he pulled the shotgun from the car and staggered across the rooftop to the prone blonde. Corey climbed out of the wreck and followed slowly, afraid the girl was dead. His fears were allayed when she groaned and raised her head.

2:00 p.m.

Cindy Raposa managed to sit up. She looked at her bloody hands, arms, and legs, and wondered how they had gotten that way. She tried to wipe the blood from her hands, thinking it wasn't hers; she felt no pain. An animalistic roar, echoed immediately by another, startled her. She looked up at the two creatures on the rooftop of the parking garage and her short-term memory returned, assaulting her with the images of everything she had witnessed since shooting up in the public bathroom back in Hudson River Park. With the memory came pain, and she understood the blood was hers.

Her arms and legs oozed blood where great swatches of skin had been scraped off. Her palms were equally bloodied from road rash. With the pain, her voice, as hoarse as sandpaper on a rusty pipe, returned, and she sobbed loudly.

"Over here! There's a door!" she heard a boy's voice calling. Suddenly there were strong hands under her arms, lifting her to her feet.

"You okay?"

It took a moment for recognition of the guy helping her to kick in, but only a moment. It was followed by an intense anger.

"Why the hell did you do that?" she shrieked, her strained voice on the edge of cracking. "Look at me!" she cried, holding out her crimson arms and hands, palms up. "You could have got us killed!"

"Yeah," the guy remarked, and pointed at the monsters on top of the parking garage. "Or you could have been dinner for those guys."

"Come on!" the boy called again.

Shrugging off the guy's helping hands, Cindy limped across the rooftop to the boy.

2:05 p.m.

The roof door opened on a narrow flight of stairs that went straight down to a heavy metal fire door. Joe led the way, cautiously, to the bottom. He put up his hand to stop the blonde and the boy and slowly opened the heavy door. It was dark beyond but with the light filtering down from the roof, Joe could see another, wider stairwell that went down a dozen steps or so to a landing, then another flight of stairs down into darkness. Joe wasn't sure, but he thought the warehouse was only four or five stories high.

"Follow me and stay close," Joe said to the blonde, who was still whimpering and picking bits of dirt from the scrapes on her arms and palms. Pouting, she ignored him, but the boy nodded and gently took her hand.

Leaving the door to the roof open for light to see by, Joe led the way down the stairs to the first landing, then down another. At the second landing the light from above faded, and the trio maneuvered the next flight of stairs in near total darkness. As the light completely disappeared, and they were enclosed in blackness so complete they could not see their hands in front of their faces, Joe stopped. The boy bumped into him, followed by the blonde.

"What the fuck?" she whined.

"Sssh! Quiet!" Joe commanded in a whisper.

From the darkness below came an airy sound—as though someone were breathing heavily into an amplified microphone.

"Is that you?" the blonde asked.

"No. You got a light?" Joe whispered as softly as possible. A moment later she touched his arm, followed it to his hand, and gave him her butane torch crack lighter.

Joe took another cautious step forward and depressed the gas button on the lighter. A strong blue flame erupted, exposing one of the monstrous man-eating beasts less than eight feet from Joe. Startled, he leaped back. The creature roared, and its head lunged at Joe, its teeth snapping closed on air not far from him. The flame went out. The blonde shrieked, tripped, and fell in her frenzy to get away from the thing. The boy burst into terrified tears and clung to Joe's leg, nearly tripping him up. With the return of darkness, the beast's snarling quieted, and it let out a mournful, whimpering sound.

"Wait!" Joe commanded the blonde, whom he could hear scrambling up the stairs they had just come down. Crouching, Joe maneuvered the kid to stand behind him, and lit the lighter again. This time the horrifying hulk let out a halfhearted, threatening roar and immediately resumed its pathetic mewling. Joe saw the reason why—the beast was trapped in the stairwell, jammed tight between the stairs and the ceiling, lying awkwardly on its side and unable to move anything but its head. Looking at it, Joe deduced what must have happened: someone who worked for UPS—probably a security guard, since it was Sunday—had fled into the stairwell to escape a chasing orb but had been unsuccessful. The flying egg had caught up with him or her—once someone transformed it was nearly impossible to determine gender—turning the person into a behemoth too large to maneuver in the low-ceilinged, narrow stairwell.

Now the thing lay trapped, emitting a god-awful sorrowful sound that was somehow worse than its menacing roars. It rolled its reptilian eyes so pathetically, Joe almost felt sorry for it.

"Here," he said to the blonde, handing her the lighter. It went out. "Light it and keep it lit," he instructed. The blonde flicked it back to life. Joe pumped the shotgun and pointed it at the beast.

"What are you gonna do?" the boy asked, still clinging to Joe's leg.

"Ah, shit, kid, I've got to kill it."

"No!" the boy replied adamantly. "You can't! It's helpless!"

"I'm sorry, kid." Joe looked to the blonde for help.

"Yeah, go ahead, kill the fucking thing," she said. The lighter's flame flickered in her trembling hand.

Joe frowned at her and nodded toward the boy. "A little help here?"

"Oh! Right," she said. She took the boy's arm with her free hand and gently pulled him away from Joe.

"No!" the boy shouted tearfully. The creature moaned as if in agreement. "That used to be a person!" the boy cried. "You *can't* just murder it!" he sobbed loudly, his breath hitching in his chest.

"Kid," Joe said, kneeling next to him, "I know that used to be a human, but it isn't anymore. Look, I'm really sorry about your aunt, but she wasn't human anymore, either, just like this thing. And remember, it was one of these things that carried your mom off and ate her. And this one would eat us in a second if given half a chance. If you think about it, we're really doing it a favor, you know? Just like your aunt—do you think she *wanted* to be one of these things?"

Sadly the boy whispered, "No." His argument defeated, he slumped against the blonde and wept.

"Could you hurry it up?" the blonde said callously. "I can't keep this lit forever. My hand's getting tired."

"Give it to me," Joe replied. As she handed it to him the flame went out.

"Please don't kill it," the boy softly pleaded in the darkness.

Joe raised the gun and lowered it. "Damn it!" he cursed softly. He lit the lighter and surveyed the situation. He leaned over the railing and looked at the landing and stairs below. He turned back and knelt in front of the boy. "Okay. I think we can climb over the railing here. We can jump down to the next flight of stairs and get by without having to kill that . . . thing."

The boy smiled and nodded gratefully.

"Are you fucking crazy?" the blonde asked, her voice shrill.

"Yeah, I guess I am," Joe said, straightening. "But then, the whole world's gone crazy, why should I be any different?" He handed the shotgun to the blonde and swung his left leg over the railing, then his right.

"You better hold this, too," he said, handing her the lighter, careful not to let the flame go out. "I'll jump down first." He looked at the boy. "Then you can jump and I'll catch you, okay?" To the girl he said, "After the kid gets down you can toss the shotgun and the lighter to me and climb down yourself."

"I don't fucking believe this," the blonde muttered.

Joe crouched, his back against the railing and jumped to the stairs below. The trapped monster bellowed and struggled to free itself and grab him.

"Okay, kiddo, your turn."

The boy deftly climbed over the railing. The monster quieted and eyed him malevolently.

"Come on, jump," Joe coaxed. "I got you."

The boy hesitated, unable to take his eyes off the beast so close.

"Let's go! We ain't got all day!" the girl nagged. The lighter flame jiggled in her unsteady grasp.

The kid took a deep breath, his eyes still locked with the reptilian eyes of the trapped creature, and jumped.

The monster's reaction this time was far more violent. It roared furiously, twisting its shoulders back and forth, snapping at the air as it tried to lunge for the boy. Suddenly, its exertions began to have an effect. The ceiling began to crack and large flakes of plaster fell from it. A fissure ran up the wall behind it. A huge chunk of the ceiling near the creature's jammed left shoulder broke off, freeing the thing's arm. It reached for the girl, but she back-pedaled away from its claws, which nearly got her. She tripped and fell on her ass, dropping the lighter, plunging them all into darkness again.

2:13 p.m.

Cindy hit the floor and bit her tongue so hard she could taste blood. She dropped the lighter and heard it clatter away from her in the pitch-dark, but she held on to the shotgun. The lost lighter was the least of her worries at that moment. From the sound of it, the trapped monster was breaking completely free. It snarled and roared, and she heard the metal railing groan as it was twisted and bent. Chunks of plaster began falling around her and on her. A moment later something heavy and sharp closed around her leg and pulled her slowly across the landing. She shrieked, kicked out with her other foot, but couldn't get free. The monster's snarling grew closer, and she could feel its hot breath. She knew she was within inches of its death-delivering mouth.

Screaming, Cindy pointed the shotgun into the darkness above her legs and pulled the trigger. The *bang* of the weapon was like a sonic boom in the tight space of the stairwell, compressing the air against her ears as painfully as when the gun had been fired in the car. The recoil caught her in the stomach, knocking the wind out of her.

The monster yelped like a kicked dog, and then it was

quiet. Hot liquid and globs of something wet and pulpy splattered Cindy.

The ensuing silence was complete except for the ringing in her ears and the air shrieking into her lungs as she struggled to inhale. She pulled her leg free, receiving a painful gash on her calf for her efforts, and her right hand brushed against the fallen lighter. She grabbed it, placed the shotgun on the floor beside her, and, with both hands trembling badly, she flicked the flame into being.

The scene revealed was sickeningly revolting. The top of the monster's head, above its eyebrows, was gone; blood gushed from the ragged flesh that had been its forehead. The wall behind it was painted with gore that used to be the creature's brains. Cindy's gasps for air became sobs as she looked at herself—her chest, arms, and legs were stained with the thing's blood and pulpy wads of flesh. She felt sick and struggled to keep from vomiting. Shaky, she got to her feet as the jock ran up to her, scrambling over the bloody carcass of the creature.

"Are you okay?" he asked, taking the lighter from her trembling hand. In shock, she could give no answer. She could only throw herself into his arms and weep into his T-shirt.

2:15 p.m.

Corey didn't want to look at the bloody remains of the dead beast on the stairs and wall, but his eyes were repeatedly drawn to it. Memories of his aunt's transformation and death, and his mother being carried off, assaulted him with renewed vigor, forcing him to face the fact that the two women he loved most in his life were really gone. He looked at the blond girl being helped past the huge corpse by the runner guy, and felt powerful guilt; his insistence that they not murder the trapped beast had almost got her killed. His refusal to give up the hope that there was still some semblance of humanness and humanity left in the beast had nearly got her eaten—had, in fact, endangered all three of them. All because he couldn't (wouldn't) believe that his aunt—the woman who had loved to babysit him when his parents went out, who took him to the movies nearly every weekend, who always helped him make the scariest Halloween costumes, and gave *the* best presents ever on Christmas and his birthday—had become a mindless, cannibalistic eating machine. Though he wouldn't (couldn't) vocalize it, he had thought that if they let the trapped monster live—maybe even helped it get free and fix its injuries—its former human self would come through and the thing would be grateful. And if that happened, then he would be justified in his hatred and desire for revenge on the runner who had killed Aunt Helen.

Now, there was no footing upon which to stand his vengeance; the runner hadn't killed his aunt; he had saved Corey from a horrible death at the hands of a horrible thing that had no longer contained anything—not one iota—of the person who used to be Aunt Helen. She was gone, and the runner wasn't the one who had killed her; it had been the sparkly flying things that had taken her, just like the other monster that had once been human had taken his mother.

"I'm sorry," was all Corey could say to the blonde.

"Don't worry about it, hon," she remarked, shakily. "I always enjoy being splattered with monster brains."

Her sarcasm was not wasted on Corey and made him feel worse than he already did. Even the runner's pat on the head and wink didn't help.

2:30 p.m.

The rest of the journey down the stairs was uneventful after the near disaster with the trapped monster. On the first floor, Joe waved the blonde and the kid back while he cautiously opened the fire door just enough to see what lay beyond. He found what he had expected; the first floor was the UPS storage warehouse and garage where they loaded packages onto trucks for delivery. It was a vast area at least a hundred yards long and fifty yards wide. At the far right end, a row of dark brown UPS delivery vans sat waiting to be loaded. To the left of the trucks was an open garage bay door next to two closed ones. In the middle of the floor a pile of cardboard boxes and packages of varying sizes sat on platforms of wooden pallets. A forklift was parked near the clos-est end of the nearest row.

Joe ventured forth, opening the fire door enough so that he could peer around it and see the rest of the warehouse. There were two much higher rows of packages stacked on wooden pallets nearly to the ceiling with a narrow row be-tween them extending all the way to the left end of the ware-house. To Joe's immediate left was the warehouse office, a small room with a large glass window through which a dis-patcher could keep an eye on things. And right next to the office door, lined up against the rear wall, was something that caught Joe's eye and made his mouth water and his stomach growl—two vending machines: a Coke machine and a snack machine.

After another quick glance around the seemingly empty warehouse, Joe closed the door and motioned his two com-panions closer. "Okay," he said in a low voice. "We're on the warehouse level and the place *looks* empty, but we still need to be careful. If one of those pods was able to infect that per-son up on the stairs, there might be more around. But . . ." Joe paused, his face brightening, "there *are* vending ma-chines close by. We can get something to drink and eat."

The boy looked eager at the latter news, but the blonde was still pouting, absorbed with picking bloody wads of monster goo off her clothes.

"Is there a bathroom where I can at least get cleaned up?" she whined.

Joe shrugged. "I didn't see one, but there must be. I think we should hide out in the office right next to the vending ma-chines, and then we can check the rest of the floor out and find a bathroom and make sure it's safe." Joe turned and opened the door again. Cautiously, he stepped through. The sound of screams from outside the open garage bay door froze him where he stood. He waited, listening to the screams falter and stop, and still he waited, ready to flee back into the stairwell at the first sight of a monster or a flying orb. Distant roars, as though the entire city had been converted into one

large zoo, were all that he heard. With a feeling of despair,
he realized he couldn't even hear sirens anymore.

Waving the boy and the blonde on, he ran behind them to
the office door. It was a small square room containing a beat-
up wooden desk upon which sat a telephone and two square
wire baskets, one marked IN and the other OUT. Next to the
desk was a computer table on which sat a brand-new Sony
Vaio computer. The back wall of the office was made up of
five tall filing cabinets. Above the cabinets was a large street
map of Manhattan and the five boroughs. There was no sign
of a bathroom.

After making sure the office was safe, Joe started for the
door, asking, "So what do you want to eat and drink, kid?"
Before the boy could answer, Joe felt his pockets and groaned.
"Shit! I don't have any money. I never take any with me when
I go for a run." He looked at the blonde. "You got any change?"

The blonde regarded him with disdain. "Who needs
money?" she asked. She fished in her shoulder bag, which was
still strung over one shoulder and between her breasts by a
thin leather strap, and pulled out a metal nail file. Quietly,
she led Joe and the boy out to the vending machines and proceeded to pick the lock on the Coke machine first, then the
snack machine.

Joe admired her skill with the file. She quickly had both
locks picked and the machines open. The boy helped himself
to a cold bottle of Coca-Cola and a bag of Skittles. Joe took
a Coke also, but wanted to have a look around the place some
more before he settled down to eat anything. The blonde
took nothing.

"There has to be a fucking bathroom in this fucking place
somewhere," she muttered, standing and peering about.

"Why do you swear so much?" the boy asked her, getting
a grimace for an answer. "My dad says people who swear a
lot are ignorant and have a low 'cabulary."

"You mean, *vo*cabulary?" Joe asked, grinning.

"Yeah, well just call me ignorant then," the blonde remarked. She answered Joe's laughter with the middle finger
of her right hand and stalked off to find a bathroom.

"Okay, stay in the office and eat," Joe instructed the boy. "I'm going to see if I can get that garage door over there closed."

Obediently, the boy did as he was told. Joe followed the route the girl had taken in search of a bathroom, to make sure she was okay. Behind the last row of pallets and packages stacked to the ceiling, he saw two doors marked MEN and WOMEN. He knocked softly on the women's door, opened it a half foot, and called, "You okay?" in a soft voice.

"Just peachy," came her sarcastic answer followed by the sound of water running.

Joe smirked and went into the men's room to wash the dried blood off his face. He took off his T-shirt and tried to wash the blood off it, also, without much success, but it made a good wet compress for his painfully swollen nose. He wadded up toilet paper and blew his nose and was rewarded with a shock of pain that went up through his eyes. For a moment, he thought he was going to pass out. When his vision cleared and the room stopped spinning, he tried to breathe through his nose but could only manage it through his left nostril.

He put the wet T-shirt back on and went out to the warehouse again. He snooped around and was glad to find the first floor was empty. If there had been anyone else there when the orbs arrived, they had either escaped the building or had been transformed like the fellow they had encountered on the stairs and had left the warehouse in search of human prey. Since it was Sunday, Joe wasn't surprised to find the place void of people.

Cautiously, Joe approached the third garage bay door, which was open. The security guard must have opened it when he heard all the commotion outside from the invading orbs. One of them must have chased him into the stairwell where it had caught up with him. Joe stood a few feet from the open door and listened. The sounds of mayhem outside had diminished a little, or at least had moved away from the warehouse. Sundays in this neighborhood were generally quiet anyway. Most people, he hoped, had still been in bed when the attack of the flying orbs had begun.

Crouching, Joe peered around the corner and had his suspicions confirmed—no monsters or orbs in the immediate vicinity of the warehouse. He ventured farther. To the right a row of large brown delivery vans parked behind a gas pump blocked his view, but to the left he could see for another block. There he caught sight of several of the enormous creatures climbing all over a brownstone apartment house. Like giant monkeys digging insects out of trees, the creatures were smashing their giant clawed hands through windows and pulling out hapless victims.

Joe stepped back into the garage and looked around for a button that would close the open door. On the side of the door, he saw it. There was a panel with two rows of large buttons—three green ones on the top row, three red ones on the bottom. Figuring the red buttons closed the doors, he was just about to press the third one when a flying egg flew past within yards of the open door. Afraid that closing the door might bring unwanted attention from monsters and orbs alike, he decided to leave well enough alone.

When he got back to the office, the kid was asleep and the blonde was still in the bathroom. Joe looked through the desk and found half a bottle of Advil. He helped himself to another Coke and gratefully took four of the capsules to dampen the pain in his nose. He ate a bag of peanuts from the vending machines and found them to be almost tasteless without his ability to smell.

3:00 p.m.

Cindy stripped naked. She took off her thong and washed the dampness and scent of urine from it. She used paper towels to wash the monster gore off and to gingerly clean the cuts and scrapes on her hands, arms, and legs that she had suffered on the rooftop and the gash from the monster on her calf. Finished with that, she washed the rest of her clothes in the sink and wrung them out. She hung her blouse, skirt, and tank top on the stall doors and tossed her torn nylons in the trash. That done, she was able to relax—get out her works and cook up a spoonful.

"God! I've never needed this shit more than I do now," she said aloud, even though she knew it had only been a few hours since her last fix. It felt like it had happened months ago—with all that she'd been through her high had faded like smoke in the wind. In retrospect, it was surreal, like when she was a teenager and seeing a movie that had such a powerful impact on her she felt like she was living it when she left the theater. As she cooked the brown heroin in her charred spoon and watched it boil, the same questions kept bubbling up: What was going on? Where had those flying things come from? How could they turn people into those grotesque man-eating monsters? And where were the authorities? Had the police, too, all become victims like the one who had tried to help them earlier? If the police had been unable to do anything, then what about the military or National Guard? Wasn't there *anyone* who could help?

Tired of thinking about it, she welcomed the relief of the drug she injected into her arm. Within moments of doing so, she was relaxed and calm, all worry gone. Her stomach growled, and she remembered she hadn't eaten anything all day. "I need something sweet," she said to no one. She put her thong and tank top back on and her works back in her handbag. She left it and the rest of her drying clothes in the bathroom while she, wearing only her top and wet, but clean, thong, went back to the office and the vending machines.

The kid and the jock were asleep, apparently exhausted by all they'd been through. The kid was curled up under the wooden desk, the guy sitting on the floor with his back against the wall, an empty bottle of Coke and a half-eaten bag of vending machine peanuts next to him. Welcoming the relief from the heat that wearing only her underwear brought, she retrieved a bottle of Fanta root beer and two packages of Twinkies from the vending machines. Feeling wiped out herself, she settled down in the corner of the office opposite the jock, ate, and was soon asleep as well.

Day Two: Monday

12:05 a.m.

Joe Burton awoke in darkness and with a sense of being disconnected from reality. His legs were stiff, his back ached, his nose throbbed painfully, and he could not immediately identify where he was. His mouth was dry and his throat raw from not being able to breathe through his nose much while he had slept. He felt a sense of displacement similar to having awakened from a dream that feels more real than reality itself. It took several moments for the feeling to dissipate as his eyes adjusted, and he took in his surroundings.

He quickly sat up, panic and fear bringing an urgent feeling to his bowels. With a soft groan, he remembered where he was and how he had got there, but he wished he hadn't. He wished he had been able to stay asleep and out of connection with the world, which had become the realm of nightmares more horrendous than any he could ever remember having.

Joe stood and looked around. The boy whose aunt Joe had been forced to kill lay sleeping, curled into a fetal position under the metal dispatcher's desk, his thumb stuck in his mouth. The blonde, Joe noticed with widening eyes, was curled up in the rear corner of the office and wearing nothing but a black spandex tank top and a black leather thong. Since her back was to him he had a good look at her posterior, and though she was too skinny for his tastes, he had to admit she had a nice butt. He also couldn't help but notice the needle marks on her arms and feet. She must have a really bad habit, he thought, if she was forced to shoot up in the veins on her feet.

Joe stretched; his joints crackled with the effort and his stomach growled with hunger. He tentatively blew his nose into a piece of paper from the desk and cleared his left nostril. The right one, too, was now drawing a little air, which was more than it had done before. He went out into the warehouse and grabbed a Coke, downing it quickly and swishing it around in his dry mouth. He looked at the open vending machines and frowned at the food choices—nothing but junk. That was fine for the kid. He probably loved having nothing to eat but junk food. And from the empty Twinkie wrappers on the floor strewn around the sleeping blond addict, she probably preferred it, too. But Joe hated junk food. A bit of a health nut, Joe tried to avoid processed foods and stuff loaded with sugar. To make it as an actor, he knew he had to keep his physique in top shape, not to mention his looks. He had learned as a teenager that foods loaded with sugar and preservatives made him break out. At twenty-two, he had a good complexion and wanted to keep it that way. He wasn't a vegan like a lot of his friends—he loved meat too much—but did believe the old adage: *You are what you eat.*

"There's got to be something else around here to eat," he muttered to the darkness. After a trip to the john, he set off to reconnoiter the warehouse again. At the opposite end of the building from the office, behind the smaller delivery trucks parked inside, he discovered the employees' break room. Inside was another vending machine for M&M's and assorted candies made by the same company in the corner. On a small counter along the side wall he found a Mr. Coffee and a mini-refrigerator.

With hope, he opened the fridge but found only a quart of milk way past the imprinted freshness date. At least I can make some coffee, he thought, but when he checked the solitary cabinet in the room he found none. It figures, he thought.

"Think, Joe, think," he muttered to himself.

Where is the closest grocery market?

He wasn't far from his apartment; it was only a block away and he had food there, having gone shopping on Saturday. He paused, trying to remember what day it was and how long ago Saturday had been. He remembered that yesterday had been Sunday—the day of the Lakers-Knicks championship game seven—so it had to be Monday morning.

Only one day?

"God, yesterday felt like it lasted a month," Joe said softly. I guess the Lakers and Knicks will never get to play game seven now, he thought. He felt like crying, then berated himself. "Of all the horrifying things you witnessed yesterday, you're going to *cry* over a stupid basketball game?" he muttered, chastising himself.

Remembering how King Street had been crawling with monsters climbing the brownstones and picking people out of their apartments like insects out of dead trees, he decided against going home. For the same reason he couldn't go to the little market on the corner.

Wait a minute!

Just two blocks away, on the corner of Washington Street and Charlton Street, was a great little Italian restaurant, Phillipi's Pizza & Pasta Parlor, which he frequented. Since it was on the same side of Washington Street as the UPS warehouse, Joe figured it would be easier and safer to go there and raid the place for food—*good* food. His stomach gurgled at the thought.

He hurried back to the office and found the kid just waking up. The blonde was still asleep. Joe crouched by the sleepy-eyed child.

"Listen, kid. I'm going to go out and get us some real food, okay? I can't keep eating the crap in those vending machines."

The boy looked suddenly terrified, shook his head, and grabbed at Joe's arm. "No! Don't go!" the boy pleaded.

"It's okay," Joe soothed. "I won't be long and I'll bring back something *really* good to eat."

The boy would have none of it. "No!" he whispered adamantly. "The 'Vaders will get you!"

"The what?" Joe asked, confused.

"The *'Vaders*," the boy stressed. "The *monsters*."

"Oh," Joe replied. "You mean *in*vaders?"

The kid nodded and Joe had to smile. The kid was bright; Joe hadn't really thought about it, but those things—orbs and monsters alike—were *invaders*, probably from outer space. It sounded crazy. He shook his head, incredulous that he could be thinking such a thing and facing it as a *fact*, as the *truth*. He felt as though he had been suddenly trapped in a science fiction movie.

"What's your name anyway, kid?" Joe asked the boy.

"Corey."

"Okay, Corey I'm Joe. Listen. I'm not going to let those *'Vaders* get me, I promise. It's nighttime and it's dark outside. Those things, hopefully, will all be asleep—I mean they probably get tired and have to sleep at night, too, right? After all, they used to be human like us." As soon as he said it, Joe wished he hadn't. The kid looked like he was about to start bawling, obviously thinking about his aunt and mother.

"Hey, Corey, it's going to be okay. You like Italian food? Spaghetti and meatballs? Pizza?"

Corey contained his tears and nodded.

This kid is all right, Joe thought, and tousled his hair. "Okay. I'll be back in a flash with pizza and other goodies. You stay here with Sleeping Beauty and keep quiet. You can use the bathroom over there in the back." Joe pointed the way. "Before you know it, we'll be chowing down on some *real* food."

Corey nodded.

Joe looked toward the sleeping blonde and inclined his head. "And no checking out her butt," he said with a grin.

Corey smiled sheepishly.

"But if she farts, you've got my permission to kick her."

Corey giggled.

Joe paused just inside the open garage door, holding the pump-action shotgun in both hands in front of him against his chest. He peered out into the night. Something was wrong—he could sense it but couldn't put his finger on it. A moment later he realized what it was—*silence*. For the first time since he had moved to the city, Joe couldn't hear *anything*. Besides being the city that never sleeps, New York was also the city that was never *quiet*. There was *always* sound of some kind, no matter what time of day or night. But now, Joe heard *nothing*. No sirens, no distant music, no hum of traffic, not even the sound of airplanes overhead—all of which were constant background noise normal in the Big Apple.

It was eerie.

"Shit," Joe whispered in the silent night. "We're fucked." For the first time since this nightmare had started, Joe felt an overwhelming sense of despair. He realized now just how *bad* things really were. This was not a dream from which he would awaken. This was not a disaster, like a fire or a hurricane, that the city and the people in it would recover from. This was not a terrorist attack that people could fight back against and rally round the flag and the president; go to war and kick some ass and get a sense of vengeance.

No. This was the end of the world.

The end of the fucking world . . .

He fought back tears of despair for several moments before he could go on. He told himself he had to—for the kid, even for the hooker. He took a deep breath and dashed to the gas pumps less than twenty yards from the garage doors. As he squatted behind them, he noticed one pump was for regular unleaded gas and the other was for diesel. Something nagged at him, but he couldn't quite figure what. He was too nervous; his level of stress too high to think of anything beyond staying alive, getting food, and getting back to the warehouse in the same condition as when he'd left it.

Joe rose slowly, one hand on the diesel pump, the other holding the shotgun, and squinted into the darkness of the street. Though he remembered the night before the moon had been near full, tonight's sky was overcast. None of the streetlights were on. He wondered for a moment if power was out, but realized the lights in the UPS break room and in the bathroom had worked. He peered closer and saw that all the street lights had been smashed. Joe figured that the creatures the kid called "'Vaders" must have done it; maybe the lights had bothered them and hindered their hunt for humans. As his eyes adjusted to the lack of light, he began to make out vague dark shapes—the wrecks of automobiles. From the many crashed vehicles strewn upon Washington Street, it looked as though escaping the invading orbs and monsters via cars had not been a successful venture for most people.

There was a row of large delivery vans to Joe's immediate right, which he ran between, keeping out of the open as much as possible. Behind the brown trucks was a tan brick wall, about seven feet high. Slowly, Joe crept along the wall, and behind the trucks, to where it ended at the sidewalk on Washington. He crouched and looked around it. On the other side of the wall was a large parking lot half-filled with cars parked in rows. About fifteen yards from him, at the entrance to the lot, was a small booth. A large sign on the booth declared parking rates were $2.50 an hour with a $5.00 minimum charge. The Big Apple insignia on the sign signified that the lot was affiliated with the parking garage across the street.

Joe paused long enough to look up at the top of the parking garage and then at the top of the UPS warehouse. He shuddered, seeing that the Big Apple garage was nine stories high and the UPS warehouse only five. If he had known just how far a jump it was before attempting it, Joe doubted he would have had the nerve to perform such a daring feat.

Something moved in the street. Joe flattened himself against the wall. What he had thought was a pileup of crashed vehicles moved again, and one of the cars rolled over onto its side with a metallic crunch and a tinkling of broken glass. One of the monsters had apparently been lying amid a multiple car wreck, and now sat up, yawned with a whining, growling, breathy sound, and lay down again. It pulled the car that had rolled over into place as a pillow. The thing rested its head on the smashed auto and was asleep again within moments.

Joe surveyed the street, his dark adjusted vision now able to pick out monsters asleep in the street, across the sidewalk, and lying atop a bed of wrecked cars. He realized that the city *wasn't* as completely silent as he had thought—he could hear the breathing, even soft snoring, of sleeping monsters. The street was a chaotic mess of sleeping creatures, crashed cars, building rubble, and detritus left from the monsters' rampage for food the day before. For a moment, he lost his bearings and couldn't tell the direction of Phillipi's restaurant. After several panicky moments, he regained his equilibrium and used the Big Apple parking garage as a point of reference to figure out that he had to go right. Remaining crouched over, Joe slipped from behind the wall and ran to the collection booth at the entrance to the lot next door.

The booth door was open. Noiselessly, he stepped inside. The structure was about eight-by-six feet. One end held a cash register and a ticket-printing machine with a clock on it for punching the time on parking slips. The other end housed a small TV and a countertop refrigerator on a shoulder-high shelf. In the middle was a tall, high-backed, plush padded swivel chair.

As quietly as possible, Joe checked the small refrigerator and snatched a pack of matches from on top. He pocketed them. Inside the fridge he was glad to find a one-pint bottle of OJ. His throat and mouth were dry with fear. He thankfully downed the cold juice, and thought he had never tasted anything so good in his entire life. Joe eyed the TV longingly, wanting to turn it on to see if the nightmare was confined to New York City alone, and if the authorities had a plan to help survivors. But he knew he couldn't risk the noise and the light the TV would surely make. He compromised by promising himself he would either grab the TV on his way back and bring it to the warehouse hiding place, or, if his arms were too full with food from Phillipi's, he'd make another trip for it.

Joe left the booth the way he had entered, bent over and staying low and less visible as he ran to the rear of a large Buick Century with a faux convertible hood. He was now at the corner of Washington and King Streets. Across Washington, and up King, less than two short blocks away, was his tiny apartment. Encouraged by the quiet and the sleeping monsters in the streets, he wondered if it might be easier after all to go to his apartment. At least he *knew* there was food there he could eat and carry back to the warehouse.

Joe started to cross Washington Street to get a better angle from which to see his apartment building, but at the curb he had to stop. Less than ten yards away, two nightmare creatures lay midstreet, huddled together, arms and legs entwined, like two lovers napping. Holding his breath and walking on tiptoe, Joe prudently crossed to the other sidewalk and dropped to one knee on the concrete. Behind him, the two monsters slept on undisturbed. Their combined breathing made no more sound than a light breeze.

It didn't matter. The moon came out from between clouds just long enough for him to see that his brownstone apartment building at 28 King Street no longer existed. Little more than a quarter of the former seven-story apartment house remained. The rest was gone, blocking King Street in a pile of brick rubble. In spite of everything that had happened to him in the past twenty-four hours or so, Joe had not lost hope— not even when he realized the world as he knew it was very possibly at an end. Realizing he no longer had a home to return to, however, caused that sense of hope to evaporate.

He had known despair before, but nothing compared to the empty feeling he had now. He fought back the urge to give up; to just sit right there on the sidewalk, bawl his eyes out like a lost little boy, and *quit*. That apartment and the things in it were all that he had in the world. Both his parents had recently passed away. He was an only child and both his parents had been only children. He had no aunts, no uncles, no family, not even distant relations—nothing but his home on King Street and his few friends in the acting community and at the Lauricella Mia Restaurant in Little Italy, where he worked as a waiter between acting gigs. He had no idea where his friends and show business colleagues were—more than likely eaten by, or transformed into, one of the monster beings terrorizing the city.

Joe's fear of being cannibalized or turned into a monster was stronger than the black despair threatening to permeate him; he knew he had to survive somehow. He had always despised cowards and people afraid to face their fears, but now he had a new perspective and with it came what he considered to be a healthy type of cowardice. The bottom line was that no matter how much he lost or how alone he became, he wanted to keep on living, no matter what.

Turning away from his former home, and in a sense, from his former life, with a feeling of finality, Joe moved on. He crossed the street again, back to the block between King Street and Van Dam, toward Phillipi's Pizza & Pasta Parlor. The street and sidewalk were an obstacle course of wrecked vehicles and rubble. Here and there Joe noticed, with a tightening of his stomach, bitten-off body parts lay strewn about crawling with insects. Halfway along the block he had to duck under an SUV with its front end impaled on a fire hydrant. Next he had to crawl over a nearly flattened yellow Cadillac Eldorado and through the open front doors of an undamaged Chevy. Upon exiting the latter he stumbled over a severed leg, still wearing a bell-bottom jean with tiny pink embroidered flowers running along the seam and hem. The foot was still clad in a delicately braided high-heeled sandal. The upper end of the leg, where it had been severed, looked ragged, like a turkey leg that has been gnawed on and discarded in favor of plumper meat. Several rats scurried away, and a cloud of flies rose around him from the disturbed limb.

Joe had difficulty taking his eyes off the leg as he backed away from it, and nearly walked right into a slumbering, half-pint demonesque creature that must have been a child the day before. The thing lay curled into a fetal position, its grotesque thumb, upon which it greedily sucked, stuck in its mouth. The child monster's face displayed a range of shifting emotions. One moment happy; the corners of its evil mouth curled up in a grin. The next, a scowl as if it suddenly found its thumb to be sour and bitter. It pulled its thumb from its lips with a wet *pop* and let out a brief high-pitched cry that was not unlike that of a cat in heat.

Twenty yards away, on the other side of Washington Street, a full-grown sleeping monster roused by the cry sat up. Joe barely had time to hit the deck before the thing looked his way after yawning and stretching. Joe lay silent on the tar, his face less than a few inches from the thumb-sucking monster's thumb-sucking mouth. The adult creature stretched again, leaned over onto its left side and farted, following that with a loud belch and lay back down, its head cushioned by a crushed fire truck.

Joe stayed where he was, waiting to make sure the monster was again asleep. It was difficult to do. Despite his injured nose, Joe could still smell the child monster's reeking breath. He realized he had never smelled the breath of anyone whose diet was human flesh and blood. He shuddered and wondered how bad it would have smelled if his nose had been completely *clear*.

Breathing through his mouth, Joe regained his footing. Stepping carefully around the child creature, he continued on, fighting a feeling of nausea as thick as his fear. His eyes were now so adjusted to the dark that he could see the sign for Phillipi's ahead, less than thirty yards away, just across the intersection with Charlton Street. Thankfully, he saw that the sidewalk and a good part of this side of the street were clear between him and the restaurant and for a good way past it. Joe hurried on.

12:40 a.m.

Sara Hailey sat in complete darkness. She had hid in a storage closet near the salad chef's counter after removing boxes of prepackaged condiments until she had enough room to sit with her legs pulled up and her knees in her face. That had been over twelve hours ago and now she was getting cramps in her calves and her feet, and her back was killing her. She was also hungry. She decided to leave the safety of her hiding place.

As cautiously and quietly as she could, she opened the closet door and peered out into the dark kitchen. Her eyes had become accustomed to the dark in the storage closet after so long, and she could see fairly well in the shadowy restaurant kitchen. Carefully, she crawled onto the black-and-white-tiled floor and lay there a moment stretching her arms and legs, all the while remaining alert for any movement, any sound that might signal the return of the flying balls of light or, worse, one of the hideous monsters the flying orbs created.

The kitchen was quiet and appeared to be deserted. Slowly, Sara stood, peering over the counter to the outside wall near the swinging doors that led to the main dining room. A bright, three-quarter moon had appeared between clouds and shown through a gaping, ceiling-to-floor, hole in the wall. The hole had been made by the restaurant's owner, Giorgi Phillipi, crashing through the wall after he had swallowed one of those weird flying things and was turned into a raging rapacious monster who had quickly devoured the head chef.

A sound from outside froze Sara in her tracks. Something was moving just outside. She ducked, dropped to all fours, and crawled backward frantically until her feet struck the closed door to Mr. Phillipi's office. Remembering something the restaurant owner had shown her the day he had hired her to paint landscape murals of the Italian countryside on the walls of a new dining room addition off the main dining hall, she reached back and turned the knob. The door latch clicked as loud as a boom of thunder in the darkness. She froze, her hand still on the knob, her eyes on the hole in the kitchen wall. She waited several anxious moments but heard nothing. She proceeded to push the door open. To her terrified senses, it creaked loud enough to wake the proverbial dead. Again she remained immobile, listening for any sign of the return of Mr. Phillipi—the monster—or any of the flying balls of light.

She heard a sound like a rock rolling on pavement, but could see nothing through the fracture in the wall. Even so the sound made her panic and the panic made her move swiftly, rising to a crouch and duck-walking to the large oak desk in the rear of the small office. If she remembered correctly, what she sought was taped to the back of the top left-hand drawer, unless Mr. Phillipi had been carrying it—something she knew he liked to do since it made him feel macho or something—when he had been transformed.

Gingerly, she pulled the left drawer open, relieved when it made no sound. A moment later, though, she was mentally cursing—she couldn't pull the drawer all the way out of the desk. She tugged on it, lifted it, and jiggled it, growing more frustrated and fretful with each passing moment. Finally, she pushed the drawer in halfway and tried to snake her hand and wrist in and over the back of it, when she felt a small lever along the back rim. Pulling the drawer out again to its stopping point, she depressed the lever and the drawer came free of its tracks, and she pulled it out of the desk. She nearly dropped it in her surprise in having succeeded. The drawer had more weight than could be caused by its contents—a few papers, and some pens and paper clips strewn over the bottom of it. The heaviness was a good sign; taped to the back of the drawer was the .45-caliber pistol Mr. Phillipi had shown her the first day of her employment. Waving the gun with bravado, he had boasted how he would never be robbed, at least not without a fight. At the time, Sara had been extremely nervous with him waving the pistol around, but now she was ecstatic to find it there.

She pried the pistol loose from the duct tape holding it to the back of the drawer. Holding the pistol in her trembling hands, she crept, hunched over, back into the kitchen.

She heard a sound.

Like breathing.

There was something right outside! It was moving over the rubble near the gaping hole in the wall!

Trembling with fear, she raised the gun in her shaky hands, but try as she might she could not keep the pistol steady. She strained to hear more but the only thing she heard now was her own panicked breathing—fast and shallow. She felt light-headed and knew if she didn't get control of herself and calm her breathing she was going to hyperventilate. She took a deep breath and held it, but it had a worse effect on her trembling hands; they now shook so badly she could barely hang on to the weapon. She was afraid that if she did have to fire the thing she had little to no chance of hitting whatever she aimed at. With a gasping renewal of her breathing, which sounded to her as loud as an explosion in the silence of the kitchen, Sara realized she was completely exposed where she stood.

She awkwardly dropped to her knees and nearly toppled over. Walking on her knees, trying to ignore the pain as she thumped over broken bits of crockery and plaster, she made it to the corner of the salad station's counter and cabinets. Now she was better concealed and had a clear shot at anything coming though the breach in the wall from outside.

Another distinct grunt from outside sent her fear and panic levels up another notch. She tensed so strongly she felt as though her muscles were seconds from ripping clear of their tendons and bones. She was so tight it hurt. It was all she could do to keep from crying out. She bit her lip, used the corner of the salad counter to steady her gun-holding hands against, and mentally told herself, repeatedly, to be calm. It had little effect.

A tall, dark figure stepped through the tear in the kitchen wall. Stifling an urge to cry out in fear, Sara tried to aim the gun, but she realized something wasn't right about the silhouette stepping cautiously through the opening and into the kitchen. It wasn't big enough to be one of the monsters, not even one of the small monsters she had seen before hiding in the closet. It was a normal human being.

Relief flooded through her, and she was suddenly so weak that she almost dropped her gun. She rose unsteadily, putting her right hand on the countertop to aid the motion, and whispered, "Hey!"

12:55 a.m.

Joe Burton whirled toward the sound of Sara Hailey's voice, bringing the shotgun up as he did, ready to blow her away. Luckily, his mind registered her voice as human and her monosyllabic word as understandable in time to prevent his finger from reflexively pulling the trigger. The moon had disappeared behind clouds again, and he couldn't distinguish her form from that of the cabinets next to her in the nearly pitch-black kitchen and didn't do so until she moved, stepping toward him.

"Shit!" Joe whispered loudly. "You almost got yourself killed." He lowered the shotgun and squinted into the darkness at the girl coming toward him. She was about five-foot-seven, with long brown hair framing her face, which had a sensual softness to it. She had large dark eyes and an attractive, small nose. High cheekbones and a dark tan made her look exotic, as did her full lips. She was dressed in a faded green Boston Celtics T-shirt that commemorated the team's sixteen championships. She wore white painter's pants rolled up to her shins and a pair of paint-spattered sneakers with no socks.

"Sorry," she whispered back, her voice shaky with emotion. Suddenly she ran to Joe, threw her arms around him, and sobbed into his chest.

Caught off guard, Joe cautiously hugged her with his free left arm, holding the shotgun away from her with his right. He could feel her shaking against him and held her tighter, bringing his right arm awkwardly into the embrace while still trying to hold the shotgun away from her body. The scent of her perfume seeped through his partly stuffy nose; after the stench of the child monster's breath outside moments before, she smelled heavenly. He was also aware of her warm softness and how good and reassuring it felt to have her close to him—to feel her arms around him.

"We shouldn't stay here too long!" Joe whispered. The girl nodded. Joe said: "I came here to get some food."

The terrified girl didn't appear to understand.

"I can't go until I get some food," Joe stressed. His words finally sunk in.

"The larder's over here," the girl said, pointing behind her to a door next to the open one to Mr. Phillipi's office. Joe squinted and, sure enough, the word LARDER was printed on the door.

Leading the way, the girl pushed the door open. A stream of cold air washed over Joe, and he paused a moment to relish its relief from the sticky humidity of the night.

"The walk-in freezer is at the back of this room," the girl whispered.

Joe gave a quick glance back to the hole in the wall to make sure no orbs or creatures were sneaking up behind them. He stepped into the room with the girl following.

"All the stuff on the left-hand shelves is precooked and only needs to be heated or served. Stuff like all the desserts and pastries. The things on the right are stock supplies," the girl explained. Joe handed her his shotgun and picked up a good-size empty cardboard box from a pile that was stacked in the corner behind the door.

Joe went down the middle aisle, grabbing food, most from the right shelf, but some from the left. This act of shopping gave him a weird sense of comfort and familiarity, something he'd had little of in the past twenty-four hours. Once the box was nearly filled with supplies, he put it down and opened the walk-in freezer door. The blast of icy air brought goose bumps to his arms and a shiver to his spine. He went quickly through the freezer, grabbing a box of hot dogs and two frozen apple pies.

He put the goodies in the box, picked it up, and said, "Let's go." She nodded but looked uncertain as to what to do with both the shotgun and pistol in her hands. Joe put the box on the left-hand shelf in the larder and took the shotgun from her. He placed it across the top of the food.

"Okay. Let's get out of here," Joe told her. "Don't use that thing—" he nodded toward the gun in her hand—"unless absolutely necessary. We don't want to attract a horde of monsters."

The girl nodded but looked uncertain. Joe had serious doubts she could even fire the pistol, much less hit anything with it, her hands were shaking so badly.

"Follow me and be quiet," he whispered, and took the lead, heading for the hole in the kitchen wall he had come through. Out of the corner of his eye he caught a glint of light. He sucked in his breath. One of the flying, illuminated spheres was in the kitchen. In that moment, Joe heard Corey's voice in his head—"*The 'Vaders will get you.*" He was tempted to run, or use his shotgun to swat the thing, but it remained near the opening in the wall, just hovering there. He wasn't sure if it had seen them.

"Don't move a muscle," he whispered as softly as possible to the girl next to him. He sensed the 'Vader wasn't sure they were there. He remembered reading once that many predators cannot discern prey from its background if the prey does not move. The way the orb was just hovering, as if surveying its surroundings and not moving directly toward them, gave Joe the impression that this thing, too, could not detect them if they remained immobile.

The orb floated slowly to the left and the girl next to him suddenly stiffened.

The 'Vader glided toward them.

The girl began to tremble with fright—at first mildly, but the closer the orb came, the stronger and more pronounced her shaking became. Joe sensed the 'Vader's awareness of them now. He and the thing moved simultaneously, and quickly, but Joe was just a little bit quicker.

He dropped the box of food and his shotgun as the orb shot at them. Joe snatched it out of the air with his right hand. As Joe had dropped the box, the girl ducked behind him. Now she looked around frantically for the orb.

"Where is it?" she asked, her voice trembling with fright.

"Shhh!" Joe commanded, putting his left index finger over his lips and holding the closed fist of his right hand up for her to see. The flesh of his fingers was illuminated from within as if he had his hand over a bright flashlight. The thing in his hand vibrated slightly at first, tickling him, but it quickly began to grow very hot and was soon burning the palm of his hand. Joe looked around for something to trap the orb in before it scorched a hole in his hand. To his right, running to the far end of the kitchen, were a series of gas burners and flat metal grills for cooking. Under them were a series of ovens lined up neatly along the wall. Overhead was a rack from which hung a multitude of pots and pans.

"Help me," he said as loud as he dared to the girl. Moving quickly, Joe stepped over the box of food and the shotgun on top of it and grabbed the nearest pot to him from the closest stove—a five-quart pressure cooker with a lid. There were latches on each side to secure the lid tightly.

"Take the lid off! Hurry!" Joe whispered to the girl.

She popped the latches with both hands and pulled the lid off.

Joe threw the burning orb into the pan as hard as he could. The thing made a loud, metallic *gong* as it struck the bottom of the pan.

The girl quickly put the cover back on.

"Ask not for whom the bell tolls," Joe muttered, snapping the latches shut immediately. "It tolls for thee, mother-fucker," he finished, grinning.

"Yes!" the girl said loudly and triumphantly. She immediately grimaced and looked toward the street to see if her exclamation had disturbed any of the sleeping beasts outside. She and Joe stood still waiting; looking to the opening in the wall. The girl looked at Joe with an expression of apology, but Joe winked and shook his head. He mouthed, "It's okay."

A moment later another gong was heard from within the pot in Joe's hand, then another and another. The pot began to shake and rattle, the bell-like sounds from within increasing in rapidity. The orb was ricocheting back and forth, and up and down inside the pressure cooker with such force the stainless-steel sides and lid began to bulge outward with each impact. The noise of it striking the metal was so loud and fast it reminded Joe of the bells on a slot machine giving up its jackpot.

Joe had to hold the pot with both hands now to keep it from flying from his grasp. The bottom of the pan was beginning to glow red with heat as if the orb was trying to melt its way through the metal.

"Open the oven door!" Joe cried in a whisper just loud enough to stress his sense of urgency.

The girl nodded rapidly. She pulled open the door of the oven in front of her. Joe shoved the bonging, rattling pressure cooker into the oven and the girl closed the door. The noise of the trapped orb pinging about inside the pot was immediately muffled but not enough for Joe.

Apparently it wasn't enough for the girl, either, for she whispered, "We gotta get outta here!" The panic on her face and in her eyes was as readable as words.

Joe nodded in agreement and turned the oven on, setting its temperature at 500 degrees.

"That should hold him for a little while," he whispered, and grinned at the girl. "By the way, I'm Joe Burton," he added.

"Sara . . . Sara Hailey," the girl stammered as if she were having trouble remembering.

"Pleased to meet you, Sara. Now follow me and keep quiet."

1:15 a.m.

Corey Aaron left the warehouse office and the girl still sleeping within, and went out to the open vending machines. Thirsty, his mouth drier than he could ever remember it being, he took a Fanta orange soda and guzzled it down. He let out a loud belch and immediately felt a cold fear-sweat break out on the back of his head and neck. The sound of his burp seemed amplified in the high-ceilinged warehouse. Thankfully, his oral expulsion of gas didn't attract any monsters. It didn't even awaken the sleeping blonde, so he figured it hadn't been as loud as he thought.

He used the bathroom and returned to the vending machines, where he opened another bottle of soda and looked over his choice of snacks from the other machine. He picked up a Snickers bar and felt a pang of guilt—his mother never let him eat chocolate; she said it made him too hyper and would rot his teeth. With the guilt came the memory of his mother being carried away by a monster. He realized she would no longer be around to tell him what to eat. She would never again do that, or any of the hundreds of other things she had done or said to him.

Tears welled inside him and grief formed a painful lump in his throat. He tried to wash it down by drinking the second soda as fast as the first, but it didn't work. His eyes still filled with water and his throat constricted around the sobs trying to seep from it. Corey threw the Snickers bar on the floor, determined to wait for Joe to bring back some good food—food his mother wouldn't mind him eating.

He walked to the open garage door to look for Joe, and take his mind off things that he could do nothing about except cry.

1:25 a.m.

Joe and Sara crossed Charlton Street. Joe tried to move as quickly as possible considering the heavy box of supplies he carried. The first half block from the restaurant was clear of any debris or bodies, allowing him and Sara to move unhindered, but giving them a fearful feeling of being dangerously exposed. At the corner of King Street, Joe stopped. With a nod of his head, he directed Sara's vision to the middle of the road, where the sleeping child monster lay.

At first, Sara didn't see the thing lying on the asphalt. Between the smashed streetlights and the overcast sky, she couldn't make out much. Having lived in the city for the last six years, she was unaccustomed to such complete lack of light. She shrugged and shook her head at Joe, and at that moment the small monster rolled over and farted in their direction. A foul odor, bad enough to make them both gag, washed over them. Sara gasped, both at the sound and the smell, and pointed her shaking pistol at the creature.

Afraid that in panic she was going to shoot, Joe put down the box of groceries, reached out, and gently pushed the barrel of the pistol down. He leaned into Sara, putting his lips right against her ear, and spoke in the softest of whispers.

"It's asleep. Shoot it now, and we'll have every one of those things within hearing distance charging down on us."

Sara nodded, but Joe could sense she was still on the edge of losing it. She was breathing rapidly; her exhalations were tremulous with fear. He squeezed her shoulder and turned her toward him, forcing her to take her eyes off the little monster.

"Keep it together, Sara," he whispered directly in her ear again. "We're almost there."

Sara nodded again and her breathing calmed slightly. Joe picked up the box and, with an inclination of his head, beckoned her to follow him across the street where they could avoid the obstacles he had encountered on his way to the restaurant. He also wanted to avoid the severed leg—he didn't think Sara could handle that. On tiptoe Sara cautiously followed. Behind her, the beast resumed sucking its thumb.

Opposite the parking lot tollbooth they crossed the street again. Joe paused and looked wistfully at the TV inside. Though it was small—its screen no larger than thirteen inches—Joe figured it was probably too heavy and too awkward for him to carry on top of the shotgun and box of groceries. And he just didn't trust his newfound companion Sara to be able to handle the thing without mishap; she was just too nervous. Determined to come back for the TV later, Joe moved on.

A second later, the night's silence was split by a loud explosion followed by another, even louder. The street for two blocks past Joe and Sara was suddenly illuminated with yellow, then orange, light. They turned back to see a plume of flame shoot into the sky from the roof of Phillipi's Pizza & Pasta Parlor.

"Oh shit!" Joe muttered, and started to run. He didn't have to tell Sara to do the same; she was right beside him, matching his stride. All around them in the street, from on top of automobile pileups and from within damaged and fractured buildings, the 'Vader monsters were wakened from sleep and drawn to the fire. From uptown and from the direction of the Hudson River and the ocean came swarms of the sparkling orbs as if to investigate. Luckily, a third explosion from within the restaurant split the night, drawing beasts and orbs alike and keeping them from noticing Joe and Sara.

Joe glanced back as they rounded the brick wall and ducked behind the row of brown delivery trucks. He saw an orb, glowing a bright angry red, emerge from the flames. All the other orbs hovered around it for a moment then flew away, going in different directions as if commanded to split up and search for something. Joe couldn't be certain, but he was pretty sure the red orb was the one he had trapped in the oven. If it was, it looked as though he and Sara were what the orbs were all now searching for.

1:35 a.m.

Cindy Raposa awoke at the first explosion, was on her feet at the second, and running toward the open garage door, wearing only her tank top and thong, when she heard the third. She saw the kid standing just inside and to the left of the opening, peering out at the flame-lit night sky. Panic and raw fear, from which she had had a grateful respite while sleeping, returned as she reached the boy and saw monsters and orbs alike streaming down Washington Street, heading for the source of the explosion, which appeared to be at least two blocks away.

"We gotta close this door!" Cindy said nervously.

"No!" the boy whispered loudly.

"Yes! We do!" Cindy shot back, her panic so great she forgot to whisper. She searched the left side of the garage door frantically looking for a button, then skittered over to the right side.

"Joe is still out there!" the boy hissed, staying out of sight on the left side, afraid of exposing himself.

That stopped Cindy's search for a moment. "Who's Joe?" she asked.

"You know, the guy who got us here? The guy who saved our lives?" Corey said.

"Too bad," Cindy said. "Trust me, kid. If he's out there now, he's dead or soon will be." She found the panel of red and green buttons for opening and closing the three doors automatically. In her panic she pressed the third green button first and nothing happened. She swore and pushed the red one. The loud grinding of machinery filled the garage bay and spilled out into the night.

The boy immediately put his hands over his ears and ran to hide behind the nearest row of wooden pallets with boxes stacked on them.

"Oh, shit!" was all Cindy could say.

1:40 a.m.

Joe and Sara were halfway along the row of delivery vans when they heard the shockingly loud noise of the warehouse door closing.

"Go!" Joe shouted, pushing Sara ahead with the box of groceries and not caring how loud his command was; it was not louder than the racket of the door machinery. They reached the end of the row of vehicles and darted to the door, which was a quarter of the way closed. They both ducked inside, where Joe immediately dropped the box of food and picked up the shotgun. He whirled around to face the door, which had reached the halfway point. He saw Cindy standing, in her underwear, off to the side near the panel of buttons for opening and closing the doors.

"What the hell are you doing?" Joe nearly screamed at her. "You want to bring every one of those things down on us?"

Within the garage, the sound of the huge door clattering closed seemed deafening compared to the previous quiet of the night. Joe fervently hoped the explosions and fire at Phillipi's would keep the monsters and orbs distracted and they wouldn't notice or hear the warehouse door closing.

His hopes were in vain.

A large, hulking monster charging along Washington Street, heading for the flames still shooting into the sky, suddenly skidded to a stop, gliding on a mix of blood and motor oil coating the street. It charged straight at the door, which still had a good five feet to go before it would be closed completely.

Joe was crouching to see under the door as it lowered. He caught sight of the beast coming and hastily fired the shotgun. Nothing happened when he pulled the trigger. Frantically, he pumped a shell into the chamber and took aim again. The monster was right outside the door, which was three feet from being closed. The creature grabbed the edge of the door with both hands in an effort to raise it again. Joe fired and the thing's eight grotesque fingers, curled around the inside of the door, disintegrated in a spray of red. Bits of flesh mixed with splinters of wood flew everywhere. Outside, the wounded beast let out a bellowing cry of pain.

The door was two feet from the ground.

Joe pumped the shotgun again and fired at the monster's feet, still visible in the narrow space remaining. The monster's right foot was ripped to shreds in a cloud of blood, flesh, and bone.

The door finally closed. There was a loud *thud* against it, and the door bulged inward as the wounded beast toppled over and fell against it. The monster yelped loudly and painfully. A moment later the muffled sounds of flesh tearing and being ravaged came through the door. Joe could picture the wounded monster outside being set upon by others of its kind and devoured.

"Come on!" Joe said. "We'd better get down to the basement before those things finish eating their friend and break in here." He handed the shotgun to Corey and picked up the groceries. Cindy headed for the bathroom.

"Where are you going?" Joe hissed.

"All my stuff's in the john," she said without a backward glance.

"Nice girl," Sara said. "Does she always run around in a thong?"

"Screw her," Joe muttered. "Corey, this is Sara. Sara, Corey," he said nodding his head in introduction. Sara grinned at Corey and he gave a short wave and a scared smile back.

Together they headed for the exit door at the back of the warehouse, where the stairs led down one more flight to the basement.

1:50 a.m.

Cindy quickly dressed before retrieving her works from her pocketbook. She frowned and took stock again of the amount of heroin she had left. She pulled her cell phone out of her purse and called her supplier, who was also her pimp, but all she got was his voice mail:

"This here's Z-Jay. You know what to do, so do it, nigga."

At the sound of the tone, Cindy left a message. "Z-Jay, it's Cindy! I'm stuck downtown and I need help. I'm trapped in the UPS warehouse on the corner of Washington and West Houston and I'm almost out of, you know. I'm scared, Z-Jay. I don't know what the fuck is going on. I almost been killed more times than I can count by those fuckin' things out there. I need you, Z-Jay. I gotta get out of here. Please, please, *please* call me back as soon as you get this message. Okay? Okay! Bye for now but call me *soon*—or better yet, come and get me."

She closed her cell phone and sat on one of the toilets to prepare a hit for herself. A sudden loud *boom* shook the entire building and almost made her drop her spoon. It was quickly followed by another and the cracking sound of wood splintering. Frightened, she thought better of cooking her smack right then and there and put everything back in her purse.

She cautiously opened the bathroom door as another cracking boom, much like thunder, reverberated though the building. It was coming from the other end of the warehouse, from the garage door she had closed. At the sound of another bone-rattling explosion, she ran from the bathroom to the warehouse office. It was empty.

"Damn it!" she said under her breath. "Where the fuck are they?" From the office, she could clearly see the garage doors. All three were bowed inward and bulging at the middle. The doors shuddered under more blows that echoed through the building, jangling Cindy's nerves. The wooden frames of the doors were cracked and in danger of giving way at any moment.

Where the hell was the jock and the brat she'd come there

with? she wondered. In her hurry to get her dope and shoot up she hadn't paid close attention to what the guy had said. He *had* been pissed off at her for closing the door, maybe he had abandoned her. She had to think; obviously they had left but she was pretty sure they hadn't gone outside, not with those things out there trying to smash their way in. Then it came to her; they had gone down to the basement. That's what the jock said, she now remembered.

2:00 a.m.

The stairway going down to the basement level was even darker than the upper one Joe and Corey had descended the day before. Joe handed the shotgun to Sara and put the box of supplies awkwardly under one arm. He felt in his pockets for the blonde's lighter, not remembering that he had given it back to her. He was relieved of his search a moment later when Sara flicked on a penlight she kept on her key chain and handed it to him.

The three went down to the very bottom of the stairwell, where a single old door confronted them. Joe put the penlight in his mouth, pointed at the door, and tried the knob, giving a sigh of relief when the door creaked open. His relief was tempered somewhat by the dank, musky smell that greeted him from within. Taking the light from his mouth, he flashed it into the darkness, illuminating a vast, creepy stonewalled cavernlike room. The walls were damp and silky with spiderwebs, which also hung from the ceiling like low cloud cover. With barely six feet between the floor and the spidery ceiling, Joe had to venture in with his head bowed.

"At least it's cool down here," Joe said, pointing out the place's seemingly sole advantage. "We won't need air conditioning."

In the dark far recesses of the large basement, they heard the scuttling of what could only be rats. The sound of the vermin was suddenly drowned out by the booming from overhead. The cobwebbed rafters of the basement shook and narrow falls of dust cascaded through the spider homes to the dirty stone floor.

Corey whimpered and Sara put her arm around him, drawing him closer. Joe put the groceries down and took the shotgun back from Sara. Corey immediately threw both of his arms around Sara and clung to her.

Joe played the light around the room, but its arc of illumination was less than ten feet. Besides looking like a dungeon or a vampire's lair from a horror movie, the place had obviously been used for storage. Against the walls were stacked moldy wooden crates and cardboard boxes. Joe went farther in and found an open door on the back wall. Beyond, the basement opened up into a vast area. Along the right wall were a series of stalls separated by decrepit wooden walls as high as his chest; they looked like old-fashioned animal pens. Guessing at the age of the structure, he figured that was probably what they had been used for, either livestock or horses back before the automotive era. From what he could tell in the dim reach of the light, there were a dozen or more such stalls, creating a succession of them that continued on into the darkness. Not too far off, in one of the stalls, he saw the building's furnace. To the left was nothing but darkness, giving him the feeling there was a lot of empty space in that direction.

As he turned back into the room, he was encouraged to see a dirty sink and an ancient toilet—the kind that has a water box above it and flushes with the pull of a chain—in the corner of the room. Unfortunately it provided no privacy, but at least they had water and a place to go to the bathroom.

"Something's coming," Sara suddenly whispered, and pulled her pistol from the waistband of her pants. She and Corey ran to Joe.

Keeping the light averted, Joe went back to the door and stepped into the stairwell. He heard the faint sound of someone breathing heavily and the intermittent squeak of a sweaty palm rubbing along the stair railing. He was tempted to close and barricade the door; he knew it was the blond hooker coming. He came very close to shutting her out—hadn't she tried to do the same to him upstairs? She hadn't cared if she stranded him out on the street full of monsters, so why should he let her in now? But he couldn't do it; especially since it sounded like the monsters had succeeded in knocking down the garage door and were now inside the warehouse. Every few seconds, he could hear a loud crash above and dust would fall from the ceiling. Regretting he wasn't more of an asshole, Joe stepped onto the stairs and shined the light up into the darkness.

"Hey!" he called as loudly as he dared. "We're down here."

The softly padding steps quickened and a few moments later the blonde traipsed down the stairs.

"Thanks for leaving me behind," she pouted.

Joe stared at her, dumbfounded.

"What the fuck did you do out there anyway?" she continued before Joe could recover enough to object. "You blow up the whole fucking city or what?" She stepped past Joe and into the basement, grimacing at the condition of the place.

"Nice digs," she said sarcastically, ducking away from a cascade of dust. She looked at Sara and nodded slightly. "Hiya," she grunted.

"Hi," Sara replied, looking Cindy up and down and coming to the same conclusion Joe had upon first meeting her—the girl was either a prostitute, a junkie, or both; more than likely, both.

"Hey kid!" she said loudly to Corey in order to be heard over the sounds of destruction overhead. The boy was the only one who looked happy to see her. "So what'd you do to light up the night?" Cindy asked again as she dusted off a crate and sat on it.

"I don't know," Joe said, shrugging. He was more interested in what was going on in the warehouse above them. "I think we'll be safe down here." A large sliver of wood and a stream of dust fell on his head and shoulders. He stepped aside and quickly brushed the wood and dust from his shoulders. "As long as they don't bring the ceiling down on us," he added.

"I think the explosion was caused by that thing you trapped in the oven," Sara offered.

Joe nodded as he ran his fingers through his hair to get the dust out. "Yeah, you might be right. Were those gas ovens?"

"Yes," Sara replied. "The orb must have got out of the pressure cooker and somehow ignited the gas line."

"What are you two talking about?" Cindy asked.

Joe explained what had happened inside Phillipi's Pizza & Pasta Parlor.

"You trapped a 'Vader in a pot?" Corey asked, his voice full of wonder and his eyes with admiration for Joe.

"What the fuck's a 'Vader?" Cindy wanted to know.

"Isn't it obvious," Joe replied, scowling at her. "Those things out there—the orbs and monsters—they're *in*vaders."

"Oh," Cindy said. "Cute, kid," she added to Corey.

"The orb got so hot in my hand just before I threw it in the pressure cooker, I wouldn't be surprised if it melted its way right through the pot, and probably did the same with the oven, only it must have hit the gas line."

"Did you kill it?" Corey asked eagerly.

Joe looked at Sara and both shook their heads.

"Nah, I doubt it," Joe said. "I'm pretty sure I saw it after the explosion, hovering over the fire." He paused, a pensive look on his face.

"What?" Corey asked, looking at him.

"It was weird, but I could have sworn that pod was communicating with all the other pods and the monsters, too. It was like it called them all to it, then sent them all out in different directions to search for us."

"That would mean they're intelligent," Sara mused. "But how do they communicate? Telepathy?"

Joe shrugged and nodded. There was an especially loud booming crash from above and they all looked up.

"What the fuck *are* those things?" Cindy asked no one in particular.

Sara gave her a sharp look. "I know you've probably been through a lot—we all have—but do you think you could watch your language, especially in front of the boy?"

Cindy stood, and stared defiantly at Sara. "Fuck you!" she said.

Sara looked to Joe, who didn't want to get involved and made a point of inspecting the crates nearest the door.

"I don't mind. Not really," Corey piped up, playing peace-maker. "My friends all talk dirty when there's no grown-ups around. Me, too, sometimes," he added, lying. He never swore; if his mother or father caught him, he knew they'd kill him.

Not anymore!

The harsh reminding voice in his mind threatened to bring back tears. He went to help Joe, hiding his watery eyes from the two women.

Cindy stuck her tongue out at Sara and sat down again. "So, like I said before I was rudely interrupted," Cindy went on, giving Sara a harsh look, "what the *fuck* are those things and where the *fuck* did they *fucking* come from?" Cindy smiled coyly at Sara's disapproving look.

"From outer space," Corey offered immediately.

"How do you know that?" Cindy asked.

Corey shrugged but Joe answered. "It's the only thing that makes sense, I think. I mean, where else could they come from? I've never seen or heard of anything like those orbs and the monsters they turn people into. There hasn't been a minute gone by since this started that I haven't felt like I was trapped in a dream and any second I'll wake up."

They all nodded. The sound of the monsters searching for them in the warehouse overhead suddenly stopped. Joe opened the door and looked up. There was one final faint crash, followed by silence.

"Do you think this is happening everywhere?" Sara asked Joe as he closed the door. "All over the world?"

"I don't know," Joe said. "There was a TV in the toll-booth of the parking lot next door that I wanted to grab to see if we could get some news, but that was before *some-one*," he looked at Cindy, "attracted all those things by clos-ing the garage door."

"Hey! Don't blame me!" Cindy countered. "You're the one who had to go blowing things up."

"So . . . what? You thought you'd close the door on us and leave us outside for the 'Vaders to eat?" Joe asked, perturbed.

Cindy looked guilty but shrugged it off. "No! I just . . . I just panicked is all. When I saw all those monsters running around I got scared. . . . "

"Yeah, right," Joe muttered.

"It ain't gonna help if you guys fight," Corey said.

Sara smiled at him. "Corey's right. 'From out the mouths of babes,' you know?"

"What the fuck does that mean?" Cindy asked, her voice dripping with sarcasm.

"It means the kid is acting more grown-up than we are," Joe interjected. "And we could learn a lot from his example."

Cindy raised her eyebrows and pursed her lips in an expression that said, "*Whatever*!" She looked at the toilet and sink. "At least we've got a crapper. Not much privacy, though."

"Maybe this will help," Joe said, pulling a couple of thick gold-colored drapes from a cardboard box that was falling apart from mildew and age. "Looks like there's a bunch of stuff in these crates that UPS couldn't deliver, or it's stuff left over from whatever this place was before UPS." He carried several of the drapes, which had black splotches of mold on them, to the corner and fastened them to nails protruding from the rafters above. The drapes made an effective, if musty-smelling, wall and door. Joe noticed a bare lightbulb with a short string on it set between the low beams of the ceiling. He pulled the string and the bulb came on, casting a feeble yellow light around the small room.

"Better than nothing," Joe said, and picked Sara's penlight off the crate where he'd left it to light the room. "At least we'll save on the batteries," he said, handing it back to her.

Sara turned the light off and pocketed it, before clearing a space on a box to sit down. Corey came over and sat next to her, getting a mean look from Cindy for it.

"So now what do we do?" Cindy asked. She was starting to feel jittery and had broken out in an uncomfortable cold sweat. She needed a fix soon.

"Well, we can eat," Joe said. He started taking food out of the box. "We got some nice hot dogs, and sandwich meat. I got some pastries, too, and a couple of pies. Oh!" he said looking at Corey. "You like cold pizza?"

Corey shrugged. "I guess. I never had it."

"It's pretty good. I eat the leftovers cold for breakfast sometimes," Sara said. "I like cold pizza just as well as hot."

"So do I," Joe said, smiling.

Cindy groaned and rolled her eyes. "Wow! You two have *so* much in common!" She got up and went into the bathroom. "I'm going to take a dump," she pulled back one of the drapes and stepped inside.

"I take it she's not your girlfriend," Sara whispered to Joe.

"You got that right," he replied.

"She's a piece of work, isn't . . ." Sara started to say and was interrupted by Cindy.

"I-can-hear-you!" Cindy singsonged from the toilet.

Sara blushed but Joe and Corey laughed.

2:30 a.m.

While the others ate, Cindy sat backward on the dirty toilet, legs spread, facing the back wall with the sink to her right. She put her purse in the sink and carefully removed her works. She proceeded with the routine of preparing the heroin for shooting up. Like most addicts, she took as much pleasure in the preparation—which was akin to a religious ritual in its importance—as she received from the actual effects of the drug. Part of it was from the heightened sense of anticipation it gave her, but more than that it was from a deep-seated instinct for habit that had meaning and provided comfort. The measuring of the brown powder into the spoon; the addition of just the right amount of water to it; and the subsequent cooking and drawing up of the liquid into the syringe was, for her, equal to any religious ceremony a priest performs, such as the preparation of bread and wine for Communion. It was the closest thing to religion for Cindy.

Tying off her arm with the length of rubber tubing she kept coiled in the bottom of her purse, she injected her version of the holy Host into her arm.

2:35 a.m.

Sara Hailey sized up her two new companions as she ate sparingly. Joe was tall and good-looking with short dark hair, parted to the side. He had white, straight teeth in a small mouth, a strong nose and chin, and the body of a man who keeps in shape. The boy, Corey, was tall for his age and cute enough to be a child model with his large eyes, silky soft brown hair that hung in bangs across his forehead, and dimples in both cheeks that were always visible and which became even more pronounced when he smiled.

After just a few bites of food, Sara stopped eating. Though she had been hungry at the first sight of it, she quickly lost her desire to eat. Sara blamed her loss of appetite on the events of the past twenty-four hours. She couldn't help thinking of the people she had witnessed being gobbled alive, and her stomach tightened and soured with nausea. It appeared Joe and Corey felt it, too, as they each put their food back in the box after only a few bites.

"So," Sara asked Joe after a long uncomfortable silence, "is this your son, or your little brother?" indicating Corey with her eyes.

Joe looked at Corey and both smiled. "Nah, we're not related," he answered.

"Oh, sorry. I just assumed. . . ."

They lapsed once again into quiet. The sound of Cindy lighting her mini-blowtorch of a lighter reached them. Joe and Sara exchanged knowing glances.

"So how did you two get together?" Sara asked, trying to distract Corey, who had heard the lighter's *whoosh* to flame and was looking curiously toward the drapes.

Joe looked uncomfortable with the question, but Corey spoke up.

"I was at the Summer Trapeze and Acrobatics School down at Hudson River Park when the 'Vaders came," Corey said with tears filling his eyes. "My aunt Helen was turned into a monster and one of them got my mom." Tears spilled from his eyes and ran over the dimples in his cheeks. "She was going to have a baby in September." His voice broke on the last word and he sobbed.

"Oh, I'm sorry," Sara replied. She pulled Corey close and put her arms around him. "I know someone who went to the acrobatic school," she said, trying to distract Corey from his grief. She thought for a moment and asked, "Did you know Maria Stephanowski?"

Corey sniffed back his tears, shrugged, and shook his head. "I just started a few weeks ago. I was late doing it cuz me and my mom and my dad just got back from Disney World in Florida," Corey said, his voice full of sadness as he spoke of his parents.

Joe jumped in to keep him talking so he wouldn't continue to dwell on what had happened to him. "I've never been to Disney World, or Disneyland in California, but I've always wanted to go," he said. "Was it fun?"

"Yeah!" Corey said, perking up a little. "It was cool. I liked the Tower of Terror the best. I rode it seventeen times straight the last night we were there." He smiled faintly with the memory, his eyes still gleaming with tears.

"Yeah, I liked that, too," Sara said. "My mom and dad took me there when I was ten. It was the best vacation ever."

Corey nodded in agreement and Sara went on.

"So did you like the trapeze school?"

Again Corey nodded, showing a little excitement. "Yeah! It was fun! We went to see the circus in New Jersey a couple months ago and the acrobats on the trapeze and the high wire were the best; they were like, flying. I want to do that when I grow up—be a pilot."

From behind the drapes came a snorting guffaw. Corey blushed and looked sad again.

Sara looked askance at the curtains, then at Joe. They knew what each other was thinking, what Cindy had just so callously vocalized—Corey's dream of becoming a pilot was just that, a dream. Things like flying, vacations to Disney World, parents, and family were all gone, Sara thought, never to return to the way they had been before the 'Vaders.

2:45 a.m.

The world is over, Joe thought again, hearing the words in his head but not wanting to grasp the totality of what the statement meant. But once the thought was thought, his mind took off with it. No more vacations and family were just the tip of the iceberg that was truly a massive glacier—the end of everything. No more TV or movies. No more government; no more morning runs. No more Broadway and the excitement of the casting call, trying out for a play on the Great White Way. No more off-Broadway. No more music; no more eating out. No more shopping or sports or . . . the list went on, running relentlessly in his head. Looking at Corey and Sara, he could see they were thinking the same thing. Corey looked like he might start bawling again at any minute. If he did, Joe thought, he might be unable to keep himself from joining the boy.

"So," he said, his voice unsteady. He cleared his throat and went on. "What were you doing before . . . all this?" he asked Sara.

"I'm an artist. I work with my three cousins. They have a studio, *Designamics*, on East Fourth Street in the Village. We do on- and off-Broadway play programs and posters, brochures for businesses, and sometimes the New York City Tourist Board. We do murals and billboards, too. That's what I was doing at Phillipi's, painting a mural on the wall of their new dining room."

"Yeah? What of?" Joe asked.

"It was a pastoral scene of the Italian countryside," Sara answered.

"Cool," Joe commented. "Do you, like, use a photograph as a model, or do you just make it up?"

"It depends, but I usually try to use a model. In this case, I had a lot of photographs of the countryside around Florence to work with. I studied there for a year at the Michelangelo School of Art."

"Wow!" Joe said, impressed. "How'd you do that?"

"I won a scholarship when I was a junior at UMass,

Amherst." She looked at Corey, who appeared quite interested. "Do you like to draw, Corey?"

"Yeah! My art teacher said I was the best in my class. I like to do lan'scapes, too," he answered. "My watercolor of a field of sunflowers was picked to be on display at the post office in Soho," he added, beaming with pride.

"Yeah? I think I might have seen it," Sara remarked.

Uncomfortable silence crept in once more until Corey, this time, broke it speaking to Joe.

"I saw you runnin' by the trapeze school every Sunday. Are you, like, trainin' for a marathon or somethin'?"

Joe looked surprised and shook his head. "Nah, I doubt if I could ever run a marathon. I can barely make it a couple of miles. I run every day to keep in shape."

"What do you do?" Sara asked.

Now? Joe thought flippantly for a moment. *Now I try not to get eaten by living breathing nightmares, or turned into one of those nightmares by those glowing flying egg whatchamacallits.* Out loud he said, "I'm an actor. I also work as a waiter at Lauricella Mia in Little Italy, and sometimes at construction in the summer for a company in Queens."

"Everyone in this town is a friggin' actor," Cindy said lazily as she stepped through the drapes and rejoined the others.

"I'm not," Sara pointed out defensively.

"Me neither," Corey piped up.

Cindy smiled indulgently at him and sneered at Sara.

"Are *you* an actor?" Joe asked, sarcastically.

"Dancer," Cindy answered. "Same difference."

Joe and Sara exchanged doubtful looks.

"So, what have you been in?" Joe asked.

"Lots of stuff. I was an understudy for the *Lion King*."

"Really?" Corey asked, his eyes wide. "I saw that movie."

"I'm talkin' about the Broadway musical, kid," Cindy said.

"What have you been doing lately? Anything I would have seen?" Sara asked.

"I doubt it," Cindy replied. "I mostly been doin' interpretive stuff at a dinner and theater club in the Bronx called Ra-bini's."

Joe hid a smile behind his hand. He knew the place; it was a strip club.

"What's your name?" Corey asked Cindy. "We were never properly introduced."

The three adults had to smile at his polite seriousness.

"Cindy Raposa, and you?"

"Corey Aaron." Corey looked to Joe and Sara. "I don't think you said your last names either."

"Burton. Joe Burton."

"My last name's Hailey, like the comet, only spelled differently."

Cindy sat on a crate near the water closet and took a pack of Mustang filtered cigarettes from her purse, along with her massive lighter. "Anyone mind if I smoke?" she asked after lighting up and blowing out a cloud of blue carcinogens. "Good," she answered herself before anyone had a chance to speak.

Sara looked perturbed. "I mind," she said crossly, and added, "haven't you ever heard that secondhand smoke is worse for kids?"

Cindy chuckled. "Not as bad as people-eating monsters." She took another deep drag and let it out slowly. "Do you mind, kid?"

"No," Corey said, shrugging.

"I don't believe this," Sara said huffily.

"You don't believe *this*?" Cindy said, smirking and holding up her cigarette. "There are flying-fucking-aliens invading the world and turning people into cannibal-fucking-monsters, and *you* don't believe *this*!" She indicated her cigarette again and laughed harshly. "That's fucked up, bee-atch."

Sara looked to Joe for help again, but he just turned his palms up in a gesture of indifference.

"She's got a point," he said to Sara.

"Goddamned right I got a fuckin' point," Cindy said slowly, her voice reflecting how high she was. "Instead of worrying about the effects of secondhand smoke, you should be worrying how you're going to stay alive in a world turned into a living-fucking-nightmare."

Sara pouted, and couldn't help feeling chastised. She knew Cindy was right, she just hated hearing the truth from someone like Cindy.

Quiet followed as Cindy's reminder brought silent consideration of their plight. Finally, Corey, who had been eyeing Cindy since she stepped out of the water closet, asked, "What are those red marks all over your arms?"

Realizing she had inadvertently pushed up her long sleeves enough to reveal her tracks, Cindy quickly pushed them down again and made a show of scratching, first her left arm, then her right. "Bug bites," she said.

Sara let out a loud and sarcastic laugh.

Cindy glared at Sara and stood as though to attack her. Not backing down, Sara stood as well, her fists balled.

"Hey!" Joe said, jumping to his feet, attempting to head off a fight. "Have either of you got a cell phone?" he asked. "I left mine in my apartment. I never take it when I go running."

"Yeah," Cindy said.

"Me, too," Sara replied, taking the small communicator from her pants' pocket. "But it's no good. I tried calling 911 about a dozen times, but all I got was a recording. I tried my cousins' studio, too, and their apartments, but all I got were answering machines or out-of-order recordings."

"What about you?" Joe asked, nodding toward Cindy.

"What about me?" Cindy asked. "I've been with you guys," she indicated Joe and Corey with her eyes, "since this shitfire started. When did I have time to call anyone?" she lied, suddenly embarrassed that she had thought only to call her dealer for more scag rather than the police or someone who might help them get out of danger.

"Try again now," Joe said to Sara.

She dialed 911, listened, then held the phone out for them to hear. Faintly, they could all hear the weird mechanical voice that is the hallmark of institutional recorded messages everywhere.

Joe couldn't understand what it said. "Well, what's it saying?" he asked impatiently.

Sara put the phone to her ear and listened. "Oh," she said after a moment. "This is different than before. Yesterday, it just said all the lines were busy and to try again later. I tried for an hour while I was hiding in Phillipi's but no one ever picked up." She listened again. "Now it says a *terrorist* state of emergency exists—level *red*. It says if we are in the vicinity of any terrorist attack we should go to our nearest police precinct station, fire house, National Guard armory, or designated civil defense shelter."

"Terrorist attack?" Cindy asked incredulously, and laughed. "They think this is a terrorist attack?" She shook her head and snorted. "Those man-eating monsters are terrorists?" she laughed at the absurdity of it. "Oh *yeah*. Come to think of it, I did see Osama bin Laden out there." She looked to Joe. "Remember that one that almost ate us? The one with the towel on its head?" Cindy laughed again, but her laughter had lost its spacey quality and was becoming high-pitched and panicky.

Joe saw it in her eyes, and it was frightening to behold. There was something about her growing panic that was as infectious as a yawn. He thought if he had a mirror that he might see the same look in his own eyes.

"Take it easy," he said, trying to remain calm. "I think they're saying that 'cause they don't have anything that even comes close to describing what is going on."

"Huh!" Cindy grunted. "You got that right." She sat again, sucked on her cancer stick, leaned back, and closed her eyes.

"So what should we do?" Sara asked Joe.

He looked at her, impressed that she did not appear as panicky as he felt and Cindy sounded.

"I'm not sure," he answered. "I guess we should do like the recording says; go to one of those places. You *know* the authorities have got to be responding to this crisis." He warmed to his words, rebuilding his sense of hope as he spoke. "I wouldn't doubt it if they've already called out the army and the National Guard and they're fighting the 'Vaders as we speak. I bet there's a lot more people who have survived like us than you think. We might even be getting help from other countries—after all we're always helping them out when there's an earthquake or a tsunami or something."

"You think this is only happening here, in America? Maybe even just in New York?" Sara asked, hope in her voice.

"Who knows?" Joe shrugged. "We don't know that's *not* true."

"Nigga, please!" Cindy said with a ghetto accent. "You don't think this ain't happenin' all over the world?" She looked at Joe then Sara. "You're nuts if you think these fuckin' things are just local. They're fuckin' eggs that fuckin' fly, man. Why wouldn't they be *everywhere*?"

No one had an answer for her.

"See? It's the end of the goddamned fuckin' world—at least as we know it—no matter who they call out. They can call out the fuckin' *marines* but it ain't gonna' make any difference." She ground her cigarette out against the wall and tossed it to the floor.

"So, what are we supposed to do? Just give up and die?" Sara asked contemptuously. "If you feel that way, why don't you just walk outside and yell, 'Come and get it!'"

"You know, you're really starting to get on my nerves, *bitch*!" Cindy said angrily. The two women stood and faced off again, ready to come to blows.

"Stop it!" Corey screamed. "Just stop it. Fighting won't help!" He began bawling loudly.

Sara and Cindy were embarrassed. Cindy returned to her seat on her crate and dug out another cigarette while Sara knelt and put her arms around Corey, apologizing in a soft whisper.

"Corey's right," Joe said, and looked at Cindy. "And so is Sara—we can't fight among ourselves and we can't give up. There has got to be some help out there *somewhere*." He paused and thought a minute, then slapped his forehead. "I'm an *idiot*! There's a *computer* in the office upstairs and a regular phone. So there's probably a phone book, too. I'll go up, see what I can learn from the Internet about how widespread this attack is. It should be safe up there by now; I haven't heard a sound for a while. If the coast is clear, I might even be able to run next door and get that TV I told you about. The important thing is that we're all safe and healthy. I bet there are a lot of people like us right now hiding out somewhere and hoping for help from the authorities."

Corey spoke up, softly, his voice tremulous. "My dad's a policeman at the Sixth Precinct. I don't think that's too far from here, because me and my mom were going to meet him for lunch after the trapeze school."

"I know where that is," Cindy offered.

Sara gave her a look that said, *I'll bet you do*, but Cindy ignored her.

"That's over on West Tenth Street in the West Village—about six blocks from here," Joe mused, thinking out loud.

"I know the other number to call there—not the 'mergency one—the one for regular calls, like from family and stuff," Corey explained. "My mom made me memorize it 'case I ever need to call him. He was workin' yesterday." He looked at Sara. "Can I use your phone to call him? Maybe he can come get us."

"Fat chance," Cindy muttered, and received a dirty look not only from Sara this time, but from Joe, too.

"Sure, honey," Sara said, smiling at Corey. "What's the number and I'll dial it for you?"

Corey recited the number mechanically, "two-one-two, five-five-five, six-nine-six-nine."

Sara punched in the number, listened for the ring, then handed it to the boy.

Corey waited, apprehension showing in his face and in his leaning-forward posture. His face brightened and he started to speak, saying, "Hello?" Then he frowned.

"I get a 'cording, too," he said sadly. "Same as you. It said, 'Try again later.'" He handed the phone back to Sara. He looked ready to cry again.

"Don't worry, Corey," Sara said, hugging him to her after she pocketed her cell. "I'm sure he's okay."

"West Tenth Street really isn't that far from here," Joe said.

"I bet we have a good chance of making it there, especially if we travel at night."

Cindy grunted and shook her head in disbelief. "It's *six long* blocks! You know how *far* that is? You ain't lived in the city for much, have you?"

"Four years," Joe said, and added defensively, "but I know how far it is. I run in this neighborhood every day."

"Yeah? But with a five-year-old kid tagging along?" Cindy shot back.

"I'm seven and three quarters!" Corey said, indignantly.

"Fine! Whatever!" she said to him, but continued with Joe. "And in case you ain't noticed, I ain't in as good a shape as you." She glanced askew at Sara. "And Mrs. Michelangelo here don't look it either."

"I jog three times a week, thank you very much!" Sara argued. "And I go to aerobics and yoga classes, too. Maybe you could do it if you didn't smoke and shoot up so much!" she added angrily.

"What's shootin' up?" Corey wanted to know, but the adults ignored him.

Cindy leaped to her feet, dropping her cigarette and clenching her fists again, ready to fight. "You keep dissin' me, bitch, and I will fuck you up *good*!"

Sara stood also, but this time she picked her pistol up from the crate beside her and pointed it at Cindy. "And if you don't back off, *junkie*," Sara challenged, imitating Cindy's tough-guy ghetto accent, "I'm gonna bust a cap in yo ass!"

Corey giggled at Sara's mimicry, and it was just the thing to defuse the tension and avoid a confrontation. Neither Sara nor Cindy could help but smile and laugh also at the boy's infectious giggle and the deep dimples that sprouted on his cheeks when he laughed.

"Oh, you think that's funny?" Cindy asked him, stooping to pick up her cigarette. "You even know what 'bust a cap in my ass' even means?"

"Sure," Corey said, still giggling. "It means she'll shoot you in the butt." He laughed heartily.

"Pretty smart," Cindy said, smirking.

Corey stopped laughing and grew serious. "But what's a junkie?" he asked.

"Never you mind," Cindy said before Sara could speak.

"You two have got to chill out!" Joe said, standing and facing the women. "If we're going to survive this and get to safety, we've got to stick together and work together." He glared at both of them and went on. "I'm going to go upstairs and see what I can find out, and I can't be worrying about you guys killing each other." He continued to glare at them until Sara nodded sheepishly and Cindy shrugged.

"I think it's best if I hold on to both guns for the time being," Joe said, holding his hand out to Sara for her pistol.

Begrudgingly, she gave it to him. He tucked it in the waist of his shorts.

"And your penlight, too," he added. "Now sit tight until I get back."

3:15 a.m.

Joe ascended the stairs slowly, the shotgun in his left hand and the small penlight in his right, creating a circle of light around him. He became aware of the sound of his own breathing, rapid and shallow. He held his breath; he heard the sound of breathing continue in the stairwell for several seconds. He became suddenly frightened that he was not alone; then it dawned on him—he was hearing an echo of his own breathing. He let out his breath in a loud sigh and heard it come back to him. He smiled and went on.

At the first-floor landing, he paused outside the fire door and clicked the penlight off and put it in his pocket. With caution, he opened the door just wide enough for one eye to peer through.

Nothing but darkness.

He blinked and waited for his eyes to adjust. Slowly, visibility emerged from the darkness. From what he could see, the first floor of the warehouse was in shambles. The boxes and packages that had been neatly stacked on wooden pallets were everywhere, most of them torn and opened, their contents spilled on the floor in a chaotic mess. He couldn't see any orbs or monsters within his field of vision and took heart from that. He opened the door wider, propped it with his foot, and leaned in, shotgun first, to look at the entire place. Beyond the litter, he could see that all three garage bay doors had been destroyed, torn from their tracks. It looked like a bomb had gone off where the office used to be. What was left of the walls were a twisted shambles, and the desk, computer, phone, and filing cabinets, were either smashed or buried under rubble. The vending machines lay facedown, a mix of the Coke machine's beverage contents pooled around them.

So much for using the computer and phones, Joe thought dismally. He looked toward the open garage doors and decided he didn't really want to risk going outside to retrieve the TV from the parking lot tollbooth. Besides, without cable, he probably wouldn't be able to get anything on it anyway. He remembered something and leaned into the warehouse farther. He was glad to see that at least the Manhattan street map still hung on the rear wall.

He slipped through the door and edged along the wall, carefully stepping over debris until he reached the map. Nervously, he tried to pull it down with his left hand, while still holding the shotgun with his right, but the map started to rip down the middle. The sound seemed deafening and he dropped to a squat, back against the wall, shotgun up and ready. There was no need, he realized. The sound was deafening to his frightened ears only.

He leaned the shotgun against the back wall and carefully removed the street map, folded it, and stuck it in the back pocket of his shorts. He paused and sniffed the air. His injured nose was much better, and he smelled alcohol—more specifically, wine. He'd had to take a four-hour-long wine tasting, serving, and appreciation course when he had first started working at Lauricella Mia. He knew the scent of wine and could tell that what he smelled was good stuff. He looked around and saw a large box lying on its side a few feet from him, and in it a case of wine. He went to it, righted it, and found only three of the twenty-four bottles broken. He pulled an unbroken one out and admired the label—it was a Reisling, vintage 1987.

An idea suddenly came to him, and he looked to the open garage doors. Outside still stood the two gas pumps, one for regular, one for diesel. He smiled and nodded. Laying the shotgun across the top of the case of wine, he picked it up and headed back downstairs.

3:30 a.m.

Sara and Cindy avoided making eye contact as soon as Joe left. Sara sat with Corey and together they removed the food supplies from the box Joe had carried from Phillipi's and arranged them as best they could on top of a dusty stack of what looked like bags of quick-drying cement.

Cindy remained sitting, nodding off. After a short time she lit another cigarette and chain-smoked two in a row until she realized she had less than a half dozen butts left. She slowed her intake, trying to stretch out the second cigarette, not knowing when she would get more. She realized a bright side to her situation as she watched Sara and Corey play house—she'd probably never have to pay for cigarettes, or food for that matter, ever again. She only wished the same were true for drugs.

Thinking of which, she took stock of what she had besides the small and getting smaller bag of brown horse. Turning away from Sara and Corey, she opened and rummaged through her purse. In a narrow Altoids cinnamon chewing gum tin, she had two and a half joints plus four roaches of primo Colombian weed. In a brown prescription bottle bearing someone else's name, she had a variety of pills: four 100-mg Oxycodone; ten 50-mg Valium; seven 100-mg Vicodin; five 100-mg Flexeril; six 300-mg Trazadone; and twelve 15-mg morphine sulfate pills. She had stolen all the prescription drugs from past tricks.

She pursed her lips and chewed on the inside of the bottom one. Her peripheral drug supply seemed adequate for the time being, but that made little difference to her. She again checked her Baggie of heroin and chewed her lip harder at the thought that even with stretching it and supplementing it with her other drugs, she'd be lucky to make it last a week.

Corey laughed at something Sara whispered to him, then gave Cindy a sidelong glance. Sure that Sara was talking about her, Cindy's face flushed with the heated red of anger. She glared back at Sara through slitted eyelids and thought the bitch was lucky the boy was there because if he wasn't she'd be all over her like a dingo on a baby.

She couldn't contain the giggle that bubbled out of her at the simile. Corey smiled at her, but Sara now looked flushed and suspicious of Cindy.

Good, Cindy thought. *That's right, little-miss-I'm-an-artist. Now I'm making fun of you. How does it feel, bee-atch?* She wouldn't admit it, but she knew her dislike of Sara stemmed from the fact that she was everything Cindy would never be but had always wanted to be. Sara was well educated, talented, well-spoken, and self-confident. Despite her bravado, Cindy lacked the latter—her apparent self-confidence was all an act. The daughter of an alcoholic, sexually abusive single-parent father, Cindy's life had mostly been one of hardship and misery. Her mother had taken off when Cindy was five, and from then until she was thirteen she had been a multitude of things to her drunken father: cook, servant, punching bag, and sexual slave—none of them roles on which to build strength or self-esteem.

She liked to tell people she was still a dancer, hoping they'd picture her on the stage and not wrapped around the pole of a strip club, which had been the truth before she had become a full-time hooker and junkie. All else was a lie. She'd never been an understudy for the *Lion King*; that had been a fellow prostitute's younger sister. Cindy had never even auditioned for anything on the stage. After running away from home and her pervert of a father at age thirteen, she had lied about her age and stripped at Rabini's for three months before being taken in by Louis Trumain, a pimp, and had started turning tricks. Working for True Lou, as he had been known on the streets, until his death in 1998 from an overdose, she had then hooked up with her present pimp and drug supplier, Z-Jay.

By the time she was seventeen she had become a junkie and looked like she was thirty. Now, at age twenty-five, she looked closer to forty. Sara, on the other hand, looked younger than she was and probably always would. That alone was enough in Cindy's petty book to hate her.

She took out her cell phone, checked it for recorded or text messages from Z-Jay, found none, and checked the battery to see if it had enough juice. It seemed all right, but she was confronted with another problem; sooner or later her cell batteries would die, and she didn't have her charger with her.

"I'm gonna go see if Joe needs any help," Cindy said, standing. She really wanted a little privacy so she could call Z-Jay again. Unfortunately, as soon as she stepped into the stairwell and closed the basement door behind her, Joe came down from the first floor. At first angry at his interruption, she forgot about it when she saw the case of wine in his arms. She took a bottle from him at the bottom of the stairs and decided Z-Jay could wait.

7:10 a.m.

Sara Hailey woke and had to squint and concentrate on focusing her eyes on her watch to see the time. Doing so, she realized she was still drunk; she had only slept for two hours. She looked at the watch again. It read 7:10 a.m. She was *drunk* on a Monday morning! A first for her. Even in college, when she had been the epitome of a party girl, she had never been drunk this early and on a Monday. Hungover, yes, but cocked? No.

She looked around the small, dimly lit basement area where she sat with a half bottle of wine cradled in her lap. Next to her, and behind the food, Corey lay on the cement sacks sleeping. Across from her, Joe Burton sat on the dilapidated box in which he'd found the drapes, his back against the wall, dozing. He had an empty bottle of wine next to him. He had spent the better part of the predawn hours bent over the Manhattan street map he had retrieved from the warehouse above them, all the while mumbling to himself. A few feet to his right, Cindy sat where she had before, near the draped-off toilet, leaning back against the dusty, webby sidewall, apparently asleep after polishing off two bottles of wine, which now lay empty on the floor.

Sara scowled at her, feeling belligerent in her inebriation. Usually the type of person who tries to befriend everyone, Sara was a bit disconcerted by her intense dislike of Cindy. After all, she had friends who were as foulmouthed as the blonde. She even had friends who were as addicted to drugs as Cindy obviously was, albeit their addictions were to lesser drugs like pot, alcohol, coke, and diet pills. Still, a drug is a drug is a drug . . . as her super-straight cousin Kathleen liked to say.

Thinking of her cousins derailed her train of thought, and she wondered how Kathleen and her sisters, Linda and Susan, were doing . . . or if they were *doing* at all.

She took out her cell phone now and tried Kathleen's home number again. This time there was no ring at all. Instead she got a prerecorded message telling her there was a problem with the line and to please try again later. On a hunch, she tried 911 again and got the same message as earlier. She called the personal police number Corey had given her and got a recording there, too. At random she tried every number she had programmed into her cell phone—Phillipi's Pizza & Pasta Parlor, and other restaurants that she called mostly for take-out, like Wong's Chinese and the Blue Thai Restaurant, plus the McDonald's on the Lower East Side that delivered—all of them rang until she gave up. She punched in numbers at random, making them up after entering the 212 area code, and got a mix of endless rings or recordings.

She called her sister who lived in Fitchminster, Massachusetts, with their mother, Rose, who suffered from advanced Alzheimer's. The phone rang endlessly without answer. She tried other numbers in Fitchminster, friends and her uncles and aunts. Nothing.

"I can't get through to anyone in or out of the city," she said, slurring her words slightly. She got up and went behind the drapes, used the toilet, and washed her face, trying to sober up. When she came back out, Joe was awake again and back to looking over the map.

She took a quarter loaf of Italian bread and several slices of provolone cheese from the food supply and ate it while trying not to think about the phones. A growing knot of panic was building in her that had started with her attempt to call someone—*anyone*—and getting nothing with every number she had tried. She felt like crying. She felt like a child, overwhelmed with fear, alone in the dark. She wanted her mommy and daddy; she wanted to be hugged—*she wanted to wake up*!

She closed her eyes, told herself it was the wine making her feel so bad, and fought back the tears. She concentrated on breathing deep, cleansing breaths, the way she'd been taught to in yoga class. To clear her mind, she mentally chanted, "OM," and imagined it sounding like a deep thrumming gong; a bass note so strong she could feel it in her bones. She opened her eyes. She felt a little better, but she still yearned for a hug—and more, for that matter. With a sly, still slightly inebriated smile, she gave Joe an appraising look. After all, liquor always did make her horny; and Joe was a pretty cute guy.

She grimaced at Cindy again. If only that slut wasn't with them. . . . With an inner laugh, Sara identified the true source of her dislike for Cindy. Considering their predicament, it was absurd, but she couldn't help it. Being tipsy and horny didn't help. Soon she couldn't contain laughing at herself for being so human and feminine and a bitch in the face of such great adversity. Giggles spilled from her.

"What?" Joe asked, looking up, a confused smile breaking across his sleepy face.

Sara looked at him and giggled louder. She placed the half-eaten bread on the floor, covered her mouth, leaned over, pressing her breasts into her thighs, and giggled until she was out of breath and incapable of making a sound. And she kept on giggling.

7:30 a.m.

What Joe at first had found mildly, if confusingly, amusing, quickly made him uncomfortable. Sara kept giggling, soundlessly, her face flushed and getting redder by the moment. It was her eyes, finally, that clued him into the fact that she was not experiencing a prolonged moment of mirth, but was actually in the throes of a panic attack. Trapped deep in silent hysteria, she was unable to breathe and on the verge of passing out.

Joe reached for her a moment too late. Sara toppled over to the floor, her eyelids fluttering, the pupils floating up into her head until only the whites remained. Joe caught her by the shirtsleeve just in time to keep her lolling head from striking the floor. Unmindful of the wine spilling freely onto the floor from an open bottle, which he had knocked over when he'd reached for her, Joe knelt in it as he pulled Sara back to an upright position. Certain that she was still not breathing, Joe leaned over, his lips close to hers, about to give her mouth-to-mouth, when her eyes popped open and her lungs sucked in air through her gaping mouth. With a loud shriek, which sounded like air escaping through the narrow neck of a kid's balloon, Sara breathed again.

Joe looked into her eyes for a moment and was thinking of kissing her when Sara beat him to it. She impulsively reached up, grabbed the back of Joe's neck with her right hand, and drew his face to hers and kissed him hard on the mouth. She closed her eyes at the moment of lip impact while Joe's widened more. Initially a fleshy collision, the kiss quickly deepened as their tongues constituted the second stage of the meeting and became familiar with each other.

"Why don't you two get a room?"

Startled, Joe and Sara broke the kiss.

Cindy sat looking at them while she lit a cigarette. Her

mouth was smirking, but she kept her gaze averted, not wanting Sara to see in her eyes the jealousy and envy she felt in her heart.

Joe mumbled something that was a cross between an explanation and an apology, neither of them understandable, and sat back fumbling for the map again as he did.

Sara stood, rubbed her face, and stretched, not meeting Cindy's eyes, either.

Cindy made no attempt to hide her dislike of Sara, grimacing as she watched her pace a few steps back and forth, trying to sober up. After a few moments of watching Sara, Cindy grunted and stood.

"I'm going to get some fresh air," she announced, and headed for the door.

"What?" Joe looked up. "I don't think that's a good idea," he told her. "The first floor is wide open to the street and the 'Vaders; it's too dangerous."

Cindy paused, her scowl deepening, and thought quickly. She didn't really want fresh air, she just wanted to smoke a joint in privacy and not have to share what little she had or endure accusatory looks from Sara.

"I'll go up to the roof, then," she quickly replied, and pushed past Joe.

"But—" Joe started to object but Cindy forcibly cut him off.

"Whatever you think, dude, you're not in charge here . . . certainly not in charge of me. I'm a big girl and I'll do whatever the fuck I want." She glanced sideways at Sara and gave her a nasty smile. "Besides, you should take advantage of my absence," she said to Joe with a nod toward Sara. "You saved her life, right? That ought to be worth at least a blow job."

She let out a short barking laugh that sounded more like a grunt and left the basement.

7:48 a.m.

Cindy climbed the stairs quietly, sulking over the obvious play Sara had made for Joe's affections. Though she had no interest in the man whose fate had become interwoven with hers, she was still angry at Sara's cattiness. It occurred to Cindy that if she was, indeed, experiencing the end of the world, Joe Burton and to a lesser extent, the boy, Corey, might be the last men on earth. She had to laugh at that—Corey and Joe as the new Adams and she and Sara as the Eves.

Outside the fire door to the first floor, Cindy paused and listened. Something was moving around and not being real quiet about it. She was tempted to believe it was another survivor, except for the volume of noise it generated. If it was another survivor, she thought, he or she wasn't going to survive for long making so much noise. After a particularly loud crash, Cindy decided that the chance that whatever was in the warehouse was human was slim. It had to be one of the 'Vaders, perhaps still looking for them.

The thought chilled her. Shivering with fear, Cindy crept past the first floor and continued upward into darkness. At each successive landing, she felt on the wall for the door and tried it; they were all locked. Just before the spot on the stairs where the monster she had killed lay rotting, she paused long enough to dig out her lighter. If possible, she wanted to avoid touching the dead beast as she went by it. The smell of its decomposing flesh was sickening. She took out the Altoids tin that held her marijuana. After several tries, she managed to light a joint. She inhaled the sweet, harsh smoke, held it in, and let it out in a blue cloud toward the stinking carcass. After another deep puff, she decided to finish the joint on the roof. Despite her nonchalant "I'll do as I want and fuck everybody else" attitude, she found herself concerned that Joe and Corey might think badly of her if they smelled the weed in the stairwell and realized what she was doing.

Cindy managed to maneuver through the obstacle course of monster body parts quickly and without getting blood or gore on her. She ran up the last few flights, pushed open the roof door, and stepped into sunshine so brilliant and the day so hot she had to visor her eyes with one hand to look around and immediately broke a sweat.

The first thing she spotted was the wrecked police car they had arrived in. It now looked like a junked convertible left to rust on the rooftop. Staying close to the small shack that housed the stairs she had just climbed, Cindy slid around it and looked back and up at the roof of the parking garage across the street. She shook her head with disbelief and wondered how they had managed to survive the jump.

Though it was quieter outside than a normal New York City Monday, it was nowhere near as quiet as Joe Burton had found it to be during his midnight foray. She could hear crashing sounds, which she imagined were being caused by monsters trying to reach people hiding inside as she and the others were. Several times she heard screams and the roar a 'Vader monster. Still smoking the joint, Cindy looked out over the city as far as she could see in all directions. To the south were thick plumes of smoke not too far away, which she figured to be coming from the restaurant where Joe had found Sara. Farther out several more smoke spirals indicated that parts of Tribeca, Battery Park City, and the Financial District also had fires burning out of control.

To the north there was more smoke. She figured it was in the vicinity of the West Village or beyond in Chelsea. To the west she could see a section of the Hudson River between two buildings, and it appeared to be void of maritime traffic. To the east, the parking garage blocked her view completely.

"Ouch!" she said as the joint burned down to a roach and singed her fingers. She dropped it, then stooped to pick it up and stub it out on the rooftop. Standing again, she carefully put it in her pot tin and gazed wistfully at what was left of her scag. She took out her cell phone and called Z-Jay again.

This time she got an answer, one of Z-Jay's crew. It sounded like Jam Man, Z-Jay's number-one homey.

"Who dis?" he questioned plaintively when she asked to speak to Z-Jay. In the background, she could hear music and voices; the sounds of a party—the normal sounds she would have expected to hear on any normal day she called Z-Jay. Every day, and every hour, was a party with Z-Jay, but she was stunned to find that seemingly nothing had changed

even with the advent of the 'Vaders' arrival and the destruction of the world.

There was muffled silence after she spoke her name, and
she could picture Jam Man with a hand over the phone as
he told Z-Jay who was calling. Within a minute, the background party sounds returned.

"He busy right now. Call later," Jam Man drawled in his
lazy, slow way of talking.

"No! I need him right now!" Cindy restated angrily but
immediately wished she could take it back.

"What? Bee-atch, I *know* you ain't takin' that tone with a
brother!" Jam Man said, his slow warm drawl suddenly accelerating and growing icy.

Cindy tried to apologize but he cut her off.

"The man sez call *later*," he repeated with emphasis and
then added with a chuckle: "If you still *alive*, that is."

The last thing she heard before the line went dead was
raucous laughter as if everyone at Z-Jay's end-of-the-world
party had been listening. Cindy cursed loudly, clapped the
hinged lid of the cell phone down, and shoved it back into
her purse. She felt like crying, but, as she often did when her
life didn't go the way she'd like, and she didn't have the luxury or opportunity to shoot some scag, she tried to find
something good in the fuck-up. This time was easy—at least
Z-Jay was still alive, and even better, still partying like always. All she had to do was get to him somehow and everything would be fine.

Fine . . . right!

Getting to Z-Jay was going to be a lot easier said than
done, she realized, especially with him hanging out way up
on West 126th Street. It might as well be California with all
the 'Vaders waiting out there to catch and eat her, not to
mention the little flying orb thingies that wanted to infect her
and turn her into some kind of freaking thing from the Saturday Night Creature Feature she used to watch when she
was a kid.

"All is not lost," she spoke silently to herself and lit a cigarette. When tears threatened again, she murmured, "At least

he's alive. I'll figure something out." A moment later it appeared that something had found her instead of the other way round. She heard a high-pitched faraway whine, which seemed to be coming from the south. She looked in that direction and saw a pyramid of dark specks coming toward the city from a great altitude.

"Now what?" Cindy muttered, anticipating the worst. She started toward the door and safety but stopped as the pyramid came closer and she saw the glint of sunshine on metal.

8:20 a.m.

Joe was pacing in the small, dimly lit basement area while Sara sat with Corey, who was now awake and eating apple pie for breakfast. On every pace that brought him close to the door, Joe leaned toward it, listening for Cindy's return. He didn't like it that she had gone out alone and liked it even less that she had been away so long.

Sara watched Joe, reading his worry in every step and in the way he paused, leaning to the door and looking up as though he had X-ray vision. She felt a pang of jealousy every time he did it. It quickly became irritating. By the twentieth pace—she had been counting—and worried look and lean toward the door, she was about to snap at him. A loud rumble of thunder followed by a sound like a rapid yet muffled drumroll stopped her. The building overhead and the concrete underfoot trembled.

8:20:30 a.m.

A grin broke across Cindy's face as she stared at the sky. The pyramid of specks grew larger the closer they came until, with a thrill of exhilaration, she could make out what they were.

"The fuckin' cavalry has arrived," she murmured. A moment later the lead speck, now clearly identifiable as a fighter jet, broke from the formation and zoomed down toward Washington Street. Rapid machine-gun fire exploded from the plane as it swooped in low, barely twenty yards above the tallest rooftop. Watching the red tracers zip toward the street, Cindy ran to the edge of the rooftop just in time to see the fruition of the jet's attack. Bullets peppered the street below, punching holes through cars, churning up the asphalt street and concrete sidewalks alike, and, best of all, ripping 'Vader monsters to pieces.

Cindy tossed her cigarette and clapped wildly. She cheered as loud as she could: "Kill the fuckers!"

The jet was past in a matter of seconds, pulling up to the right before descending upon another part of the city, but it was immediately followed by another bullet-spitting jet, then another. She looked up to see jets in the sky all over the city breaking off their formations and diving into strafing runs.

Overjoyed, Cindy ran back to the roof door, down the stairs to the fire door, and threw it open, shouting into the echoing darkness of the stairwell: "Hey! You guys! Get up here! You got to see this! The cavalry is here, goddamn it! The *fuckin'* cavalry!" She ran back to the roof.

8:25 a.m.

Joe stopped pacing when the building started shaking. Sara and Corey stared at each other in confusion, but Joe thought he knew what they were hearing.

"Give me your penlight!" he shouted at Sara. He ran to the door with it and into the stairwell. Corey immediately followed, but Sara hesitated, suddenly wary that the noise was somehow being caused by Cindy to get attention.

At the second landing, Joe heard the roof door open and Cindy shout down, but it was hard to hear exactly what she said with the continued roar and staccato explosions from outside.

"What did she say?" Joe asked, turning to Corey who had paused for a breath behind him.

Sara, who had just caught up with them, shook her head and shrugged her shoulders, not caring. She still thought Cindy was up to something.

"I think she said the cavalry is coming, and then some swearwords," Corey piped up.

Joe nodded. That's what he thought he'd heard, also. And it jibed with the thunder and drumroll sounds. Turning on the speed, Joe sprinted up the remaining stairs two, sometimes three, at a time, slowing only when he had to go by the stinking monster remains. Corey followed the bouncing light from the penlight and tried to keep up as best he could. In the rear, Sara took her time but went quickly by the dead 'Vader with her hand over her nose and mouth. Its stench did not mask the smell of marijuana in the stairwell, however, which only increased her suspicions that Cindy was up to something.

Joe opened the door at the bottom of the rooftop stairs and saw Cindy framed in the open doorway at the top, looking to the sky, an expression of joy on her face. She turned and saw Joe coming up the last flight of stairs to the roof.

"It's over!" Cindy cried. "It's fuckin' over! The cavalry has arrived to save the fuckin' day!" She jumped up and down, clapping her hands as she watched the jets zoom by, spraying death upon the 'Vaders in the street below.

Joe reached the roof just in time to see the strafing run of the third jet from one of the many formations now flying over the city. A wide grin broke across his face—this is what he had thought all the noise meant. He was ecstatic to be proven correct.

"Yes!" he cried, pumping both fists in the air. He and Cindy embraced, then started jumping up and down with excitement.

"Get 'em, boys!" Joe shouted, and laughed wildly. "Kick some ass!"

Corey reached the rooftop, confused as to what was happening, but his face reflected the adults' excitement. "What's happening?" Corey yelled watching Joe and Cindy jump around. He giggled at their antics.

"We're saved, kid!" Cindy shouted, grabbed his face with both hands, and planted a wet kiss right on his mouth. "Come on!" She ran to the edge of the roof.

Corey giggled with embarrassment as Joe scooped him up in his arms and carried Corey over to where Cindy stood at the edge of the roof.

"It's the military, Corey. At last we get to fight back!" Joe explained as another jet made its run.

The streaking plane turned the street below into a smoking mess. Cars were demolished and the street was churned up as though a giant farmer had worked the asphalt with an enormous hoe. But what made the three survivors on the roof cheer was the number of 'Vader monsters that had been dispatched. At least a dozen lay sprawled and bleeding in the space of the two blocks Joe, Cindy, and Corey had a clear view of. Several more had been put on the run, ducking down narrow side streets and heading for the river.

Sara emerged onto the roof in the middle of the fifth jet run. The noise of the jet engines combined with the rapid-fire explosions from its gatling gun cannon were deafening. Displaced air swirled around the rooftop in the jet's wake so fiercely that Joe, Cindy, and Corey had to take a step back from the edge for fear of being pulled from the roof. The jet-induced wind staggered Sara also as she tried to join the others. Excitement was rising inside her, too, when she realized what was going on. Unfortunately, her excitement had no chance to grow.

Appearing seemingly from nowhere, the air was suddenly filled with the glowing, flying orbs. They flew above the city en masse, and formed into small oval swarms before zipping up and away. Rising above the building tops, each swarm headed straight for one of the jet formations in the sky over the city.

It was obvious to Joe that the orbs were acting in unison and in their own attack pattern much like the air force jets. With a sinking feeling, he put Corey down and stared at the sky where another jet was descending to start its attack run. A swarm of orbs raced head-on toward it.

8:45 a.m.

Lieutenant Darcy Cornwall eased the nose of his F-16 down, pointing it at the city below. As he began his descent, the swarm of orbs coming at him was camouflaged, appearing to Lieutenant Cornwall to be nothing more than an optical illusion caused by the sun reflecting off the water below and the Hudson River to his left. Though he, like every other man in the squadron that had been the only one able to deploy from Otis Air Force Base, had witnessed the infecting and transforming powers of the invading orbs, he didn't think they presented a threat to him or his fellow pilots inside their planes. The transparent canopy on his cockpit was made of a bulletproof polymer, so he doubted a tiny, sparkly spore no larger than a marble could do any harm.

He was wrong.

The swarm parted as he went through it, scattering the glowing balls to the wind. But *that* was the true illusion; instead of scattering haphazardly, the orbs divided into smaller swarms and some of them sped off toward other jet targets. Lieutenant Cornwall laughed as the lights were seemingly dispersed in his wake, but his laughter was cut short when one of the flying marbles hit his canopy and stuck there.

"What the hell?" Cornwall muttered. A moment later, the stuck orb glowed red. Before Lieutenant Cornwall's unbelieving eyes, the sphere slowly melted through the cockpit canopy. The tiny spore burst into the cockpit, driven by the force of the air behind it coming through the hole it had made. It flew directly at Lieutenant Cornwall's face and attached itself to his flight mask.

The mask began to melt.

Lieutenant Cornwall tore it from his face. Air blasted through the tiny hole in the cockpit with a high whistling sound. He didn't notice the orb detach from his flight mask and felt only its heat as it flew up his nose and down his throat.

Lieutenant Darcy Cornwall, USAF pilot, had just enough time to think, *I'm fucked*, before his body transformed. It burst from his flight suit with an explosion of shredded material and quickly grew so large the cockpit quickly ran out of room to contain him. With a scream that was part roar and part anguished human cry, his head, shoulders, and upper body burst through the canopy, jettisoning it as if he had deployed the ejection system. At the same time his expanding legs punched through the bottom of the plane.

Out of control, its aerodynamic stability destroyed, the plane tumbled through the air, losing altitude quickly and falling toward the city.

8:55 a.m.

"Oh no. Please, God, no," Joe Burton muttered in despair.

"What's going on?" Corey asked, looking up from the dead monsters in the street below. He followed Joe's gaze skyward just in time to see Lt. Darcy Cornwall's legs poke through the bottom of his airplane. At first Corey had the urge to laugh; the legs sticking out of the bottom of the plane reminded him of Fred Flintstone's stone-age automobile. But when the jet went into a nose-over-tailfin-tumble toward the ground, the urge to laugh passed, replaced by shock.

"I don't fuckin' believe this," Cindy said, her voice heavy with emotion.

The first jet to crash slammed into the ground just above the site of the World Trade Center Memorial. Though Joe and the others could not see it impact the earth, they heard it, and felt it—a loud *wham-bang* combination of sound and earth tremor as though a giant hand were slamming shut the cover of a gigantic book. To the three adults it was eerily reminiscent of September 11, 2001. Mere seconds after the crash, a narrow pillar of flame amid a thick plume of black smoke rose into the sky.

9:00 a.m.

Maj. John Jamison, 1st squadron leader, watched Lieutenant Cornwall's somersaulting F-16 slam into a five-story building, demolishing the structure, itself, and its pilot-now-turned-monster. In shock at what he had just witnessed, the major didn't notice the small swarm of orbs rushing at him. Instead of burning through his canopy, the swarm split in two, like a pair of reaching arms, and passed by the cockpit. Growing red-hot, one arm of the swarm rose above the jet and then turned and swooped down into the plane's wake. It shot directly into the F-16's exhaust and into its single engine. The other arm of the swarm continued on heading for the next fighter jet.

With his cockpit seat close to the jet's fuselage, Major Jamison didn't feel a thing when it exploded, killing him instantly.

All over the sky above the city, the scene was repeated again and again.

The quartet of survivors stood on top of the UPS warehouse and stared in shock at the plight of the jets that a few moments before had seemed to be their salvation. They watched in horror as one by one the jets ran into the swarms and either exploded in midair or the pilots transformed inside the jets, causing them to crash. The much repeated sound of multiple explosions and crashes echoed throughout the city. With each thunderclap signifying the death of another jet, the hopes of Joe, Cindy, Corey, and Sara sank lower and lower.

9:20 a.m.

Driven back into the basement when it became apparent that the jets were not going to save the day, the group was quiet. Sara and Corey returned to their seats atop the crates along the left wall while Cindy resumed her position opposite them, near the bathroom. Joe remained upright though leaning his shoulders against the closed door behind him. Every few moments there was another faint *boom*, and he shook his head, sometimes muttering inaudibly, as though engaged in an argument with himself.

By noon, the sounds of the battle were over. The day wore on with none of them speaking much. They each slept intermittently, but more often than not, their sleep was not restful, bringing fantastic nightmares instead of escape from the *real* nightmare they were living in. They each used the bathroom at least once. Occasionally, one of them rummaged through the food supply that Corey and Sara had neatly stacked on a crate next to the one they sat on. Cindy drank a bottle and a half of wine, picked at the food the most—mainly consuming the pies and anything else that was sweet—and smoked two of her last three cigarettes. She and Sara avoided making eye contact.

Around midafternoon Joe finally resumed his seat on a crate and hunched over the Manhattan street map again.

"Why are you even bothering with that?" Cindy asked, her words slurring a little from the effects of the wine. "If the fuckin' army can't do anything against those things, what makes you think the cops could?"

"Look," Joe replied, sighing. "What happened this morning doesn't mean all hope is lost. In fact, I think it means exactly the opposite. Think about it; if the military is still able to send a squadron of jets to battle the 'Vaders, then it's logical that other government forces, like the cops and the National Guard, must be doing something, too."

Cindy remained unconvinced. "There are so many of those little flying fucks . . . you saw what they did to those planes. If those jets couldn't stand up to those, whatever they are, then neither can the cops or anyone or any *thing* short of a nuclear bomb." As soon as she said it, it occurred to Cindy, as well as Joe and Sara, that the military might just do that as a last resort. After several minutes of uncomfortable, contemplative silence, Sara finally broke it.

"Do you think they would really do that? Drop the bomb on us?" she asked, addressing the question to Joe and ignoring Cindy.

"Fuck, yeah!" Cindy shot back and laughed halfheartedly before Joe could respond.

"They're going to drop a nuclear bomb on us?" Corey asked, mispronouncing the word as *nuc-u-lar*. His face revealed the fear he felt at such a prospect.

Cindy laughed again, a nasty, mocking laugh that caused Corey to blush with embarrassment.

"How the hell do you know about nuclear bombs?" she asked, mocking his pronunciation.

"I saw somethin' on TV," Corey mumbled.

Cindy continued, "Yeah? And what did they say about it?"

Corey appeared to be on the verge of tears as he replied, "It could blow up the world and then it would be like winter every day." By the time he finished the sentence, tears were brimming his eyes and rolling down both cheeks.

Sara pulled him close, wrapping her arms around him and casting an angry look in Cindy's direction.

"It's okay, Corey," she soothed. "That's not going to happen. Don't worry."

Cindy scoffed at her comment. "Why you lying to the kid?" she asked laconically.

"Why don't you just shut up?" Sara commented through clenched teeth.

Cindy sneered back at her. "You know, if you didn't have that gun, I'd kick your ass into the middle of next week."

"Why don't you both shut up!" Joe commanded, his voice stern. He looked at Corey. Corey he said, "It's going to be okay, kid. No one's going to drop the bomb on us." He glared at Cindy, who had begun her mocking laughter again. It quickly withered under his angry gaze.

Corey nodded, grateful for Joe's assurances.

"So what now, oh great leader?" Cindy asked.

Joe ignored her as best he could and spoke softly, his jaw tight with anger. "We wait until nightfall, then we make our way to the Sixth Precinct. We should be able to get some help there." He paused and looked gravely at his three companions. "There's just one problem, I checked the shotgun and it's out of ammo, and your pistol," Joe pointed at Sara, "holds only six bullets. That's all we have to defend ourselves out there."

Cindy smirked.

Corey and Sara looked apprehensive.

"But," Joe continued, "we do have another weapon at our disposal." He picked up one of the empty wine bottles on the floor. "There's a gas pump just outside the garage doors upstairs. If we can fill a bunch of these bottles with gas and tear those drapes," he indicated the moldy gold curtains he'd put up around the toilet and sink, "into strips, we can stuff them into the bottles as wicks and make—"

"Molotov cocktails!" Sara finished for him.

"That's right," Joe said, grinning.

Cindy remained unimpressed. "Yeah?" she questioned. "Who's going to go topside to fill the bottles?" Her tone indicated it would not be her.

"I will," Joe replied, calmly.

"Me, too," Sara backed him up.

"Me, three!" Corey piped up, his face eager.

Joe smiled at him and tousled his hair. "Sure. You can be our lookout."

Corey beamed.

"You, too," Joe said to Cindy.

"Fuck that," Cindy scoffed. "And fuck you, too. I ain't goin' out there on some harebrained, half-baked plan and become a chew toy for those things."

"No," Joe said, his voice angry. "Fuck *you*! If you won't help, I'll leave you behind."

"Go ahead!" Cindy challenged. "I've got everything I need right here," she said, nodding at the supply of food.

"Uh-uh," Joe said. "We're taking that with us."

"How are you going to carry it?"

"We'll manage," Joe answered.

Cindy scowled at him. "You'd leave me here to starve?"

"Fuckin-A," Joe replied.

"And how the hell are you going to carry the Molotov cocktails?"

"We can make a sack out of the drapes," Joe answered.

Cindy didn't look happy.

Joe grinned at her, eyebrows raised as if to say, *How about that?*

"Fine," Cindy growled. "But at the first sight of those things coming anywhere near us, I'm gone. I'm coming right back here."

"Sure, just as long as you let us know they're coming," Joe told her.

Sara regarded Cindy with distrust.

Reading her expression, Corey spoke up. "Don't worry, I'll be watching, too."

Sara smiled, then gave him a hug and a kiss on the cheek. "Thanks, Corey."

He blushed and smiled.

"Nigga, please!" Cindy said under her breath, and turned away in disgust.

10:00 p.m.

The night was cool and damp; the air filled with a soaking mist. Rain fell from the sky intermittently, first pouring, then becoming a drizzle, then stopping altogether before it began the cycle again. Through the rain and fog, the street, without streetlights, was hard to see.

Joe and Sara stood just inside and to the right of the three demolished garage doors with Cindy and Corey behind them.

"Maybe we should wait until the fog lifts," Sara suggested.

Joe shook his head. "No. I think this might be better. The fog provides cover and the rain should, too. They won't be able to hear us so good."

He turned to address Corey and Cindy.

"One of you stand on each side of these doors. Corey, right here, and Cindy, over there." He pointed to the other side. "Keep your eyes and ears open. If it looks or sounds like *anything* is coming our way, let us know." He turned and pointed outside at the gas pumps that were less than ten yards away. "We'll be close enough to hear you if you whistle or call to us."

Corey nodded eagerly, but Cindy just raised her eyebrows and *harrumphed* softly.

Joe glared at her until she nodded and reluctantly took up her designated post. He and Sara knelt next to the box of empty wine bottles at their feet. The bottles had been emptied into the basement toilet, except for a few that Cindy had insisted on keeping for herself.

"You ready?" Joe asked Sara.

She nodded. Joe noticed she was sweating, and it wasn't from humidity; the rain and mist made the night cooler than normal for this time of year. Her hair clung to her forehead and the sides of her face, and she was breathing rapidly.

"Okay. Calm down," he told her, and placed a hand on her shoulder. "Take a deep breath, like this." He inhaled deeply and let it out slowly. Sara followed suit.

"Again," Joe said. They sucked air deep into their lungs together and let it out slowly. "Once more," Joe commanded, and they repeated the exercise for the third time. "Now, when we get out there, I'll work the pump. You hand me the empty bottles, and I'll hand them back to you when they're full. Then you put them back in the box. Okay?"

Sara nodded.

"Good. We'll use the diesel pump since it's closest to the door," Joe added.

Sara shook her head.

"Why not?" Joe asked.

"Regular gas ignites easier than diesel," Sara told him. "My dad used to own a gas station when I was a kid," she added by way of explanation to his questioning look.

"Thanks," Joe said. As he picked up the box, his left hand slipped and he nearly dropped it. The bottles clinked against one another, sounding as loud as church bells on a Sunday morning.

Sara's face drained of color, and both of them held their breath.

Joe hugged the box to steady it and prevent further noise. Slowly, carefully, he stood and Sara followed. They both let out their breath in mutual sighs.

"Let's do this," he said.

Stepping into the misty night, both Joe and Sara shivered at the touch of the cool, damp air on their skin. The eerie silence riveted Sara to the spot for a moment until Joe nudged her toward the pumps. Looking at the fog-filled night, it seemed that the entire sky over the city was aglow with a soft, faint light. Joe assumed they were fires burning out of control caused by all the jets that had crashed earlier. An

overwhelming sense of pity crept over him for the poor pilots, bringing back with it the sense of despair he had been
fighting since this madness had begun. He concentrated on
the task at hand to battle the feeling.

At the gas pump, which was the one farthest from the
door and closest to the street, Joe put the case of bottles
down, careful not to jostle and rattle them. He crouched by
the box and turned to Sara, who copied his position next to
him.

"Oh, shit," he whispered.

"What?"

"I just realized something. We've got to go back."

Picking up the box of bottles again, he followed Sara
back into the garage.

"What's the matter?" Cindy sneered. "Chicken out?"

Sara ignored her. "What is it?" she asked Joe, who had
put the box of bombs-to-be down again and was scanning
the inside of the garage.

"The nozzle on the pump is too big for the bottles. We'd
get gas all over the place trying to fill them. We need a fun-
nel or something else; something with a bigger mouth to put
the gas in, then we can fill the bottles downstairs and add the
wicks. It'll be safer."

Sara agreed, and together they searched the debris-strewn
warehouse for a container to fill with gas. After a half hour
of searching, Sara found what they needed—a five-gallon
gas can—behind the seat of the only small van parked inside
the garage that had not been damaged. She also found a
small, portable chemical fire extinguisher.

Joe, who had been growing anxious and finding it harder
to keep despair at bay, was so overjoyed with her finds that
he threw his arms around her and kissed her passionately,
leaving Sara breathless.

"Come on," Joe whispered.

Leaving the box of bottles inside, Sara carried the fire extinguisher, and Joe the gas can, back to the pumps. Joe ran
head-on into more disappointment; the pumps didn't work.

Try as he might, he could not coax even a drop from the nozzle.

Sara whispered, "I remember now! The pumps need to be turned on. Daddy always shut them off at night so he wouldn't get ripped off. The switch should be inside the mechanic's garage."

Leaving the gas can and extinguisher by the pump, they went inside. Sara looked around, scanning the wall beside the door. "There!" she said as loud as she could whisper. She pointed at a small gray metal electrical box about a foot below the red and green buttons for operating the doors.

She ran to it and dropped to a knee in front of it as if it were a holy relic and she a pious pilgrim. She opened the rectangular metal box to reveal two clearly marked switches—the left one for *diesel*, the right for *petrol*.

"Yes!" Sara said, drawing out the final consonant like a snake hissing. "We're in business," she said, smiling at Joe.

"If you two are through fuckin' around, could we get on with it and get the hell out of here?" Cindy rasped, trying to shout at the top of a whisper.

Sara flipped her off then flipped the petrol switch on. A loud electric hum filled the mist-laced night, accompanied by an even louder crackling sound. The gauge showing gallons pumped and the price lit up on the pump.

"What the fuck?" Cindy gasped, backing farther into the shadows away from the door.

On the other side, Corey let out a soft scared whimper.

To the four of them, the illuminated gas pump looked as bright as a lighthouse beacon.

Certain that the light would attract 'Vaders like the proverbial moths to a flame, Cindy kept backing away, then turned and ran for the basement door.

Joe and Sara scowled at each other.

Corey looked uncertain as to what to do. He shared Cindy's fear, but he didn't want to abandon Sara and Joe.

A minute passed that felt like a day. All remained quiet outside the door. After two minutes and no sign of monsters or orbs coming out of the fog, Joe looked at Sara, raised his eyebrows, and nodded toward the pumps.

Sara took a deep breath and shook her head, yes.

Joe looked to Corey and mouthed the word, "Okay?" and held his right hand out, thumb up.

Corey nodded and gave a thumbs-up back at him. He resumed his position by the door as Joe and Sara went out to the pumps again.

Joe unscrewed the spout on the gas can, wincing at every little metallic squeak it made. Lifting the spout free of the can, he handed it to Sara. He carefully lifted the nozzle from the gas pump and pushed up the lever under it to allow the gas to flow.

10:50 p.m.

Corey tried to keep his eyes focused beyond Joe and Sara at the pumps, but it was hard to do. The street was invisible to him. The only things he could see clearly were Sara and Joe and the gas pumps. He watched as Joe inserted the nozzle into the gas can and pressed the trigger. A moment later the smell of gasoline filled the air.

Corey grew nervous; if he could smell the gas ten yards away in the garage, then anyone (or anything) could smell it in the opposite direction, out on the street, where there were monsters. Corey tried his hardest to cut through the fog with his vision, attempting to see even the slightest movement that might indicate the approach of a 'Vader.

A loud *ding*! pierced the night. Corey jumped at the sound of it, as did Joe and Sara. They both looked nervous, but Joe kept on pumping. Joe leaned over and said something to Sara. She nodded and came back into the garage.

"Joe wants me to help you keep watch since you-know-who chickened out," she said.

"What was that bell?" Corey whispered.

"The gas pump," Sara replied. "It dings for every gallon that is pumped. It's a wicked old pump," she explained further. "The new ones don't do that."

From outside came another loud *ding*! as the second gallon went into the can. To Corey it was too loud for comfort.

11:00 p.m.

Joe Burton was not a religious man, but in desperation he found himself bartering with God through prayer as the second gallon bell sounded from the pump. *Please God, let me live through this and I'll never do a bad thing again in my life, ever!*

"Dear God, please let me get through this, and I'll do everything I can to protect Sara and Corey and keep them from harm," he whispered.

He looked to the garage and the objects of his prayerful promises as the third-gallon bell rang. Only two more and still no sign of danger. He repeated his prayers more fervently.

Just as the gas pump rang for the fourth time, Corey saw something move in the fog beyond where Joe crouched. He saw it only for a moment before the mist swirled to cover it, and he wasn't sure that his eyes weren't playing tricks on him. He looked at Sara who was scrutinizing the foggy landscape as vigilantly as he, but she did not appear to have seen anything; she showed no alarm.

The *ding*! registering the final gallon going into the five-gallon can gave Corey a start even though he was expecting it, and he bumped Sara. He startled her and she let out a short, high-pitched squeak. She looked at Corey with concern.

He smiled sheepishly at her, and she grinned back, touching his arm reassuringly as she did. At that moment, the largest 'Vader Corey had yet seen came lumbering out of the fog. Corey froze, unsure of what to do; afraid to warn Joe with words and attract the monster to him and Sara, and afraid *not* to warn Joe so that he could either hide or make a run for the garage. But the monster appeared so suddenly, coming out of the fog so close, it was doubtful Joe would have time to make it back inside.

Sara saw the beast at the same time as Corey and found

herself subjected to the same dilemma. She made up her mind more quickly than Corey and was about to risk attracting the monster to the garage when Joe leaned forward to look around the pump at the street and saw the hellish creature less than ten yards away. Leaving the gas nozzle running in the can, he quickly ducked back between the row of delivery vans parked behind him.

The pump rang again as the gas overflowed the can. The smell of the spilling fuel grew stronger, attracting the large 'Vader to the gas can. Using two of its fat, grotesque fingers, the thing picked the nozzle free of the can with a motion much more delicate than it appeared capable of.

With Joe having set the pump's trigger on automatic feed, gas continued to pour from the nozzle as the creature pulled it free of the can. Still holding it with two fingers the way a mother might hold a dirty diaper ready for disposal, the monster brought the nozzle close to its face and sniffed at it, dousing itself with the fossil fuel in the process. Next, the monster apparently decided a taste test was in order as it stuck out its massive tongue for a lick.

Its dislike of the gasoline's flavor was immediate. It made a bitter face, contorting its already abnormal features even further, and dropped the gas handle, which continued its flow all over the monster's feet and beyond, forming a narrow rivulet running toward the open garage door. The giant former human spit repeatedly, shaking its head in an attempt to rid itself of both the taste and the smell of the toxic fluid.

The pump bell rang gallon seven as the flow continued unabated. Another 'Vader, slightly smaller than the first, appeared through the cloaking mist, attracted by the sound of the pump and the smell of its spilled contents.

The first and larger 'Vader backed away from the pump as it tried to wipe the gas from its body and bumped into the second monster. The latter creature took a deep sniff of the former and covered its nose with its right hand, grimacing at the smell. The first monster seemed to take offense at this reaction and snarled at the smaller one before giving it a hard shove. The beast leaped at its bigger brother and both tumbled to the asphalt, locked in mortal combat.

Joe couldn't breathe; fear and panic had stolen his ability to do so. Hiding between two UPS vans, he realized he had come within mere inches of being discovered by the 'Vaders. If he had not looked around the pump when he had, he would now be chewed up and in pieces in the horror's gut. Of course that was still a very real possibility with the two 'Vaders fighting, but with them distracted, Joe saw a chance for escape.

Duck-walking out from between the trucks, Joe went behind the gas pump and stopped. From there, he grabbed the fire extinguisher and put it by his feet. Next, he grabbed the full gas can and screwed on its lid, his hands shaking so badly he could barely complete the task. On the other side of the pump, the two monstrous gargoyles rolled about, snapping and clawing at each other with their teeth and talons. The fight attracted more 'Vaders from out of the fog, drawn to the battle of the titans like drunks to a bar fight.

Joe pressed his body against the pump hiding him as he tried to keep from being spotted. He could see at least four 'Vaders now at the edge of the UPS driveway, all watching the fight and still, thankfully, unaware of him. He realized that if he tried to make a dash for the garage now, he would most certainly be seen by one of the spectator monsters and that would bring all of them chasing after him and into the garage where Corey and Sara were. The battle between the two 'Vaders was not enough of a distraction to allow him to get back inside undetected.

He got an idea. He pulled out the pack of matches he had found in the tollbooth of the parking lot next door. He opened the cover. There were only three inside; he hoped it would be enough. As a kid playing with his GI Joe action figures, he used to use matches like rocket bombs by placing a loose match on the striking strip, then flicking at it with his middle finger sprung off his thumb. If done correctly, the match head would flare as the match sailed through the air, sometimes as far as four or five feet depending on how hard he could flick it. To his youthful imaginative eye, it had looked like a missile.

Now he tried the same thing. Keeping a wary eye out for 'Vaders, Joe crouched on the side of the pump away from the monsters. He pulled a cardboard match free and placed it on the flint strip at the bottom of the packet. He held it close to his body to shield it from the mist until the right moment. A few seconds later, it presented itself as the two creatures fighting rolled within a foot of Joe.

He flicked the match head and missed. The match fell to the wet ground. Joe pulled another free and placed it on the flint, huddling over it again. The light drizzling rain stopped. At last, Joe thought, maybe my luck is changing.

Out on the driveway, the smaller monster struck the larger, gas-soaked 'Vader a vicious blow to its stomach. The bigger beast fell over, holding its gut, and rolled to within a yard of the pumps.

Joe flicked at the second match, hit it, and sent it sailing . . . but it didn't ignite.

He was down to his last match. The big one got up and charged the smaller one. Both were back near the street. For a moment, Joe thought he could make it back to the garage, but before he could act, the brawlers were tumbling in his direction, again coming within a couple of feet of the pump.

Joe quickly tore out and placed his last match. He looked up; the larger 'Vader's head was a mere foot away. The smaller one was on top and strangling the larger beast trapped beneath it. In its struggle to free itself, twisting its head to and fro to break the choke hold, the big monster caught sight of Joe crouched by the pump. Their eyes met a half-second before Joe flicked the match straight at it.

There was a spark, a flare, and the match arched through the air aflame. Just as the monster reached for Joe, the burning match struck it on the nose, bounced off, and landed on its gas-soaked chin. With a sound like a strong wind blowing through a narrow space, the face of the creature burst into flames that spread like a tsunami across the island of its body.

The creature on top tried to jump off the sudden inferno beneath it, but the burning monster wouldn't let it. It wrapped its incendiary arms around the smaller 'Vader and locked it in a fiery embrace. Now twin howls of pain rose from the flaming duo, answered by bellowing roars from the onlookers. The ball of fiery monsters rolled into the midst of the spectators, making them scatter.

It was the moment Joe had been waiting for. Grabbing the gas can and the extinguisher, he sprinted for the warehouse.

Corey and Sara had retreated into the darkest shadows of the garage interior without losing sight of Joe and his predicament. They had watched in terror as the battle between the 'Vaders ensued. They looked at each other questioningly, trying to figure out what Joe was doing with his matches. Realization came with the monsters bursting into flames. They cheered silently and urged Joe on as he ran and joined them, puffing from fear and the exertion of carrying the heavy five-gallon gas can. Sara picked up the box of empty wine bottles and, together, the three of them headed for the basement, secure in the thought that the inferno of fighting 'Vaders had covered their retreat.

It had, but what they didn't see, and thus didn't know, was that the broad rivulet of gas that had flowed from the pump into the garage soon ignited when the brawling, burning monsters came in contact with it. Like a fuse, the fire burned the length of the fuel stream and into the warehouse, where it quickly spread. In the other direction, the fire ran back to the pumps. With a sound that compressed the air with its volatility, and a bright, blinding flash of flame that left the monsters around it stunned, the gas pumps exploded and engulfed the throng of creatures in a fiery wave.

11:44 p.m.

Cindy Raposa had returned to the empty basement room mumbling to herself.

"What a bunch of fuck-ups. If they want to get killed, it don't mean I have to join 'em."

She had stood under the weak, yellow lightbulb and looked around as if searching for someone to agree with her justification. Then she sat on her crate and lit a cigarette, cursing the fact that it was her last. She popped several Vicodin and washed them down with wine from one of the bottles she had kept. While she had sat smoking and drinking, she had tried to figure out how she was going to get to Z-Jay's place without getting eaten or turned into an alien nightmare. She wondered if the subway ran automatically. If it did, getting uptown to Harlem would be easy.

She pulled out her cell phone and tried Z-Jay's number again, but, unlike Sara, she couldn't get a signal in the basement. Soon after, an explosion rocked the building seconds before Joe, Sara, and Corey came through the door.

11:46 p.m.

"That must have been the gas pump exploding," Joe said, a worried look on his face as he looked up at the ceiling. "We'd better get busy." He placed the gas can on the floor. He didn't look at Cindy, treating her as though she no longer existed. Sara, on the other hand, glared at her as she put the case of empty wine bottles on the floor next to the can.

"Thanks for your help up there," Sara said, her voice stiff with sarcasm.

Cindy shrugged. "Don't mention it," she replied, calmly, refusing to let Sara rile her. But Sara wasn't about to let it go.

"We all could have been killed up there, thanks to you!" Sara went on in an accusing tone.

"Maybe," Cindy said nonchalantly. "But you weren't. There was probably a better chance of you getting blown up. It seems every time you guys go out there's a fucking explosion."

"Doesn't it bother you that a kid of seven"—Sara indicated Corey with a pat on his shoulder—"has more *balls* than you do?"

Cindy smiled but it was more of a sneer. "Of course he's got more balls, he's a boy and I'm a girl." She laughed. "And I wish you'd watch your language in front of the child," she added in a stilted, phony tone of voice.

Exasperated and furious, Sara let out a growling sigh and clenched her fists at her side as if she were about to pummel Cindy.

Cindy remained cool, yet tensed inside, ready to defend herself and more should Sara actually try to attack her.

"Would you two knock it off?" Joe grunted. He was sitting cross-legged on the sagging cardboard box next to the wooden crate that held more of the moldy old drapes. With a good deal of effort, he was ripping the heavy gold-colored fabric into strips. Corey sat next to him, laying each new strip in a neat pile and looking nervous at the women's bickering.

"But Joe," Sara said, "aren't you going to say *anything* to her? I don't think we should take her with us—she hasn't helped *at all*."

Joe shrugged and kept tearing strips using his teeth to bite a fray into the edge of the material before ripping it.

Sara shook her head and sat heavily opposite Joe and Corey, her arms crossed over her chest, a look of exasperation on her face.

Cindy smiled sweetly at her and winked playfully.

Sara stuck up her "fuck you" finger and Cindy made a mock display of shock at it, delicately covering her mouth with one hand and widening her bloodshot eyes in feigned outrage.

"Forget about her; she's useless," Joe told Sara. "Help me out with this stuff, would you? We need to do this pronto; if the gas pumps and their tanks have blown, we may need to get out of here fast." He indicated the gas can, bottles, and torn strips of drapery.

With one last look of disgust at Cindy, Sara asked, "What do you want me to do?"

"Well, for starters you can fill each of the wine bottles about three-quarters with gasoline. Then we'll soak the strips of curtain with gas and stuff them into the necks for wicks."

"Okay." Sara knelt next to the box of wine bottles and picked up the gas can.

"While you do that, I'm going to search the rest of the basement and try to find something to carry our Molotov cocktails in," Joe told her, getting up. He turned on Sara's penlight, and with her pistol tucked in the waistband of his pants, he ventured into the darkness of the basement beyond the rear door and the feeble reach of the bare lightbulb overhead.

Sara and Corey watched as Joe walked cautiously into the thick shadows that closed about him until even the faint glow of the penlight was no longer discernible.

Cindy made a show of not caring and cleaned her nails with a small sliver of wood pried from the crate she sat on, but she, too, watched out of the corner of her eye. Sara ignored her and kept up a constant conversation with Corey while they worked, questioning him about everything from school and friends to family and his favorite TV shows, cartoons, and movies.

For the most part Corey happily obliged, talking freely and openly about his former life without realizing it *was* now *former*. It was painfully obvious to Sara, though, and to a lesser extent, Cindy. Both women felt pity and sympathy for Corey, who spoke so eagerly about his life as if it still existed somewhere unchanged and as innocent as it should be. Only once did Corey falter and grow sad; when he talked about how excited he was that he was going to have a little brother or sister to play with when his mother had her baby. As soon as he said it, he buried his head in Sara's shoulder, but didn't cry—which bothered Sara much more than if he had. After a few minutes, he lifted his head and smiled wanly at her. His eyes, though red with emotion, were dry.

"You know, we're going to hook up with your dad," Sara said, trying to ease the pain she saw in Corey's hurt yet tearless eyes. "I can feel it. When we get to the Sixth Precinct, he'll be waiting there for you. Just wait and see."

Corey nodded thankfully, and his countenance brightened.

Across the room, Cindy rolled her eyes at Sara's, "every-thing is going to be hunky-dory" speech. She opened her mouth to say something needling and sarcastic, but the eager hope on Corey's face stopped her. Though part of her said it was cruel to lead the boy on with such bullshit, she still couldn't bring herself to say anything negative, even if the kid was going to end up crushed when he discovered the truth. She doubted his father, or anyone else for that matter, was holed up at the Sixth Precinct. Hadn't all the police cars and cops they had seen on the first day of the 'Vaders attack been from the Sixth Precinct? From what she remembered witnessing that day, she doubted any of them had survived.

Instead of raining on the kid's parade, Cindy stood— hands on her hips—and leaned back, loosening up muscles sore from sitting too long. What she really wanted was a nice fat syringe full of junk. Unfortunately, if she was going to make the little bit she had left last until she could get to Z-Jay's place, she had to conserve. The next best thing was a dose of Valium followed by a joint and some more wine. The Valium she could take—and did, washing it down with more wine— without Sara or Corey being any the wiser. Smoking a joint, though, presented a problem, especially with the basement room full of gas fumes.

By the time Joe returned, Sara and Corey had filled all the wine bottles with gas and still had at least a gallon of the fuel left in the can. It had been a messy process, though, and the room was thick with the smell of spilled gasoline. They were a little more than midway through the process of inserting the drapery wicks into the bottles and were getting dizzy from the fumes.

Cindy was getting up to go into the stairwell to the upper floors where she could get high undisturbed.

"I found a tunnel!" Joe said, excited, as he stepped through the door into the light. "I think it leads to the next building on this block, or it might even run under the whole block and further. We might be able to gain access to a subway tunnel. I don't know, but I think we should explore it to see how far we can go."

"Yeah!" Sara agreed. "That would make it a lot safer than traveling the streets."

Ignored by Joe, Sara, and Corey, Cindy continued to the stairway door and her rendezvous with a joint on the upper floor. Passing into the stairwell, she considered what Joe had just said. She hoped the tunnel he discovered *did* connect with the subway. Even if the trains were no longer running, she figured she could get uptown by walking through the tunnels—couldn't she? In answer, she thought of all the times she had been on the subway when the train had been forced to stop between stations for one reason or another. She remembered how she had looked out at the dark, creepy interior of the underground and thought, I'd hate to be trapped down here and have to walk out.

She shuddered at the combined memory and thought that she might have to do just that if she wanted to hook up with Z-Jay again. She took a deep breath and tried to push the fear from her mind. After all, it wouldn't be the first time she'd had to do something she was afraid of (or disgusted by) to get a fix. And in this scary new world, she doubted it would be the last time.

Cindy left the basement and started up the stairs, her head down and focused on her open purse as she got out the chewing gum tin that doubled as a joint holder. After a few steps, her eyes began to sting and her nostrils detected the acrid smell of smoke. She looked up.

The stairwell was clouded with smoke. It flowed down the stairs, heavier than air, and wrapped its blinding arms around her and stuck its gagging fingers down her throat. The smoke overcame her so fast she became disoriented and unsure of which way was up. Only after twisting away from the billows of gray and slipping off the step she was on, stumbling down the few stairs she had just climbed, was she able to reorient herself.

The smoke chased her back down to the basement door, and tried to overtake her, wanting to put her to sleep forever by filling her lungs with deadly, smoky somnolence. She reached for the doorknob, but the cloud beat her to it. Suddenly the door handle was gone. She couldn't find it no matter how hard she tried. She stubbed her fingers and scraped her knuckles searching for it, but it was no use. The smoke and growing heat that followed the suffocating cloud like a tagalong little brother were quickly taking away her ability to see, think, and act clearly.

She coughed raggedly and stumbled into a hard, cold, smooth surface. Hoping it was the basement door, she slapped both hands on it, pounding it with the heels of her palms. Just when she thought she was a goner, that she had breathed her last breath because the nasty smoke and heat had consumed all the air, the hard surface under her hands moved.

The door opened and large strong hands grabbed her by the arms and pulled her inside.

Day 3: Tuesday

12:10 a.m.

Joe Burton immediately closed the door behind Cindy, who fell to the floor, coughing and gasping for air. Though the door had been open less than ten seconds, the fast-moving smoke managed to get into their basement hideaway, filling it with enough smoke to roll over the floor and rise to form low-lying clouds that hung just beneath the cobweb-strewn rafters as if ready to spew lightning and clap out thunder.

"What the hell?" Sara exclaimed, perplexed by the sudden inrush of so much choking smoke. "What did you do?" she asked Cindy accusingly.

"What did *I* do?" Cindy got out before being seized by a spasm of coughing so strong she nearly puked. "I didn't do nothin'," she answered, her voice hoarse, when she was under control again. "The fucking building's on fire!" She glared at Joe and Sara. "I think *I'm* the one who should be asking *you* what *you* did, 'cause I wasn't the one playing with gasoline upstairs!" she finished righteously.

"No!" Sara immediately countered. "*You* ran *away* and didn't care if we lived or died up there."

"Big fucking deal," Cindy shouted, regaining her feet.

"At least I didn't set the fucking place on fire. Now we can all die down *here* instead of up *there*!"

Corey burst into tears at their fighting. "Please stop," he blubbered. "Please don't fight."

Joe just shook his head at them and turned to the door. He placed the palm of his right hand on the door and quickly removed it.

"This is really hot," he said softly, as if thinking out loud. "I guess now we have no choice," he said, facing the others. "We're going to have to go through the tunnel I found."

He bent over and quickly completed stuffing the remaining wick-strips into the bottles. To Sara he directed, "Take down that curtain." He pointed at the drape hung as the door of the water closet. "We'll have to use it as a sack for carrying these."

Sara did as told and pulled one of the drapes free. She lay the drape on the floor and eyed it, trying to figure how to convert it to a sack. She was surprised when Cindy pulled a switchblade out of her bag and made a deep slit in each corner of the curtain. Then, folding opposite corners toward each other, she tied them together until she had made a sack typical of the hobo stereotype—the kind that can be hung on the end of a stick carried over the shoulder.

While drying his eyes on the front of his T-shirt, Corey watched with rapt fascination and now declared the homemade sack "cool!"

"Yeah," Joe agreed. "Nice job," he told Cindy.

She shrugged off the compliment and, with effort, did not smile or show how pleased she felt to be appreciated.

Sara, too, nodded and gave Cindy a thumbs-up sign, although reluctantly.

While Joe held the sack open, Sara carefully placed the fire extinguisher and a dozen of the Molotov cocktails in it. Though they had made twenty, the sack held only twelve. To make use of as many as possible, Sara and Cindy each carried one. Joe slung the sack over his shoulder, snaking his arm though the top, and carried one more in his left hand and the penlight in his right.

"We'll have to leave the food behind, and I'm going to need your lighter," he said to Cindy.

There was a prolonged, tense moment as Cindy considered whether or not to give up her lighter; it was her only means of cooking her heroin and lighting her joints. She finally acquiesced but only because she knew she wouldn't be able to shoot up until they made it somewhere safe. She had a small box of wooden kitchen matches in the lining pocket of her purse if she needed to light a joint.

Joe thanked her as he took the lighter and exclaimed: "Yeah, *this* should do the trick!"

12:30 a.m.

Following the dim circle of light cast in front of them by the penlight Joe held, Corey, Sara, and Cindy followed Joe through the vast cellar. The going was treacherous; the floor of the cellar beyond the section they had sheltered in was uneven and strewn with rubble and debris. The cobwebs were more numerous, thicker, and hanging much lower. Some of the webs were massive, stretching from the stone floor to the wooden ceiling like something out of a horror movie.

Joe tried to keep the light concentrated on the floor in front of them. He kicked aside loose bricks, broken glass, gravel, and rusting empty cans as best he could. Several times during their flight through the cellar, either Corey or the women, or all three, gave out frightened shrieks when rats scuttled through the light or their red eyes gleamed from the peripheral darkness.

The cellar seemed to go on forever. Before long, smoke began to seep through the cracks in the rafters overhead. As the smoke grew thicker and its pungency more noxious, they began to hear a soft, rustling sound that became louder and louder. At first, Joe thought it was the muffled crackling of the fire in the warehouse above them. When it got steadily louder, he feared it meant the fire was burning through the warehouse floor, which was their ceiling. He became frightened that the entire upstairs was going to come crashing

down on them in a fiery inferno, but when he turned to urge
the others to move faster, he was able to suddenly pinpoint
the direction the sound was coming from—behind them, not
above.

The sound grew louder and clearer. Instead of the crackling of a fire, it was now a continuous pattering, like rainfall
on a tin roof. For a moment, Joe wondered if he was mis-
taken about the sound's direction and thought it might actually be water raining down on the floor above from the
warehouse's sprinkler system. The sound expanded quickly,
spreading out until it was coming from all around them, and
he was certain he was right . . . except for a new sound akin
to the squeaking of many rusty wheels.

He realized how wrong he was when Cindy screamed.
Her vocalization was immediately imitated by Sara and
Corey. Joe turned, playing the light back over the band of
followers, then nearly dropped the flashlight in shock.

The cellar floor was thick with rats of all sizes scurrying
frantically in the same direction the foursome was heading.
Joe was stunned to inertia at their numbers; the floor was a
squirming mass of rodents, scrambling and climbing over
one another, three and four furry bodies thick in some spots.
The initial wave parted and rushed around and by them, but
the second and third waves of vermin were too thick and
panicked to bother avoiding the slow-moving humans in
their way. They scurried over feet and tried to climb to
higher ground up the humans' legs.

Cindy, Sara, and Corey felt tiny claws digging into the
flesh of their legs as the rats tried to climb their bodies, some
nipping at human flesh as the group frantically tried to brush
the rodents off. They were appalled and disgusted by the on-
slaught. They danced and slapped at the filthy creatures.

Because of the light, which was painfully blinding to many
of the vermin, whose entire existence had been subjugated
to blackness, Joe had fewer rats clambering over his feet or
trying to scale his legs. But he was as horrified as the others
by their numbers. There were so many it seemed as if every

rat in New York City was in the dungeon with them, and all were trying to escape the fire by the same route as Joe and the others.

"Keep moving and they won't climb on you!" Joe shouted. "This way!"

Crying, shrieking, and swearing, Corey, Sara, and Cindy followed him and discovered he was right—if they kept moving the rats didn't try to climb up their legs. Within minutes, the tidal wave of rodents began to thin out as the bulk of them passed on, disappearing into whatever narrow means of escape they could find.

The foursome collectively breathed a sigh of relief, but not for long.

They noticed what they thought were bits of wood and pieces of dirt dislodging from the low ceiling overhead and falling on them. But when the bits and pieces began *crawling* on them the terrifying truth came to light, literally, as Joe flashed the beam over his own body, then the others'. Hundreds of spiders, centipedes, and cockroaches—perhaps thousands— were dropping from the smoky ceiling. They crawled with incredible speed over the four humans. A multitude of the insects dropped to the ground around them, but it seemed like most of them dropped into their hair, onto their shoulders, and down their shirt collars. They crawled en masse over the uneven floor around them, over their footwear and up their legs, under Cindy's skirt, Joe and Corey's shorts, and Sara's rolled-up painter's pants.

Cindy and Sara screamed and frantically crushed and brushed off the insects. Corey didn't scream but wiped the bugs off just as frantically. Joe realized they had to keep going. Even as he brushed the creepy crawlers from his body, too, he noticed that the smoke coming through the rafters was thicker than before. The fire was driving the insects, as it had driven the rodents. Like the humans, the bugs were just trying to escape the death trap of the burning building above.

"We're almost there!" Joe shouted, trying to talk above the women's screams. A spider crawled into his mouth, and he bit down on it before spitting it out. He shined the light in front of them, through the shower of bugs, and saw the end of the cavernous cellar, where a battered wooden door hung crookedly on its hinges at the opening of the tunnel. Some of the insects were retreating under that door, but many more were disappearing into cracks and holes in the wall, following the rats' avenues of escape.

Before the quartet reached the door the flow of insects grew thinner, and by the time they reached it, the only insects that remained were the ones hitching a ride in their hair or under their clothing.

At the door they paused, and the four of them did a panicky dance to get the insects out of their hair and clothing. They rapidly groomed one another for bugs, removing them and crushing them underfoot, until they were all deloused as best they could be.

Even when they were done, Cindy couldn't stop trembling, squirming, and scratching, especially her head as she felt phantom bugs still infesting her. She sobbed quietly, emitting a constant high-pitched whine that vibrated with every shudder that passed through her body. Every few moments, her voice went up in pitch and her body jerked involuntarily. Her hands flew to her hair, and she raked her fingers through the tangled, snarled mess.

Sara's true nature surfaced then, and she helped Cindy finger-comb her hair, reassuring her in a low, soft voice that she was okay, it was over, she was all right now. Gradually, Cindy grew quieter, and Sara wrapped her arms around her former enemy and hugged her close until her trembling also quieted.

While Sara took care of Cindy, Joe crouched next to Corey and picked several cockroaches and spiders off the boy's head. Despite this, the boy seemed to be doing much better than the adults.

"You okay, Corey?" Joe asked, trying not to shudder or shriek like a girl as he picked bugs off the boy and himself.

Corey nodded. "I like bugs," he proclaimed.

Behind him, Cindy broke into a nervous, hysterical laughter. "Well, you can have mine, kiddo," she joked, her voice as unsteady as her still-trembling hands.

The smoke was gaining on them. It now poured from the rafters in slow-motion waterfalls.

"We need to go into the tunnel," Joe said to the others, a wary eye on the descending smoke. He pulled open the wooden door and it fell from its hinges, clattering to the floor and raising a cloud of dust to mingle with the smoke.

All but Cindy nodded their heads in agreement. She pulled back, looking at the dark rectangle of the tunnel with trepidation.

"Come on," Sara coaxed softly, gently taking Cindy's arm.

Cindy pulled away. "No!" she whimpered, her voice shaky. "The bugs and rats went in *there*!"

"Yeah, but they're gone now," Sara answered.

Cindy shook her head fiercely. "No!" she repeated, the negation sounding more like a groan than a word. She scratched herself, her hands scrambling wildly over her arms and through her hair. Transfixed by the darkness inside the open doorway, she shuddered and whimpered as she scratched.

Corey coughed from the smoke and put a hand over his mouth.

Joe dropped to one knee next to the boy, coughing also as he tried to get under the choking smoke. "Cindy," he said sternly, "we are going to *die* if we stay here."

It made no difference to the terrified Cindy. She continued to tremble and cry, shaking her head back and forth and trying to scratch everywhere at once.

"Cindy, please," Sara gasped, coughing.

Though gasping for breath, Cindy retreated from the door while Sara tried to pull her toward it. Cindy yanked her arm free and barked a loud, *"No!"*

The smoke grew thicker as it tried to enfold them in its deadly embrace.

"Goddamn it!" Joe rasped between coughs. "We've got to go *now*. If you won't, then we'll leave you behind. But *we* are *going*!"

Cindy's frightened eyes went from Joe to the dark doorway and back. A spasm of coughing racked her body. Tears flew from her eyes, snot from her nose, and saliva from her hacking mouth and blubbering lips.

Sara leaned close to her and whispered something in her ear. Again Cindy pulled away.

"That's it!" Joe said angrily. "Fuck her. Let her stay here and die. We gotta go, *now*!"

Sara turned on him fiercely. "Don't be so mean!" she managed to get out, coughing the words as much as speaking them.

Joe looked at her with disbelief. "Half an hour ago you were ready to shoot her," he complained, his voice raw from the smoke.

"Oh, shut up!" Sara spat out.

"You know what?" Joe said, standing again and turning to the tunnel entrance. "Both of you can stay here and suffocate." He nodded at Corey. "Let's go, kid."

Joe stepped into the tunnel but Corey hesitated, looking from Joe to Sara and Cindy. "Please, Cindy," Corey rasped, and started to cry. "I don't want you to die, too," he blubbered.

The boy's tears and caring words were the catalyst Cindy needed to keep going. She drew her eyes from the darkness of the tunnel and looked fondly, if sadly, at Corey.

"Please come with us," the boy pleaded.

Coughing and wiping the snot from her nose, Cindy nodded. Clinging to her former nemesis, she let Sara lead her.

1:45 a.m.

In the claustrophobic darkness of the tunnel, Joe felt every sense heightened, and every sensation magnified and exaggerated. Despite the penlight's illumination, the darkness around them seemed darker, blacker than any darkness he'd ever experienced. The musky, dank smell seemed to push itself into his sore nose, reaching up into his partially clogged sinuses and clogging them more. It affected them all. To breathe they had to open their mouths, and when they did the darkness tasted like moldy bread. The air in the tunnel had *texture* that could be felt, slippery and slimy, yet somehow sticky at the same time. But worse than that were the sounds—scurrying, scuttling, *crawling*—that gave the darkness life.

The sounds, combined with the feel of the air on her skin, drove Cindy to the brink of madness. Every few steps she let out a whimper and clawed at a part of her body, digging her nails into her track-marked arms, or snaking her hands inside her clothing in search of crawling things she could feel but couldn't see. At times, her scratching, twitching fingers flew to her head to become entangled in the web of her hair in which she was certain spiders were weaving webs of their own.

About ten minutes into the tunnel, she shrieked loudly and dug her index finger into her right ear, hopping around on one foot and shaking her tilted head like a swimmer with water in her ear.

"Get it out! Get it out!" she screamed.

Joe, Sara, and Corey crowded round her. Joe flashed the light on her head while Sara pushed Cindy's hair aside with one hand and pulled her digging finger out of her ear with the other.

"It's just your hair," Sara explained when she found nothing. "A strand of your hair was tickling your ear."

"My hair?" Cindy asked vaguely, as if the words were unfamiliar to her.

"Yeah," Sara said, nodding and rubbing Cindy's back soothingly.

Joe returned the light to the floor in front of them, careful not to let it linger on the walls of the passageway, which were festooned with webs and spiders of varying sizes. Thankfully, Cindy was too distracted with her own phantom insects to notice the real ones close by.

"I think we should try to keep the noise down, people," Joe said in a low voice, turning his head to address the others as he led the way. "We don't know how close we are to the street, and I think the 'Vaders have very sharp hearing.

We don't want them tracking us and waiting in ambush wherever we happen to come out."

"Do you think they can do that?" Corey asked, his voice trembling with nervousness.

"No," Joe replied quickly, "not if we can keep quiet." He shined the light on Cindy, who promptly gave him the finger.

"You're okay." Joe chuckled, and led on.

The floor of the tunnel passage was as rough as the cellar they had traversed. Loose stones and shattered pieces of concrete made it tough going. Joe had to proceed slowly and whisper back warnings about the bad spots. Since the passageway was narrow, they had to walk single file: Joe first, then Corey, with Cindy followed by Sara who kept her comforting hands on Cindy's shoulders.

A sudden loud rumbling and crash from behind them stopped the four of them in their tracks. A moment later they could smell smoke again.

"That had to be the warehouse collapsing," Joe said. "I think the fire is spreading this way. We need to pick up the pace, folks."

After what seemed like miles and hours of walking, the floor became firm and unbroken, suggesting a newer part of the tunnel. The walls, too, became smoother and less knitted with cobwebs. Instead of rough stone with cracks and crevices where rats, mice, spiders and all other kinds of vermin and insects could hide, the walls were now tiled, much like in a subway station. They had outdistanced the smell of smoke as well as the musty, moldy smell. The air was fresher.

Joe told the others he thought they were close to a subway station. A moment later the right wall fell away into dark empty space. Joe played the light in that direction and they all could see that they were, indeed, walking along a subway tunnel. They proceeded, walking on a service walkway that followed the tunnel; it was no wider than a catwalk. It dropped off on the right a good ten to twelve feet to the subway tracks below. They rounded a bend and breathed a collective sigh of relief—there was a light ahead; they were coming to a station.

Joe held his hand out to the right, palm facing backward, for them to stop. He motioned Sara to the front of the line and handed her the penlight. He leaned close to all of them and spoke in a soft whisper. "Stay here. I'm going ahead to check it out."

Sara and Corey nodded agreement in unison while Cindy scratched herself.

Joe slung the sack of homemade bombs off his shoulders and laid it carefully on the floor. He also put down the Molotov cocktail he had been carrying in his hand and pulled Sara's revolver from his waistband. Holding the gun up next to his head with both hands the way he'd always seen actors in movies and on TV do, he proceeded, back against the wall, sliding along.

The closer he got to the station, the more he could smell something burning, but he saw no flames or smoke ahead. This was a burned smell that he was unfamiliar with. It was nothing like the smell of the warehouse or trash burning, or like firewood, which, unlike the other smells, he found pleasant. This was a *nasty* burnt smell, like melting hair and rubber combined. It was more pungent than the smoke they had left behind in the warehouse. Joe had to cover his nose and mouth by pressing them into the crook of his left arm while still holding the revolver with both hands.

A faint crackling sound reached his ears. He noticed an electrical, ozone scent mingled with the other smells. Joe slid to the end of the wall where it opened up into the loading platform for the trains. He turned around, flattened his chest against the wall, and inched his head out until he could see around the corner with one eye.

The platform was empty. Joe looked up at the wall and saw he was at the Christopher Street/Sheraton Square station. He realized they were now in the West Village; just one block away from the Sixth Precinct on West 10th Street. He turned around and faced the edge of the platform and tracks again. At that moment he caught a glimmer of light, just for a second, from the darkness beyond the platform's end. The flash of light was accompanied by a crackling sound like static on a radio, and he got a whiff again of ozone.

Holding the pistol in front of him, ready to fire, Joe approached the edge and found the source of the light, the noise, and the smell. On the tracks below, stuck to the high-voltage third rail, was the decapitated head of a 'Vader monster. Its hair was burning and its face was frozen in a grotesque grimace. By the looks of the ragged edge of its throat, Joe guessed another monster had ripped its body free of the head. Apparently the 'Vader before him had accidentally fallen on the third rail and been electrocuted. Joe realized the monsters were getting into the subways. He had thought his entourage might hide out in the subways if they couldn't get to the Sixth Precinct, but now that didn't seem like such a good idea.

He turned away in disgust and went back to the others.

"Okay," he said, kneeling in front of Sara and Corey, who had taken the opportunity to sit with their backs against the wall and rest. Cindy remained standing and scratching.

"We're at the Christopher Street station," he said. "We're not too far from Tenth Street."

"Good," Cindy grumbled. A long, sinuous centipede crawled out of her blouse's collar and up the left side of her hair. Joe saw it and stood. He snatched it off her, flinging it away into the darkness a second before Cindy's reaching hand could find it.

"What was that?" Cindy asked, jerking her head away from Joe's hand. Her voice was shrill with impending panic.

"Nothing," Joe said quickly. "Just some cobweb."

Cindy scratched at the side of her neck. "It felt like something crawling on me," she said in a small scared voice. She shivered with disgust at the thought.

Joe hid a smile behind his hand and winked at Corey, who looked confused.

"Why don't I go up to the street and check things out." Joe looked at his watch. "Wow! I don't believe it. It's almost 3:30 a.m. We've still got about two hours of darkness to travel by. If I remember correctly, we're only a block from the police station. I don't think we want to arrive in the dark, but it's going to be a lot tougher to get there in daylight when the 'Vaders are out and about. The best thing we can do is get there right at dawn when it's light enough to see and be seen, but still early enough that we won't have to contend with a lot of monsters. From what I've seen, the 'Vaders seem to like sleep as much as humans."

"They used to *be* humans," Corey reminded him in a small, sad voice.

"Ah, yeah . . . right," Joe said slowly, as he exhaled a sigh. "Sorry."

3:30 a.m.

Ascending the stairs as quietly as possible, and carrying nothing but Sara's pistol, Joe found himself holding his breath and had to make a conscious effort to keep breathing. He reached the street level and remained on the top step of the subway entrance, checking out the situation. The first thing he noticed was the smell of smoke. He looked south— the sky was glowing. Joe realized the warehouse fire must have spread, burning out of control with no fire department to put it out.

He looked back at the neighborhood around him. The street was chewed up from the attack of the jets, and several vehicles in the road had been completely demolished during the aerial attack. There was a liquor store to his right called Spy's. It and the store next to it had scaffolding rising two stories up the face of the building. A few feet away was a street sign indicating that he was at the intersection of Christopher and Bleeker Streets.

Joe had to pause and get his bearings. He knew West 10th Street was north, but as he crept from the subway entrance to the curbside he saw that way was blocked by a massive car pileup involving a tractor trailer that was twisted as badly as a pretzel across the road. If that wasn't bad enough, a cluster of sleeping monsters had bedded down against the wreckage, using it as pillows and backrests. From what Joe could see, there were at least seven 'Vaders sleeping together; four large ones and three smaller. If he didn't know better, he might have thought it cute the way they were nestled against each other like kittens seeking comfort and warmth from each other.

"Kittens from Hell," Joe muttered under his breath.

Doing a quick visual recon, Joe surmised they would have to go down Christopher Street, which appeared clear except for a few abandoned cars, to Hudson and hope it was clear enough for them to cut over to West 10th Street and the police station.

He heard Cindy's whimper before he even reached the bottom of the stairs and the loading platform. He ran to where he had left the other three and found Cindy on the edge of full-blown, "screaming at the top of her lungs" hysteria.

"Shut up!" Joe commanded her in as loud a voice as he dared.

Cindy was against the subway wall trembling and quivering, both hands fluttering over her body. Like scavenger birds her hands dove into and under her clothing, digging around, clawing and scratching at invisible bugs, only to emerge again and flutter nervously to another part of her body. Her whimpering only increased at Joe's command to be quiet.

Next to her, Sara looked nonplussed, wanting to do something to keep Cindy quiet but flabbergasted as to what.

Corey huddled on the floor, his knees drawn up to his chest, both arms wrapped around his legs as he rocked back and forth.

"What's wrong with her?" Joe whispered to Sara when Cindy paid him no heed.

Sara shook her head as if to indicate it was a lost cause. "She's flipping out," Sara said softly, but urgently. "It's the bugs. She thinks they're still under her clothing."

"I can *feel* them crawling all over me!" Cindy suddenly cried so loud it sounded like a sonic boom in the silent tunnel.

"Shhh!" all three hissed at her at the same time, but she

wouldn't be shushed or calmed. Her fidgeting, hand-fluttering dance grew more frantic.

"They're under my clothes!" she cried, trying to keep her voice low but not succeeding.

"Shit!" Joe cursed, and looked at Sara, then Corey. "Take your goddamned clothes off, then!" he commanded in a loud rasping whisper. "Corey, cover your eyes," he added.

Cindy started pulling at her clothes but was so near full-blown hysteria she couldn't seem to remember how to undress. She pulled at her flimsy garments as if she were wrapped in gift paper that could be ripped off and discarded. The more she pulled and tore at her clothes the more frustrated she got, and the more frustrated she got, the louder she whimpered.

"Help her out, for Christ's sake!" Joe implored Sara. He kept looking nervously over his shoulder, expecting the 'Vaders, in either of their forms, to hear her and seek them out for nutrition or transformation.

"Okay. Okay. Okay," Sara soothed. She grabbed Cindy's frantic hands and put them gently at her sides. "Look at me," she whispered, and Cindy obeyed. Sara kept talking to her in a soft reassuring tone while she unbuttoned Cindy's blouse. Still cooing calming words, Sara pulled the shirt off Cindy and was shocked at how skinny she really was—her shoulders were nothing but bones, and her collarbone protruded through her pale skin. Sara's shock turned to pity as she got the blouse completely off, but then turned to disgust. There was a good reason for Cindy's thinking she was infested—she was. Tiny spiders, no bigger than the head of a thumbtack, crawled over Cindy's chest and belly, disappearing and reappearing from her tank top and the waistband of her miniskirt.

Sara let out an involuntary shriek and backed away from Cindy, who looked down. She saw the spiders and began screaming in short grunting bursts that were a cross between choking and gagging sounds.

Her shrill, staccato screams galvanized Joe into action.

He did the only thing he could think of to quiet Cindy before every monster within hearing distance came chowing down on them. He coldcocked her—a right cross to the chin—and she was down and out for the count.

Sara started gasping loudly as she, too, began tearing at her own clothes. When a few bugs dropped from her, the gasps became soundless shrieks of air as she inhaled and exhaled rapidly. She frantically pulled the rest of her clothes off as quickly as possible, leaving on only her bra and bikini briefs.

"Get 'em off! Get 'em off! Get 'em off!" she pleaded with Joe, fighting to keep her voice low and coming close to losing that battle. There were fewer tiny spiders on Sara. With Joe's help she got them off quickly. Sara ran a hand under her bra and panties for the final debugging and then did a bug-crushing two-step on the minuscule creatures trying to scurry away from where they weren't wanted.

Corey, who had started crying softly when Joe hit Cindy, stood and lifted his shirt to explore his chest and stomach, finding fewer spiders than Cindy had.

"Turn around. Let's see your back," Joe said to the boy. He picked a few more off the boy.

Corey bent over and shook his curly locks. Two cockroaches fell from his hair and he giggled.

"Cool!" he said, and quickly put a hand against Sara's leg to keep her from stepping on them. "No!" he said seriously. "They didn't hurt me."

Joe grinned until he felt things crawling under his T-shirt and shorts also. Trying to keep his cool in front of Corey, he turned his back and pulled down his shorts and picked quite a few of the tiny spiders from his skin. He did the same with his chest. And took off his shirt to clear his chest while Sara wiped them from his back.

Clean of their unwanted guests, they got dressed. Sara made sure Cindy was completely bug-free before trying to wake her.

Cindy came to with violence, both vocal and physical.

She woke screaming and slapping at the insects that had been crawling on her but were now gone, leaving behind the phantom feeling of their feathery legs against her skin.

Sara immediately shushed her, covering Cindy's mouth with both hands and whispering that she was free of bugs but in danger of bringing the 'Vaders down on them.

Still in just her tank top and thong, Cindy checked herself and quieted quickly when she found no more spiders. She dressed and stood against the subway wall, working her jaw back and forth with her left hand while crying softly. Joe mumbled an apology but couldn't meet her eyes. She ignored it and smoothed out her clothing, scratched at a couple of insect mirages, and clung to Sara's arm.

"Okay," Joe said softly when it became apparent there would be no more outbursts. "Bleecker Street is blocked, so we have to cut down Christopher and over Hudson to get to West Tenth." He looked at his watch. "We got maybe an hour and a half or so to do that before daylight. Hopefully, we can get to the Sixth Precinct station house without having to deal with any of the 'Vaders." He picked up the sack of home-made bombs and slung it over his shoulder. He picked up the one he had been carrying in his left hand and took Cindy's lighter back from Sara.

"Ready?" he asked them.

Corey and Sara nodded. Cindy just sobbed.

4:00 a.m.

They could still smell the earlier rain on the street when the wind blew the smell of the fire away from them. The predawn air was cool for summer, but then, none of them had been up and out this early in a long time. They were used to venturing forth much later in the morning, when the sultry heat of summer had already claimed the city streets, causing the air itself to feel sweaty. Now, despite its coolness, the air smelled hot. It smelled of smoke and the skyline glowed, indicating many fires raging out of control.

They went in single file, Joe leading, Corey second, Cindy next, and Sara bringing up the rear. Outside the subway entrance and just around the corner on Christopher Street was a deli/variety store whose glassed-in entrance had been demolished. It looked like a bomb had gone off inside. Glass crunched under their feet as they skirted broken pavement and the store's broken neon sign that read ONNIE'S DEL on the largest, still intact, piece. Joe remembered the place— Ronnie's Deli and Food Mart. He had passed by it twice a week on his way to acting class and had often stopped in to buy gum or Danish and coffee. The place had always smelled good enough to make his stomach grumble. Now, he remembered something else, too.

"Wait here," he whispered to the others. Stepping gingerly over the broken glass and rubble of the storefront, he disappeared inside. Less than a minute later, he reappeared, holding up a handful of colorful plastic butane lighters, which he distributed to the others. Cindy declined and took her blowtorch lighter back from Joe.

"Take another one anyway, in case yours runs out," he whispered.

He resumed the lead, cautiously pioneering a trail through the wilderness of urban destruction. Less than twenty yards beyond the demolished deli they came upon a monster about ten feet tall lying across the sidewalk, sleeping. Joe almost laughed; it looked so comical. It wore a very tight T-shirt with the word DOOM emblazoned on the front. Joe figured the creature must have been a teenager before it changed and the T-shirt, in the fashion of teenagers, must have been huge— a good four sizes too large. That would explain how it still fit the monster.

Waving the others to follow, Joe crossed the street. He paused in the middle, behind an overturned city bus that was riddled with huge bullet holes from the jet attack. There was a loud, ground trembling *thud* followed by a loud *slap*. The group remained behind the bus, huddling together in terror and trying to figure out the direction of the noise. Again they felt and heard it. The ground vibrated under their feet, followed by the sound of a heavy hand smacking something hard and wet. Joe peered around the front end of the bus and saw the source of the sound. Coming up Christopher Street was an enormous 'Vader that was slapping its huge belly first with its left hand, then with its right as it walked leisurely toward them. If they hadn't crossed behind the bus at the precise moment they had, the thing would have certainly seen them.

The creature leaped over the length of the bus and came down with a tremendous *thump* as both feet hit the road, cracking the asphalt five feet from where Joe and the others huddled. The creature paused, crouched, and let loose a pile of feces before it resumed its belly-smacking stroll.

It was all the group of survivors could do to keep from gagging and coughing as the malodorous wind from the monster's waste washed over them. Joe didn't think he could keep from coughing—and if *he* couldn't, he doubted the women or the boy could either. He motioned them onward as the monster disappeared around the corner. They ran the rest of the way across the street. Ahead was a tall wrought-iron gate that opened onto what looked like an alley and beyond that maybe a courtyard. Joe pushed through the metal gate, letting out a mental sigh of relief at its silence. He led the others into the safety of the alley.

They paused to rest, backs against the walls on either side, and breathed deeply of the relatively clean air—compared with what they had just smelled. A loud squeak startled them and they turned as one to look at the iron gate, but it had not moved. They heard the squeak again, and realized it was not a metal sound, but an organic one, and it was coming from the courtyard ahead.

It was coming closer.

At the end of the alley, where it turned left into a small courtyard, several trash barrels overflowing with garbage were stacked in a corner. Scurrying over the top of the barrels, and in and out of the torn trash bags, were several black rats. Looking at them, Joe thought for a moment they were the source of the squeaking.

Until it came again. Louder.

A shadow, dark and large, slipped over the trash barrels

and the rats feasting. One of the vermin looked up, let out a shrill squeak—much softer than the one they had just heard—and tried to burrow into a rip in the trash bag. A huge snout sporting two top teeth like pickaxes lunged from around the corner and tore into the rats and the trash pile, consuming the rodents and a good chunk of the bagged garbage in one huge noisy nasty bite. Two red eyes, as big as footballs and with the same shape, turned toward the humans. The eyes sat above the massive snout that sprouted whiskers as thick as arms on both sides. The snout ended in a black rubbery-looking nose with dual nostrils that twitched as they caught the scent of humans. Behind the eyes rose a huge head with large furry ears on top.

"No," Cindy whimpered. "No more rats. I'm sick of fucking *rats*!"

The mutated rodent was as tall as a Great Dane and as massive as a rhinoceros in sheer body width and bulk. It scuttled into the alleyway and once again sniffed in the direction of the humans. Its normal instinct was to run as soon as it caught the scent of humans. Enough of the instinct still remained in the brain of the monstrosity to make it wary now.

The foursome froze at the sight of the behemoth rat. A high-pitched terrified squeal escaped Corey's lips, and the rat paused, turning its head quizzically in his direction and emitting an answering squeal as if speaking to the boy.

"Don't make any quick moves," Joe told the others in a low voice. "Back up slowly." He glanced quickly at his companions and jerked his head in the direction of the gate that was less than five yards away.

Sara was closest to the gate, but she let Cindy go by her as she waited for Corey, putting a reassuring hand on his shoulder and guiding him backward.

Joe stepped away from the building and faced the rodent, a Molotov cocktail in his right hand, a plastic lighter in his left. He was ready to light and toss the bomb if the rat pursued them. He knew that would risk waking any nearby 'Vaders and would place them in even greater danger. He hoped he could get through the gate and close it before the rat made its move.

The beast pointed its snout upward and its nostrils twitched. It took a tentative step toward Joe and sniffed the air again.

Joe cast a quick glance behind him. Cindy was through the gate. Corey and Sara were within a few steps of it. Joe himself had less than five yards to go. A large shadow above and to his right caught Joe's attention. Before he could look up to see what it was, the shadow ballooned in size and a huge black object came hurtling down into the alleyway.

A black cat, as big as an SUV, landed on the monster rat with a triumphant yowl. Its extended claws, bigger than meat hooks, dug into the vermin's back as easily as a toothpick inserted into Jell-O. The rat let out a deafeningly shrill squeal of pain and terror that was immediately silenced when the cat bit the back of the rat's neck, snapping the rodent's spine between its dagger teeth and massive jaw.

The rat's head jerked upward; the beady eyes bulged from its sockets. They glazed and its body twitched as its legs gave out. It flopped to its belly on the filthy alley floor. The rat's body twitched once, twice, and a small stream of blood flowed from its nostrils.

The cat kept its teeth clamped in the rodent's neck as it went through its death throes. The cat made a deep growling, purring noise as it held on, bringing death to its prey. The rat stopped twitching. Without relinquishing its hold, the cat picked the rat up and shook it the way a puppy might shake a chew toy. After a couple of shakes, the cat tossed the rat into the air, flipping it over. It landed a few feet away. As soon as the rodent hit the ground, the cat pounced on it again and repeated the action, obviously playing with the thing before eating it.

Sara and Corey slipped through the gate. Joe backed toward it. As long as the cat was preoccupied playing with the dead rat, Joe hoped it wouldn't be interested in making any of them into kitty treats.

The cat flipped the rat aside and turned toward the humans.

I should know better than to hope for anything, Joe thought. He was still two yards from the gate.

The feral cat knew how to survive, and one of its primary instincts learned on the streets and in the back alleys of New York was to hunt any living thing smaller than itself. Even though it had a meal in the rat ready at hand, it saw the potential for dessert in the puny frightened human backing away.

It crouched, ready to pounce, but suddenly stopped. It looked at Joe and the others with uncertainty, then bounded away, leaving Joe and the other three, plus the rat, untouched. Joe wondered why but not for long. From behind him came the sound of a huge hand smacking against a fat belly. As one, the group turned to face the slap-happy beast that now had them cornered in the alley.

The monster threw its head back and let loose a horrible warbling sound that Joe and the others could only interpret as gleefully demented laughter.

Joe lit the wick on the Molotov cocktail in his hand and chucked it at the 'Vader. As if brushing flies away from a meal, the monster knocked the bottle away with a backward sweep of its hand. The flaming bottle flipped end over end and smashed to the road, breaking open and releasing a blossom of flame a good ten yards in diameter. The sudden appearance of fire so close distracted the monster just long enough for Joe to pull another bomb from his homemade sack and light it. Sara followed his example, but shoved her bottle's wick up to his lit one, igniting it.

Having learned from the error of his first throw, Joe shouted, "Throw it at his feet!"

Sara did as he said, tossing the bottle bomb at the same time Joe threw his. Joe's and Sara's bottles smashed just in front of the beast's deformed feet. Gas quickly turned to flame and sprayed from the broken bottles, splashing against the monster's feet and shins and setting them on fire. Cindy used her blowtorch lighter to ignite the wick of her Molotov cocktail and tossed it underhand a few feet shorter than the others, but it was effective in helping to set up a wall of flame like a barrier between them and the creature.

The now-blazing horror gave out a new cry that was far removed from the hideous laughter it had been emitting a few moments earlier. The creature backed away from the flames while trying to beat out the fire consuming its feet and legs and stepped in the pile of its own dung. To the thing's dismay, the mound of shit ignited, causing the fire on its legs to burn higher and climb its hairy torso. The rubbery smell of burnt hair, crap, and flesh filled the air in accompaniment to the monster's screams of pain.

All around on the street, the sidewalk, and from within the ruins of buildings, sleeping 'Vaders were awakened.

4:40 a.m.

Corey was the first of the group to see other monsters approaching, drawn by the fire like insects to a light. The first to appear was the creature that was sporting the too-tight T-shirt. It woke up with a start, being the closest 'Vader in proximity to the flaming monster. The being scrambled to its feet, watching the larger kindred flail about as it tried to get away from the engulfing flames. The look on the T-shirted monster's face was a mix of fascination and anticipation for a cooked meal. It seemed unaware of Corey and the others.

The second creature Corey saw, drawn by all the flaming commotion, was a squat, hulking gargantuan that came at a trot from the intersection with Bleecker Street. It stopped in the middle of Christopher Street, a few yards from the T-shirted monster and regarded its flaming compatriot with a similar expression of hungry anticipation.

As if trying to outrun the flames engulfing its body, the enormous 'Vader sprinted down Christopher Street, turned left onto Hudson, and kept going. Still unaware of Joe and the others, the other two 'Vaders took off in pursuit of their escaping flame-broiled dinner.

"Yes!" sobbed Cindy. She was shaking so hard Sara and the others could hear her teeth chattering. Joe and Sara looked excited that the firebombs had worked so well.

"We got company," Corey said, putting a damper on the grown-ups' joy. Three 'Vaders—two from the wreck of a build-

ing farther down Christopher Street and one who crawled out
from behind the now-destroyed Ronnie's Deli—were drawn to
the ring of fire in the street.

Cindy panicked and let out a short involuntary scream.

It was enough to draw the 'Vaders' attention.

Cindy started to run in the wrong direction, toward Bleecker
Street. Sara grabbed her by the arm, causing the blonde to
whirl violently about under the force of her own momentum.

"This way!" Sara shouted.

With a look of fury, Cindy raised her arm as if she meant
to slug Sara but was distracted from it by the charge of the
three monsters. Bellowing, they stampeded toward the group.
Sara pulled Cindy in the correct direction, and Cindy let her.

Spurred on by Joe, Corey was already running down the
sidewalk in the direction of Hudson Street.

As Sara ran, she looked back just in time to see Joe toss a
flaming bottle at the attacking trio of 'Vaders. He followed it
with another one from his makeshift shoulder bag. She saw
the first one hit the rear tire of the overturned bus in the road.
It bounced off and landed behind the creature nearest it. Up
sprang a wall of flame.

Joe's second toss bounced off the middle 'Vader's chest
and smashed on the street at its feet, but the creature was
moving too fast and had already passed the bottle when it
broke and burst into flame. Only a little of the gas got on the
monster's feet, setting them on fire. Unfortunately, they didn't
burn long; its feet slapping against the pavement put out the
flames.

Joe didn't see the second bomb's little effect. He was already running as fast as possible with the sack of clinking
bottles on his shoulder. As he ran he pulled out another bottle and tried to light it, but the jerky motion of his body
while running and the ensuing headwind made it difficult to
ignite the lighter. Ahead, he could see that Sara, Corey, and
Cindy were almost to the corner of Hudson Street. As far as
he could tell, there were no more 'Vaders threatening them
other than the three chasing him. Joe's lighter finally ignited
long enough to catch the gas-soaked wick and set it aflame.

He glanced over his shoulder, made a quick estimate of the distance between him and the closest 'Vader, and threw the flaming bottle straight up in the air. He ran as fast as he could, the way he always did for the last hundred yards of his daily run when he imagined himself to be nearing the finish line in a close race. The bottle tumbled end over end and came straight down a few feet in front of the three monsters. Joe heard the tinkling of the glass breaking followed by the *whoosh* of the gas igniting.

The flaming gasoline got on the leader's legs and arms. It did a mad dance, hopping about and slapping at the flames with its hands, which caught on fire also—it was a losing battle. The creature tried to escape the sudden ring of fire, but ran into a streetlight pole, snapping it in two. The burning beast staggered back, and the top half of the pole fell on the monster's flaming head. The 'Vader fell straight back and lay burning in the road. The pole severed an electrical wire running from the closest building. It sparked and whipped down and into one of the other 'Vaders, making the fiend jitterbug as its insides fried.

The creature was dead before it hit the ground.

4:55 a.m.

Sara was torn between worrying about Cindy and a growing desire to leave her behind before the sluggish blonde slowed them all down so much they became 'Vader food. Fear commanded her to dump Cindy, while compassion urged her to continue on.

They reached the corner of Christopher and Hudson Streets and stopped. Cindy immediately slumped out of breath against the outside of a place called Partners' Bakery. Corey ran a little way past, then came back, panting and looking worried.

"I don't think we should stop," Corey said.

Sara turned and looked back at Joe, who was ten yards behind and running hard. Behind him, in the road, one monster was still giving chase. She couldn't see the other two monsters, but she did notice the street behind Joe was ablaze.

"Take this!" Joe shouted to Sara as he caught up. He handed her the sack of gas cocktails and pulled the pistol out of his waistband. Joe aimed the gun with both hands.

"Keep going!" he shouted at Sara, Corey, and Cindy. Corey didn't need any more encouragement and immediately started running. Cindy, however, stayed where she was slumped against the bakery wall, shaking her head wearily.

"Come on! We've got to go!" Sara shouted at Cindy, and grabbed her arm, pulling her along.

Joe pointed the gun at the beast and pulled the trigger. The recoil staggered him. He stumbled back and both arms jerked in the air.

The sole 'Vader still giving chase fell on its chest to the street. Joe was about to crow joyfully at killing the monster, but a moment later the 'Vader rose to its feet.

Joe's cheer died in his throat as he realized the thing had only stumbled—his shot had missed. Joe aimed again and fired. This time his shot found monster flesh as it ripped into the 'Vader's right shoulder, slowing it, but not stopping it.

The thing was less than twelve yards away and still coming as fast as before.

Joe fired again and saw the creature's head jerk; and it fell heavily, bounced on the pavement, and slid to a stop. Joe's hands were trembling; that had been too close for comfort. He turned and ran after the others.

5:05 a.m.

Overhead the night sky turned to dark gray, and the first sunlit fingers of dawn reached across the sky. The light filtered down through the tall buildings of the city and illuminated streets rife with devastation. Joe ran faster, not wanting to be caught in the open when the sun rose completely. He caught up to Sara and took the sack of bottle bombs from her. He then led the way down Hudson Street as quickly as possible. He looked back and saw that Cindy was slowing Sara down. He went back and grabbed Cindy's other arm to pull her along faster. They passed a small store called the Spy Shop, which was one of the few shops on the street that was still intact and still had its nighttime protective cage in place over its entrance, giving the electronics store the appearance of a jail.

Corey could have run ahead, but only because Cindy was slowing down Joe and Sara so much. Corey kept pace with them. As they ran past a liquor store, Cindy tried to reach out to it longingly as though she wanted to embrace the place and by doing so become inebriated.

Joe looked back and saw four new 'Vader monsters pursuing them. If that weren't bad enough, several monsters that had been sleeping in the middle of Hudson Street, parallel to Joe and the others, were now waking up. In fact, all around, the 'Vaders were rising with the sun.

Joe looked up. Two glowing orbs, moving with speed and precision, came soaring from the sky. "Keep moving!" he shouted as he and Sara pulled Cindy along. They were almost to the intersection with West 10th Street. In the growing light, Joe could see the names of the stores they were running by—the Hudson Deli, the Hudson Middle Eastern Restaurant, and across the street, Lucy's on the Hudson. The place had outdoor tables and chairs, which remarkably were still set up as if waiting for customers. Next to that was the Beauty, Body, and Health Store.

"Keep going," Joe told Sara as he disengaged from Cindy's arm. He stopped running just long enough to light another bomb and throw it into the street. Its explosion into flame didn't catch any 'Vaders, but it did slow them down. The flames, however, had no effect on the two flying spores that flew well above the conflagration and dove at him like bees pursuing a hive marauder. Joe got an idea and pulled the fire extinguisher from the bomb sack, yanked its pin out, and sprayed the orbs with monoammonium phosphate foam just as they were about to fly into his face. The flying 'Vaders immediately took off, gyrating crazily in the air as they tried to shed the chemical.

At the corner, Joe again pulled out another Molotov cocktail, lit it, then used the flaming wick to light another bottle. One he tossed into the intersection to head off the monsters that had been sleeping and were now giving chase. The other one he threw back at the other four coming after them.

Another orb appeared and swooped down, buzzing within less than an inch of Joe's face—close enough to tickle his nose hairs. He jerked away and sprayed it from behind with the extinguisher. The thing flew off as if shot from a cannon. Joe laughed with triumph as the orb spun wildly trying to slough off the foam. He ran after his companions who were already around the corner and running up the right-hand sidewalk on West 10th Street. Suddenly a loud rumbling sound emerged and the ground trembled beneath his feet. As Joe caught up to the others, just past a shop called Gotham Antique Watch and Clock Repair, the entire front of the place exploded outward as a 'Vader inside broke through into the street. Glass, clocks, wood, metal, and bricks flew into the street in front of it, catching several more low-flying orbs that had taken up the chase. They were buried under the debris. From the shop's shattered display window, one long, sharp sliver of metal, at least a yard long, was launched into the air like a javelin and straight through the neck of a tall monster who had managed to leap over the flames in the road and continue its pursuit.

The creature grabbed at its neck and emitted gurgling, choking sounds. It toppled facefirst to the road. The monster from inside the shop staggered into the street and tripped over the dead monster. The other monsters giving chase were pelted with glass and building debris, but none were injured enough to keep them from pouncing on the bounty at hand. In a violent rumble of tearing claws and gnashing teeth, they set upon the fresh kill and feasted ferociously. The monster from within the shop, lying atop the impaled dead one, was caught up in the feast and found itself being eaten alive.

Joe and the others had to stop. The sidewalk ahead was impassible; several cars blocked the way, and farther on there appeared to be some sort of barricade. Joe turned left into the street, and the others followed.

Joe stopped in the middle of West 10th Street. He couldn't believe his eyes. The entire width of West 10th was blocked

off. A barricade of wrecked vehicles stretched from one side
of the street to the other. At the left end of the barricade was
a white building with a sign in gold letters: NYPD 6TH PRE-
CINCT. The barricade was made of trucks, cars, and building
debris of stone and brick. Across the roofs of the barricade
vehicles, barbed wire had been loosely strung. Large metal
spikes, which looked like the sharply pointed wrought-iron
pickets of the cages that protected shops from burglary at
night, had been driven through the roofs of the top layer of
cars—two spikes to each car roof—with their business ends
pointed skyward to deter any monsters trying to climb over
the wall. A gray, paint-stained tarpaulin, eight feet high and
strung on the barbed wire, stretched from one end of the barricade to the other, blocking any view of what lay beyond.

At first, Joe was exhilarated to see the barricade. At last it
appeared they had reached a safe haven, a place of authority,
a place with a plan for survival; maybe even a place with a
plan of attack for defeating the feared 'Vaders. His exhilaration weakened when a shot was fired from behind the barricade and the bullet struck the pavement less than a yard in
front of him. His exhilaration died when a loud voice amplified by a bullhorn blasted out at him:

"Turn back! Do not come any closer or you will be shot!"

5:20 a.m.

It was patrolman Brian Aaron's sleep shift, but he couldn't
sleep. He lay in his sweat-stained, wrinkled uniform and
stared at the ceiling. Since the world had become an insane
nightmare two days ago, he figured he had slept less than
four hours total. The first twenty-four hours of the attack, he
hadn't slept at all. There had been too much to do, especially
after Captain Tillis had ordered the barricades be built at
both ends of the precinct building to keep those . . . *things*
out. It was fortunate that the city had been working on the
road directly in front of the precinct and a private contractor
had been tearing down the brownstone next door. Without
the heavy equipment—backhoe, bulldozer, and wrecking
ball and crane—they couldn't have barricaded the street so

fast. After he and several other patrolmen and construction
workers had put the finishing touches on the barricades by
puncturing the roofs of the cars with iron spikes, he finally
slept. And then it had been the sleep of exhaustion, fraught
with nightmares.

Now, he couldn't remember when that had been—he had
lost track of time; had lost all *concept* of time. He knew that
sooner or later exhaustion would overtake him again and
then sleep would return, but he couldn't invite it in and ask it
to give him a few hours on demand just because the captain
said it was his turn. He wouldn't relax until he found his
pregnant wife, Kathy, and their son, Corey. Until he knew,
absolutely, whether they still lived or had died, exhaustion,
total exhaustion, would be the only thing that could make
him sleep.

Even though sleep would not come, and he wouldn't even
try to coax it, he lay on the makeshift bed on the floor of the
precinct locker room and rested. A sufferer of insomnia even
before all this (back when the world had been normal, which
now seemed like some unbelievably happy, sappy movie he'd
seen ages ago and could barely remember), he had learned
that just lying still and being quiet was almost as good as
sleep.

Almost.

But then, back in that fantasy movie world that had been
his life—that world that he had *thought* was reality—he hadn't
worried about where his wife and son were as he lay unable
to sleep in the darkness. He hadn't had to worry about them
being eaten by monsters. After all, monsters weren't real. He
had told that to his son time and again after Corey had watched
some scary movie or had awakened crying from a nightmare. And he hadn't had to worry as he lay in the darkness,
his thoughts racing, replaying the events of the day gone by,
or pre-playing the events of the day to come, about his wife
and son becoming monsters.

Monsters aren't real. The only *real* monsters are the
human kind; the kind who kill people; the kind who abuse
and molest children; the kind who rape and assault women.

That's what he had always believed; as a policeman it was what he had always known . . . and it had all been a big, fat, stupid, *fantasy*! It had been a lie.

The sound of a shot and Captain Tillis's shouting through the bullhorn roused him from his thoughts. The alarm was going round. The monsters that shouldn't be real must be attacking again, he thought. Since he and the other cops of the Sixth Precinct, combined with a number of people who had lived on this section of West 10th Street or had been working there at the time of the initial attack, had worked furiously to build barricades at both ends of the building the monsters had attacked four times, each time in greater numbers. And each time the men of the NYPD Sixth Precinct—the same men who had faced the horror of September 11th and had helped the public on that insane day—had repulsed every attack.

But now they were running low on ammunition, and everything else for that matter. During the last meeting with the captain, Brian had noticed a difference in his superior officer as he had told everyone that their food was being rationed; cut in half. The captain didn't look or sound like the man of confidence he had always been. He was nervous and his voice trembled. To Brian, he seemed to be on the verge of a complete breakdown. When he had asked for non-police personnel to volunteer for a foraging party—claiming the officers of the Sixth Precinct were too valuable as marksmen to send—he had been unable to meet the eyes of two construction workers who had come forward. They had gone out yesterday, and not returned. After that, the captain got worse.

When Brian volunteered to join the search for food, the captain refused; his voice shaky as he repeated his reasoning that officers were too valuable and Brian too good a marksman. Brian had accepted that; everyone knew that their flimsy barricade couldn't stop the monsters; it was up to the police marksmen to keep the creatures from getting close enough to breach the barrier.

The hardest and scariest time had been while the barricade was being constructed. While construction workers, civilians, and precinct clerical personnel had worked non-stop building the barricades, Brian and his fellow officers had spent their breaks from working on the barricade perched atop the roof of the station and the two brownstones across the street where they had picked off attacking monsters. But that wasn't all. In addition to shooting the huge gargoyle creatures, Brian and his comrades had had to watch out for the infecting eggs. If an orb managed to invade anyone working within the barricades, then that person had to be shot before he or she could transform.

Although a difficult thing to do, it hadn't been as hard as what the captain had ordered next: that anyone shot or dying for any reason was to be tossed over the barricade for the monsters on the other side to fight over and devour. Brian knew this was done to help stave off attacks from the creatures, and so far twelve bodies had been tossed over the barricades like sacrifices to some evil pagan god. Though he knew they had to do it, he didn't have to like it.

Rising from his sleepless sleep shift, Brian ran to the rooftop and looked down on the commotion. Policemen, construction workers, and civilians scampered about the compound below between the two barricades, running to their assigned positions given to them by Captain Tillis. Sixth Precinct officers were mainly on the roof of the station and atop the buildings opposite, or in the third- and fourth-floor windows across the street. The ones on top of the brownstones had to be ready to open fire on the monsters outside the barricades, while the ones in the third- and fourth-floor windows had to target any potential threats within the barricades.

"What's up?" Brian asked Dave Wozkowicz as he opened his service revolver and checked it to make sure it was loaded. Wozkowicz had an M-16 rifle, as did nearly all the policemen on the roof, but Brian preferred his service revolver. He checked his belt and swore silently; he had only one speed-loading cartridge left. After that, he would only be able to throw his pistol at the monsters.

"The apes are up to something!" Wozkowicz replied, using the nickname the cops and civilians in the compound had given the monsters. Brian thought they looked more like demons from Hell than apes but kept that thought to himself. "Apes" was short and simple and made the monsters seem less frightening than they really were, and more capable of being defeated in everyone's mind. You could kill an ape, but a demon?

"Better pick your shots carefully," Wozkowicz said condescendingly to Brian, as if Brian didn't know that already. But then, he and Wozkowicz had never got along; had, in fact, been enemies from day one. Brian was sure Wozcowicz would not shed a tear if he was grabbed by one of the monsters, and would be more than happy to put a bullet in him if one of the flying eggs invaded him, or even came close.

Brian looked around. The night's rain had stopped. The horizon sky was pale blue-gray and brightening, promising a hot and sunny day. The temperature was already at seventy-two. The lightening sky was smudged by several columns of smoke billowing from the fires burning out of control. The light of dawn had not yet reached 10th Street; the compound below and the street beyond the barricade were still cast in night's shadows. Brian could see two good-size fires burning in and around the Hudson Street intersection. By their position, Brian figured they had to be car fires since the flames appeared to be shooting up from the middle of the street and the intersection. He could hear a tumultuous mix of bellowing and roaring, plus the occasional animal cry of pain. Brian Aaron knew the sounds all came from "apes." Nothing on earth sounded like that; it was too unnatural.

Brian turned and looked to the other end of the roof and beyond. Police marksmen were in position training their rifles on the upper section of West 10th Street outside the barricade, but as yet none of them had opened fire. Nothing was burning close by in that direction, though the lighter the sky became, the more plumes of smoke appeared above the horizon. So many smoke plumes were visible during the day that it looked as though a good third of the city was on fire. The thickest was coming from the south, around King Street, Brian figured. Last night there had been a loud explosion from that area and the sky was lit from what had to be a huge, raging fire. Brian had guessed a gas station must have blown up, perhaps having caught fire from one of the crashed jets. He turned back, facing Hudson Street again, and heard a voice come out of the shadows on the other side of the barricade.

"Hello? Help us! Let us in!" a strong male voice cried. Two female voices took up the pleas for help; both of them sounded as though they were walking a tightrope between hysteria and relief.

No one from within the compound answered. Brian looked down and saw a group surrounding Captain Tillis, listening to his commands. The group dispersed and Captain Tillis stepped up to the barricade with a bullhorn in his hand.

"Turn back! Do not come any closer! You people must turn back!" the captain said into the horn, which broadcast his voice loudly. "We have no room or provisions for you."

Brian couldn't believe what he was hearing. Was Captain Tillis actually refusing to help those poor people? Next to Brian, Dave Wozkowicz was grinning fiercely and nodding his head just as strongly.

"You tell 'em, Cap!" he muttered.

"What the hell is wrong with you?" Brian asked him. "If we leave those people out there, we might as well just shoot them. Those things will get them as sure as the sun rises if we don't help them."

Wozkowicz sneered at Brian. "Ask me if I care! Better them than us," he said sarcastically. "It's every man for himself now."

"No!" Brian cried fervently. "It isn't. We're still NYPD Blue and we have a sworn duty to serve *and protect* the population. Or did you forget that?"

Wozkowicz ignored him.

Holstering his pistol, Brian Aaron headed down to the compound. Behind him Wozkowicz muttered, "Pussy!"

5:35 a.m.

Fifteen yards in front of the barricade protecting the Sixth Precinct, a black Cadillac and a large red heavy-duty tow truck, with the logo *Gotham Towing Inc.* on its doors, sat tangled together where they had crashed. The tow truck was a heavy hauler, the kind with four wheels on its rear axle and used for towing eighteen-wheel trucks. When the shot and warning had rung out from behind the barricade, Joe had motioned for the others to make for the Cadillac while he tossed three Molotov cocktails to block West 10th Street as far down its length as he could throw. A wall of flame had swelled up; fingers of fire had stretched skyward through the tree branches overhead. It was enough to keep the monsters at bay so he and the others could get close enough to plead for help from the inhabitants behind the barricade. Luckily, so far no more orbs had appeared.

But now, it seemed it had all been in vain; Joe couldn't believe what he was hearing.

No room?

No! That couldn't *be* what he had heard.

He stared dumbfounded at Sara, Cindy, and Corey. The shocked looks on their faces told him he had heard correctly.

The flames were going to die down soon, and when they did he didn't want to think about what would happen. Joe looked in the makeshift sack and counted three homemade bombs left. Just three.

5:37 a.m.

Brian Aaron reached the first floor and heard a woman's voice from outside the barricade cry, "Please let us in!"

Incredibly, Captain Tillis's response was, "I'm sorry. Please believe me. I am very sorry but I can not, and will not, risk the lives of everyone in here. We have too many mouths to feed as it is. . . ."

Brian sprinted through the station house lobby and out the glass front doors of the station.

"Aaron, get back to your station!" Desk Sergeant Tom O'Malley shouted at him as he went by. Brian ignored him. He kept going outside and across the compound to the middle of the barricade where the captain stood, his bullhorn pointed through the open window of a wrecked Buick on the barricade wall.

"You got this far," Captain Tillis was saying as Brian reached him. "You should be able to make it to the—"

Brian grabbed the captain by the arm holding the horn to his mouth and cut him off.

"What the hell are you doing?" he yelled at his superior officer. "We can't say no to these people! We can't leave them out there! That's as good as murder!"

Captain Tillis's face was a portrait of shame—shame at what he was doing and shame for something else; something so strong it overwhelmed all his senses, all logic, and all conscience; warping his understanding of right and wrong. That something had been born in Captain Tillis on the first day of the invasion and it had grown every day since until it was so overwhelmingly strong he had to bow to its every whim; he had to cower before its irrationality. That something was *fear*. Pure abject fear—a terror so deep and malignant it had eaten his spirit, his soul, and his conscience. By the lack of protest from those around him—officer Aaron was the only one—to turning the strangers away, it seemed the same had happened to every other man and woman living on borrowed time between the barricades. It gave Captain Tillis a sense of justification—a sense that he was doing the right thing.

Even so, Tillis couldn't look at Brian, couldn't meet his eyes. Two former construction workers came running over and grabbed Brian; ordered to do so by Desk Sergeant O'Malley who followed behind them.

"I'm sorry," was all the captain could mumble weakly as the burly construction workers pulled Brian Aaron back.

Sergeant O'Malley ordered, "Take him inside and lock him in a cell."

5:40 a.m.

Outside the barricade, huddled with the three grown-ups in the V formed where the Cadillac had run into the rear left side of the tow truck, Corey Aaron looked at the fear on the faces of Cindy, Joe, and Sara and got an idea. He went a few feet around the Cadillac, toward the barricade, and cupping his hands around his mouth shouted as loud as he could, trying to be heard despite the sound of the monsters roaring beyond the fire behind him.

"My daddy is in there. Patrolman Brian Aaron is my daddy! Are you there, Dad? Please let us in. *Please!*"

5:41 a.m.

Brian Aaron's body stiffened.

Was that Corey?

He'd heard only a couple of words, but it was enough for him to realize there was a child out there, and that child might be his son, Corey. He turned back, struggling against the strong arms holding him and pulling him across the compound to the station where a cell awaited him.

"That's my boy!" he cried, his eyes wild. "We've got to let him in! That's my son!"

The construction workers stopped, uncertain what to do. They turned around with questioning looks on their faces for Desk Sergeant O'Malley. The sergeant, in turn, looked back at the captain who kept his eyes down, but slowly shook his head, *no*.

"Then let me go! Let me leave to be with my son!" Brian pleaded. Again Captain Tillis couldn't meet his eyes and again fear spoke for him and through him when he said, "I'm sorry, but no. We can't afford to lose you. You're too good a marksman. We need you. Besides, we couldn't open the barricade now, during an attack." As if to bolster his argument, several monsters made a charge at the opposite barricade and were shot down by the marksmen on the roofs. The sound filled the air of fallen ones being cannibalized by other monsters. A moment later a squadron of orbs flew out of the gray morning sky and dived at marksmen on the roofs and others within the compound.

"This is fucking crazy! You're all fucking crazy!" Brian spat out the words, looking from face to face, from the captain to the sarge to the two guys restraining him. The pure terror he saw on their faces, especially when the swarm of orbs entered the compound, made him realize they could not act rationally. Their fear of the orbs, however, did give him a chance to break loose.

"I'm going!" Brian shouted. He brought his right foot down hard on the left instep of the burly construction worker holding his right arm. The man howled with pain and let go of his arm. Brian swung around and slammed his fist as hard as he could into the other man's head. His fist hit the man's ear just right, creating a pressure pulse of air that instantly exploded the man's eardrum. He, too, cried out in pain and dropped to his knees holding his head. Sergeant O'Malley's reaction was too slow for the adrenaline-pumped Brian. The sarge reached to restrain him and got a kick square in the balls for his effort. He collapsed with a girlish shriek spilling from his lips.

"Corey! I'm coming, buddy!" Brian Aaron shouted. It was a shout of futility that Corey and the others outside the barricade could not hear over the roars of the monsters, the shots ringing out from the roofs within the compound, and the screams and cries of terror from those being attacked by the flying orbs.

Brian sprinted toward the end of the barricade nearest the precinct station where there was just enough room for him to slip by the barrier. The asphalt less than a foot in front of him suddenly cracked, and a plume of dirt, dust, and fragments of tar were thrown into the air. Almost immediately, he heard the report of a shot. One of the bits of tar struck him on the left cheek, stinging him and drawing a trickle of blood. It felt warm as it dripped down his face. He stopped and looked up. Wozkowicz was on the precinct roof, his M-16 pointed at Brian, who now realized the first missed shot had been on purpose—a warning. Wozkowicz was too good a shot to miss by accident. Brian also knew Wozkowicz hated him enough that he wouldn't miss again.

He bolted left, feinted right, then back to the left again. A second bullet buzzed so close by Brian's head he could feel the displaced air like a tiny breeze against the skin of his left ear. He heard the deadly projectile's whine as it spun by, then slammed into the asphalt, too, puncturing it and kicking up a small cloud of black tar, dirt, and dust.

Wozkowicz's next shot didn't miss. It caught Brian in the upper arm and shoved him hard to the right. Like a bee sting followed by a hard punch, it burned so badly he wanted to rip the skin from his arm to stop the fire. The bullet slowed him, but didn't stop him. With his right arm dangling uselessly by his side, he struggled on toward the end of the barricade wall.

Wozkowicz fired again, and the bullet hit Brian in the left thigh, went right through it, and lodged in the street after ripping through the flesh and bone of his leg. This bullet was more painful than a burning bee sting. It felt like an ice-cold metal rod had been thrust through his leg. In a few seconds, the ice turned to fire and the burning started. He fell hard to the street and tried to reach his pistol.

Before Brian could unholster his gun, Wozkowicz fired a final shot—the killing shot that struck Brian Aaron in the neck, severing his carotid artery before burrowing through tissue and muscle and coming to rest against his left scapula.

5:55 a.m.

Pandemonium reigned. It began the moment Corey ended his plea for his father. Twenty yards behind where he, Joe, Sara, and Cindy hid, hoping for salvation that they were quickly realizing was not going to come—not from the Sixth Precinct, at least—the fires caused by Joe's bombs had lessened. The 'Vaders that were least fearful of the fire broadjumped over and through the dying flames.

Shots rang out. Corey felt Joe's large hands on him, pulling him back to the relative safety behind the tow truck and the Cadillac. Joe looked down the street and saw monsters jumping over the diminishing wall of flames and knew he and his companions had to get out of there fast.

Corey thought he heard someone call his name from the other side of the barricade across West 10th Street. He strained to hear more, but it was impossible between the sound of shots being fired, the roaring of the 'Vaders, and the pavement-pounding thunder of their footsteps as they came up the street. He couldn't tell if it was his name or anyone else's.

"I thought I heard my dad!" Corey nonetheless told Joe, but Joe was too intent on the 'Vaders breaking through his wall of fire.

"We've got to get out of here!" Joe yelled. He pulled a Molotov cocktail from his bag, lit it, and tossed it at the closest 'Vaders coming up 10th Street. It landed several yards in front of the creatures, slowing them for the moment.

"The tow truck's keys are in the ignition!" Sara shouted to Joe who was ready to light another bomb.

"Then let's go—fuck them!" he answered. He lit the bomb and tossed it stiff-armed the way a soldier throws a hand grenade. The bomb exploded at the feet of a monster that had run around the pool of flame from the first bomb. Its legs were suddenly engulfed in flame. The thing howled with pain and fear, turned tail, and ran back through the low flames behind it, shoving aside its compatriots as it did.

"Come on, kid," Joe cried, and scooped Corey up with one arm as he ran around to the driver's side of the tow truck.

"Wait! My dad!" Corey cried.

"Sorry, kid, but he ain't here," Joe said, and lifted Corey with both hands into the cab of the tow truck where Sara and Cindy waited, after climbing in on the other side. Sara grabbed Corey and helped him in, pulling him onto her lap. Joe climbed in after and pulled the driver's door closed.

"Let's hope this baby starts," Joe muttered. "Hallelujah! Christ be praised!" he cried when the engine responded on the first try. He threw the truck into gear and stepped on the gas pedal. With tires spinning out a cloud of black smoke, the rear end fishtailed to the right and pulled free of the Cadillac. The truck took off. Joe swore under his breath. He didn't see a lot of options for escape ahead. Coming toward them on the right side of West 10th Street was a crowd of monsters, huddled together as they ran to avoid the flames still burning in the street. Going left was not an option. The fire had spread to an old rag-top convertible, which, along with the rubble from the destroyed clock shop, blocked the road in that direction.

"Fuck it!" Joe muttered fatalistically, and stomped on the gas pedal. He pointed the truck straight at the middle of the street where the flames were lowest and into the path of the 'Vaders.

6:00 a.m.

The people behind the Sixth Precinct barricade—the policemen, city and construction workers, the men, women, and children civilians who had been living on borrowed time hoping for rescue—found their time was up. The books that were their lives were due. The rescue they had hoped for had indeed come, just not the type they had hoped for. Their escape from the terror of their daily nightmare existence came in the form of death; a horde of attacking monsters trampled over the upper barricade. The people within were killed and eaten as there were just too many of the monsters this time for the marksmen to keep them out. That, and the fact that the glowing, flying orbs descended on the rooftop gunman and quickly turned most of them into monstrosities, soon made the area inside the compound a bloody cafeteria for the 'Vaders. Anyone who avoided becoming fast food soon became a consumer by the flying orbs.

Captain Tillis was the first to become one of the nightmare creatures he had been so afraid of. As patrolman and marksman Dave Wozkowicz ran out of ammo and jumped from the roof of the station to avoid the orbs, Tillis caught him and ate his fill.

There would be no more rationing for the captain.

6:01 a.m.

The truck raced on, Joe clenching the wheel with white-knuckled hands. He hunched forward over the steering wheel, his face set in a maniacal grin, his eyes wild. In the back of the tow truck, the towing apparatus—consisting of a metal derrick, a thick braided metal tow line that fed off a motor-cranked wheel set into the derrick, and a large thick metal hook at the end of the line—rattled and four feet of the line with the hook at the end of it swayed free behind the speeding truck.

The closest monster beyond the flames saw the tow truck coming straight at it. The creature hesitated, confused by this aggressive behavior; it had become used to humans and vehicles running away from it, trying to escape. Two more 'Vaders behind it also paused, confounded by the actions of the first.

The three creatures reminded Joe of bowling pins. Laughing, he aimed the bowling ball of a truck at the lead 'Vader-pin.

"What the hell are you doing, Joe?" Sara asked. She sounded frightened.

"Bowling," Joe muttered, and laughed again—not a reassuring sound.

6:01:30 a.m.

Jammed between Joe and Cindy and with the not so small or light Corey on her lap, Sara found it hard to see or breathe. Combined with the jolting this way, then that way, as a result of Joe's frenetic but necessary driving antics, to avoid the monsters and the fires he had started, Sara couldn't do much but hang on tightly to Corey and try to gulp air as best she could. That, she was finding, was not as easy, or as pleasant, as one might think. The air smelled poisonous; full of gas vapors and the stench of burning hair and flesh, making her feel sick. She closed her eyes and hung on.

6:01:45 a.m.

As sick as Sara felt, Cindy Raposa felt worse. She was badly in need of a fix and was starting to experience withdrawal. She broke out in a cold sweat while at the same time having hot flashes. One moment she was sweltering, the next she was freezing. A hammer-pounding headache banged between her ears so hard and hurtful she could feel her eyes bulging in their sockets with every pulse. Her mouth was so dry, her tongue was glued to its roof, and she could taste copper. With every hot flash, her stomach soured and she felt dizzy. Her heart raced; she could feel it like a drumroll in her chest. Her skin crawled with the memory of the shower of insects she had endured, and she squirmed in her seat.

Not ready for cold turkey, and unable to shoot up in the cramped cab, Cindy clawed through her pocketbook looking for something to take the edge off. She found it in the prescription bottle of assorted pills. She fumbled the bottle open, nearly dropped it, but managed to grab six morphine sulfate pills and four Valiums. She dumped the rest of the bottle's contents, and the empty bottle, into her purse. She struggled to dry-swallow the pills, despite the desert her mouth and throat had become, and nearly choked. She managed to get all but one of the pills down. The one that refused to go stayed lodged in the back of her throat, slowly dissolving and leaving a bitter, bad taste.

Within a few moments, though, it didn't matter; she was almost as senseless as she wanted to be; oblivious to her surroundings and danger, for a short time anyway.

6:02 a.m.

Scant seconds before the tow truck reached the first 'Vader, the burning convertible a few feet to the left of the three of monsters exploded as the flames reached the fuel tank. The two 'Vaders behind the lead one were immediately consumed by the explosion. Their burning death screams were horrible to hear. The lead 'Vader was caught off guard by the explosion. It gave up on the truck and decided a hot meal—offered by its burning fellows—was better than a cold one, and the truck sped past.

Joe felt a sudden lag in the truck's forward momentum and glanced in the large side-view mirror. He was shocked at what he saw: a small 'Vader monster—not more than twelve feet tall—had come stampeding up West 10th Street, drawn by the attack on the precinct. As the truck zoomed past it, the short creature had grabbed the tow line and hook and was now being dragged on its stomach, roughly bouncing and tumbling over the pavement that had been churned up during the strafing runs of the jets the day before.

Joe cut the wheel hard to the left, then back to the right, trying to shake off the monster, but it wouldn't relinquish its hold on the towing hook. As the truck neared the intersection with Hudson Street, Joe kept his foot on the gas pedal, careening the truck brazenly around the corner. The truck nearly flipped over, yet the creature held fast.

Why doesn't it let go? How can it stand it? Joe glanced in the large side mirror outside his window. The creature was leaving a bloody wake behind the truck as its flesh was rubbed off by the asphalt. A closer look revealed that the monster wasn't holding on to the tow line's hook; the hook was holding on to the monster. It had pierced the small monster's left hand and the creature couldn't let go. As a result, the 'Vader's flesh, blood, and bone were being spread over the road like butter smeared on toast.

"Uh," Cindy grunted, her face pale. Her hands went quickly to her mouth. The back-and-forth rocking motion and the constant jolting as the truck rumbled over the torn-up street combined with the bitter pill dissolving in her throat to make her sick. "I think I'm going to puke!" she moaned.

"Don't puke on me!" Sara shouted, and slid closer to Joe, jamming him right up to the door and nearly causing him to lose control of the truck.

"Watch it," he yelled at Sara. He cut the wheel hard to the right, pumped the brakes to keep the truck on the road, and came within inches of sideswiping an overturned police paddy wagon. He took his eyes off the road for a moment to look behind at the 'Vader still being dragged, and when he looked back there was another ten- to twelve-foot tall 'Vader standing atop a metro bus that was lying on its side, blocking the left side of the street. The creature grinned with gleeful anticipation as it watched the truck's approach. It leaned forward on its haunches, arms raised, clawed hands outstretched toward the approaching vehicle.

To the right of the bus was enough room for the truck to

get by, and Joe steered in that direction. The truck raced
through the narrow pass. The monster on the bus leaped at
the tow truck . . . and missed. Instead it landed on the back
of the monster being dragged. The latter screamed in pain as
the front of its body was forced deeper into the road surface.
A bright red spray of blood flew from its braised chest, forming an even higher V-shaped crimson wake in the air. The
creature on the unfortunate beast's back got to its feet precariously and teetered and tottered like a novice surfer taking on his first wave. Arms outstretched for balance, the 'Vader
crouched and gained a surer footing as the truck traversed a
smooth section of the street. With a very humanlike gesture—
an echo perhaps of its former self—the thing raised both fists
in the air in a declaration of triumph and roared.

Its victory was not to last.

Hudson Street was littered with car wrecks and the rubble
from destroyed buildings along both sides. Joe was forced to
spin the wheel right, then left, and back again. The bodysurfing
monster behind the truck was thrown off and slammed into
the back of a yellow taxi and flipped head over heels onto the
top of a white Ford Explorer. The creature that had been used
as a surfboard slid under the taxi and became stuck. The hand
impaled by the tow hook was ripped free of the monster's
arm as the truck sped away.

The truck slalomed on and reached the intersection with
West 11th Street.

On the far corner of West 11th and Hudson, two bloody,
fat 'Vaders who still held partial human torsos, each with an
arm and a leg still attached, paused from their feasting to
watch the truck go by and traverse the short city block between West 11th and Bleecker Street in less than a minute. The
truck turned right on Bleecker, and Joe was surprised at how
free of abandoned vehicles it was. The truck was able to travel
in a straight line for a change, much to Cindy's gratification.

6:05 a.m.

"Are we going around in circles?" Sara asked, spying the
sign for West 10th Street coming up. Being squashed behind

Corey and between Cindy and Joe, she couldn't see much and had no idea of the direction they were travelling.

"Seems like it, don't it?" Joe remarked, and grunted as he turned the wheel to the left. In the middle of the West 10th and Bleecker Street intersection, a City Public Works yellow protective cage surrounded the open manhole in the middle of the street. Four fluorescent cones around the Public Works apparatus made the combination look like a miniature playground jungle gym. The road around and beyond the manhole was broken up as if by a jackhammer.

Joe felt the hand of luck as he approached the torn-up intersection—it was empty of 'Vaders. They had all been drawn to the fireworks and destruction of the upper barricade that had been protecting the Sixth Precinct farther down West 10th Street. He pumped the brakes, slowing the tow truck down, while he leaned forward over the steering wheel to look at the havoc going on less than a hundred yards away to the right.

The barricade on this side of 10th Street looked as though it had been breached by the 'Vaders. The Sixth Precinct police station was on fire. Beyond the barricade of scattered cars, a mob of 'Vaders feasted on the bounty of human flesh that had been so easy to grab with all the people herded together so conveniently between the barricades for them.

A few folks had managed to escape the monsters and the orbs and leave the enclosure. Two had climbed a tall oak tree growing out of the right-hand sidewalk. From within their leafy hideaway they waved to the truck and called pleadingly for help. A third young man had started climbing the same tree, but when he saw the tow truck he dropped to the ground again and started toward it, then changed his mind and ran into the apartment building on his left.

As the two in the tree climbed down, Joe hit the gas and turned the wheel, steering the truck around the Public Works detour and up West 10th Street away from them. Though Cindy and Sara had seen the two people in the tree climbing down with the obvious intention of running to the truck for help, they said nothing when Joe drove off. Corey didn't see them;

he kept his face buried in Sara's shoulder, sobbing silently. An uncomfortable, guilty silence settled over Joe and the women as the truck put the killing field of the Sixth Precinct behind them.

The upper block of West 10th Street, between Bleecker and West 4th Street, provided fairly easy passage. Joe drove fast but not recklessly past a Laundromat, dry cleaner, and several small shops before the commercial buildings gave way to attractive brownstones lining both sides of the street. For one small stretch of pavement, the city appeared normal; the way it should have. For one short half a city block they saw no sign of 'Vader monsters or flying pods; they were all too busy with the bounty offered by the Sixth Precinct. For the space of a few minutes and less than twenty-five yards, they could fantasize that everything that had gone before had been nothing but a bad dream.

6:09 a.m.

The pills weren't cutting it for Cindy Raposa; they were not strong enough to keep the withdrawal symptoms at bay. Sounds became distorted to her ear; some reverberated in her head while others, especially speech, seemed muffled like noises heard underwater. Many sounds felt like physical blows, as if someone were boxing her ears. The truck's engine roar made her ears ache and her eyes water. Tiny dark specks swirled at the edges of her vision.

Every movement of the truck felt like a blow to her stomach, causing her to exhale loudly and leaving her dizzy, panting, and in danger of hyperventilating. Motion within the truck became thick as if everyone moved in slow motion. She could feel every pulse in her body pounding like hammers on anvils. Her head and neck throbbed; her wrist, groin, and thighs—indeed, every joint in her body—ached.

The events of the past forty-eight hours were jumbled, like a nightmare half-remembered for its scariest moments, leaving her wondering—when she could think straight, which was growing rarer by the moment—what had happened in between that got her to where she was now. She drifted in and out of lucidity, sporadically viewing her companions as people she thought she should know very well, but, like a victim of Alzheimer's, she had trouble connecting them to her life and remembering how she had met them. At one point, Cindy looked at the girl next to her, with the boy on her lap, and thought she remembered not liking her. She was pretty sure, however, the girl had helped her recently and had been very kind. But that was a contradiction and didn't make any sense to her heroin-starved mind.

Frequently, her skin still crawled with the phantom feeling of bugs. The illusion, bordering on hallucination, was brought on more by drug withdrawal than by what had actually happened to her in the cellar of the UPS warehouse. In addition to the maddening feeling of insects on her skin, hot and cold flashes ran rampant. A wave of intense heat, usually starting in her forehead or at the back of her neck, made sweat spout from every pore. Almost immediately, the clammy perspiration would turn ice-cold, making her shiver despite having the appearance of being overheated. She felt restless—her legs jerked involuntarily—yet tired at the same time.

Her nose ran with yellow snot, but that didn't keep her from smelling the rank sweat that oozed from her pores with every hot flash. More foul than ordinary body odor, it was a combination of fear and her body's craving for the heroin it had become dependent on. As if the odor oozing from her sweat glands wasn't bad enough, her intestines became locked with cramps, and the gas that seeped from her bowels was all the more deadly for being silent.

6:13 a.m.

Joe was the first to comment on the smell in the cab of the truck. "Whoa! *Christ*, what is that?" he said loudly, rolling down his window.

Sara pulled Corey close and buried her face in his back, trying not to laugh or breathe the malodorous air.

Corey's whimpering stopped and he sniffed the air, making a face as he did. "Who cut the cheese?"

Sara burst out in nervous laughter, as did Joe. Corey couldn't help but giggle, too. All three looked at Cindy, who was slumped against the door, her face hidden by her greasy, stringy hair. Her stomach gurgled loudly and an audible emission of gas escaped from her. The others groaned and gasped, but couldn't help laughing.

"Corey, roll down her window before we're all gassed to death!" Joe gasped, and Corey obeyed, leaning over Cindy to get at the window handle.

"I don't feel good," Cindy whined pitifully as Corey got the window down.

"You don't smell so good, either," Joe said, and their laughter grew louder.

It didn't last long.

They were halfway up West 10th, heading for West 4th Street, when three large 'Vaders suddenly blocked the intersection ahead. One monster jumped out from behind a bar called the Diablo Royale Saloon. The other two came around the corner of West 4th Street, where they had been sleeping against the side of a building housing the Chow Hound Restaurant.

Joe hit the brakes, bringing the tow truck to a jarring stop. He threw the gearshift into reverse and stepped on the gas. He looked in the side mirror and hit the brakes once more. The refugees from the Sixth Precinct who had been running to the truck hadn't made it far. As Joe had guessed—and his reason for driving on—they had quickly been overtaken by the 'Vaders that had invaded the police station compound. The two humans were now being devoured, but they had attracted a dozen monsters in pursuit. A few of the 'Vaders fought over the human flesh—a leg, arm, head, or portion of a torso—but the rest quickly keyed on the moving tow truck.

They were coming.

Joe looked to the front. The three 'Vaders there had now multiplied to seven waiting for the truck to deliver breakfast to their ripping, clawed hands and their hungry, gnashing mouths.

"Oh, shit," Joe exclaimed, looking back, then forward,

then back again. "We are caught between the rock and the fucking proverbial hard place."

"What are we going to do?" Sara asked.

"I don't know," Joe said. "But we ain't giving up. Not now, not ever."

The monsters behind them on West 10th were coming at a full jog. The monsters in front of them, at the intersection with West 4th were moving toward them slowly and spreading out.

"What are we going to do?" Corey fearfully repeated Sara's question.

Joe didn't answer. He kept switching his gaze between the side mirror and the monsters to the rear, to looking forward at the monsters coming at them from the intersection.

Corey asked his question again; his voice more panicky than before. Again he got no answer from Joe, who was preoccupied with looking back and forth. The knuckles of Joe's hands were white from tightly clenching the steering wheel. The set of his jaw was grim as he ground his teeth.

Corey slid from Sara's lap and crawled under the truck's dashboard. There was little room with Sara's and Cindy's legs and feet in the way, but he managed.

"Joe, what are you doing?" Sara asked. She could see the monsters in front of the truck but was jammed too tightly between Joe and Cindy to turn and see behind the truck. She leaned forward, looked past Joe, and caught a glimpse in the driver's side mirror of the monsters behind them.

"Oh no!" Sara gasped breathlessly. Next to her, Cindy rocked back and forth, her head down, her arms hugging her cramping abdomen, and crying softly. Her sweat-dampened hair obscured her face.

Sara looked over at Joe, but he kept his eyes averted and continued his front-back vigil. She prodded him with words. "Joe? Joe? Don't you think we should get out of here?"

He just kept looking back, then forward, and remained silent.

"Joe?"

"Not yet."

"Not yet?" Sara looked at the monsters closing in the front. They were less than fifty feet away. "Uh . . . Joe . . . if not *yet* . . . when?"

"Soon," Joe said calmly, looking *anything* but. He clenched the steering wheel so tightly the whiteness had spread from his knuckles to his hands and wrists. Cords of muscle stood out on his arms and neck. Sara could see a pulse under the skin on his neck and in the clenched mandible of his jaw.

"Give me that last bomb," Joe told Sara.

Moving with difficulty in the tight cab, Sara managed to get the bottle out of the sack, which had been wedged between Cindy and the passenger's side door. She held it up for Joe, who grabbed it with his right hand.

"Light it for me," he said.

Sara patted herself down, looking for the lighter Joe had given her.

Joe shook the bottle, indicating that she should hurry up.

She finally found the lighter, stuck in the hip pocket of her jeans. She squirmed trying to get it out.

"Come on. Come on!" Joe urged.

"It's stuck," Sara said a moment before she managed to pull the lighter free. "Yes! Here it is!" She held the blue plastic butane lighter up to the bottle's wick and spun the flint wheel. The lighter sparked but no flame resulted. She glanced through the windshield at the 'Vaders bearing down thirty feet away and closing. She glanced quickly to the left. In the driver's side mirror she could see the 'Vaders behind were crossing the Bleecker Street intersection.

"For Christ's sake, *light it*!" Joe commanded.

Sara struck the flint wheel again, spinning it with her thumb. She got a lot of sparks and a momentary flame that quickly died.

"What the fuck are you doing?" Joe snarled at her.

"I'm sorry!" Sara wailed. "I'm trying!"

The monsters in front of the truck were trotting now. Sara could hear the slap of their feet on the pavement and could feel the truck vibrating as the monsters' combined weight shook the very earth with each step.

Sara tried the lighter again with the same result.

"Come o-on!" Joe urged, shaking the bottle bomb in Sara's face. "We're running out of time here," he shouted in a sing-song manner.

Sara looked up—the monsters were so close she could see dry blood spots on their chests. She tried the lighter again.

Finally, flames spouted from it.

"Yeah!" Joe cried.

"Yes!" Sara said at the same time, and accidentally blew out the flame.

Joe groaned and Sara squealed in panic.

She tried again—got nothing but sparks. On the next try the flame returned.

Joe immediately shoved the gas-dampened wick into the flame. The blue fire crawled up the rag a second before the lighter went out; a victim again of Sara's breathy excitement. Joe put the flaming bottle in his left hand and grabbed the steering wheel with his right.

"Hold on!" he yelled. He hung his arm and the bottle out the window and gave one last glance at the monsters coming up in the rear. He pushed the gas pedal to the floor and let out the clutch. The drive wheel spun, the back end of the truck slid a few feet to the right, and Joe tossed the Molotov cocktail at the 'Vaders now charging full speed from the front. The truck took off, screeching and burning rubber, leaving black smoke behind.

The bottle bomb smashed a half foot in front of the middle monster in the charging line ahead of the truck. With an acrobatic graceful move for such a large, awkward-looking creature, the thing leaped into the air while rolling to its left. It came down on two of its fellows, sending them sprawling. Miraculously, the erupting flames did not touch them.

The truck flew forward, a step ahead of the monsters coming up from behind. Joe expertly steered through the wall of fire and between the 'Vaders on both sides who had shied away from the flames. They watched the truck race through their midst and turned to give chase just as the monsters that had been pursuing from behind reached them.

The two monster groups collided.

The front group was so intent on avoiding the flames while charging the escaping truck they didn't see the other group of beasts. Grotesque creatures on both sides went sprawling in all directions. Two of them were shoved into the ring of fire as the others tried to get by. The flaming gas stuck to their flesh and they ran amok, bellowing and howling in pain. The first flaming monster ran into another and some of the flaming gas rubbed off. In flames, all three ran pell-mell down West 10th Street, back toward the precinct barricade.

A fight broke out among the remaining monsters. The creatures that had been approaching from the front turned on the other monsters that had run into them and a full-scale brawl of slicing claws and gnashing teeth was soon under way. In the melee, the escaping truck was forgotten as it sped through the West 4th Street intersection and kept going.

6:20 a.m.

Feeling the truck in motion again, Corey emerged from his hiding place under the dashboard. Sara helped him squeeze past hers and Cindy's legs until he was again sitting on Sara's lap. Wrecked and abandoned cars lay everywhere; some showed signs of multiple bullet holes that the air force jets had rained down upon the city, others had obviously been caused by accidents. Still others were untouched, but vacant, left behind when their drivers had been pulled from them and eaten, or had tried to escape on foot. Some of the vehicles were on the sidewalks, and quite a few had crashed into buildings. The street surface was torn up, too—both from the aerial attack and the weight of the largest 'Vaders. The buildings on both sides had suffered as well. Many were ruined, looking as though something had either smashed into or out of them.

Corey looked around. Despite the destruction he saw every-where as the truck went up West 10th, he recognized the neighborhood. He had walked this way often with his mother on treks uptown for shopping or entertainment. His apart-ment at the corner of James and Bedford Streets was not far. Though the area looked as if it had been bombed or had been through a tornado or hurricane, he could still tell they were approaching the end of West 10th Street where it merges with 7th Avenue South. He knew he was correct when he saw Smally's Nightclub advertising, "Jazz from dusk till dawn," on the left corner of West 10th and 7th Avenue South.

He remembered the day, two years ago, when he had asked his mother what "jazz" was, and what did "from dusk till dawn" mean. In answer to the second question his mother had explained the phrase meant *all night long;* dusk was when the sun set and the sky grew dark, and dawn was when the sun rose and the day began. In answer to his first ques-tion, though, his mother had taken him farther along West 10th Street, past the Gourmet Garage Restaurant, the New York Sports Club, and a stretch of the street where all the trees and brownstones on both sides were covered with lush green ivy. She took him to the next corner, the intersection with Waverly Place where the Free Times Bookstore sat on the corner. Inside, his mother had taken Corey to the music department and bought him his first CD: *The Jazz Tree—A Collection of Modern Jazz.*

Back home he had been allowed to use his dad's stereo for the first time. He loaded his new CD into the stereo, and the music he heard had captivated him. Music by John Coltrane, Miles Davis, Charlie "Bird" Parker, and Ramsey Lewis, among others. But his favorite artist and song on the CD was Dave Brubeck playing "Take Five." After listening to that CD so many times that his father said he'd wear it out, Corey had asked his parents to take him to Smally's Night-club so he, too, could listen to his new favorite music from dusk till dawn. Sadly, he had learned that Smally's was a place for grown-ups only. Kids weren't allowed. His disap-pointment hadn't lasted too long, though. The next day, his mother bought him a two-volume four-CD collection of Dave Brubeck's music. Corey had been in jazz heaven.

Looking at Smally's now, Corey remembered how he had begged his mom for a piano so he could learn to play like Dave Brubeck. She had promised he could start lessons in the fall, after the new baby came, and if they went well, she would get him an electric piano for Christmas. Tears filled Corey's eyes at the memory. *That was never going to happen now.* He was never going to take piano lessons, never even get a piano. He was never going to Smally's to listen to music from dusk till dawn no matter how much of a grown-up he became. He was never going to play his favorite music for his new little brother or sister. In fact, he sadly realized he might never ever get to listen to Dave Brubeck again. That thought made the tears flow ever harder.

6:24 a.m.

Joe was surprised at the lack of monsters and orbs as the truck traversed the short block between 7th Avenue South and Waverly Place. He figured most of the creatures they had just escaped must have come from this area and had been on their way to the Sixth Precinct compound, drawn by the sounds of attack and its abundance of human flesh all in one place. He doubted the easy going would last, though, and wasn't disappointed. Right after the Waverly Place intersection, something large, furry, and black came charging out of an alley between the Café Torino and a jewelry store called NYC Bling-Bling! It moved so fast Joe barely had time to see it. It was a dark blur in the corner of his eye before it rammed headfirst into the back of the truck.

Initially Joe thought a monstrous bull had charged the truck, head down. Upon impact, the rear wheels of the truck left the ground and the entire vehicle swiveled to the right, turning completely around to face its attacker. The truck nearly turned over but managed to land with all six tires on the road. When the thing barked as loud as an explosion, Joe realized what it was, or had been.

Though nearly as big as a trailer truck, with mouth and

fangs almost as long as Joe was tall, there was still enough of its original form to tell it had been a black Newfoundland dog. Its eyes were red with bloodlust. The dog-monster's enormous nostrils flared. The fur around its serrated mouth was clumped and filthy with matted strands of bloody drool as thick as telephone poles that dripped from its jaw, lazily falling toward the street until the thing shook its head and the bloody, gooey saliva flew in all directions. One gob of the spit took out a huge glass window in nearby Little Jack's Sandwich Shoppe, shattering it. A tongue as large as Joe's living room rug slurped from the monster canine's mouth and ran along one side of its massive jaw.

The canine's snout was elongated, thus stretching its bloody maw and making its dangerous mouth even more so with the addition of more razored teeth. Four stubby horns protruded from the top of the thing's head, between its ears, looking like swollen lumps from a severe beating. Its eyes were large and slanted, the pupils reptilian in their diamond shape. The whites were blood red with lust for the kill.

The former dog's now-giant body was rippling with massive musculature. Its legs bulged beneath fur that resembled coiled steel cabling more than hair. Its paws had swelled; its normally blunt claws had become rapier sharp, sticking out from its bulging toes like spears at the front of a phalanx. Its bushy tail, nearly as long as a telephone pole, could take out a whole building with one wag.

For a moment, Joe was captivated by the strangeness of the abomination before him, but Sara's and Corey's screams pushed him into action. Despite the wrenching blow the tow truck had just received, the engine was still running. He pounced on the gas pedal and pulled the wheel to the right as the truck took off. The giant Newfoundland barked explosively at the truck, but, surprisingly, didn't attack. The reason for its nonaggression quickly became apparent.

As the truck turned it was confronted by a Chihuahua as big as a pony. The Chihuahua trembled and growled—a sound not unlike the tow truck's engine—and yipped—an irritating, screeching noise. Forming a half-circle behind the

Chihuahua, a motley pack of monster dogs of varying sizes and breeds, both pedigree and mongrel, stood, eyes bloodshot, snouts bloody, jaws drooling.

The pack blocked the way completely.

6:27 a.m.

Cindy Raposa felt sicker than she ever had in her life. She felt *beyond* sick. She felt ready to *die*. The jarring ride, the smell of gasoline, the burnt smell of the air in general, and the smell of her own farts—all had nauseated her. Now the smell of dogs nauseated her. It was the one smell in the world that she couldn't stand. Her father had bred dogs—pit bulls—and had treated them better than he had ever treated her. Growing up, there were always at least six dogs living in their hovel of an apartment.

Sometimes she dreamed she was back in that apartment with the dogs and their stink. She was having that dream now, only she was awake.

Wasn't she?

She couldn't be sure. She was deliriously sliding in and out of consciousness; slipping in and out of reality. One moment she was back in her father's dog-stinking apartment, the next she was crammed into the cab of a tow truck somewhere downtown. The only constant between the two states was that they both smelled like *dog*.

She needed a fix, and she needed one badly. She knew it; it was the reason she felt so horrible. The last time she had gone this long without a fix had been a *long* time ago when True Blue had died, and she had wandered the streets with nowhere to go and no one to supply her with the brown horse she so loved to ride.

She came to in the truck, briefly unable to remember who the pretty brown-haired girl was sitting so close to her. A memory of a dream worse than the recent one of being back in her father's dog-infested apartment came back to her, adding the trembling of remembered terror to the withdrawal tremors racking her body. She tried to speak, to tell the girl next to her—whose name was on the tip of her tongue—about her dream, but her tongue was too swollen for audible speech.

She pushed her greasy hair back out of her face and eyes. She looked up and thought she was still dreaming.

A white poodle bigger than a horse was sniffing the windshield right in front of her.

6:30 a.m.

Sara Hailey loved dogs; she always had. The toughest decision she had ever faced was giving up her dog, Boo-Boo, when she took the job with her cousins and moved to New York City. She'd had Boo-Boo since she was ten and when she moved he was fifteen years old. If he had been younger, she might have brought him, but when she got her apartment on the eighth floor of a brownstone on Van Dam Street she knew she couldn't bring Boo-Boo; he'd never be able to climb eight flights of stairs day-in, day-out. Besides, her roommate, Cheryl, who was a friend of her cousin, Susan's, was allergic to all furry animals. Poor Boo-Boo had died within a month of her moving away.

Looking at the four-legged monster fidos in front of her now, the odd thought that she was glad Cheryl wasn't around made her want to giggle and cry at the same time. As the pack of hounds surrounded the truck, Sara pushed back into the cushioned seat as if to disappear. She had never been afraid of dogs. In fact, she used to like to paraphrase Will Rogers and tell people she had never met a dog she didn't like.

Until now, that is.

She twisted away from the dogs sniffing the front of the truck and finally got turned enough that she could see out of the narrow rear window. The black Newfoundland that had initially attacked them was sniffing the side of the truck. It turned around and lifted its hind leg to spray the back of the truck with urine, thus marking the vehicle as its own. The overpowering smell of ammonia filled the air. Sara coughed and covered her mouth and nose, trying to keep the strong odor out.

Following the Newfoundland's lead, the rest of the pack took the opportunity to scent-mark the truck. Sara thought it strange that the mutant dogs could still pee without any noticeable organs for that purpose. It was even stranger that they were more curious than threatening, but she was glad for that.

6:31:22 a.m.

Corey Aaron had always wanted a Chihuahua, but a small one, not one big enough to eat him and still have room for dessert. Despite the initial scariness of the dogs' appearance, Corey found them fascinating. After a moment of fear at first seeing them, he now felt no threat from the monster pack around the truck. While they had been transformed into gigantic, deformed caricatures of their former selves, Corey sensed that at heart they were still just dogs; after all, they still peed like dogs. This was proven even more within the next few moments.

A brown-and-white mutt, a cross between a collie and a cocker spaniel and as large as the truck, began sniffing the right front fender after it peed on the front bumper. It followed its nose along the fender to the passenger door, then up to the open window. It stuck its huge, rubbery blood-stained nostrils into the passenger window and took a good sniff of the interior and its human contents.

Sitting closest to the window was Cindy, and Corey was shocked and delighted when she suddenly roused herself from her stupor, slapped the mutt hard on the nose, and said, "Bad dog! Bad! Go lie down!"

Miraculously, the dog *obeyed*.

6:32 a.m.

Joe Burton couldn't help but join in with Corey's laughter. He never would have thought that a slap on the schnoz and a "Bad dog!" would work on the demon dogs around them. The brown-and-white mutt let out a little yelp, backed away from the truck with its tail between its legs, and lay down in the street. Joe didn't know which was more unbelievable—

Cindy slapping the monster mutt and commanding, or the thing obeying her.

For the moment at least.

Joe didn't know how long that moment would last, but there were other more important worries at hand. Like the eighteen-foot-tall formerly human monster that had just come out of the same alley as the dogs. Several of the flying orbs swirled around it like an escort. The black Newfoundland, who was the largest, and obviously the alpha male of the pack, lowered its head and growled at the sight of the approaching 'Vader and its flying companions. The hair on the massive canine bristled. As if its snarling were a command, the rest of the pack followed the Newfoundland's lead. Closing ranks with their leader, the other dogs faced the monster, bristling, growling, and showing their teeth.

The message was clear: *The truck and its contents are ours!*

The two-legged monster had other ideas, though. It squared its shoulders and filled its lungs with air before leaning forward and letting out a loud, bone-rattling roar.

The trembling Chihuahua and the once-upon-a-time poodle whined in fear and backed away. The Chihuahua's trembling went up a notch in speed, but the rest of the pack stood firm alongside the Newfoundland. When it snarled and barked back, they menacingly joined in.

"Dad, will you tell those stupid dogs to shut up? I'm trying to sleep!" Cindy suddenly called out, her eyes closed, oblivious to the reality of the situation.

Corey laughed nervously and covered his mouth with both hands.

"This just keeps getting weirder and weirder," Joe muttered, shaking his head. The moment of humor quickly passed as the monster bellowed at the dogs again; its roar was even louder than the previous one. Several more of its kind emerged from the alley behind it and squared off opposite the dogs. Still, the monster canines did not back down.

"Joe, look!" Sara said urgently. Joe followed her pointing finger and felt his mouth go dry.

The flying eggs—four of them—that had been zipping around the first monster 'Vader's head were now floating past the dogs and coming toward the truck. The dogs paid them no mind; the orbs were no threat to them. The orbs came on slowly until they got behind the pack, then they began to speed up as if they had spotted the human occupants in the truck.

"Time to go, kiddies," Joe said softly. "And I think we should close that window again," he said to Corey, who leaned over Cindy and rolled the glass up. Shifting the gears and popping the clutch, Joe set the truck in motion as he looked in the rearview mirror. The pack of dogs turned at the sound of the truck leaving and were giving chase. Behind the dogs, the 'Vader monsters were following.

But there was a more immediate danger. Just outside the truck's windows, on both sides, the orbs had caught up. They didn't try to crash through the windows right away, but seemed content to just follow, as if observing the humans in the truck, or keeping track of them for the monsters following. Joe pushed the truck as fast as he dared and still be able to weave through the vehicular obstacles in the road and avoid the parts of the asphalt that had been churned up by the jets. As he did so, a senseless Cindy flopped around in her seat.

"Can you get a seat belt on her?" Joe asked Sara as he cut the wheel left, then right, to maneuver by a pileup.

"I'll try," Sara said. "Corey, I need you to just scoot down where you were before, for just a minute."

Corey nodded and slipped off Sara's lap into the narrow space under the dashboard in front of Cindy. Sara leaned over the semiconscious blonde and grabbed the seat belt buckle hanging by the door. As she did, Joe had to cut the wheel hard again to avoid a hunchbacked, grizzled, old-looking monster that leaped out at them from within a fire station— Squad Company 18. The fire station's garage doors were open and the monster had been hiding inside. Knowing the fire house was there, Joe had hoped to find help, or at least a place to hide. He quickly realized, however, the fire station would provide neither. The creature had nearly got a hand on the truck, but Joe's quick reactions kept them just out of its reach and the monster fell flat on its face. Before it could rise, the largest monster dogs at the head of the chasing pack pounced on it and put their massive jaws to bloody use. By the time the rest of the pack—consisting of the smaller, but no less ferocious, dogs—reached the fallen old 'Vader, its throat had already been torn out. It lay twitching in the street as the dogs tore chunks of bloody flesh from its body and wolfed them down.

Because of the fallen monster and the dog pack feeding on it, the street was effectively blocked, preventing the other beasts that had been drawn to the chase from continuing as fast as they had been. They dispersed to the left and right at the intersection with Greenwich Avenue, seeking alternate routes around the pack.

Joe gunned the truck past the Jefferson Market Library, which sported scaffolding hung with large green plastic tarpaulins along the entire length of the side on West 10th Street. The orbs kept pace; all four still on the driver's side of the truck. As the truck sped along the short stretch between Greenwich Avenue and 6th Avenue—also known as the Avenue of the Americas—Joe was forced to play a dangerous game of dodgeball as the small flying orbs finally went on the attack and took turns careening toward his window in attempts to smash through it, or attach themselves to melt a passage inside. Joe did his best to keep that from happening. He jerked the wheel right and left, worked the brakes and gas to swerve, slow, then speed up and was able to keep the orbs out.

Nearing the intersection with 6th Avenue, one of the flying pods managed to attach itself to Joe's window and started melting through. Joe grabbed the fire extinguisher he had shoved under his seat when they had procured the tow truck, and blasted the red-hot pod just as it was about to get inside. The orb retreated leaving a spiderweb of intricate tiny fissures that spread throughout the glass. Another of the orbs tried to zip through the first one's hole, but Joe blasted the window with foam, sending just enough through the hole to chase the thing off. Another careened head-on toward the windshield. Joe cut the wheel hard left, then hit the gas again, making the truck jump the curb at the corner as he made a left and headed north on 6th Avenue. In doing so, he not only dodged the attacking pod but also avoided a nasty pileup of vehicles that had blocked the intersection of 6th Avenue and West 10th Street. A police car and a fire truck had collided, and other vehicles had apparently then run into them until there were at least a dozen cars blocking the road.

6:50 a.m.

After hooking Cindy's seat belt, Sara was jostled back and forth by Joe's maneuvering, but with Corey still on the floor in front of Cindy, she was able to use her hands to brace herself against the dashboard. She grabbed on to Cindy's relatively immobile seat-belted body when the truck went hard right or left. The truck cleared the curb and sidewalk and headed up 6th Avenue, which was torn up worse from the jet air attack than any of the roads they had yet been on. As the truck zigzagged around abandoned and wrecked cars in the road, Sara silently prayed the Hail Mary—the only prayer that came to mind.

Sara was raised Catholic and had attended after-school catechism classes while growing up. She had continued to attend church with her father until his death when she was eighteen. When her dad had first been diagnosed with lung cancer, and was given no more than a year to live, Sara had prayed fervently daily, asking God to let her father get better. When her father died seven months after being diagnosed, despite chemo and radiation therapy, Sara turned away from her religion and prayer. The loss of her father followed by her mother's succumbing to Alzheimer's had made Sara bitter. She took on the attitude that if God could ignore her and her needs, then she could ignore Him.

Now she rattled off the Hail Mary more as a way to expel nervous energy than as an actual plea to the Mother of Jesus for help. Two-thirds of the way through the prayer she stopped, her mouth open as if awaiting the next word of the prayer, but it never came. Instead, the next word out of her mouth was, "Dinosaurs?"

Next to her Joe muttered, "What the fuck?" and she knew she wasn't seeing things.

In the middle of the intersection of 6th Avenue and West 11th Street, a live dinosaur sat watching the truck's approach.

6:50:16 a.m.

Joe thought he had seen *everything* since going out for his morning run on Sunday, two days ago. He had seen people turned into giant cannibalistic gargoyles. He had seen monster pigeons big enough to eat a man, and colossal rats, cats, and dogs more than large enough to do the same. After all that, Joe thought *nothing* could ever again surprise him; he was certain of it, but he now knew that certainty was dead wrong.

He hadn't counted on seeing dinosaurs.

Like the one eyeballing the approaching truck as if it were a moveable feast.

The thing reminded him of a movie he had seen and loved as a kid: *One Million Years B.C.* with Raquel Welch. Of course, one of the biggest reasons (make that two big reasons) he had liked the film was because of Raquel Welch wearing tattered animal skins that barely covered her incredible breasts. The other reason was the film had not used animated dinosaurs or miniature models like the ones in the original *King Kong*, which had always looked fake to him. Instead, *One Million Years B.C.* had used lizards, superimposing them on a back screen behind the actors. The best part of the movie, besides Raquel's cleavage, was when two of the dinosaur lizards fought. When he saw the monster in the road ahead he realized that it looked almost *exactly* like the lizard dinosaurs in *One Million Years B.C.*

"A lot of good *that* knowledge does me," he muttered.

"What?" Sara asked.

"Nothing! Hold on!"

With the intersection of 11th Street and 6th Avenue cluttered with cars and trucks and the dinosaur sitting smack-dab in the middle of the only empty pathway through the vehicular wreckage, Joe saw only one possible escape route. Jerking the wheel hard to the left around a dumped motorcycle and up onto the left sidewalk, he cut it hard to the right again, turning in a wide arc like an elderly driver making a turn.

Joe gunned it then and the truck shot across 6th Avenue and hit the right curb. The result was exactly what Joe hoped for; the truck jumped the curb, its front end reared up like a wild horse, and it crashed into and through the corner front entrance of the New School for Social Research, taking out both sides of its triangular-shaped, glassed-in entranceway in an explosion of broken glass, shattered wood, and twisted metal.

Amazingly, neither front tire was damaged, and only one of the four rear tires caught a jagged edge on the smashed window frame and went flat. The truck cleared the entranceway, hit the sidewalk on West 11th Street, and shot between two small compact cars. The cars were pushed aside and the truck reached open pavement.

There was an immediate loud *crash* from behind. Joe looked in the side mirror just in time to see the dino-lizard trying to give chase, but it stumbled over an abandoned car and landed flat on its stomach on another car.

6:50:33 a.m.

"Whoo-hoo!" Sara howled, unable to contain the thrill she felt at what had just happened. She had her left hand braced against the dashboard and her right arm hooked in Cindy's left arm. Cindy was still seat-belted and out of it. Under the dash, Corey had wrapped both his arms around Cindy's legs in order to keep from pinballing back and forth from the truck's gyrations.

Joe shared Sara's excitement but only for a moment—ahead in the middle of West 11th Street stood a man wrapped in the coils of a yellow snake thicker than a telephone pole and longer than a city block. And directly behind the snake-entwined man, another two dinosaur-like lizards, smaller than the one they had just avoided, but still at least eight or nine feet long, were creeping stealthily toward the snake and its human victim.

A quick glance in the large side mirror confirmed to Joe that they were now trapped between the lizard behind them, which had regained its feet and was lumbering after them, and the three reptile monsters in front. A strange thought entered his mind—one so absurd it almost made him laugh out loud, but he had the feeling that if he did start laughing, he might never stop: *I've heard of being caught between two lovers, but never caught between two lizards.*

6:51 a.m.

Crammed into the small space under the dashboard, Corey had been less jostled about than the others. With his right arm braced against the wheel well and his left wrapped around Cindy's right leg, he had been fairly secure both from being thrown about, and from seeing any of the dangers confronting them. Neither had Corey minded being sheltered and cut off from everything. Since the debacle at the Sixth Precinct police station and the realization that his father wasn't there or was dead, Corey had felt a strong urge to withdraw and, seated where he was, accommodated that urge.

Though the knowledge that he was alone—both parents probably gone—was prominent in his mind, it stood apart from him. It was like when he was younger—probably four or five—and he had learned the truth about Santa Claus. That fact had occupied center stage in his thoughts for a long time before he could acknowledge and accept it as real. It was the same now; he knew his folks were most likely gone—the proof was almost as incontrovertible as that which had convinced him of Santa Claus's nonexistence—but he just couldn't, or didn't want to, accept it as fact just yet.

The human mind is an amazing thing, especially in the way it protects itself against catastrophic hurt, both physical and emotional. Its capability for compartmentalizing severely shocking news is amazing. Corey's mind was performing that feat superbly, keeping him from breaking down and/or shutting down; both dangerous to his survival at present. It allowed him to function almost normally, as if nothing had happened to change his life and future so drastically.

His mind was protecting him so well that even though it operated in its most primal state—the fight-or-flight mode— it was still capable of showing interest and curiosity at something new and unusual.

Like hearing Sara say there was a *dinosaur* in the road.

It took a minute for that statement to sink in, but once it did his curiosity was piqued enough that he had to take a look. Right after the truck jumped through the store windows and he heard the crash of glass, he used Cindy's leg for leverage and pushed off the floor with his right arm. He managed to slide up onto her lap just enough to be able to see over the dashboard and through the passenger's side window.

For as long as Corey could remember he, like most children—especially boys—had been fascinated and in love with dinosaurs. One of his favorite movies of all time—ranked up there with the *Harry Potter* films—was *Jurassic Park*. Now here in New York City, in the so-called *real* world, was a *dinosaur*. Once Corey regained his position on Cindy's lap, he could see not one, but three dinosaurs and a giant yellow snake bigger than any he had ever seen. Not realizing, at first, that the massive snake was wrapped around a man, the sight of it thrilled Corey, but he was a bit disappointed in two of the dinosaurs. Being such an avid lover of dinosaurs, he was very good at identifying the many different kinds, but he had never seen any like the two small dinosaurs creeping up behind the snake, or the larger one he saw in the side view mirror just outside the passenger window. None of the creatures looked like any dinosaurs from any of his books at home, including his favorite, *The Illustrated Encyclopedia of Dinosaurs*.

Still, they *were* reptiles, and they were very large—the one behind them was as big as an actual dinosaur and the other two were almost as big as the tow truck. Corey knew that the word *dinosaur* meant "terrible lizard" and by that definition, the larger-than-life lizards he was looking at certainly qualified. But were they *actual* dinosaurs? He didn't think so. Considering what the flying 'Vader orbs had done to so many other normal-size creatures, it wasn't hard for Corey to figure out that the monster lizards must have been regular size before being transformed by the 'Vaders.

The proof of this Corey saw just to the right of the snake. There was a shop with a sign over the sidewalk depicting lizards, parrots, snakes, cats, and dogs. It read: EXOTIC PAM-PERED PETS GROOMING & SUPPLY SHOP. Corey looked back at the snake and with a sickening turn of his stomach realized it was wrapped around a man as it disengaged its jaws to begin swallowing him whole.

"Grab the kid!" Joe yelled at Sara, who reached out and grabbed Corey off Cindy's lap. Corey was glad she did; he didn't want to look at the horrible sight of the man being eaten but was mesmerized by it even though the sight nauseated him. Sara's grabbing him forced him to look away. Next to him, Cindy didn't look too well either. She was pale and shaking, her face dappled with perspiration. In fact, her legs also were coated with sweat, as Corey had noticed when he was on the floor holding on to her right one; it had felt clammy. He noticed now that she had large sweat stains under the arms of her blouse and down the front. But most of all, though she looked pretty bad, she smelled even worse almost as bad as the farts she had been stinking up the truck with.

6:52 a.m.

Cindy Raposa *felt* worse than she looked or smelled. The effect of the pills she had taken was gone. Continued waves of alternating heat and cold flashed over her. When she was hot, she felt like ripping her clothes from her body, but then just as she was about to undress a clammy coldness would overtake her, starting in her scalp and quickly moving down and over the entire length of her body. At the onset of the cold wave, she began to shiver and continued until the shivering became shaking. The shakes were so bad she could feel her teeth rattling in her head and in every other bone in her body. The shakes were so bad she swore she could actually *hear* her bones rattling.

The hot and cold flashes, the sweating and the shakes, weren't even the worst of it. Her mouth was so dry her tongue felt like it was welded to her palate. The dryness extended to her nasal passages and her throat so that if she tried to breathe through her nose, her throat clamped shut and her uvula and tongue melted together, sealing her airway shut. She had to gasp for air, opening her mouth as wide as possible to tear a tiny breathing hole between the sealed flesh, top and bottom, at the back of her throat. The fear of suffocation when this happened brought on a panic so severe she felt it as a weight against her chest, crushing her.

Nausea was constant and strong but not strong enough yet to bring on vomiting. At least if she could vomit she might feel a brief moment of relief from having expelled the sickening contents of her stomach, but she was denied even that slight, short relief. Her stomach held nothing but candy, pastry, soured wine, and the prescription drugs she had consumed. The contents of her stomach roiled about, refusing to be digested, and refusing to come out. It was probably just as well that she couldn't digest it; her intestines were tied in knots so tight that if she were standing, she'd be doubled over from the intensity of the cramps that grabbed and twisted her lower abdomen every few minutes.

The cramps came on again, and she experienced the worst so far. She bent over in the seat, her arms cradling her stomach as she shook and moaned.

"What the hell is wrong with her?" she heard a man's voice ask. Cindy couldn't identify the voice, but she could identify the stress and fear in it. Her thoughts were a mess; jumbled and confused. This confusion ruled her memory. Minute to minute she was unsure whether she was dreaming or awake. Lifting her head and peering at the world around her was no help. Every time she tried, she saw either giant gargoyles or dinosaurs. That should have convinced her she was dreaming, but everything looked and felt so *real* that, taken with what she remembered—or thought she did—she couldn't be certain. She hoped it all was a bad dream brought on by withdrawal. She hoped she would come to any minute to find Z-Jay shooting her up.

6:53 a.m.

In the past two days, Joe Burton had seen enough gore and gruesome violence to last a lifetime, but nothing so far had been as grotesque or as disgusting as what he now saw. In the middle of the street, not more than twenty feet away, some poor schmuck was being devoured headfirst by a massive yellow python.

Joe slammed on the brakes and the truck skidded to a screeching, shuddering halt. He and Sara sat speechless for several moments, horrified at the snake's gaping dislocated jaws inching down over the guy's head. When the stretched mouth reached the victim's shoulders, the python tightened its coils, squeezing the shoulders together enough so that the snake could get its jaws around them and continue on down the man's body. Joe was glad Sara was holding Corey's face to her shoulder so he couldn't see, but even twenty yards away, and in the truck, they could all *hear* the sickening *crack* and *crunch* of the man's bones breaking as his shoulders and chest were compacted to fit in the snake's mouth. Thankfully, the man seemed to be already dead by then and was no longer suffering.

A heavy, metallic crashing sound, accompanied by the sound of glass breaking, pulled Joe's eyes from the horrid sight in front of him. He looked in the large side mirror. The huge dinosaur behind them was coming closer, scrambling awkwardly over the abandoned and wrecked cars in the street. The vehicles slowed the thing down but couldn't stop it for long. Fortunately, when it stepped on a car and crushed it, either the noise or perhaps the steel or glass cutting it made the giant lizard pause and proceed with caution, looking for empty spots on the street in which to place its feet.

"We got trouble behind us," Joe said, a little startled at the calmness in his voice.

"We got trouble ahead, too," Sara said.

Joe looked to the front. One of the two, truck-size, pale gray lizards that had been sneaking up on the yellow python had apparently changed its mind and was now focusing on the truck and the tasty inhabitants. The lizard crawled up the front of a building on the left, using windows and ledges to cling to, and bypassed the cars blocking its way. It paused and flicked its tongue, which was a good three feet long and a beautiful shade of blue, at the truck, smelling the air with its oral appendage much the same way as snakes do.

Apparently, it liked what its tongue smelled. Despite the approach of the much larger lizard coming from behind the truck, the lizard with the blue tongue continued forward.

Which way to go? Joe wondered. The street ahead was blocked by vehicles except for a too-narrow passage between the wreckage next to where the yellow python was feeding. If the road had been clear behind, Joe could have run the snake over, but it wasn't. Turning around and heading back to 6th Avenue looked like just as bad an option as proceeding, but looking in that direction gave Joe an idea.

"Hang on," Joe grunted, and turned the wheel hard as he hit the gas and let the clutch out. With a groaning sound, the engine revved. The truck lurched forward and to the left, toward the lizard scrambling over the face of the building. The lizard stopped, a little startled by the truck's movement, and took a moment to test the air again with its blue tongue.

Joe stepped on the brakes, depressed the clutch, and ground the gears into reverse. The transmission gave forth a strangled cry. He backed the truck up in a wide arc to the right so that the front end now pointed to the right of the giant lizard. There was just enough room on the sidewalk for the truck to squeeze through. Before proceeding, though, Joe hesitated a moment, looking from the great lizard in front of them to the smaller one coming up on their right. The latter had regained the street and now stood half on the sidewalk, half on the street, its colorful tongue flicking in and out of its mouth rapidly. It seemed to be weighing its options. The giant lizard in front of the truck was doing the same, licking the air.

Suddenly there was a rush of movement and sound behind the truck. Joe, Corey, and Sara, as well as the two lizards hunting the truck, all looked that way. The other blue-tongued lizard was making a move on the feeding python. With the python in a vulnerable position, having half of the man's body in its mouth, the lizard pounced on the end part of the snake's body that was not wrapped around the man. Even with five or six coils tightly wound around its victim, the snake still had a good twenty or so feet free lying in the street behind it. The lizard clamped on to it, sinking its teeth into the smooth yellow flesh, and tried to tear a chunk free.

The snake's reaction was swift and effective. Without regurgitating its human victim, the reptile used the rest of its body to immediately coil around the blue-tongued lizard several times. Thus wrapped up, the lizard could do little except bite harder, which it did to little avail. With the lower half of its body, the serpent easily squeezed the fight, and the bite, out of the lizard. It was forced to give up its toothy hold on the snake and tried to claw at the tightening coils around it.

If the snake had not been midway though a hearty meal, the lizard would have found itself hard-pressed to escape the serpent's embrace. But with the python busy with a meal, the lizard's clawing at its body was just painful enough for the snake to loosen its coils and allow the reptile to scramble free. The blue-tongued monster wisely used its freedom to skitter away quickly down 11th Street and around the corner onto 5th Avenue and out of sight. Rid of the distraction, the snake went back to its methodical swallowing of its hapless human victim.

6:55 *a.m.*

From the first moment that she had laid eyes on the giant lizards, something about them had tugged at Sara's memory. When one of the smaller ones revealed its long, blue tongue, she remembered. When she was in high school, her best friend, Stacy Cline, had worked at a petting zoo that had had many exotic animals, including normal lizard versions of the monsters now before her eyes. She racked her brain trying to remember the names of the lizards, and they came to her as she watched one of the smaller ones run away.

"Those are blue-tongued skinks!" she said proudly. She pointed at the largest one in front of them. "And that's a water monitor lizard!" She beamed at Joe and Corey.

6:55:15 a.m.

Joe looked at Sara and shook his head slowly. "That information will certainly be good to know if that thing catches us." Despite his sarcasm, he *was* intrigued by how *human*-hand-like the giant lizard's feet were. Each one had five long fingers extending from a palm, and each finger had a long sharp fingernail growing from it. So fascinated with the reptile's hand-like claws, Joe almost got them caught by the smaller lizard. It had reached the sidewalk and was scrambling toward the truck. Joe saw it just in time, popped the clutch, and stepped on the gas. The wheels spun and screeched as the truck took off.

"Hang on," Joe shouted.

Corey was knocked off Sara's lap by the truck's forward momentum. He hit Cindy in the face with his left hand, and his head butted against the rear window of the truck between Sara's and Cindy's heads.

"Oh!" Corey yelled as his forehead hit the glass.

"What the fuck!" Cindy groused as Corey's hand hit her cheek.

"Sorry," Corey said softly while he rubbed his forehead.

"What are you doing?" Sara yelled at Joe as the truck careened across the street seemingly out of control and diagonal to the great lizard. The beast's head jerked up, following the truck. At the same time it shifted to the left and its front foot slipped on the roof of a station wagon as it moved to intercept its prey before it could escape.

The smaller lizard also made its move when the truck took

off. At first, Joe had been confused at the smaller lizard's interest in the truck. Though the lizard was as big as the truck itself, he thought it would not attack it. Watching it creep along the building face, apparently stalking the vehicle, he wondered if it was able to discern that there were living people—food—inside the cab of the truck. But then, when its attention was distracted by the snake and the other small lizard fighting it, Joe saw what the stalking lizard was after. Trailing out behind the truck was the towing cable and hook, and still attached to the hook was the hand of the 'Vader monster that had been snagged on it. That severed and bloody chunk of flesh was rapidly decomposing in the rising heat and humidity of the day, and the blue-tongued lizard had apparently smelled it with its forked tongue. Unlike the gigantic lizard that was obviously hunting the smaller truck, seeing it as prey, the blue-tongued lizard was after the carrion still attached to the tow line's hook.

Joe was counting on its intent to get the juicy chunk of free meat to help them escape the dangerous attention of the giant dino-lizard.

The truck reached the sidewalk and jumped the curb, causing the front end to bounce a couple of feet off the ground, and the back end to hit the curb with a loud clang as the rubber on the one flat tire ripped free, exposing the metal rim to the granite curb.

Like a cat chasing a piece of string, the smaller lizard ran after the tow line and its meaty tidbit.

As soon as the front end landed Joe floored the gas pedal and the truck moved faster but unevenly along the sidewalk, due to the missing rear tire; the ride was akin to what it felt like to walk with one shoe on and one shoe off. The large lizard tried to move sideways and nab the truck with its huge snout, but abandoned cars between it and the escaping truck proved to be enough obstacles to slow it down. Before it could get clear of the cars, the truck squeezed through a narrow space of sidewalk between a cement streetlight pole on the left and a building on the right. Sparks flew from both sides of the truck as it scraped through the narrow space.

The sound of metal against stone grew louder for a moment, setting the passengers' teeth on edge. Cindy screamed at the noise and Corey and Sara clasped their hands over their ears.

Behind the truck, two things happened almost simultaneously. The small blue-tongued lizard scurried after the chunk of meat on the tow truck as it hit the curb and bounced in the air. The lizard caught the meat in midair. The giant lizard made its move at the same time, but being larger and thus slower and more cumbersome in its movements, its lunge missed the truck entirely. Fortunately for the larger lizard and unfortunately for the blue-tongued one, it was able to catch the smaller lizard in one quick snap of its jaws.

Watching in the side mirror Joe was ecstatic, but as the truck reached the end of the sidewalk, the tow line played out to its limit and the truck was jerked to a sudden stop. Joe, Sara, Corey, and Cindy all were flung forward. Looking back, after cracking his forehead on the steering wheel and receiving a blood-red welt there, Joe saw the problem. The large dino-lizard now had the smaller dinosaur, with the hook still in its mouth like a fish on a line hooked by the bait.

The truck's engine raced at a high pitch and smoke poured from the burning tires. The noise was horrendous. In the cab, Joe kept his foot on the gas and screamed at the truck to break free. He wasn't able to hear himself over the squeal of the rear drive wheel as the rubber was scorched from it. On the seat next to him, Corey was crying, having bashed the side of his head against the windshield when the truck was brought up short. Cindy appeared to be completely unconscious now. She remained leaning forward, suspended by her seat belt. A trickle of blood dripped from her nose. Only Sara remained free of any visible injury, but by the way she was holding her hand to her neck, Joe had a pretty good idea that she had suffered serious whiplash.

"Fuck!" Joe swore, looking in the mirror. Now that it had a meal in the smaller lizard the huge one was taking its time dining on it, despite the acrid smoke blowing toward it from the truck. Though it was being eaten alive, the smaller lizard still refused to let go of its meal on the hook. As soon as the tow line had played out to its limit the smaller lizard had clamped its jaws tighter on the meaty hook to keep it from slipping away.

With the tow line so taut, it could have been plucked to emit a musical note. The truck revved at high speed and pulled on the line with every bit of torque the engine had. Something had to give sooner or later. Looking at the extreme tension on the tow line—it was stretched so tight it began to hum—Joe thought it would give and snap.

But he was wrong.

The lizard colossus was the stalemate breaker when it delivered the killing bite to the blue-tongued lizard in its mouth, driving its teeth through the reptile so completely the smaller lizard's head and tail were severed while its torso went down the giant lizard's gullet.

The truck lurched free with such force Joe and the others were now flung backward, then forward again. The back of Corey's head found the bridge of Sara's nose, splitting it and nearly crushing the cartilage within. The back of Cindy's head said a bloody hello to the rear window, cracking the glass. If she wasn't out cold before this, she was now. Sara let out a yelp of pain and blood spurted from her nose all over Corey and down the front of her T-shirt.

The truck took off so unexpectedly and, with one of the four rear tires devoid of rubber, Joe found it hard to steer. It careened wildly, clipping the back fender of a white Mercedes-Benz, shoving the luxury car aside as it plowed onward. Next it ran over a motorcycle lying in the road. The truck was heading for a collision with a fire hydrant and a streetlight pole side by side on the opposite sidewalk when Joe regained control just in time to avoid the collision that surely would have stopped the truck cold and exposed them once again to the dino-lizard. As it was, the mammoth reptile looked as though it were going to give chase when the truck broke free and sped off, dragging the head of the smaller blue-tongued lizard behind. If not for the python dining on the man less than twenty yards away from the big lizard, it probably would have given chase to the truck. But seeing an easier, and much slower meal, closer, Lizard Rex sucked up the severed tail of its dinner and went after the yellow snake for dessert.

7:00 a.m.

The truck screeched around the corner and regained 6th Avenue. Corey was tossed from side to side and had to grab hold of something to keep himself from being flung into Joe and causing an accident. The thing he grabbed on to, without realizing it at first, was Sara's right breast. The funny thing was, and Corey was glad of it, she didn't seem to notice. He immediately pulled his hand back even though it spilled him onto Cindy who was still bent over.

"Sorry," he said quickly to Sara, blushing hotly. Thankfully she didn't notice that, either. "Sorry," he repeated to Cindy, but she was too out of it to hear him anyway.

Sara had both hands cupped over her nose and though she didn't sound like she was crying, Corey was pretty sure she was. He felt bad but didn't know what to do. He thought about times he had been hurt, or sad, and had cried, and what he remembered most about those times was *not* wanting anyone to see him bawling like a baby. From that he figured no one, no matter what age, liked to have anyone looking at them while they cried.

Squeezing himself onto the edge of the seat between Sara and Cindy, Corey sat and braced himself by holding on to the dashboard with both hands. Thus stabilized with his back to Sara, he looked up and saw a strange thing; something that brought a smile to his lips and a memory. From where the truck was on 6th Avenue, Corey could see the top of the Empire State Building. At first glance, he couldn't believe what he saw there. At the top of New York City's tallest building, Corey could clearly see King Kong hanging on by one hand as he railed at the city below.

Corey looked at his companions, but each of them was too wrapped up and distracted. He looked back again and was delighted to see *two* Kongs now clinging to the top of the Empire State Building, one on each side. Even though he knew the King Kongs had to be 'Vaders, Corey couldn't help but giggle, drawing the attention of Sara.

"What are you laughing about?" she asked, taking her hands from her face.

Corey pointed, and she followed his finger.

"Oh, my God," Sara said softly. "First dinosaurs, now King Kong."

"What Kong?" Joe said, glancing at Sara and Corey as he maneuvered the truck up 6th Avenue. There were no 'Vaders in sight, but his clear line of vision was severely restricted by a fire in several buildings at the intersection of 6th and West 13th Street, where one of the downed jets had crashed. There was a wall of black smoke across the road and no way to tell what lay beyond it on the Avenue of the Americas.

"On the Empire State Building," Corey explained.

"Yeah, dummy. Where else would King Kong be?" Sara joked.

Joe stepped on the brake and brought the truck to a slow stop. He looked skyward and said, "I'll be damned," as he shook his head in wonder.

"Once again life imitates art," Sara murmured softly. She began sobbing.

Corey looked at Joe, who shrugged; both were nonplussed by Sara's reaction.

"Don't cry, Sara," Corey said softly, touching the side of her face gently. His concern only made her cry harder. Her tears were infectious and Corey's eyes also filled with tears that brimmed over.

"I'm sorry," she spluttered. "I just . . . I just. . . ." Her mouth opened and closed but no words came out.

"What?" Corey asked tearfully. "You just . . . what?"

Sara smiled at his show of empathy. "I just . . . ," she tried again. "I just . . . don't *get it*!" she finished and blubbered loudly.

"What don't you get?" Joe asked, confused. He looked to the Empire State Building, which was now obscured by the blowing smoke from the fire ahead. "King Kong? Is that what you don't get? It really isn't King Kong you know—it's just the damn 'Vaders."

Sara gave Joe a sour look and rolled her eyes at Corey. "I know that!" she snapped. "You think I'm stupid? That's not what I mean."

Joe sighed in exasperation. "Then what the hell do you mean?"

Sara shook her head angrily. "You don't get it!"

"*I* don't get *it*. *You* don't get it! Make up your fucking mind!" Joe said in exasperation.

"I don't get *this*, okay?" Sara shouted at him, and put her arms out, palms up. "I don't get *why* this has happened!" She went on shouting. "I don't get *where* these things come from. I don't get *what* they are, or *why* they are here!" Her shouts softened into sobs once again. "I'm only twenty-one. It's not fair. I had a *life*."

"We all had lives," Joe retorted. Movement in the side mirror caught his eye. "And if we want to keep the ones we have now, we've got to get the hell out of here." He shifted the truck into gear and stepped on the gas.

Sara pulled Corey protectively into her arms. Over her shoulder, Corey saw what Joe had just seen in the side mirror: the dogs were back and the Newfoundland had the blue-tongued lizard's head, and the hook, in its mouth. The truck's tow line hung from between its teeth as it chewed on the head and swallowed it.

The engine revved; the rear wheels spun with the smell again of burnt rubber, but after a few feet, the truck went nowhere. Twenty to thirty yards behind the Newfoundland, the rest of the pack was coming on fast. Behind them, one of the two-legged monsters that had been detoured by the dogs was catching up. Watching the giant dog as it braced against all four legs to tug on the line reminded Joe of his dog, Jasper, that he had growing up. Like the Newfoundland—and all dogs as far as Joe knew—Jasper had *loved* to play tug-of-war. Joe had even had a special length of thick rope with a knot on one end that his father had brought home from work at the Portland Shipyard. It had made the perfect tug-of-war toy for Jasper. An image of Jasper holding on to the rope so tightly that Joe had been able to lift the dog by his teeth and swing him around in the air popped into Joe's head.

Suddenly the truck slid violently from side to side as the Newfoundland shook its head back and forth, trying to break the tow cable free. Joe and the others were tossed to and fro. Joe gave the engine more gas, and the truck managed to creep forward a few inches but no more.

The rest of the pack reached their leader and the truck. The alpha-male Newfoundland growled threateningly at the other dogs as they sniffed the tow chain. The monster dog did its head-shaking tug on the line again, jerking the rear end of the truck left and right, and actually pulled it back a few feet in the process.

A golden retriever almost as large as the Newfoundland walked to the front of the tow truck and sniffed the grille before working its way over the hood to the cracked windshield. Finding the scent of the humans inside the cab, the retriever whined and yelped at the glass keeping it from getting at Joe and the others.

Behind the truck, the Newfoundland kept up its tug-of-war while the other dogs whined and sniffed about on the street or scratched themselves. The retriever gave one roaring bark at the windshield and bounded back to the Newfoundland, where it barked again, first at the leader of the pack, then at the others.

Suddenly, the tow cable snapped. There was a whining, whirring, *zip* noise as the thick line lashed through the air. The severed end of the wire cable whipped across the Chihuahua's face as it stood next to the Newfoundland, catching it in the left eye and leaving a deep, bloody gash from the eye down its snout to its black rubbery-looking nose. The dog's eye was sliced open by the cable and pulpy white goo that looked like partially cooked egg whites spewed forth.

The Chihuahua yelped with pain, flinched, fell backward, and kept on yelping. It was a sound so pitiful it brought tears of sympathy to Corey's and Sara's eyes. It even brought a lump to Joe's throat, though he'd never admit it.

With the scent of blood flying in the air from the gash on the Chihuahua's cheek, the other dogs in the pack quickly lost interest in whatever they were doing and converged on the hapless, bloody Chihuahua. They tore it to pieces in a feeding frenzy.

Joe took advantage of the situation and got the truck out of there. Unfortunately, there was only one way to go and that was through the wall of black smoke dead ahead. Joe took a deep breath, checked that the dogs were still busy, and pointed the truck into the smoke. He gave the truck a little gas and it crept forward, through the dense black cloud. Joe felt as though he was driving blind. Even with all the windows up, he, Corey, and Sara could smell the smoke, and it was not pleasant. The smoke was acrid with the scent of burning plastic and rubber. Sara pulled Corey's T-shirt up over his mouth and nose and told him to hold it there when he breathed. She did the same even though it exposed her stomach and bra. Joe tried to keep his eyes on the road.

Swirling in the dismal smoke he could see movement to the left and right and had to fight the urge to go faster. The only thing good about going slow was that the ride was less jolting over the broken asphalt of 6th Avenue where the jets must have made a majority of their strafing runs before being destroyed. Joe told himself that the 'Vaders couldn't see much better than him, and probably worse since they had the irritating smoke right in their faces and in their eyes and were breathing it into their lungs. The smoke shrouded 6th Avenue for almost an entire block between West 13th Street and West 14th. As the truck neared 14th Street, the smoke thinned rapidly.

The first thing Joe could clearly see was a 'Vader. In its left hand it held the remains of what looked to be a man, and in its right it clutched an uneaten red-haired woman who hung limply over the fingers of the 'Vader's fist. A large billboard for the Chipotle Restaurant, on the top of a low building behind the 'Vader, caught Joe's eye.

KNOW THY LUNCH—INGEST NO EVIL! it read in Gothic-style lettering.

Joe felt surreal. Not for the first or last time he had a strong urge to laugh and keep on laughing until he went either insane or became lunch for one of the 'Vaders. In that moment, he finally understood completely what Sara had just been trying to convey. He, too, wanted to know *why* the world had suddenly become a madhouse. He felt like he had awakened in a Dalí painting. The thought brought a joke to mind that his friend Roger had recently told him: How many surrealists does it take to screw in a lightbulb? *Fish!*

Reality made about as much sense as that joke—no, he thought, present reality actually made less sense.

The more the smoke cleared, the more they realized things were no better in midtown Manhattan. While the 'Vader they had just encountered was too preoccupied with its double-fisted meal, it quickly became apparent there were many more who were still on the hunt, and the Avenue of the Americas from 14th Street northward was the hunting ground. About the only good thing he had noticed since their debacle at the Sixth Precinct was that there were a lot fewer orbs now. Perhaps most of them had invaded and transformed their hosts into monsters, but Joe couldn't shake the growing suspicion that somehow the orbs were communicating with each other and had warned their flying brethren of his scalding fire-extinguishing foam.

"We need a place to hide," Joe said, stating the obvious.

7:30 a.m.

On the roof of the Zion Gourmet Deli at the corner of West 25th Street and 6th Avenue, thirty-one-year-old Hiram Zion, dressed in red plaid Bermuda shorts, no shirt, and bare feet, had his head well protected with a paisley bandanna over his nose and mouth, like a Western outlaw, and cotton stuffed in both ears for protection against the alien flying eggs. Next to him was a brown blanket, roughly the same color as the rooftop, under which he could hide if he saw orbs coming. He crouched behind the tin façade of battlement that ran around the edge of the roof, which added to the building's already unique appearance, and searched the streets below through a pair of binoculars.

Built in the shape of an arrow pointing to the middle of the intersection with 6th Avenue, the building that housed the Zion Deli was an architectural throwback to the nineteenth century when it had been built. Its point fit snugly into the corner of West 25th and the Avenue of the Americas and was adorned with a cast-iron rococo relief of flowers and vines that had originally been bright yellow and green. Now the adornment was brown with dirt and corrosion. The cast-iron relief started at the second floor and extended upward two more floors to the roof's battlement façade. In its original state, the relief had started at ground level and the ground floor had had only two lancet windows, one on the 6th Street side, the other on the West 25th Street side, to light the first-floor entrance.

The deli had originally been the townhouse of William Waterman, one of New York City's richest men in the late 1800s and early 1900s. He lost everything on Black Tuesday, and less than a year later Abe Zion, Hiram's great-grandfather, bought the building for a song. Abe Zion had been one of a very small group of investors who had not lost everything in the crash of 1929. On Monday, October 28, that year, the day before Black Tuesday, Abe had liquidated all of his holdings at the behest of his wife, Ruth. She had had a dream that Abe's cousin Rupert, his partner in an investment firm, was going to cash in all of the firm's holdings and leave the country. The dream, needless to say, did not come true. Instead, Rupert, like so many other investors, lost everything on Black Tuesday. He blew his brains out on Wednesday.

Abe's grandson, and Hiram's father, Herschel, had opened the Zion Gourmet Deli on the first floor, while the family lived on the top three floors, in 1959. From the very start, Herschel disliked the lack of large display windows. For years, he had saved to purchase another deli that was more functional and visible at street level. Fortune shone on him, however, when a city plow truck lost control during a blizzard in 1962 and smashed into the point of the building. With the insurance and a decent settlement from the city, Herschel Zion had the damaged area replaced with display windows that met at a large glass door in the peak of the pointed building.

Herschel had wanted even larger windows that would have wrapped around the peak with no interruption, but the remodeling company told him it was impossible; it wouldn't be able to support the load of the three stories above it. As it was, the construction boss had told him the old building was already leaning slightly toward the corner and that he had been lucky the front part of the building hadn't collapsed after the truck had slammed into it. Though Herschel doubted what the construction company had told him—he thought the boss was only saying that so Herscel would have to pay more for steel support posts integrated into the display windows' design—he went ahead with the supports, though smaller than what had been recommended. The construction boss had warned him that should another such accident occur and the smaller support posts be damaged, the entire front of the building, and maybe even the entire building, could collapse. But Herschel felt confident that such a thing would never happen—such accidents were a once-in-a-lifetime occurrence. He figured the law of averages was on his side.

"What's up, Hiram?"

With the cotton in his ears, Hiram didn't hear the voice addressing him. He lowered the binoculars through which he had been watching the Hell-spawn climbing the Empire State Building, and rubbed his eyes. "Hell-spawn" was his father's word for the aliens that had invaded the city and presumably the world. Hiram had tried to explain to his father that the flying glowing pods had to be aliens from outer space, but Herschel refused to believe that and insisted they were sent by God to bring about the end of the world and the end of humankind. Herschel was seventy-three and was stubborn in the way of the elderly, so Hiram didn't push it. Besides, maybe the old man was right. Who knew? With all the insane things Hiram had seen since Sunday, it wouldn't surprise him in the least if his father was right about the whole wrath-of-God thing. Actually a part of Hiram *wished* his dad was correct—at least then it would make a sense that he could get his mind around.

He felt a light tap on the shoulder, startling him. He turned to find his ten-year-old cousin, Beth, wearing a sweatsuit that had the sleeves and legs cut short. Hiram pulled the cotton from one ear and frowned at her.

"What are you looking at? Let me see." Beth asked, and reached for the binoculars, but Hiram held them away.

"You're not even supposed to be up here," he told her.

"I can, too," Beth pouted.

"No, no, no," Hiram replied rapidly. "You're not supposed to be up here during the day."

"You can't see anything at night," she groused. Suddenly, she put a shading hand over her eyes and pointed downtown. "There's a truck moving."

Hiram raised the binoculars and looked.

"It's coming this way," Beth said.

At first, Hiram couldn't see what his cousin was talking about. With half of the city burning from where the jets had crashed yesterday morning, when hope was reborn and murdered in the space of a few hours, it was difficult to see anything on the ground more than a few blocks away. He silently admired his little cousin's vision, *if* she was really seeing something and not just making it up so she could stay out on the roof longer. Hiram was beginning to think the latter when he did catch movement that was not one of the creatures. Quite a ways downtown he saw what looked like a tow truck, the heavy-duty kind that could tow a bus. By his estimation, the truck was down around 16th Street and heading north on 6th.

"Maybe it's someone coming to rescue us," Beth said.

Hiram doubted it. In fact, he doubted that the truck would ever get as far as the deli at the corner of 25th Street. He estimated that the truck might make it to West 22nd Street but no farther. What Hiram could see that the driver of the truck

couldn't was were several Hell-spawns on both sides of 22nd
Street, to the left and right of the 6th Avenue intersection.

"Do you think they're coming to rescue us?" Beth asked,
repeating her hope.

Hiram didn't answer. Up until the air force jets had failed,
Hiram had believed, along with the rest of his family, that
someone—army, navy, marines, NYPD, fire department, or
National Guard—would come to rescue them. He had believed that, and so had everyone else in his family, except his
father, who were surviving and hiding in the three floors
above the deli. To *not* believe would leave them with nothing. To survive and keep their sanity in an insane world, they
had to have hope, had to believe someone, or something,
would deliver them from evil.

The morning of the failed air force attack, a strange thing
had happened to Hiram. Upon realizing there was no hope
for rescue and, thus, no hope for surviving very long—especially once the food supply in the deli ran out—Hiram had
not been filled with despair. In fact, the opposite had happened. He had felt suddenly *exhilarated*, even *liberated*. The
old world—the world he had hated and despised—where he
was nothing but a thirty-one-year-old nerd and fantasy-role-
playing-game-geek still living with his parents, was gone. It
would never return and Hiram was only too glad to say
good-bye to it.

Hiram realized that his plate was suddenly wiped clean;
with the old world gone, so was the old Hiram if he so
wanted. The only thing holding him back, holding him to the
stereotype of aging geek-nerd, was his family, both immediate and extended, who were hiding in the rooms below and
praying to Yahweh for deliverance.

If I could just get away from here.

"Can I look *now*?" Beth demanded, interrupting and irritating Hiram as she always did. Hiram shoved the glasses at
her and shaded his eyes with both hands cupped on his forehead. The thought occurred to him that the tow truck might
not be coming to rescue the Zions, but he might be able to

use it as a rescue and escape for himself. At the very least, he could use the commotion the truck was bound to cause, if it made it as far as the deli, to cover his escape from the house into the wilds of alien-occupied Manhattan.

Too many years of near total immersion in Dungeons and Dragons and video games caused Hiram to believe, which was much better than hope, that in the aftermath of the alien invasion the world was going to become a place with a reality not too far from his favorite role-playing and video games. Hiram longed to be a warrior battling the monstrous Hell-spawn like a character from Dungeons and Dragons.

"I should go tell everyone that we're going to be rescued!" Beth said full of excitement, but she didn't move. She remained by Hiram, the binoculars to her eyes, as if she, too, sensed that the truck would not make it to the deli.

"Give them back now," Hiram said, trying to sound like an adult. The problem was that, even though he was thirty-one, no one in his family—especially his younger cousins—treated him like one. Of course, he never stopped to think he never acted like an adult. He didn't even think of himself as grown up. In fact, he didn't feel a day over thirteen. He was caught in a vicious cycle of immaturity and adolescence.

"You better give me those right now and get inside," Hiram warned. "You don't have any protection on, and I saw a couple of those flying things around. You don't want to get turned into a Hell-spawn, do you?"

That got Beth's attention. She lowered the binoculars and looked up and around nervously. "Yeah, right," she said sarcastically.

Hiram snatched the binoculars out of her hands.

"Hey! Quit it!" Beth complained.

"Get below, you little turd," Hiram said, feeling quite victorious.

"I don't have to if I don't want to," Beth remarked petulantly.

"Suit yourself." Hiram shrugged. "Wait around for those things to come and turn you into a big fat Hell-spawn. See if I care." Hiram paused and grinned. "It shouldn't be that hard since you're already a skinny little monster!" He laughed at his own cleverness, but Beth was hurt. She started to cry.

"You're mean, Hiram," she bawled. "I'm going to tell my daddy."

Those words—that threat—were Beth's best weapon against Hiram. He hated Beth's father, but more important, he was afraid of him. Married to Hiram's cousin, Gladys, Joshua Silver had been an Israeli commando fifteen years ago when he had met Gladys while she was vacationing in Israel. Joshua often bragged that he could snap a man's neck, killing him instantly, with just a quick twist of the head.

Hiram believed him. Joshua was a walking advertisement for bodybuilding. As Hiram's mom liked to say—which always got Hiram's dad upset—Joshua had, "muscles on his muscles; he is such a *mensch*!"

"Ssh! Ssh!" Hiram hurried to quiet Beth. "I'm sorry," he added, and pushed the binoculars into Beth's hands to placate her.

She sniffled once and smiled. Hiram frowned; Beth's eyes were dry. She was a little faker.

I wish you *would* swallow an alien! Hiram thought.

Beth held the binoculars up to her eyes and looked downtown where the truck was weaving in and out and around the many cars littering 6th Avenue. "I think they're going to make it," Beth commented, without lowering the glasses.

"I wouldn't bet on it," Hiram said. He stood and stretched. Beth moved into his spot as soon as he stepped away. For a moment, Hiram thought how easy it would be to just push the little pain in the ass over the edge and then go tell everyone she slipped and fell. The Hell-spawn below on the street would gobble her up; she'd be manna from Heaven for those creatures. Her body would be gone in seconds without a telltale trace behind.

I wouldn't even have to tell anyone she fell, Hiram thought, warming to the speculation and trying to rationalize it into a logical thought and a doable action. I could just play innocent—"Why no, Josh, I haven't seen the little bitch, oops, I mean *darling*."

Hiram smiled at the fantasy and eyed Beth. One little push, that's all it would take. She was so close to the edge it wouldn't be hard. A new thought occurred to Hiram and he frowned.

She'd probably scream all the way down and everyone in the house would hear her and blame me.

The urge, the moment of courage, and the window of opportunity to do it faded. Hiram tried to resurrect it by imagining different scenarios. He imagined running downstairs sobbing, hysterically telling everyone Beth had tripped and fallen. Or better yet, she had been attacked by the flying Hell-spawn and had fallen off the roof in her attempt to get away. She wasn't supposed to be up there anyway without protection.

It was a good plan; it worked perfectly in his mind, but what he could imagine and what would really happen were generally miles apart. He knew he could never pull it off; he was a terrible liar and even worse than Beth at faking crying, much less being hysterical. The moment of conviction, of uncertainty—the moment for *action*—was gone. Sighing, Hiram decided to go down to the deli and see if he could sneak something to eat.

7:40 a.m.

The truck managed to get past the intersection at West 15th Street without any trouble. There was a bicycle store and the Okee-Dokee Family Restaurant on the right corner, and a GMC Store and another restaurant, the Left Bank, on the left-hand corner. As the truck sped through the intersection, Joe glanced down East 15th Street and saw several 'Vaders pulling down the rear side wall of the Left Bank restaurant. It reminded Joe of a nature program he had seen on PBS once about bears. It had shown a bear mother and her cubs demolishing a tree to get at a beehive rich with honey inside.

Joe didn't look for long; his attention was needed forward. Between 15th and 16th Streets, there were four abandoned cars and a three-car wreck plus a motorcycle crashed on the left sidewalk. Joe maneuvered the truck deftly past the wrecks and by the abandoned vehicles, but the truck caught the attention of a 'Vader who was in a narrow alley behind the Okee-Dokee Family Restaurant. This small 'Vader was able to move much faster than its larger, lumbering cousins. It came charging out of the alley and chased the swerving truck.

Joe kept his foot firmly on the gas pedal, pushing it to the floor. Besides the fleet-footed monster chasing the truck, Joe had a new worry: he had just noticed that the needle on the gas gauge was hovering just above empty. As the truck reached 16th Street, the chasing 'Vader made its move, a half step behind the truck. It reached out with its right hand as it ran bent over and tried to grab the derrick winch on the back of the truck. Monster fingers brushed the derrick at the same moment Joe cut the wheel hard to the left, clipping the back fender of a brand-new Honda Civic. The compact car spun around from the impact, right into the 'Vader's left foot.

The monster's tenuous reach failed and it tripped over the lime-green Honda. Unable to check, or slow, its forward momentum, the 'Vader sprawled facefirst on the street and tumbled heels over head into the double glass door entrance of the Blue Moon Deli and Grill on the far right corner of 6th Avenue and West 16th Street. The doors gave way to the crashing 'Vader. Amid the sound of glass breaking and wood and metal being crushed, Joe thought he heard the sound of women screaming.

Joe realized—and saw by the looks on Sara's and Corey's faces—there were people hiding inside. He realized many people were probably hiding in stores, offices, apartments; anywhere they could, trying to stay alive and hoping for rescue. It occurred to Joe that the guy who had been eaten by the snake on 11th Street may have been drawn outside by the sound of the truck's approach. He might have thought it was help on the way, but instead it had brought death.

Joe wished he could broadcast to any people hiding inside along 6th Avenue that the truck and its inhabitants were *not* there to rescue them and to stay hidden. Unfortunately even if there were a way, all it would do is attract more 'Vaders.

Like the swarm of orbs flying after the truck now.

"Damn it!" Joe swore at them. With a quick glance in the side view mirror, he estimated at least eight orbs were flying after the truck.

"Look out!" Sara shouted. He looked to the front again. There was a motorcycle lying in the middle of the street. With abandoned cars on both sides of it, there was no other way to go but up and over it, which the truck did roughly, bouncing Joe and the others around violently.

As the truck leveled out again, Cindy suddenly leaned forward and vomited all over her legs and shoes. The vomit stank of soured wine.

"Oh God!" Sara cried, turning toward Joe and burying her face in his right shoulder.

"Gross!" Corey commented emphatically. He pulled his shirt up over his nose and mouth again.

"Ugh!" Sara complained. "Put down your window."

"No!" Joe replied firmly. "We've got visitors."

Sara looked through the rear window just as the flying 'Vaders made their move and encircled the truck.

The air was suddenly filled with a loud booming noise. From around the corner of 17th Street just ahead came a massive 'Vader, at least twenty to twenty-five feet tall. Its feet drummed out the thunderous beat as they hit the pavement. Seeing the approaching truck, the creature hopped over a Poland Spring truck and slid feet first across the intersection like a baseball player sliding into home plate, ending up on its side. The move shook the ground. The creature's supine body almost blocked 6th Avenue completely. Only a narrow spot to the left of the monster's feet was still passable. Joe cut the wheel and headed for it.

One of the orbs attached itself to the window on Cindy's side and melted through in seconds. Immediately it, and two more orbs, flew into the cab.

"Look out!" Sara yelled.

"Keep them away from me!" Joe yelled, trying to steer

the truck and avoid the intruders while bringing the fire extinguisher up from between his legs where it rested. Just as the truck was about to go through the narrow passage between the 'Vader's feet and a Cingular cell phone store, he managed to get off a spray at the orbs, which were very close to invading Sara and Corey.

The three pods crashed through Cindy's window, shattering it in their haste to escape.

Seeing where the truck was heading, the monster 'Vader sat up, reached for it, and grabbed the derrick in the bed of the truck. The vehicle came to a dead, lurching stop with its motor still running.

"Come on!" Joe shouted. He opened his door, grabbed Corey, who was already off Sara's lap and scuttling across the seat on his butt toward him, and jumped out, one arm carrying the extinguisher, the other, Corey. Sara was right behind. Joe staggered backward toward the door to the Cingular store and let Corey's weight and his own backward momentum push him into the recessed entrance of the cell phone store and through the door, which was slightly ajar due to something bloody on the floor wedging it open. Joe tripped over the thing, kicking it out of the doorway and into the store before tumbling inside after it with Corey on top of him.

Sara came in behind them. "Cindy!" she cried, immediately spinning around. The truck was gone, shoved out of the way of the door by the 'Vader. The door swung closed before she could yell again for Cindy.

Corey rolled off Joe and both smelled what had tripped them up—rotting meat—before they saw it, and what they saw didn't really register at first. They looked closer and realized what it was—a severed arm and shoulder, nothing else; still clad in a dark blue business suit and covered with flies and maggots.

Sara saw and smelled it at the same moment as Joe and Corey. She let out a short cry of disgust, put her hand over her mouth and nose, and backed away. Outside, the giant monster suddenly slammed its fist into the door. The glass and metal door ripped from its hinges. A high-pitched screeching sound erupted when the door broke free. The tinkling of glass shattering accompanied the door as it went flying across the store less than a foot above Joe and Corey. Sara managed to jump out of the way just in time. The metal frame of the door hit a glass counter holding a display of various cell phones and shattered it, too, sending the small plastic phones and pieces of glass in every direction. The door ended its violent journey when it crashed into the wall behind the counter and was embedded in the plaster and wallboard.

A cloud of flies rose from the putrid body part and settled again.

The 'Vader's massive hand was too big to get through the opening. It tried but cut its fingers on the wrecked door frame's jagged edges and cried out. The creature stuck its bloody fingers in its mouth and sucked on them.

Joe got up and, without thinking, kicked the stinking bloody piece of torso out into the street. The air was filled with buzzing as the flies were disturbed again. The finger-sucking 'Vader was only too happy to scoop up the rotting human meat for a snack. It was enough to distract the creature from further attacks on the store—for a little while.

"Cindy's still out there! In the truck!" Sara cried, getting to her feet. She started for the door, but Joe grabbed her and held her back.

"We can't do anything about that now," Joe told her.

Sara looked at him angrily, but knew he was right.

Still sitting on the floor, Corey yelled, "Look out!" Outside, the 'Vader had finished its snack and was on its feet again. It kicked the storefront. Both display windows on either side of the wrecked door frame shattered, spraying a blizzard of glass throughout the interior of the store.

Joe threw himself on top of Corey to protect him.

Sara ducked but not quickly enough, or low enough, for her to avoid catching an inch-long sliver of glass in her right shoulder, and a large triangular piece in the side of her head just over her right ear. Several more pieces stuck in her side and back as she fell to the floor, screaming and twisting away from the glass explosion.

Joe immediately got to his knees to examine her.

Joe picked the fire extinguisher off the floor and handed it to Corey. "Get in there!" he yelled at the boy, and pointed at a door just behind the demolished display counter.

Corey followed his command and scrambled to it as quickly as he could.

Joe knelt next to Sara and felt glass digging into his bare kneecaps. He grabbed her left arm and dragged her toward the rear door. Going by the shattered display case, he slipped and fell against it, getting a sharp piece of glass in his upper thigh, but he didn't stop. He pulled it out and grabbed Sara under both arms and dragged her the rest of the way to the door that Corey had opened and was holding for them.

Outside the Cingular store, the giant 'Vader hopped around on one foot, its other cradled against its knee and held with both hands. Three of its toes were bleeding as a result of kicking in the storefront. It whined like a hurt puppy.

7:47 a.m.

In the truck, which was now five feet beyond the entrance to the Cingular store and resting against a yellow taxi that had flipped over, Cindy lay sprawled across the front seat. She was semiconscious and totally unaware of where she was or how much danger she was in. Luckily, for her, the flying 'Vaders that had not been chased off by Joe's fire extinguisher hadn't seen her stay in the truck. They had tried to follow Joe, Corey, and Sara into the Cingular store but were forced to veer off as the giant attacked the front of it. They hovered above and behind the monster 'Vader while it punched and kicked the storefront in a rage similar to a child's tantrum.

7:48 a.m.

"Hurry!" Corey yelled to Joe. He was holding the fire extinguisher under his left arm and the door open with his right elbow. The room beyond appeared to be an office. Joe dragged Sara in. Corey followed and shut the door behind him.

The room was thrown into complete darkness, and the only sounds were Joe's heavy breathing and Sara's soft sobs.

"Corey," Joe whispered, "is there a light switch?"

Corey put the extinguisher down against the door and felt on the wall where he found the switch. He turned the lights on. The office was small and windowless. A cheap metal desk stood against the back wall and a file cabinet next to it. Boxes of cell phones were stacked to the ceiling against every other wall in the office.

Joe propped Sara against the wall next to the door. "Don't move," he told her. She was crying, her face bloody from the shard of glass stuck in the side of her head. Joe knelt next to her, his hand on the glass.

"I'm going to pull this out, so don't move. I don't want to break it and leave a piece in you." Before Sara could answer, Joe yanked the glass out as fast as he could.

Sara screamed, and cried harder.

"Sorry," Joe said.

"I wasn't ready," Sara complained.

"I know," Joe said. "That's why I did it. You weren't antic- ipating it so you were less likely to move."

Sara's crying turned to hopeless laughter.

"What's so funny?" he asked her.

Again, before she could answer, he pulled the large glass sliver from her shoulder.

"Oww!" she cried, followed by, "Damn it! Don't do that again!"

"Sorry." Joe winked at Corey, who looked like he was going to start crying, too. Corey smiled weakly back at him.

There was a sudden loud *thoom*! and the office shook. Several boxes stacked on the left wall fell to the floor.

"Holy shit!" Joe cried, nearly losing his balance and falling on Sara.

The three of them looked up at the ceiling. Another loud booming noise came and the room shook again. More boxes fell to the floor and several ceiling tiles joined them.

Sara tried to regain her feet but gasped at the pain in her side from the glass daggers that were still stuck there.

"Easy," Joe said, ducking his head as more ceiling tiles fell near him. "Can you lock that door, Corey?"

The boy turned around and looked at the round brass knob and pointed to a button in the middle of it. "Is this it?" he asked, and Joe nodded.

"It ain't much, but it's all we've got," Joe said. "Push it in."

Corey did.

"I'm sorry, Sara," Joe said in a low voice. "But I've got to pull these out, too."

"Oh God!" she groaned, but turned and presented her injured side to Joe. He examined the glass, which, like the one in her shoulder, had punctured her flesh through her T-shirt. Joe figured the fabric may have prevented the glass from going deeper. The pieces were smaller than what had been in her head and shoulder. He had them out before Sara realized.

The building shook again and the entire right wall of cell phone boxes toppled over and scattered on the floor.

"What's going on?" Corey asked. He was scared, trying not to look. "Is it an earthquake?"

Boom! The sound came again and the room rattled, as did everything in it, including the people.

"My guess is it's our friendly neighborhood 'Vader—you know, the one who just kicked in the front of this place and gave Sara her edgy piercings."

Sara grimaced at him. "Thanks."

"What about Cindy?" Corey asked next. "She's still out there. What are we going to do?"

Sara couldn't look at him. Joe shrugged and shook his head. "I doubt if she's still out there, kid—or, I should say, still out there *alive*. I know this sounds harsh, but we've got to take care of ourselves. There's nothing we can do for her now."

"She's probably better off," Sara muttered.

Corey looked at them, trying to be brave and act grown

up, but he couldn't do it. His eyes filled with water and large tears rolled down his cheeks. He fought it, but his mouth slowly twisted into a grimace. He cried; a low, keening whine came from his lips.

"Aw, shit!" Sara swore, looking at Corey. "Come here, honey." She motioned him over with her hand and wrapped him in her arms.

Joe looked away and turned his back on them as he wiped a tear from his own eye and tried to hide it by running his hand through his hair. "We've got to get out of here," Joe said, looking at a spot on the ceiling from where several tiles had just fallen. "I can't believe there isn't a back door to this place." No sooner had the words left his mouth when another room-shaking crash sounded, and the cell phone boxes against the back wall collapsed, revealing a metal, fireproof emergency exit door. Stumbling over boxes on the floor and kicking others out of the way, Joe went to the door and tried it.

"*Figures!* It's locked!" There was a keyhole in the knob but no key. Joe quickly searched the desk drawers but found none. The next thundering explosion brought half the ceiling down, along with some chunks of concrete and strands of electrical wiring.

"We're going to get crushed if we stay in here!" Sara shouted.

Joe staggered around the new pile of rubble, waving his hand through the cloud of dust from the fallen building materials. "Pick your poison!" he shouted. "Get crushed in here, or eaten out there." He pointed to the door they had just come through.

"I'll take my chances out there," Sara said. With one arm around Corey, she went to the door. She picked up the fire extinguisher and handed it to Joe.

Joe took it and nodded. "Okay, let's go."

7:52 a.m.

Outside in the truck, Cindy regained a semblance of consciousness and sat up. Her eyes were bloodshot and blurry, but she could see well enough to grab her pocketbook and dig out the pills she had dumped in the bottom. Not bothering to look, or care, what she was taking anymore, she dry-swallowed as many pills as she could find.

"Ohh!" she groaned. The pills refused to go all the way down. They were threatening to come right back up and bring the rest of whatever was left in her stomach with them.

Attracted by her moans and groans, one of the flying orbs left its fellows, who were still hovering around the giant 'Vader trying to punch its way through the side of the Cingular store to get at the human goodies inside, and headed for the truck.

In the vehicle, Cindy fought against the urge to vomit. Pushed over the limit by the pills, her stomach contents were in revolt that she sought to keep contained. But, like most revolutions, sooner or later there is no longer any way to keep the insurgents down, and so it was with Cindy. Just as the lone flying 'Vader zeroed in on her as its target and zipped through her broken window, heading for her gaping mouth, the rebels in her stomach won their first battle.

Rushing up through her throat and out her mouth, the pills, and whatever else was still in her stomach, gushed forth and drowned the glowing orb just as it was about to enter her oral orifice and claim her as one of its own. As soon as the vomit hit the floor of the truck, Cindy bent over and started picking out the still-intact pills, shoving them back into her mouth one by one. She spied one pill partially hidden behind the puke-covered orb. She plucked the orb out of the mess and flicked it back out the passenger window. She then retrieved the last pill, which followed the others down her gullet again.

"I need a drink," Cindy mumbled. Seeing nothing in the truck's cab, she opened the passenger door just as the orb she had discarded was making a comeback. The door caught the flying 'Vader as it rose from the gutter toward the window again and sent it recoiling back to the gutter, where it bounced twice and rolled into a nearby sewer.

7:54 a.m.

The front display area of the Cingular store lay in shambles. Corey, Sara, and Joe stood just outside the back room doorway assessing the danger and destruction, and looking for an avenue of escape. Joe held the extinguisher up and ready as he took a cautious step into the front room and craned his head to look outside to the right, through the shattered side display window. He could see part of the giant 'Vader's leg.

The building trembled again as the 'Vader pummeled the roof some more. In the back room, behind Corey and Sara, a large portion of the ceiling and the network of concrete, metal, and wire above it came crashing down.

"Okay," Joe said, "let's—" His voice stopped abruptly, and he stared with astonishment at the street.

Corey and Sara had been fearfully watching the falling ceiling in the room behind them, but now looked forward. They, too, were astonished by what they saw.

It was Cindy, staggering along the sidewalk as if it were a normal day and she was out for a stroll. She stopped in front of the partially razed Cingular store and looked across the street at the Poland Spring delivery truck crashed against the entrance to a pizza place at the corner of 6th Avenue and West 16th Street. Cases of bottled water and individual bottles were strewn on the asphalt around it. Licking her dry lips, Cindy stumbled off the curb and into the street. She nearly fell.

"I can't believe it," Joe muttered.

Sara called to Cindy as loudly as she dared, trying not to attract the attention of the orbs or the 'Vader around the corner that was continuing to demolish the Cingular store.

Cindy paused a few feet from the gutter and looked around, unsure where Sara's voice had come from, or if she'd even actually heard it.

Sara, walking hand in hand with Corey, followed by Joe carrying the fire extinguisher, stepped gingerly over the glass and debris, trying not to make any noise as they went out to Cindy.

"Cindy! Behind you," Sara called.

Cindy turned around and fixed her bloodshot, bleary eyes on Sara and smiled. "Hey! What's up?" she asked loudly.

Sara, Joe, and Corey shushed her at the same time.

"What?" Cindy asked, not lowering her voice.

Sara grimaced and held her finger to her lips while motioning with her other hand for Cindy to keep it down. Just as Sara, Corey, and Joe stepped out of the wreck of the Cingular store and onto the sidewalk, the hammering sound from the side of the building stopped. The three of them froze where they stood, each looking to the corner of 16th Street.

"Do I know you guys?" Cindy asked as loudly as ever, walking over to them.

Joe looked left at the same moment that Sara and Corey were looking right, and he saw the truck still upright but missing its derrick and tow winch on the back.

To the right, Sara saw an even larger shining squadron of orbs around the corner. They hovered in the air for a moment, as if sizing up the situation. One of them disappeared down West 16th Street while the others made their move, swooping down on the four humans.

"Run!" Sara shouted.

"To the truck!" Joe added on the tail of her command.

Sara grabbed Corey's hand and Cindy's, pulling both of them along with her as she ran to the truck.

Joe faced the orbs, pointed the fire extinguisher at them, and muttered, "Come and get it, boys."

As if they recognized the red fire extinguisher, the orbs suddenly veered off. A moment later the giant 'Vader came around the corner of East 16th Street, with one of the orbs buzzing around its head.

"Let's get the hell out of here," Joe yelled as he reached the driver's door. Behind them the giant 'Vader let out a bellowing roar that was answered by several more close by. Joe didn't like that sound. He pulled open the driver's door and was assaulted by the smell of fresh vomit.

On the opposite side of the truck, Sara and Corey stood with the passenger door open, looking very reluctant to get in. Corey involuntarily gagged at the smell. Sara did the same when she saw the seat and floor awash in puke.

Simultaneously, Sara and Joe looked back at the 'Vader coming around the corner of 16th Street and quickly gauged the odds of their being able to run and find escape or another vehicle with keys still inside. Unfortunately, those odds looked slim to none as the creature advanced. They then looked at each other and knew they had no other choice.

"Get in!" Joe yelled.

Holding their breath, Corey and Sara climbed in. Sara pulled Cindy in after her.

Joe put the fire extinguisher on the driver's seat and took the pistol from his waistband. He didn't know how many bullets were left, but he hoped there were enough. He held the gun in two hands and took quick aim at the 'Vader's head. As he squeezed the trigger, one of the flying orbs flew into his hands and the bullet missed the beast completely. Joe quickly aimed and fired off two more rounds. The second and third bullets found lodging in the monstrous 'Vader's left shoulder and chest, respectively.

The beast howled with pain and clutched at its chest.

Joe fired again, but the trigger clicked empty.

The 'Vader staggered back and tripped on the corner of the Cingular store. The gargantuan fell heavily on its right side, its head crashing through the entrance to a pizza parlor on the opposite corner of East 16th Street. Howling in pain, it lay in the ruins.

Joe tossed the pistol aside and jumped into the truck. He put the fire extinguisher on the floor next to his right leg and within easy reach and started the engine. He cut the wheel to the left, let out the clutch, and hit the gas, launching the tow truck through the obstacle course of the cars ahead.

8:00 a.m.

Hiram Zion walked extra slowly up the back stairs to the roof. In his right hand was a chunk of salami and in his left, a handful of Greek olives he'd snitched from the deli's rationed supplies on the first floor. He wolfed the food down as he climbed at a snail's pace. He knew if his young cousin Beth saw him with food, she'd either tell on him—it wasn't mealtime, the only time they were allowed to eat the carefully rationed portions that Beth's father doled out—or, more likely, demand he share with her.

Hiram didn't like either option; he stuffed the last of the pungent, oily salami into his mouth and then crammed in the few remaining Greek olives. He stood on the last step at the top of the narrow stairs leading to the roof and chewed furiously, painfully swallowing large chunks of food. When he was done, he licked his fingers and hands before wiping them on his dirty Bermuda shorts and opening the roof door.

Beth was still in the same spot as when he'd left her. Though he should have given her his protective gear when he left the roof, he hadn't, hoping the flying aliens would get her. He had left it piled near the stairs. He put it on and walked across the roof. Beth heard him coming and turned, saying something he couldn't hear due to the cotton in his ears. She was pointing down 6th Avenue.

Hiram pulled the cotton from one ear and asked, "What did you say?"

Beth gave him a sour look. "Those people in the truck?" she said, shaking her head and widening her eyes at him as if to imply he was stupid for not hearing her.

"Yeah, what about them?" Hiram answered, her attitude irritating him.

"They're still coming! You missed it," she replied smugly. "You should have seen it. They almost got caught by a really big Hell-spawn, but they managed to hide in a store. At the corner of Fifteenth or Sixteenth Street, I think. Then, the Hell-spawn was wicked mad; it was *so* funny. The Hell-spawn was so angry it kicked the front of the building and hurt its foot. It was crying and hopping around on one foot like you do when you stub your toe."

"I don't do that," Hiram said sullenly.

Beth let out a huffing sigh and rolled her eyes. "I didn't necessarily mean *you*. I meant everyone or anyone who has ever stubbed their toe. Haven't *you* ever done that?"

"No. I'm not a klutz like you!" Hiram said meanly.

Beth shook her head and looked at him askance. "How *old* are you, anyway?" Her tone was biting.

"Old enough to know you're a *bitch*!" Hiram said hastily in anger.

Beth's eyes widened and her mouth opened.

A chill of fear crawled up Hiram's back.

"I'm telling my father," Beth proclaimed.

The fear chill continued up the back of Hiram's neck and on over his scalp. "Aw, come on, Beth," he cajoled nervously. "Can't you take a joke?"

"You *swore*!" Beth accused.

"That's not a swear. A swear is only when you use God's name in vain. You know, like 'Goddammit.' *Bitch* is just a word. It means female dog," Hiram explained.

"I know what it means, and I also know how *you* meant it, and it wasn't nice. Even if you meant it as a female dog, it still wasn't nice of you to call me that."

"I'm sorry," Hiram said, putting on a sad face, hanging his head and looking up at her with sorrowful eyes.

She wavered. Hiram saw it and pounced on the advantage. "I'll show you something cool if you promise not to tell."

Beth looked wary and curious at the same time.

Hiram enticed her with: "It's *really* cool."

Beth regarded him skeptically. "It had better be good or I will tell," she said.

"You've got to promise, first."

"I *said* if it's good I won't. But if you're trying to trick me I'll tell about your swearing *and* that you stole salami out of the deli."

Hiram could feel his face flush hotly with guilt. "What?" he asked. "I didn't do that!" He was not a good liar; his voice quivered and betrayed him. He could see by the look on Beth's face that he wasn't fooling her.

"You stink of it, Hiram," she said, her eyes narrowing.

"You must smell something else," Hiram replied with a nervous chuckle.

Beth shook her head. "I don't think so," she said conde-scendingly. "I don't even have to tell my dad about the salami," she said, smiling wryly. "Don't you think he keeps track of how much food we've got? Don't you think he's going to no-tice what you took?" She grunted, "Huh," and added, "Are you *that* stupid? Because my dad's *not*!"

"I'm telling you, I didn't take anything," Hiram said un-convincingly. He knew Beth was right and that knowledge was making the salami-and-olive snack he'd eaten turn ran-cid in his stomach.

"We'll see," Beth said matter-of-factly, smug in her con-viction that she was right and would be proven so. "Anyway, what's so cool that you have to show me?" she asked doubt-fully.

"Over here," Hiram said, and walked to the edge of the roof. "Give me the binoculars for a second."

Beth handed them over. Hiram turned west, training the glasses on the Empire State Building. There were still two Hell-spawn on the building, and now they appeared to be battling each other for the top spot on the skyscraper.

"Look," Hiram told his cousin as he took her arm and pulled her over to stand in front of him. He handed her the binoculars. "Look at the Empire State Building," he in-structed.

She held the glasses to her eyes and focused them.

Hiram again thought of giving her a shove; she was so close to the edge—like him, she had no fear of heights—it wouldn't take much of a push to send her over.

"Oh, wow!" she cried, interrupting his evil thoughts. "That *is* cool!" she said, her voice excited. "It's like *King Kong* come to life!"

"Yeah," Hiram said, feeling proud that he had impressed her. "That really is the coolest thing ever, right?"

Beth shrugged but didn't lower the binoculars. "I don't know if it's the *coolest* thing *ever*, but it is pretty cool." She lowered the spyglasses and gave Hiram a begrudging smile. "I guess it's cool enough that I won't tell what you called me."

"Thanks," Hiram said with a sense of relief that was too brief as Beth added:

"But you're on your own about the salami. I won't tell on you for that, either, but I won't lie for you. My dad *will* notice, so I'd get cleaned up and brush my teeth if I were you."

Hiram nodded, thinking that was a good idea.

Beth raised the binoculars again. "Whoa!" she said suddenly. "I don't believe it."

"What?" Hiram asked, shielding his eyes with his left hand and looking toward the Empire State Building.

"One of the Hell-spawn that was fighting just fell off," Beth exclaimed.

"Let me see," Hiram said, and reached for the binoculars.

Beth shrugged away from his hand. "You can't now; it's gone, but it was *really* cool. Now *that* might have been the *coolest* thing ever!"

Hiram frowned at her and came very close to getting in trouble again verbalizing the expletives that immediately came to mind. Fortunately, he stopped himself in time.

Beth looked down 6th Avenue again. "I don't see the truck anymore," she said with concern.

"I told you they wouldn't make it."

8:05 a.m.

As the truck went through the 17th Street intersection, Joe looked back to see several 'Vaders pounce on and tear to edible shreds the one that Joe had shot.

Sitting on Sara's lap, Corey kept his T-shirt over his nose against the smell of vomit and also saw the scene through the rear window. He was horrified by it but unable to look away. Corey counted eight monsters in the dinner party—five large ones and three small—that looked like the ones that had been chasing them before with the dogs. More important, he saw the orbs that had been following them from the Cingular store turn around and return to the crowd of feasting 'Vaders. As if the orbs were telling them the truck was escaping, the monsters—especially the smaller ones who were having trouble getting any part of the dead 'Vader with the larger ones around—turned and watched the truck maneuver up the block between 17th and 18th Streets.

The three smaller 'Vaders gave immediate chase as if they figured they had a better chance of catching the truck and eating its inhabitants than they did of getting a fair share of the 'Vader carcass the larger ones were feeding on. Nimble and quick, the three smaller 'Vaders—none of whom were taller than twelve or thirteen feet—jumped, hopped, and danced over and around the discarded vehicles littering 6th Avenue as they raced after the truck.

In the side mirror, Joe saw them, too, and didn't like how fast they were gaining on the truck.

"We *still* need to find a place to hide, and *fast*," Joe said, sounding frustrated.

8:07 a.m.

In the middle seat next to Joe, Sara felt sick from the stench of puke mixed with the smell of gasoline left over from the Molotov cocktails and the stinging acrid smell of the fire extinguisher foam. She tried to breathe through her mouth, but imagined she could *taste* the smell when she did, and that was *much* worse. Adding to her feeling of nausea was the motion of the truck as it swerved from side to side. She tried to brace herself with one hand on the dashboard in front of her, the other on the seat, jammed between hers and Cindy's legs, but it was hard with Corey on her lap. The boy seemed to notice and moved over to sit on Cindy's lap, even though she was covered in regurgitated filth.

Sara's side, where she had been stabbed by the glass daggers, throbbed with aching pulses of pain. She could feel warm blood still flowing from the wounds, soaking her T-shirt and drying quickly, gluing the fabric to her side. Her head hurt, too, where she'd taken glass hits when the giant monster kicked in the storefront, and from when Corey's head had rammed her nose. Though her head didn't hurt as badly as her side, it bled more. She remembered having read somewhere that scalp wounds tended to bleed more, even superficial ones.

She hoped so. The large amount of blood oozing from her head was scary. The wounds on the right side were covered with matted hair from the drying blood. Her right ear was filled with blood and her neck under the ear was caked with it. There was so much blood it had soaked her hair and begun to run in thin rivulets down the right side of her face and into her right eye. She could smell its coppery odor, which didn't mix well with the odor of vomit, as it flowed past her nose and into the corner of her mouth. The blood was hot and tasted sour and salty at the same time.

Every time Joe cut the wheel to swerve around or avoid a car or truck in the street, the pain became as sharp as needles being thrust into her side and head. She bit her tongue to keep from crying and screaming at the pain.

All she could do was hold on.

8:08 a.m.

Corey didn't like the gooey feel, or the stink, of Cindy's puke as he sat on her lap. Sara was still wincing in pain even though he had moved to Cindy's lap. Sara looked pale and the blood flowing down the side of her face brought fear to Corey—fear that she was going to die. He had felt the same fear when he saw his mother carried off and his aunt Helen transformed into a 'Vader intent on eating him. Though he was too young to verbalize it, or even understand it, Sara had become like a second mother to him, and the thought of losing her, too—of watching her die by bleeding to death or at the hands of the 'Vaders and their appetites—was too much to bear.

He wanted to do something to help her, other than staying off her lap, but he couldn't think of anything. He could see the pain in her face every time the truck swerved and jostled her. He wanted to yell at Joe to slow down and stop hurting Sara, but he knew it wasn't Joe's fault; he was driving the way he had to to avoid being caught and killed by the monsters.

Sitting sideways, the way he was on Cindy's lap, Corey could see clearly out the narrow rear window at three 'Vaders chasing them. Corey knew from what Joe had said earlier that they probably had been teenagers or children before they had been infected and transformed by the flying 'Vaders. Watching them getting closer and closer as they chased the truck, Corey felt a mixture of fear and sympathy for the creatures. He knew he very easily could have been one of them, and would have been, or dead, if not for Joe.

Thinking of all that had happened recently, it was difficult to remember that it had only been two days since the 'Vaders' arrival. It felt like months to Corey.

The truck suddenly swerved to avoid two huge 'Vaders that came charging out of West 19th Street at the intersection with 6th Avenue. Corey was nearly tossed to the floor but saved himself by grabbing the dashboard with his right hand and Cindy's arm with his left. The smell of Cindy's puke and the sticky feel of it on his legs was bad, but not as bad as the thought of being thrown into the puddle of puke on the floor in front of Cindy's seat. That was enough to make Corey feel sick to his stomach.

He smiled grimly, thinking that a little while ago, just before he had seen the poor guy being eaten by the giant snake, he had actually been hungry. That hunger was gone now. He looked at Cindy, who appeared to be out of it again. Even if she hadn't vomited all over the inside of the truck and herself, she still smelled bad enough for Corey to lose any appetite that might have returned.

There was a thundering sound followed by a chorus of roars as the truck sped up the block between West 19th and West 20th Street. The road was nearly clear except for several churned-up spots and a Mack truck with the sign FROM AMERICA'S HEARTLAND. It lay on its side, blocking part of the road between Filene's and a place called the Container Store. Two full-grown 'Vaders leaped out from behind the overturned trailer, where they had been stuffing themselves with the truck's contents just as the three smaller 'Vaders reached the overturned trailer truck. The larger, adult monsters faced off against the smaller ones and a fight ensued.

8:13 a.m.

"Look! Look! Look!" Beth cried, jumping up and down. "They're fighting!" she shrieked, shoving the binoculars at Hiram. "Look!" she commanded, and pointed down 6th Avenue.

"Who?" Hiram asked, disgruntled by her excitement. He scanned the wide Avenue of the Americas and went past the oncoming truck before he realized it. He dropped the field glasses and squinted. The sun was bright and hot and made his eyes water; the day was turning into what his father liked to call "a real scorcher."

"You see? You see?" Beth was giggling with excitement.

Hiram raised the binoculars again and found the truck weaving a crooked path as it wound between abandoned traffic. He estimated it was approaching West 20th Street, but it was strange that it was traveling free of any harassment from Hell-spawn or the flying things.

"I don't see any fighting," he said to Beth.

"Go back! Go back!" Beth shouted. "They're farther back."

"No, they're not," Hiram said, misunderstanding her. "They're right down there at Twentieth Street. They're just passing Kinko's."

"Not the truck, *stupid*. Look farther back, down around Nineteenth Street."

Hiram bristled at her calling him stupid. For a moment the comeback, "I'm telling that you called me stupid," sat on the edge of his tongue, but then he thought, who would I tell? He could just hear Beth's father if he told him.

"Hey, the kid's only speaking the truth," he'd probably say, and laugh at Hiram. And if Hiram told his own father, he'd probably berate Hiram for not acting like an adult. "What's the matter with you?" he'd probably say as he had so many times before. "Feh! You act like a child. Grow up for crying out loud you meshugina. Stop being such a nebbish."

"What am I supposed to be looking for?" he asked, and got the answer as he saw the crowd of Hell-spawn just past the 19th Street intersection. He couldn't believe it, but Beth was right; the Hell-spawn *were* fighting and it looked like an all-out tooth-and-nail old-fashioned street fight, as though two rival gangs were going at each other.

"Wow!" was all he could say.

"You see them?" Beth asked, still excited.

"Yeah," Hiram replied. "I see them, but it ain't going to help those people in the truck."

"What? Why?" Beth asked anxiously.

Hiram lowered the field glasses long enough to give Beth a smug, superior look. "*That's* why *I'm* the lookout and you're not. I know what to look for." He made a big show of handing the glasses back to Beth.

"Look to both sides of the Twenty-second Street intersection," he instructed her, his voice condescending.

Reluctantly, Beth took the binoculars and looked where Hiram had indicated. Having heard the truck's engine approaching, 'Vaders lay in wait just around both corners of 22nd Street.

"Oh no!" Beth gasped. "They'll be ambushed!"

"Yeah," Hiram said almost gleefully as he enjoyed her distress.

"We've got to warn them!" Beth cried.

"Yeah, right," Hiram said dismissively.

"No, really!" Beth said. She looked pleadingly at Hiram, her eyes full of tears. "We've got to help them! We've got to warn them!" She started to cry.

Nervous that someone—like Beth's father—would come up to the roof, see her crying, and blame it on him, Hiram took a more gentle tone with her. "I'm sorry, Beth, but I don't see how we can help."

Beth looked down at the truck again, then back at Hiram. "There's got to be something we can do."

8:15 a.m.

"That's it! Kill each other, you bastards!" Joe cried, slapping the wheel when he saw the gang of 'Vaders battling rather than chasing the truck. Even better, the intersection with West 21st Street dead ahead was clear of cars *and* 'Vaders.

Maybe our luck is changing.

"Keep your eyes open for someplace where we can hide, like a restaurant or a grocery store. Someplace that will have food."

At the mention of food, Cindy threw up on herself again.

Corey quickly slid back onto Sara's lap.

With her head lolling on the top of the seat behind her, the vomit bubbled up out of Cindy's mouth and dribbled down her chin. Suddenly she began to choke on it.

"Oh, my God!" Sara cried. "She's choking!" Despite being hurt, and despite the fact that every movement brought pain to her body, Sara reached over and yanked the greasy hair on the side of Cindy's head, pulling her head forward so that the vomit would run out of her mouth and onto her chest.

Cindy coughed and gagged. Her eyes opened wide, and she tried to breathe.

She couldn't.

With a sound like hoarse hiccups she tried to suck in air, but the vomit she had inhaled was lodged in her windpipe, blocking it. She gasped, her mouth gaping and a look of panic on her face.

She grabbed Corey's arm tightly with her left hand and the dashboard with her right, and leaned over, her chest heaving but still not taking in any air.

Her eyes were wild with fear.

Sara tried to slap her on the back, but between the pain in her arm and being too cramped to be able to gain more leverage, she couldn't do more than give Cindy a weak pat.

"Pull over!" she ordered Joe. "I've got to give her the Heimlich maneuver. I can't do it in here."

"That's not a good idea," he replied to Sara.

Joe had kept his eye on the mirror and the battle of the beasts behind them. A few seconds ago, he had seen the orbs that had been urging the smaller 'Vaders on were now flying around the group of brawlers. As though the orbs had some sort of command over the monsters, the beasts stopped fighting and looked around to see the truck almost too far away for them to catch. With the orbs leading the way, every 'Vader that had been fighting gave it up and ran after the truck.

It had become obvious to Joe that the orbs were not mindless, but possessed intelligence and the ability to communicate with, command, and control the deformed abominations of nature they turned living beings into.

"We've got to do something!" Sara said, panicking. "She's choking to death."

"Corey," Joe commanded, "reach over Cindy and grab the door handle. Can you get it?"

Corey tried but Cindy was leaning forward and in his way.

"Hold her back for a minute, Sara," Joe told her. "Now try, Corey," he said after Sara put her right arm across Cindy's chest and pulled her back against the seat.

Corey leaned over and was able to grab the door handle this time.

"Good," Joe said. "Now open the door."

Corey looked unsure of what to do; he looked from Joe to Sara.

"You can't just kick her out!" Sara cried, outraged.

Joe smiled and shook his head. "No, no. If he opens the door, you can swing her about and get your arms around her and do the Heimlicking thing."

Sara immediately saw what he meant and that it would work. She nodded at Corey, who looked relieved that they weren't going to just dump Cindy out the door and leave her for the monsters.

Corey grabbed the door handle and tried to push it open but couldn't against the force of the truck's forward momentum.

Joe saw it and slowed the truck. "Hurry," he commanded.

Corey grabbed the handle again and shoved the door open.

"Help me turn her," Sara grunted.

Through all this, Cindy continued to try to breathe, but she was growing weak. She grabbed at Corey and Sara and her head jerked back and forth. Her body squirmed to the point of convulsion.

Sara could barely get her arm around Cindy's midsection. Without Corey's help, as he knelt in the vomit on the floor and pushed Cindy's kicking legs toward the door, Sara never would have turned her.

Once they managed to do so, and Cindy was facing the open door with her legs hanging out, Sara had trouble getting both arms around her due to the pain from her own wounds and Cindy's panicky movements.

"Come on. Come on, hurry," Joe urged, slowing the truck to a near halt and keeping an eye on the monsters coming up 6th Avenue.

Sara finally got both arms around Cindy and clasped her right hand into a fist with her left hand over it, just under the middle point of Cindy's rib cage. She found the right spot for the Heimlich maneuver easily.

Sara pulled her fist abruptly back into Cindy's midsection. Cindy convulsed once and her head flopped back and forth, but her throat remained blocked. Sara tried again and got a loud, reeking fart from Cindy but nothing else. She did manage to open a rasping, tiny stream of breath, but it wasn't enough to sustain Cindy. Sara felt her growing weaker.

Sara gave one more tug, as hard as she could, knowing this would be her last attempt due to the excruciating pain in her side every time she tried. Cindy's head snapped forward, she coughed, and something flew from her mouth, followed by a gush of vomit that went all over her own legs and sprayed on the door.

"Got it!" Sara yelled. With Corey's help, she pulled Cindy back so that she was facing front again.

"Good!" Joe replied, and stepped on the gas. Cindy's door slammed shut. The truck took off through the 21st Street intersection with the gang of monsters twenty yards behind. As the truck wound around three wrecked cars littering the road just after the intersection, Joe noticed one of the silvery glowing orbs that had been flying along at the head of the pursuing gang of gargoyle-ish 'Vaders, as if leading them, suddenly flew far forward of the pack at a great speed until it drew alongside the truck.

Figuring the pod was looking to infect one of them, Joe swerved away from the thing, but instead of following, it continued past the truck so fast it became a blur. Distracted at that moment by Corey almost falling off the edge of the seat, where he sat wedged between Sara and Cindy, and into the puddle of vomit on the floor, Joe didn't see where the speeding orb had gone—whether it had continued on up 6th Avenue or if it had turned off at the 22nd Street intersection.

8:20 a.m.

Beth was a jiggling bundle of worry as she stood at the front corner edge of the roof and watched the truck down on 6th Avenue head for certain destruction.

Hiram's joy at seeing her so distressed was short-lived and turned sour. Though she was frequently a thorn in his side, and had on more than one occasion caused him trouble with both her father and Hiram's own father, he could not help but feel bad for her now. Out of that sympathy for her came a sudden idea.

"I know what we can do," he said. While Beth anxiously looked on, Hiram knelt and pulled a cardboard box from under the lawn chair. In it he kept things like the binoculars and his cell phone, among other supplies. At the bottom of the box were two automotive flares that Beth's father had put in there in case rescue came at night.

"Ta-da!" Hiram sang out as he triumphantly held up the flare.

Beth asked, "What's that?"

"A flare," Hiram answered, unwrapping the tip of the stick that held the striker for lighting the flare.

"What good will that do?"

"For one thing, it will let them know we're here. If I wave this around and then throw it toward them, they'll look up and see us. We can use hand signals like a traffic cop to tell them to stop or back up and go another way." Hiram was quite proud of his brainstorm and showed it, beaming at Beth. She, on the other hand, regarded him and his plan dubiously.

"What?" Hiram demanded of the skeptical look on her face.

She just shook her head.

"Hey, listen. It's the only thing we've got right now. I don't hear you coming up with any plans."

Beth had to face the truth of that statement and shrugged. "I guess it's better than nothing," she grudgingly admitted.

"Darn right. In fact, it's better than most things and it's certainly better than anything else we've got."

Beth raised the binoculars and looked down at the truck again.

"You better hurry," she said. "They just went through Twenty-first Street."

"Okay," Hiram said. "Stand back. Here goes," he exclaimed. He struck the end of the stick on the flint paper that was on the cap. He got nothing but sparks. He grinned and tried again. Same result—a lot of sparks but no flame.

Beth shook her head in disgust.

Hiram was about to try the flare a third time, but Beth suddenly pointed over his head and cried, "Look out!"

Hiram turned and saw a flying orb coming straight at him. Too late, he realized he had taken his right earplug out in order to hear Beth. He tried to duck, but the orb anticipated his move and ducked with him. He tried to swat it aside, but it swerved, grew smaller as it did, and went in his ear.

8:22 a.m.

Joe piloted the truck through the 22nd Street intersection and his unspoken question of where the other orb went that had flown past the truck so quickly was answered. It reappeared from the right side of the intersection, followed by three more hungry-looking 'Vaders. If that wasn't bad enough, four more 'Vaders entered the intersection from East 22nd Street to the left. Together, all seven 'Vaders now gave chase, followed by the original group less than fifteen feet behind.

Joe never let up on the gas and was happy to see that 6th Avenue, for several blocks ahead, had few obstacles, other than broken pavement, blocking the road. Behind the truck, the monsters who had been fighting each other caught up with the new 'Vaders from 22nd Street. They formed a mob of demoniacal nightmare creatures.

Joe managed to stay well ahead of the hungry crowd through the 23rd and 24th Street intersections. As the truck approached 25th Street, it staggered in its forward motion and the engine skipped a beat. Joe looked at the gas gauge and saw the needle on *E*.

"Oh no! Not now! God, please not now!"

Pumping the gas, Joe urged the truck on toward the Zion Gourmet Deli just ahead. He figured if they could just get close enough to the deli on the corner of 25th Street before the truck ran out of gas, they could run the rest of the way on foot and hopefully get inside.

Joe pushed the truck on at top speed, hoping to find enough left in the tank to propel them the twenty-five yards more they needed to reach the deli.

8:23 a.m.

On the roof of the Zion Gourmet Deli, Hiram Zion was discovering for real just how different his life was going to be since the invasion of the creatures his father had named the Hell-spawn. He staggered back toward the middle of the roof as he felt the orb go in his ear, tickling like water does after a swim. But the tickling sensation quickly became a piercing pain that exploded in his head and sent out tentacles of burning torture that reached along every nerve and sinew of his body. A strobe light went off in his eyes and his mind— his personality—the *things* that had made Hiram Zion, Hiram Zion, ceased to exist.

His cousin Beth watched in mute horror as Hiram's head snapped back, his eyes rolled up into his head, and his entire body began to vibrate. Like a balloon inflating, Hiram inflated, growing out of his clothes, which fell to the rooftop in shreds. He dropped the unlit flare and the striking cap and staggered back a few steps, his body never letting up from its shimmy-shimmy dance.

Beth wanted to cry for help. She opened her mouth to do

so but all that came out was a weak little squeal, the kind of noise a squeeze toy would make. She wanted to run to the roof door to escape her transforming cousin but found she couldn't do that, either. Hiram was blocking the way. And his transformation happened so fast her running became a moot point.

She was trapped. Worse, she was trapped at the edge of the roof by Hiram, whom she had sensed hated her when he was human, and now seemed to hate her even more as a Hell-spawn by the way he was looking at her.

As Hiram Hell-spawn reached his full monstrous size of eighteen feet and looked down hungrily at Beth, she saw only one chance to escape. She reached down without taking her eyes off the monster in front of her and picked up the flare and striker pad.

Hiram Hell-spawn opened his mouth, now filled with row upon row of jagged spiked teeth, and appeared to grin at Beth. His huge arms and hands reached for her, and the deadly grin grew as his mouth opened wider.

At the last second, just as Hiram the monster leaned over, his massive hands coming together to grab her, Beth struck the flare on the flint pad on the cap. It spit and burst into flame. The sparks and sight of the burning flare caused Hiram Hell-spawn to pause just long enough for Beth to make her move. She lunged forward, jammed the burning flare into the top of her former cousin's left foot, and did a tumble and roll between his legs.

The flare seared an instant hole in Hiram's now-huge foot, and stuck there, burning deeper. He let out an inhuman howl, both of pain from the flare and anger at Beth's escape. He tried to turn to give chase while at the same time reaching for the flare. He lost his balance.

As she ran for the roof door, Beth glanced back just in time to see a look of surprise on her former cousin's grotesque face as he teetered on the edge of the roof . . . and went over.

8:24:35 a.m.

"Almost there," Joe muttered to himself. He glanced in the side mirror and saw the truck was pulling away from the pursuing monsters. Joe kept the gas pedal to the floor, all the while keeping an eye on the mirror and the pack chasing them. Though the needle read empty, the truck continued on as fast as it could go.

Just as the truck reached the Zion Gourmet Deli, a shadow fell over it. From out of the sky came the body of a 'Vader. It hit the pavement five feet in front of the truck and splattered on the asphalt. With the truck going so fast, Joe was barely able to turn the wheel enough to avoid it. The swerve sent the truck crashing through the 6th Avenue display window of the Zion Gourmet Deli, and its front end smashing out the other side through the 25th Street display window.

After the shattered glass and the building debris and dust had settled, the only noise was a moaning, creaking sound from the building itself, with two of its front supports no longer there to hold it up as it leaned toward the 25th Street and 6th Avenue intersection.

8:25 a.m.

Beth Silver ran to the edge of the roof and stood transfixed as she watched her former-cousin-now-monster fall to his death. For a moment she was mesmerized by the grace of the huge, deformed body as it fell, somersaulting head over heels until it hit 6th Avenue. Blood and other fluids erupted from the grotesque carcass, flying in all directions. She saw the truck veer toward the deli to avoid the fallen body of her monster-cousin, and a moment later the building shook beneath her feet as the truck crashed into the first floor.

Beth was running for the rooftop exit when she felt the building begin to sway.

8:33 a.m.

Joe woke with his face against the steering wheel. He sat back, staring at the blood on the wheel and on the front of his T-shirt. For a long moment, he didn't know where he was and was unaware of anyone else in the truck with him. He came to awareness with a sharp, surprised inhalation of air. He looked around. Corey was upside down, his head and shoulders on the floor at Cindy's feet, in the drying vomit. His legs and feet were twisted around, his right foot on Cindy's left shoulder and his left foot in Sara's face. Her nose bled freely all over Corey's sneakers.

Sara and Cindy both appeared to be unconscious, but Corey was moaning and moving. Joe reached over and grabbed the back of Corey's pants. He pulled the boy up to the seat. Corey was crying as he came up. His head and the right side of his face were covered in Cindy's puke.

Corey touched a hand to his head, looked at it, gave it a sniff, and cried harder.

"It's okay," Joe said, fighting a chuckle in his voice, and reached for Corey. He paused in mid-reach and listened to an ominous groaning sound. He had to kick the driver's door to get it open. He jumped out, his sneakers crunching broken glass underfoot, and looked around.

The former deli was in shambles. An elderly, bald-headed man lay propped against one of the deli counters. Joe couldn't tell if he was dead or unconscious.

In the truck, Sara and Cindy were coming to. Joe reached in, took Corey in his arms, and pulled him out of the truck.

"You okay?" he asked the boy, who seemed to be moving all right, if a little dazed. He put Corey down outside the truck and heard the groaning sound again. He realized the sound was coming from overhead. Dust showered down on him and Corey. He looked where the truck had knocked out the wall and could see the top half of it was slowly moving downward.

The groaning grew louder.

"Let's go, ladies!" Joe shouted at Sara and Cindy, who were looking groggy and stupefied.

Joe leaned past the truck cab to look out into the street. The pack of 'Vaders that had been pursuing the truck were now crowded around the monster that had fallen in the street. Joe reached in the truck and grabbed Sara's arm. Pulling her across the seat to him, he whispered, "We need to get out of here before the pack out there finishes its meal and remembers we're here for dessert."

Sara nodded, though she was too dazed to understand what Joe meant. When the truck hit the Zion Gourmet Deli, Sara's forehead had connected with the windshield, starring it into a five-pointed crack. Her mouth was full of blood from biting her tongue when her head met the glass. She let Joe pull her along the seat. She reached out with both arms and embraced him as he lifted her from the truck.

The building overhead groaned again, louder. A heavy torrent of plaster and dust poured down. Joe looked around and was certain that the edge of the wall was definitely moving. The building was swaying, off balance. There was no doubt about it. He put Sara down next to Corey and turned back for Cindy and was surprised to see that she had already slid across the seat and was climbing out without his assistance.

Sara and Corey were standing next to the truck's right front fender, looking at the old man on the floor. As Cindy got out of the truck, Sara went over to the man and knelt next to him. She put two fingers to his neck, feeling for a pulse.

"Is he dead?" Corey asked in a low voice.

Sara shook her head. "I don't know." She leaned closer to the old man's face. "I think he's breathing, but it's hard to tell."

"Come on," Joe said to her. He pushed Corey and Cindy toward the smashed front end of the truck, where there was just enough of a gap between the truck and the demolished wall for them to squeeze through.

"We can't leave him!" Sara complained.

Joe looked up at the ceiling from where plaster dust still fell like a fine rain. "I don't think we can take him, either," Joe said. "We need to get out of here *now*!"

From the rear of the deli came the sound of voices. A door opened and a young, heavyset woman came bustling out.

"Uncle Herschel?" she called before she saw the man on the floor with Sara bent over him.

"What have you done to my uncle?" the woman shrieked, charging across the debris-strewn floor.

Sara stood and backed away from the prone old man.

A small crowd of people of various ages with features similar enough to reveal they were all related followed the upset woman. They were halfway across the room when the building groaned again and leaned a little more toward the intersection.

Outside, the largest 'Vader that had been the slowest in pursuing the truck and had arrived last heard the voices from inside the building. As the rest of the beasts ate their fill of Hiram Hell-spawn's remains it came closer, listening and trying to see inside to grab a meal. At that moment, Hiram's elderly mother opened a second-floor window and looked out. The huge 'Vader saw her and leaped up to try to grab her. It was just short of the window, but its jump carried it far enough that it could grab hold of the edge of the building's rococo dressing, adding its weight to the already leaning structure.

With a groan louder than the rest, the building leaned forward and kept leaning until it fell over, collapsing with a rumbling sound not unlike thunder into the 6th Avenue intersection. The building came down so fast the mob of feeding monsters in the street had no chance to avoid it. Those that weren't killed instantly were buried alive.

8:40 a.m.

Lying flat on his back in the middle of East 25th Street, Joe came to, sat up, and spit dust from his mouth. Next to him, Sara, Corey, and Cindy did likewise, rising from the dust of the destroyed building. In unison they all looked at the pile of rubble that had been the Zion Gourmet Deli. Only part of the building's rear wall remained standing. The outer limit of the debris line was less than five yards from their feet. Looking at it, then at each other, they realized that had been the distance between death and life.

Corey stood first, an inch-thick coating of dust falling from him as he did. The dust was everywhere, under his clothes, in his mouth and nose, and stuck to the blood and vomit on his face and head. Much of the dust in his hair and on his upper body fell away when he stood, but just as much stayed where it was caked to the blood and puke.

For a moment, Corey was dazed by what had just happened. He was amazed that they had escaped. Once again, he realized Joe had saved his life. The family in the Zion Deli, though, was nowhere to be seen. The last thing Corey could remember was the large woman from inside the deli rushing toward Sara. At the same moment Joe had yelled, "It's coming down!" and snatched Corey up in his arms. Carrying him, Joe had run out of the deli, ducking under the hole the truck had punched through the opposite wall and window. Corey had caught a glimpse of Sara running right behind them, pulling Cindy in tow. One moment Corey was looking at the top of the building, then at the blazing sun where the building had just been. Darkness had followed.

He realized now that when the building had collapsed, practically on their heels, Joe and the girls had either been knocked off their feet or had dived to the ground to avoid flying material from the building. Whichever it was, Joe had landed on top of Corey, but not with his full weight, and both of them had lost consciousness. Squeamish needles of apprehension shot through Corey's lower abdomen as he remembered the large pack of 'Vaders that had been chasing them. He looked around furtively, making a complete circle, but there was no sign of them; no sign of anything alive in his immediate vicinity except for Joe, Sara, and Cindy, who were now rising and shaking off the remains of the Zion Gourmet Deli, and a lot of flies that were being attracted by the upchuck that was mostly all over him and Cindy, and to a lesser degree, Joe and Sara.

8:45 a.m.

"Oh, my God," Sara said weakly, looking at the destruction around her. She spit out building dust and blood came with it.

"I can't believe we got out of there," she mumbled to no one in particular.

When Joe had yelled, "It's coming down," inside the deli,

Sara hadn't known what he was talking about. At first she had thought a 'Vader was coming down on them, but from where she had no idea. Only her instincts and trust of Joe had got her moving right behind him, grabbing Cindy's arm as she followed Joe. It wasn't until she was ducking under the gap in the wall that she realized the building was unstable and going down. A rumbling sound had filled her ears as she ran onto 25th Street. The next thing she knew she was lying on her stomach, barely able to breathe for all the dust in her mouth, nose, and everywhere else.

"Are you okay?" Corey asked her, coming to her side and taking her hand.

"Yeah, I think so," she answered. But as she turned to him, the multitude of her recent injuries cried out in pain, belying her words. She groaned and grabbed at her side where her fresh blood stuck to bloody, filthy T-shirt like glue.

"Are you sure you're okay?" Corey asked, his voice full of concern and worry.

Sara inhaled sharply and with pain. "Yeah," she grunted; she was anything but okay. Her head was both pounding with a thick headache and throbbing from the wounds on her forehead. She sneezed suddenly and shrieked at the pain she felt radiating from her nose over her entire face. Blood flew from her nostrils and gushed over her lips and chin. Her ears began ringing with a high-pitched tone so loud she could barely hear anything else. Every joint and muscle in her body felt as though it had been torn apart and glued back together incorrectly. She didn't know which hurt the worst, her head, her nose, her side, or her neck and back. From the waist up, she was a walking example of acute pain; from the waist down, she hurt less, but not by much.

Realizing they were exposed where they were, she nervously looked around. "Now what are we going to do?" she asked Joe, who, likewise, was on his feet. His face was bloody but he looked beyond the blood at their situation.

Joe looked at his watch, but it was broken.

Sara looked at hers. "It's 8:45," she told him.

"We'd better find someplace to hide quick," Joe said. "I

get the feeling this spot is going to be swarming with 'Vaders soon."

8:46 a.m.

Cindy Raposa stood, feeling pain similar to Sara's, yet worse. Hers was not just physical pain due to the wounds and bruises to her flesh. Hers was also a pain of want, of need—a deep-seated ache for the thing her body craved, the thing she thought she couldn't live without. And by this point in her life, she may have been right; if she didn't find a place to cook and shoot up her junk soon, she was going to find out.

She stood in the street, covered in as much dust and blood as the other three, but more dazed and stunned than the others. The events of the last eight or nine hours were a hodge-podge of images in her mind; pictures flashing and revolving randomly like a slideshow projector out of control. The imagery of the here and now that her eyes were perceiving made little more sense than the carousel of photos spinning in her head.

"We'd better get moving," a good-looking guy said to her and a familiar woman next to her. The man held the hand of a young boy. Looking at them, the names *Joe* and *Corey* came to mind, but she was unsure which name belonged to whom. The girl next to her brought no name to mind, just a mix of feelings—dislike, gratitude, and an overall feeling of sadness and envy—without a clue as to why she felt that way.

The enigmatic girl took her hand, asking, "Are you okay?" to which Cindy nodded, despite her outer and inner pain. Her head felt disconnected from her body, as if it might roll off her shoulders if she nodded too much. She hunched her shoulders and pressed her chin into her neck to prevent that from happening. With the cute man—Corey or Joe— leading the way, and the girl who brought such a diverse array of emotions pulling Cindy along by the hand, they turned right heading for the corner of East 25th and 6th Avenue, where they had to climb over rubble and be careful of sharp-ended debris amid the devastation. Cindy looked around at the destruction, the pile of stone that had been a building, and had no clue how it happened.

In the distance, she heard a howling unlike any dog or animal she had ever heard. The sound made her skin crawl with fear. With the fear came the shakes and she trembled from head to toe.

8:48 a.m.

Joe Burton was not a religious man. Like Sara, he had been raised Catholic and had received all the sacraments up to and including Holy Confirmation. Since then—the eighth grade at St. Bernard's School in Portsmouth, New Hampshire—he had pretty much distanced himself from the church and religion in general. When it came to God, he had decided on the agnostic view—the I-don't-know dogma—until the invasion had descended on humanity.

Since then he had come to the unwanted, but inevitable, conclusion that what was happening *was* the end of the world—the Apocalypse. At his first realization of that, he had thought the 'Vaders were proof positive that there was no God. But as things had unfolded since Sunday—which seemed years ago—he was no longer so sure. When his life wasn't in any immediate danger he had been forced to think about, consider, and attempt to solve the riddle of where did the 'Vaders come from and why was this happening. A lot of what he had been taught about God and religion now began to make sense. He had, in fact, now reached the opposite conclusion, in a roundabout, subconscious way, that the 'Vaders were proof *positive* of God's existence.

Though Joe had not been religious or God-fearing (or loving for that matter) in the pre-'Vader days, he had considered himself to be a spiritual person. As far as certain religious teachings went, such as the Ten Commandments and Christ's creed of love and forgiveness for everyone, he would have acknowledged that, in that manner, he could be considered a Christian. As a spiritual person, Joe had been drawn to any and all philosophical discussions, explorations, investigations, and representations of God and religion. Most of these had come to him via television; in particular though the History Channel, the Discovery Channel, and public television programming.

Now, in the few spare moments during which he could actually think about such things, he had begun to see the 'Vaders in the same light as Noah had seen the Flood: sent by God to "weed out" humanity, so to speak. At least that's what he hoped. His, Sara's, Corey's, and even Cindy's continued survival despite the odds and all that had happened to them seemed to him to reveal that the 'Vader apocalypse, while being the end of the world as it had been, it was *not* the end of humanity. He didn't know what was going to happen; whether surviving humanity was going to have to adjust to not being top dog on the food chain anymore, or if they would discover some way to defeat the monsters or get rid of them. If it was the former, life was going to get bad and return to a primitive level of existence for mankind. If the latter, it would probably get worse before it got better, but it *would* get better, then there would be a period of rebuilding and a lot of change.

Change was the important word, the important lesson to be learned from all this.

These thoughts ran through Joe's head as he, Corey, and the girls ran up 6th Avenue in the bright morning sun and heat. Joe was afraid that all the 'Vaders within hearing distance of the deli's collapse would soon be as thick as the flies that now followed.

8:52 a.m.

Corey was afraid, as afraid as he had ever been at the worst times in the past few days. He didn't like being out in the open and exposed. Being on foot also scared him. The truck might not have offered much protection, but he had felt safe there. At least in the truck they could try and outrun the 'Vaders. On foot . . . they didn't have a chance.

Running up 25th and 26th Streets, looking for a place to hide, Joe tried every door along the block, but they were all locked.

As they approached 26th Street, Corey heard a faint rumbling sound approaching. "You hear that?" he asked the others in an urgent, low voice.

They all nodded.

Joe led them into a parking lot just before the 26th-Street intersection, and they hid behind an SUV parked just inside the gate. A few moments later a whole troop of 'Vaders passed by, accompanied by several pods that buzzed around the monsters like the flies that buzzed around Corey and the others. One of them stopped as it went by the parking lot. It hovered in the air as if sensing the presence of the humans, but then, finding itself alone, sped off to catch up with the others. Corey and the three adults with him let out a collective sigh of relief.

"Maybe we should check these cars out," Sara whispered to Joe, "and see if we can use any of them, so we're not so exposed."

Joe looked around, but shook his head no. "I doubt if we'll find the keys in any of them," he replied. "This is a secure lot. People pay big bucks to park here so their cars *won't* get stolen. Besides, using a car now would just attract attention. We need to find a place to hole up and hide until dark or we can figure out what to do."

"What's to figure out?" she said hopelessly. "All we need to figure out is how to stay alive . . . and I'm not even sure if there's a point to *that* anymore."

"Don't say that," Corey said. "There's always something to live for." He said it so seriously and sincerely it made Sara blush. She met Corey's eyes and felt like crying.

"Like you said before: 'From out of the mouths of babes,'" Joe said softly, bringing Sara even closer to tears.

"I'm f-f-freezing," Cindy said suddenly. Her teeth were chattering in time to her body's delirium tremens.

Sara, Joe, and Corey looked at each other with disbelief. The air was so hot and muggy they could have cut it with a knife. They each had sweat making rivulets through the dust on their faces. Their hair was damp with sweat, which, as much as the drying vomit on them, attracted nasty flies, large and small.

"What are we going to do with her?" Joe asked Sara.

"What can we do? We take her with us." Sara swatted at flies and noticed Corey looking from her to Joe nervously. He reached out and squeezed her hand. She squeezed it back and smiled at him.

Joe said, "Do you think she can keep going like this? I mean look at her."

"She needs an f-i-x," Sara spelled the word, hoping to keep Corey in the dark. It didn't work.

"I can spell, you know," he said so seriously Sara and Joe felt like laughing.

"Sorry," Sara said.

"Why would you spell *fix* anyway?" Corey asked, suspicious that Sara and Joe were keeping secrets from him. He shooed tiny black flies from around his eyes. "You guys need to get fixed as much as she does," he added.

"He's got us there," Joe whispered, and chuckled.

"Thanks, Corey." Sara smiled, and whispered, "I guess we could all use some fixing up. You, too."

"Shh!" Corey said suddenly. "I hear more 'Vaders coming."

8:55 a.m.

On the roof of Cho's Chinese Restaurant, on the corner of East 27th Street and 6th Avenue, New York City patrolman Duane Murphy and Louie Lafayette, a former bookie and owner of Shangri-La Imports next door to Cho's, lay on their stomachs, facing south. Officer Murphy was wearing his dark blue NYPD summer uniform with its dark blue short-sleeve shirt and matching pants that he had cut the legs off above the knees for relief from the heat. He held the telescopic lens of a camera to his eye. Lying next to him, Lafayette, a small, grubby individual, was a bundle of nerves. With balding blond hair and fair, but pockmarked, skin, Louie Lafayette

felt like a neon sign next to Murphy who, as Lafayette thought
of him, was, "blacker than midnight in a grave."

Lafayette was sweating profusely compared to Murphy,
but Louie was wearing a long-sleeve dark blue sweatshirt
and pants with high-top black sneakers whose white rubber
soles he had blackened with a permanent marker. Louie
wanted to blend in with the black rooftop as much as possible and not make it any easier for the glowing globe things,
or the monsters, to see him and do him in.

Louie raised his head and looked south, but ducked again
almost immediately as two twenty-foot terrors came loping
down 6th Avenue heading south.

"Jesus," Lafayette whispered. "They're having a regular
family-fucking-reunion down there, pardon my French, ain't
they?"

Murphy didn't answer or acknowledge Louie in any way.

Louie scowled at him.

"What do you see?" he asked. "Any sign of them?" A
barely perceptible negative shake of the head was Murphy's
answer. It was more than Louie expected. "I told you they
wouldn't make it."

Since he had first seen it, Murphy had kept tabs on the
tow truck making its way up 6th Avenue. Right after the truck
had crashed two blocks away, and the building it had crashed
into had collapsed, Murphy had seen a man, two women,
and a boy going from door to door between 25th Street and
26th, but had lost sight of them when he'd had to duck as
monsters headed down 6th Avenue to the site of the building
collapse, where they picked through the rubble, eating anything and everything, living or dead, that they found.

Personally, Louie was glad. In his opinion, there were already too many people living in Cho's Restaurant and
Shangri-La Importers. If he had been in charge, as he
thought he should be since he owned the building housing
the restaurant and his import store, instead of Officer Murphy and Professor Ligget, some egghead from NYU, he
wouldn't be wasting his time on the roof looking for more

people to bring in, more mouths to feed. At least not more *men*. Some good-looking broads would be nice, though.

"Get below," Murphy said to him in that low rumbling voice of his, "and tell the professor I think they've gone to cover until nightfall somewhere on the next block. Tell him I'm going to stay up here for a while longer."

"Sure, sure," Louie whispered nervously. He hated the fact that every time Murphy spoke to him, no matter what he said, he scared the shit out of Louie. Murphy's being a cop and Louie's being a bookie, among other illegal things, was the main reason for his fear, but he thought even if he, himself, were a straight arrow Murphy would still scare him. And it wasn't because he was black, either—he was just a scary guy; there was something menacing about him. Of course, his being six-two and bulging with muscles helped.

As soon as Louie went through the lift-up trapdoor that led to the top-floor storage area of the restaurant, Officer Murphy relaxed, lowered the binoculars, and pulled out a round can of Copenhagen long-cut chewing tobacco. He took out a clump and put it in his mouth between his front lower teeth and gum. Murphy had been a heavy smoker but had given it up three years ago. It hadn't been that hard, really. It had got so he couldn't smoke anywhere except in the privacy of his own apartment, anyway, so he had switched to the chew. Before D-Day—*Doomsday,* his name for the day the alien pods had invaded—he had figured that sooner or later, the way things were going, smokers would soon become an extinct breed. Murphy smirked and spat out tobacco juice.

Now the entire human race was an endangered species.

9:00 a.m.

Three buildings away from the parking lot, Joe found the door to a small dry-cleaning shop unlocked. He, Corey, Sara, and Cindy slipped inside a few seconds before two more monster 'Vaders came rushing down 6th Avenue, following the others that had gone by before. They didn't notice the foursome and there were no orbs with them.

Inside the dry-cleaning store, the air was hotter and stuffier than outside. Though there was an air-conditioning system, Joe cautioned against turning it on since it was in the window over the front door and vented into the street. He was afraid it would attract attention, and they had all seen what the monsters could do to a building.

As soon as they were inside and out of immediate danger, Sara took Cindy into the shop's decent-sized bathroom so they could both wash off the blood and puke. Cindy revived quickly, and when Sara went out into the shop to get her some new clothes, Cindy locked the bathroom door and cooked a spoonful of scag for her much-needed fix. Sara came back and knocked on the door when she found it locked, but Cindy called out, "I'm taking a dump." Twenty minutes later she opened the door, and Sara gave her a pile of clothes to choose from. She came out wearing a long-sleeve New York Jets sweatshirt over a pair of black culottes, and looked like her old high self. She didn't say anything, but she looked embarrassed when Corey asked her if she had got "fixed up" in the bathroom.

Joe came to her rescue saying, "Yeah. Now it's your turn to get fixed up."

Sara helped Corey wash off the blood, dust, and dried vomit. She washed his hair with Ivory soap and carefully cleaned his cuts and scrapes. He put on a pair of neon-green bathing trunks Joe brought him and a black sleeveless T-shirt with the Nike logo on the breast.

Sara finished cleaning up next, taking care to clean all her wounds, and came out wearing a light-blue cotton sundress.

Joe was the last to use the bathroom and, after carefully washing and cleaning his wounds as well, changed into gray sweat-shorts and a matching gray T-shirt with ABERCROMBIE AND FITCH stenciled across the front.

When everyone was washed and dressed in new clean clothes, Joe searched the front of the store. From a first-aid kit he had found under the register counter, Joe doled out aspirin to everyone except Cindy—who refused it—and applied antibiotic ointment to their wounds. He put Band-Aids

on the smaller wounds. Then, using the clothes that hung
from a circular pole that ran around the entire perimeter of
the back room, he and Sara made comfortable beds for
themselves and Corey with the clothing on the floor. Exhaustion quickly set in and by 10:30 Joe, Sara, and Corey
were deep asleep.

Cindy put some towels on the floor near the bathroom
and lay on them, feigning sleep until she was sure the others
were out. She quietly went back into the bathroom and cooked
another spoonful of junk and injected it, even though she
didn't need it right away. She figured she had earned the
extra boost, even if she was getting low on the stuff. The past
hours had been hell for her. Though her mind remembered
little of what had happened, her body seemed to remember it
all, every ache and pain. Before she had got cleaned up, she
felt as though she had been crumpled up, dunked in sweat,
and wrung out to dry. There wasn't a muscle, joint, or tendon
in her that didn't hurt.

The first fix she had given herself as soon as they were all
inside had calmed her nerves and returned her mind to normal. But the second was the one she'd really needed; the second one put an end to the physical pain of withdrawal and
everything else that had held her body in tortured captivity.
It made her feel like herself again.

After the shot settled in, and she felt that wonderful sensation like sinking into warm Jell-O, she took stock of her
prescription drug supplies. She was horrified to find that all
she had left were two Valiums. Her heroin supply wouldn't
last more than a couple more days, even if she rationed it,
and she was tired of rationing. She longed for the good old
days when she could, as her best friend Linda would say,
"Ride the horse, twenty-four/seven, turning tricks for a daily
slice of heaven."

At the thought of Linda, sadness welled inside her. The
last time she had seen Linda was Saturday night, the night
before she had started living this nightmare. They had done
a high-class bachelor party together up on Park Avenue in a
penthouse overlooking Central Park. She pulled out her cell

phone and dialed Linda's number. No answer. No message. No ring. Nothing.

She fought back tears and told herself it didn't mean anything; it didn't mean Linda was dead. A little voice in her head said, "It doesn't mean she's *alive* either." Cindy ignored it. Linda is a big girl, she thought. She can take care of herself.

"I've got my own problems," she muttered, wrapping her cloak of indifference around her as she had so many times before; as she had learned to do so long ago. She punched in Z-Jay's number on her cell and felt a thrill when it rang, but it rang only three times, then nothing. She closed the phone and tried to think. While the others slept the rest of the day and until well after dark, she dozed intermittently, went into the back room of the cleaners to smoke a joint, tried Z-Jay's number repeatedly, with no success, and fought the urge to shoot up the rest of her smack.

Day 4: Wednesday

3:00 a.m.

Officer Duane Murphy awakened to a light tap on the shoulder. He opened his eyes, saw that he was lying chest-down on a black pebbled and tarred surface, and, for a moment, was unsure of where he was, or even if he was awake at all. Someone whispered, "Officer Murphy," in his ear, and it brought back memory and solid reality. He turned and looked at white-haired Professor Ligget, who was down on all fours next to him.

"You know," the professor said, "you really shouldn't sleep up here. There's no telling when one of the alien eggs could come upon you and then . . . well, you know what happens then."

Murphy smiled. "I blend in up here," he said, touching the black surface of the roof.

Professor Ligget looked uncomfortable with the comment and turned away to the south, squinting to see farther than his aging eyes were capable of.

"Any sign of them?" the professor asked.

"Nope," Murphy answered. He looked at his wristwatch. "I haven't been asleep that long; an hour at most. Bill had the shift before me and said he saw no sign of them. The last any of us saw of them was when I lost sight of them yesterday morning. I figure they holed up in one of the buildings between here and Twenty-sixth Street, but I expect they might travel by night. Unless, of course, they've found someplace to hide that has enough food for them, but I can't think of anything between here and Twenty-sixth Street where they would have."

"They may be injured and unable to travel by night or day," the professor offered.

"Yeah, I thought of that. If they don't show their faces in another twenty-four hours I'm going to go out and search for them."

The professor nodded. "What of the aliens?"

Murphy shook his head. "After the rush and the big feast at the collapsed building, they've been quiet. Too quiet, if you ask me."

"Oh?" the professor asked, eyebrows raised. "Don't tell me you've changed your mind about them." He smiled like the proverbial canary-eating cat.

Murphy shrugged. "I'm not saying they're intelligent, I'm just saying they're being too quiet; I don't like it."

"And you don't like it because . . . you think they're up to something?" the professor said with a smile.

"Yeah, I guess, but even animals, especially pack animals, can get up to something when they need to hunt. That's what these things are; just pack animals."

"Even the flying eggs?" the professor prodded. "You've seen as well as I have how they communicate with and control their offspring."

"Yeah, I guess . . . but does that mean they're intelligent, like us?"

"Well, they *are* the ones with the upper hand, and we so-called *intelligent* humans are hiding like frightened rabbits from weasels."

"If you define intelligence by who's at the top of the food chain, then I agree with you," Murphy said. Though he wasn't ready to admit it, the more he watched the aliens the more he had to agree, though begrudgingly, with the professor, that the aliens—at least the flying-egg ones—did seem to have some intelligence.

"It does seem awfully quiet," the professor observed, changing the subject. He looked up at the buildings around them shining in moonlight, all taller than the building housing the Chinese restaurant and Shangri-La Importers. "It's too bad we have such limited surveillance," he mused.

Murphy shrugged. "If we were higher up, we'd be more visible to the eggs. I'll trade better surveillance for safety any day."

The professor said nothing.

"How's Mrs. Volk doing?" Murphy asked.

The professor shrugged and shook his head. "The same," he said. "She didn't have any panic attacks last night, which is a good thing, but she woke up crying when her husband got off his shift up here on lookout and was still crying when I just left."

Murphy frowned at the tone in the professor's voice. "She can't help it, you know. Having a baby, especially your first, is a scary thing under normal circumstances. And these sure as hell ain't normal circumstances."

It was Professor Ligget's turn to frown. "Women had babies without any help for thousands of years before the advent of medicine. She's got everything she needs already built in. She just needs to relax and let nature take its course."

Murphy didn't reply. The conversation brought forth memories of his wife and their first baby.

"What if there are complications?" Murphy asked, not looking at the professor. "My wife had complications. The doctors decided to do a C-section, but she had an allergic reaction to the anesthesia. She and our unborn son died on the operating table."

"I'm sorry," the professor said softly. After a few moments of trying to think of something to add to that, all he could say was, "You should go and get some breakfast. I'll stay and keep a watch for them."

Murphy nodded. "I hope, for Mrs. Volk's sake, that she

can have a natural childbirth." Murphy turned and started for the roof door. "Call me if there's any sign of them," he said in a low voice.

The professor waved his hand, put the telescopic lens to his eye, and scanned the street below.

3:20 a.m.

Sara's dad was teaching her how to play golf. They were on the public baseball field in Billy Monday Park near their house. She held a driver in her hands like a baseball bat while her father showed her the interlocking grip that golfers use. She tried it but couldn't get it. Her father laughed at her, and a small, round silvery shining globe came out of his mouth.

She woke sweating and fearful, surrounded by darkness, not sure of where she was and afraid to move lest something in the dark reach out and bite her. Quickly, though, her breathing deepened and sleep returned to her exhausted body. In time she reached the dream stage again. She was an inmate in a prison. She sat on the lower bed of a bunk bed and stared at the gray cement floor. She became aware that there was someone in the bunk above her. She looked up, saw Cindy lying there—in the next moment she found herself standing in the doorway of a large gymnasium taking tickets for a high school dance.

She turned around and her mother and father were standing behind her, only they were Siamese twins grotesquely joined at the face and chest, with two stubby arms sticking out of their abdomens. Flies, in the hundreds, crawled all over them.

Sara awoke again and sat up. She shuddered at the memory of her last dream and tried to focus on something else to drive it away. Next to her, lying on a pile of winter coats, lay Corey curled into a ball. To the right of him, Cindy slept, her arms folded across her chest like a corpse at a wake. Up against the back of the dry-cleaning machine, Joe slept on a pile of clothing on his right side, his arm tucked under his head for a pillow.

It was muggy and stuffy in the shop, and her sleeping companions' faces were all damp with perspiration. She looked down at herself, taking in the large sweat stains under each arm, and frowned. A lot of good a fresh change of clothes had done her, she thought.

Unable to sleep any longer, she got up slowly, feeling soreness in every muscle and joint it seemed, and pain, more pain than she had ever felt before in her life, not all of it from her physical injuries. She fought back the urge to cry, feeling that if she did, she might never stop. She felt like she had when her dad died—waking each morning, often from a dream that he was still alive, only to realize the cruel truth. Like then, she wanted to deny the truth that was reality now; so wanted the power to be able to *change* the horrifying reality she found herself in. But, now, as then, she knew she couldn't. She knew she had to go on. Her father would never want her to give up; not even now when the entire world was ending in an insane nightmare.

Quietly, she got up and went into the bathroom to gingerly wash with cold water, cleaning her wounds and reapplying antibiotic ointment and bandages where she could. The cold water gave some relief from the heat. On top of the toilet tank she found Cindy's syringe and silently cursed her. She was glad she was the one to find it instead of Corey. She debated whether or not to throw it away, but decided against it. Not wanting to touch it, she picked it up and cautiously wrapped it with a wad of paper towels from the metal dispenser by the sink.

After washing, she opened the bathroom door and came face-to-face with Cindy, who was waiting to use the john.

"I think this is yours," Sara said, placing the wad of paper towels in Cindy's hand. Cindy frowned until she realized the paper towels' contents.

"Thanks," she mumbled, her eyes averted, unable to look at Sara.

Sara had been ready to give her a speech, scolding her and asking her to consider the effect her drug use would have on Corey if he found out, but when Cindy humbly, even guiltily, took her works and couldn't look Sara in the eye, Sara changed her mind, sensing that anything she could say would be nothing Cindy hadn't heard before, or even said to herself. Feeling sad and hungry, Sara went about the dry-cleaning shop looking for fresh clothes and something—anything—to eat.

3:45 a.m.

Cindy closed the bathroom door, unwrapped the paper towel around her syringe, and stood in front of the small square mirror above the sink. She looked from her reflection to the syringe in her hand and back again. Tears ran down her face and her sore nose became clogged with mucus. She tried to dig up anger at Sara but couldn't; only self-pity came, with shame in tow. After a few moments, it got so bad she couldn't even look at herself anymore. She silently cursed Sara, Joe, Corey, the 'Vaders, and God for making her feel like this, but placing the blame elsewhere did no good this time. She couldn't convince herself anymore that her life—what she had become—was anyone else's fault.

Her days of buck-passing were over, whether she wanted them to be or not. But this harsh reality, this no-holds-barred self-awareness was more than she could stand. She took out her packet of tinfoil wrapped inside a plastic sandwich bag that held her favorite brown powder. *To hell with it.* She spooned out a large amount of powder and cooked it up, telling herself: *It's okay; I'm probably going to die today anyway.*

4:15 a.m.

Corey woke sneezing from the mustiness of the clothing he lay on. His head hurt when he did. Joe woke from the sound of Corey's sneezing and both of them looked about as if confused by their surroundings until Sara joined them with a half-empty box of Ritz crackers.

"This is all I could find for breakfast, guys," she said, making it sound like an apology.

Joe grabbed the box and pulled out a small stack of crackers.

Corey got up and headed for the bathroom.

"I'd wait a bit, hon," Sara said hastily. "Cindy's in there."

"Getting fixed *again*?" Corey asked, grinning innocently.

Joe and Sara glanced at each other.

"Boy," Corey went on, "she must be really broken, huh?" He was proud of his joke and his grin widened.

Sara and Joe looked at each other again and laughed softly.

Cindy came out of the bathroom. Moving slowly, she joined the others and nearly toppled over when she tried to sit on the pile of towels she had slept on.

Joe and Sara exchanged a look that Corey saw, but didn't understand.

"Are you okay?" he asked Cindy. "Are you fixed for good this time?"

She didn't answer.

"Go, use the bathroom and wash up," Sara said, distracting him. "And wash good because you are still wicked stinky!" she teased, even though there was some truth in that for all of them; washing in the sink had not been adequate to remove the smell of vomit and blood that seemed to linger, lurking nearby and paying a visit to their noses every once in a while.

Corey looked insulted at first until he realized she was kidding. "At least I don't need to change again," he shot back, pointing at the stains under Sara's arms.

Joe looked at his own sweat stains and smiled. "He's got a point."

While Corey took care of business in the bathroom, Joe and Sara collected more clothing to wear. Cindy declined a blouse and a pair of shorts that Sara offered her, and stayed with the black culottes and long-sleeve sweatshirt she had put on the night before after she had washed all the blood and dried puke from her body. She also declined crackers and aspirin from Joe.

Joe turned in his Abercrombie and Fitch T-shirt for a white cotton short-sleeve shirt with a button-up front that he left unbuttoned. Sara changed her sundress for a denim skirt and a blue tank top. Being the only one of the group without sweat stains on his clothing, Corey stayed with the same bathing trunks and shirt he had slept in.

"I've been thinking," Joe said after he, Sara, and Corey had finished the half box of crackers. "There's a restaurant up the street; a Chinese place called Cho's."

"Like General Cho's Chicken?" Corey asked eagerly.

Joe and Sara laughed.

"I love Chinese food," Corey said, blushing. "Sorry, Sara, those crackers were good, but I'm still hungry."

"Yeah, me, too," Sara said and ruffled his hair.

"Great," Joe said. "I've eaten there a couple of times and it's good. Of course, that was when the food was cooked by a professional. . . ." He shrugged.

"I can cook Chinese," Sara piped up.

"Excellent," Joe said. "And the nice thing is there's a CVS just a couple doors down from the restaurant. I figure I can get to it over the rooftops or by sneaking over at night and we can get better first-aid supplies and medicine." He glanced at Cindy, who had looked ready to pass out but perked up at the mention of the CVS.

"How far is it?" Sara asked.

"It's on the corner of the next block, at the intersection of Twenty-seventh and Sixth Avenue. I would have liked for us to get there while it was darker outside, but I didn't expect us to sleep so long. I guess we needed it, though. I don't know about you guys, but I feel better for having slept."

Sara and Corey nodded in agreement. Cindy stared into space.

"We've still got a half hour or so before full daylight, so I guess now's as good a time as any," Joe added.

4:30 a.m.

Professor Ligget heard the roof door slam and looked over, frowning, as Louie waved to him and proceeded to cross the roof walking stooped over.

"Sorry, Doc," Louie whispered when he reached the professor's side. "I didn't mean to slam the door like that," he added, all the while nervously searching the lightening sky for any sign of the flying alien eggs.

"Hello, Louie," the professor said softly, breathing through his mouth—Louie reeked of tobacco and body odor—and returned to watching 6th Avenue to the south with the camera lens.

"So . . . what's shakin', Doc? Murph says them people are holed up somewheres between here and Twenty-sixth Street."

Professor Ligget frowned beneath the binoculars. He found it odd, and annoying, that Louie referred to Officer Murphy as "Murph" only when Officer Murphy was not around. He also didn't like Louie calling him "Doc," or Louie's lack of hygiene. Just because it was the end of civilization and the world as they had known it, there was no reason to stop being clean. However, considering himself to be a refined gentleman in the old-fashioned way, the professor felt it was important *not* to communicate that to Louie.

"That appears to be the situation," Professor Ligget replied.

Louie eased himself into a prone position next to the professor, lying on his side so he could talk and still keep an eye on the sky. "You know, Doc, I don't know why you and Murph are so hell-bent on finding more people. Ain't we got enough staying here already? I mean, I don't want to sound like a heartless fuck or anything—pardon my French—but I was checking the restaurant's food supply, and we are getting awfully low on just about everything. Them Chinks that ran the place got their weekly food supplies each Tuesday, and, in case you ain't noticed, the supplies didn't come yesterday." Louie chuckled at his joke and went on. "Or maybe them Chinks had trouble getting cats lately, if you know what I mean." He laughed again and looked at the professor. When he heard no reply, he continued.

"I could understand it if we was to let some broads in,

you know. I mean, shit, I ain't been laid in fuck knows how long. Pardon my French. And if this alien invasion thing is what I think it is—you know, lights-out for the world and all that—then we are definitely going to need lots of fresh pussy around, if we're gonna, you know, repopulate the earth and keep our kids from being born retards. You get me, Doc?"

Professor Ligget bit his tongue and took a long slow breath. When he spoke there was no indication in his tone of voice that he found Louie Lafayette to be utterly despicable. "Louie, I wish you would please stop calling me, 'Doc.' As I've told you before, quite a few times as I recall, I'm not a doctor. I'm merely a biology professor. As to your question, while repopulating the earth is certainly an important undertaking if we all survive, it is not why Officer Murphy and I, and the others, too, I might add, look for survivors to join us. It's simply the right thing to do."

"Oh yeah, yeah," Louie blustered in agreement. "But, you know, at the same time, we got to look out for ourselves, too. You know?"

So now we get down to brass tacks, thought the professor. He said, "But, Louie, what good would it be just to save ourselves? How could we live with each other and be able to look each other in the eye if we didn't do everything possible to save others like ourselves?" The professor had no doubt that Louie would have no problem forgetting about other people and putting himself first. He was, after all, a sociopath, a person devoid of conscience who thinks the right thing to do is whatever is best for him.

"Yeah, yeah, you got a point," Louie said hesitantly. After a few awkward moments of silence, Louie spoke up again. "You want I should take over for you, so you can get something to eat? It's almost time for my watch, anyway."

The professor thought twice before rising to his knees and handing Louie the telescopic lens. "If you see *any* sign of them, come down and tell us *immediately*. Understand?"

"Sure, Doc, uh, I mean Professor. Sure."

Wearily shaking his head, Professor Ligget left Louie to keep watch on the roof.

4:45 a.m.

"Oh, God! Why is it so hot in here?" Cindy groaned. She was standing with the others just inside the dry cleaner's front door. Joe had the door open just enough so he could stick his head through and reconnoiter 6th Avenue. He was tempted to tell Cindy it wasn't much better outside. Cool mornings are rare in New York City during summer.

"Okay, the coast is clear," Joe said. "Whatever food the 'Vaders found in the rubble of the deli must be gone because that intersection is empty now. So, let's do this the same way as how we got here. Single file, and keep close to the building. We'll stop at any storefront that has a recessed entrance." The women nodded, but Corey frowned with confusion.

"I thought recess was something we had at school," he stated.

"Just hang on tight to Sara's hand and follow her. And keep your sharp ears open, Corey, for any sound of the 'Vaders approaching," Joe told him.

Corey nodded proudly; he liked the fact that Joe had realized he had the best hearing in the group.

"Okay, let's do this," Joe said. "I'll go first, Sara and Corey follow behind me, and Cindy, you take up the rear."

Cindy nodded her head, but Joe thought it looked like she had to make a great effort to do so. He had good reason to want her taking up the rear; she couldn't slow Sara and Corey down, and maybe get them killed, if she was at the end of the line. Joe wasn't trying to be heartless, just pragmatic; Cindy was so doped up she was a liability. They had been lucky so far with her, but Joe knew they couldn't go on carrying her through danger after danger, keeping her safe without paying for it with their own lives. She was like a kid—worse than a kid. At least Corey kept up when they were on the run. And Corey hadn't retreated emotionally from the horrors he had seen. Joe was continually amazed at the boy's resiliency, and Cindy's lack of it.

4:50 a.m.

Louie Lafayette was lying on his back, looking up at the sky lest any of the flying alien eggs sneak up on him. He jumped up a moment later, thinking he'd heard someone coming up the ladder steps to the roof. He rolled onto his stomach while picking up the telescopic lens in the same motion. He tried to look like he'd been keeping watch all the time. After a few moments, he realized it was nothing—just a false alarm. But, before he put the lens down, he caught movement down the street.

On elbows and knees, Louie scuttled sideways for a better angle on the sidewalk below. He slowly surveyed the sidewalk to the south for as far as the telescopic camera lens let him see in the poor light. There was nothing there now. He lowered the lens and rubbed his eyes, wondering if he'd started seeing things. He almost had himself convinced that it had been nothing when two women, a boy, and a man darted quickly up the sidewalk toward him in single file until they reached the next store and ducked into the store's small entrance alcove, which was a regular feature on nearly every shop on 6th Avenue.

Louie quickly put the lens back to his eye and watched the women for as long as they were in sight. He liked what he saw.

"Oh, yeah, baby," Louie mumbled. "Come to Papa." Despite his eager lechery, Louie made no move to report to the professor as he had been instructed. Instead, he racked his brain for some idea of how he might get rid of the guy and the kid—keeping the two hot broads—and make it look like an accident.

4:55 a.m.

Sara held Corey's hand tightly and followed Joe, sprinting from the storefront next to the dry cleaners to the next recessed front entrance of a leather accessories store called Piglet's Purse Emporium. The sun rising over the city offered little light—skyscrapers left them in gray shadow, which was fine as far as she was concerned. The heat, though, quickly became as oppressive, if not more so, than it had been in the close confines of the dry cleaners. Sara felt as though she were walking through a curtain of moisture, the humidity was so thick.

She stood against the door to the leather shop, still clasping Corey's hand tightly though it was just as clammy with sweat as her own. She looked at Cindy, who was barely managing to keep up. Her hair had quickly become stringy with sweat that ran down her face and dripped from her jaw. Just looking at her wearing the heavy long-sleeve sweatshirt added to Sara's heat discomfort. Though she, herself, was clad in a short denim skirt and tank top, the heat was almost unbearable.

"Everybody okay?" Joe asked, panting slightly.

Sara and Corey nodded.

Cindy bent over, hands on knees, and breathed heavily, saying nothing.

"All right then. Let's go." Joe slid along the foyer wall until he could look out and check both directions of 6th Avenue. He motioned for everyone to follow as he stepped out and turned left up the sidewalk.

Sara followed, her heart racing, her breathing rapid, and her eyes darting everywhere—above, behind, in front. She hated the feeling of being so exposed, and hated the way it made her body respond. At any moment she expected the monsters to leap out. That expectation made her so tense her muscles hurt, and the wounds in her side and head throbbed. Though she knew their destination was only the next intersection, it seemed too far. She now regretted agreeing to make the run to Cho's Chinese Restaurant. She wished they had stayed at the dry cleaners, and holed up there for a couple of days more to let herself heal, or at least until dark. If it hadn't been for the promise of food and medicine, she would have preferred to stay there.

5:00 a.m.

Louie Lafayette never heard Officer Murphy come onto the roof, and didn't realize he was there until the policeman tapped him on the shoulder. Startled, Louie almost sent the telescopic lens over the edge.

"Oh! It's you, Officer Murphy. You nearly scared me to death," Louie said.

Officer Murphy smiled, but it wasn't a good-natured, friendly smile; it was the smile of a predator. "Did I catch you daydreaming, Louie?" Murphy asked in his slow, deep, rich voice.

Louie found his voice to be almost as unnerving as the policeman's ability to sneak up on him soundlessly. "Ah, no, no," Louie said quickly and truthfully. "Ah, just thinking. Just thinking." Again he was speaking the truth, but he didn't tell Murphy he had been thinking about how to bump off the guy and the kid down below with the two babes.

"Any sign of them yet?" Murphy asked, looking over Louie to 6th Avenue.

"Um, no," Louie said, returning to his most familiar form of communicating—lying. "Course, I haven't been looking for them as best I could," he added just in case Murphy saw the foursome approaching while he was on the roof. Louie was hoping to prevent that and get Murphy off the roof, or at least distracted, until the foursome got by the restaurant.

In the past few minutes, watching the two women, man, and boy methodically and cautiously make their way up 6th Avenue, Louie had pondered every way he could as to how to get rid of the guy and his kid and get the two women inside. He had managed to come up with a couple of things.

First, there was a pile of loose bricks and gray concrete building blocks on the rooftop, about six feet away from the front edge. A couple of well-aimed bricks and he figured he could take out the guy and the kid. The only problem with that plan was how to cover up that it was him dropping the blocks from the roof. He thought long and hard on that, trying to come up with a reasonable and believable lie, but couldn't find one.

Next, he had pondered how he might attract one or two of the twenty-foot alien monsters to the intersection to get rid of the males while he, Louie, came to the women's rescue, thus securing a place in their hearts that could easily lead to a place between their legs. It was a nice plan; it was an even better daydream. Louie was very rarely honest about anything with other people, but he had a knack for being honest with himself. It was why he had managed to survive, and that was before the invasion. Now that everything had changed, his knack for self-truth still came in handy. This was one of those handy times. Louie knew, and could freely admit to himself, that he was not the rescuing type. He was not a hero. Thus, his second plan was even less feasible than the first.

However, Louie believed in his old man's words of wisdom and his favorite saying: *The third time's the charm*. It wasn't a plan that would provide *everything* he wanted—that would be having a shot at both honeys out on the street—but it was a plan that would help keep him alive and fed. The only problem was kneeling next to him; Officer Murphy. If Murphy, or the professor for that matter, saw the four people down on the street, they'd signal them and bring them in. But four more mouths to feed was competition he didn't want.

That would be bad, but even worse, he knew that if the professor and Murphy did see the new survivors and tried to signal and rescue them, it could, and probably would, bring the twenty-foot eating machines down on them; instead of surviving to repopulate the earth, they would all become lunch for the aliens.

"What do you mean, you haven't been looking much for them? That's what you are supposed to be doing up here," Murphy barked as loud as he dared.

"I know. I know, but, I think there's something weird going on with the alien fuckers. Pardon my French," Louie said quickly to cover himself and to draw Murphy's attention away from the street.

"Yeah? How so?"

Louie stammered, "W-w-well for one thing, the gang that was feeding at the wrecked building two blocks down ain't there no more. They're all gone. And another thing, I don't see none of them sleeping in the streets or anywhere else, the way they been doing."

A moment later Murphy reacted exactly as Louie had wanted him to; he went below to consult with the professor.

5:08 a.m.

Cindy quickly became too tired and too hot. The sun was rising and bringing with it even more heat and mugginess than she had felt in the dry cleaners. Before leaving the dry cleaners she had made plans to leave the others when they got to the Chinese restaurant, and continue on herself to Z-Jay's—after a stop at the CVS Joe had mentioned, to get something to hold her over until she made it uptown to Z-Jay's crib. At first, despite the heat, she had tried to psych herself up to keep going alone, but after just a short time in the unbearable humidity and heat, she lost her resolve. Part of it was the fact that she was wearing the long-sleeve sweatshirt and was just too damn hot to have much energy. The rest of it was from just being too wasted and not in shape for such a journey.

She felt pathetic when she realized she could barely walk a block without wanting to give up and just sit and cry. How was she ever going to walk nearly one hundred blocks to Z-Jay's on 126th Street in Harlem?

She trudged along behind Sara and Corey, barely keeping up, trying to think of some way she could find some smack without having to trek all the way to Harlem. She knew the CVS pharmacy would have something similar to, or as strong as, junk, whether it be morphine, methadone, or Oxy-Contin, but she worried that Joe and Sara would keep it from her to protect Corey. Also, though any or all of those drugs would help, they couldn't satisfy her like the real thing. Morphine or methadone in liquid form that she could shoot up would be great, but she doubted the pharmacy would have that. They were more likely to have those drugs in the form of pain patches and pills. They might have OxyContin in liquid form for cancer patients.

But, with all that had happened to her lately, she *desper-*

ately needed the *real* thing; substitutes weren't going to cut it.

Suddenly, Sara grabbed her hand, and she was forced to stumble along to the next storefront. She leaned against its glass door, gaining some relief from the cooler-than-air surface. She tried to think while Joe stuck his head out and looked around.

Cindy was starting to feel downright miserable. The long stretch of going cold turkey prior to her most recent fix was catching up to her with a vengeance. Now she understood why junkies feared going cold turkey so much. Besides being so painful and difficult to sustain, if you didn't make it all the way through to the other side and sobriety, you ended up with a bigger monkey on your back than before.

I feel like I've got a friggin' gorilla on my back now, I want a fix so bad.

An idea came to her. "Hey, Joe? Maybe we should just grab another car or truck and head uptown."

"Why?" Joe asked, frowning.

The disapproving look on his face pissed her off, and she wanted to shout: *"'Cause I need a fucking fix!"* Instead, she came out with the first thing she could think of: "Maybe there aren't as many 'Vaders uptown." As soon as she said it she knew it was lame.

"I doubt that," Joe said, his voice smug and condescending.

Cindy caught him giving Sara a quick look and rolling his eyes. To Cindy's surprise, Sara came to her rescue. "That's not a bad idea—going someplace where there aren't as many 'Vaders," she said. "I bet if we could get out of Manhattan there would be less of them around, like if we headed for the country. Up to Connecticut, maybe."

Cindy quickly jumped on the suggestion. "Or Jersey even. If we could get to the George Washington Bridge we could go either way." Z-Jay's crib was on the way to the bridge.

"Why go so far uptown?" Joe reasoned. "We could just take the Holland Tunnel or the Lincoln Tunnel."

Again Sara spoke up and came to Cindy's rescue. "No

way. After our underground trip, I'm not going through an-other tunnel again for as long as I can help it. Didn't you ever read Stephen King's *The Stand*?"

Joe shrugged. "No. Why?"

"Trust me, if you had, you'd never consider going through either of those tunnels," Sara said with finality.

Cindy nodded her agreement, though she hadn't read the book, either. Joe was nodding slowly at the idea, giving Cindy hope. If they headed for the bridge, she could ditch them near Harlem and walk a few blocks to Z-Jay's if necessary.

"How can we know if things will be any better in Jersey, or anywhere else for that matter? We could be endangering our lives only to find ourselves in the same bind, but in coun-try we're unfamiliar with."

"For one thing," Sara said, "there's a lot more room. Peo-ple are packed into this city like sardines. If we headed into the country away from all the cities, we probably would see fewer 'Vaders. I mean, it makes sense, right? They're going to be where the people are, and in the cities, people are just easier to get at."

Cindy could have kissed her at that point.

Corey even joined in, earning Cindy's appreciation also. "Yeah! If we went deep into a forest or up on a mountain, I bet there wouldn't be any 'Vaders around at all."

"That's right," Cindy spoke up. "You're smart, kid. Real smart." She smiled at the boy and gave Joe a dirty look, but he was oblivious to it.

Corey, though, beamed proudly.

Joe pursed his lips in consideration. "Yeah . . . I guess that ain't a bad idea."

Cindy's pulse quickened with excitement as Joe surveyed the cars nearby.

"Okay," he said finally.

Yes! Cindy thought triumphantly, feeling a sudden rush of adrenaline until Joe went on.

"But we're still going to stop at Cho's for a few days and stock up on food and get healthy. We all need a rest. Plus, I want to get medicine and first-aid supplies from the CVS. I can go to it at night and look around for a car at the same time."

Cindy's adrenaline rush slowly deflated.

"We're going to need weapons, and another fire extinguisher—I left the other one in the truck when the deli collapsed on us. We'll need guns. It's foolish to go anywhere without some protection. We'll use Cho's as a hideout while we try to get all the stuff we need. It might take a while, but it's better than just charging off unprepared. As soon as we have everything we need, we'll head out of the city."

Cindy wanted to argue for leaving right away, but couldn't think of any good excuses. She knew Joe was right. All she could do was hope that she could get something from the CVS pharmacy to tide her over, and that it wouldn't take Joe long to obtain weapons so that they could leave.

5:10 a.m.

By the light of dawn the Avenue of the Americas between 26th and 27th Streets was still—too still. In fact, as far as he could see, north and south on 6th Avenue, it was quiet.

Too quiet for Joe Burton.

It was eerie being out in the city on a weekday and have it be as silent as a meadow in the dead of winter. No sounds of cars, no sirens, no airplanes flying overhead. No people talking. Nothing but the sound of pigeons cooing from their ledges on the buildings above. At least that was reassuring.

They were at the halfway point between 26th and 27th Streets when Joe realized there was something wrong—there were no 'Vaders sleeping in the street, snoring and breathing loudly. He'd noticed this the moment they stepped out of the dry cleaners. He had looked south to see nothing at the pile of rubble that had been the Zion Gourmet Deli, but he had thought they would come across some sooner or later. Yesterday the 26th Street intersection had been a feeding ground, and last night the feeding had continued. Joe had got up twice after midnight to cautiously stick his head out the shop's front door. The sounds of gluttony had been clear each time. By dawn, however, the cooing pigeons had replaced the sound of the feast, and 'Vaders were nowhere to be seen.

He wondered as he, Sara, Corey, and Cindy took refuge in the alcove of a small music store called Lunar Tunes: Where had all the monsters gone? He couldn't help but grin as the latter question became the lyrics to the Pete Seeger anthem, "Where Have All the Flowers Gone?"

"What's so funny?" Sara asked.

Joe shook his head.

"Come on, tell us," Corey pleaded.

"I was just. . . . You ever hear that song by Pete Seeger? You know, 'Where Have All the Flowers Gone?'" He sang the last part.

Sara nodded but Corey shook his head, no. Cindy was indifferent.

"It's stupid, but it keeps running through my head. You know: Where have all the monsters gone?"

Sara gave him a weak smile. Corey offered a weird look. Cindy rolled her eyes.

"I told you it was stupid," Joe retorted, embarrassed.

"So?" Corey asked, still giving Joe a weird look.

"So what?"

"So," Corey said, "where *have* all the monsters gone?"

"Good question, kid. I'd feel a whole lot better if I knew the answer."

5:15 a.m.

Murphy and the professor were huddled in Louie's office at the rear of the import store. The others were still sleeping, or next door in the restaurant getting some breakfast.

"I think we need more information before we make any decisions about what we can do," Murphy said.

The professor nodded slowly and hesitantly. "I agree, but there's no point in rushing out there and getting someone killed. When the people we saw get here, I hope they'll be able to give us some helpful information."

"I wouldn't count on it," Murphy replied.

"Who's on the roof now?"

Murphy looked at his watch. "Louie should just be get-ting relieved by Rico."

5:16 a.m.

On the roof, Rico, a tall, thin, dark-haired Latin American, knelt next to Louie and looked south where Louie had the telescopic lens pointed.

"You see anything, man?" he asked Louie. His effeminate voice had a thick Brazilian accent.

Louie shrugged and didn't answer. "Nothing but fucking flying rats. Pardon my French."

Rico looked confused. "Flying rats?"

"Yeah, you know, garbage-eating filthy pigeons."

Rico shrugged. "Yeah, whatever, man. I came to relieve you. Go have some breakfast and get some sleep. It's my shift."

Louie shook his head. "Nah. That's okay, I ate earlier and I ain't tired. You can go below, Rico. I relieved the professor late so I don't mind doing a double shift up here."

"You sure?" Rico replied, trying not to sound too enthusi-astic. He hated doing lookout. He felt like a fly trapped in a big spiderweb, just waiting for something horrible to pounce on him.

"Yeah, I'm sure," Louie replied.

Rico didn't argue. "Thanks, man. I owe you," said the tall, scrawny Brazilian as he backed away, hunched over, to the roof's trapdoor.

"Fuckin' faggot," Louie muttered as soon as Rico went inside. Once again, as he had done so many times in the past few days, Louie imagined how *he* would do things if he was in charge. And the first thing Louie would do would be turn those two fags, Rico, the Brazilian homo, and his boyfriend Juan, the Dominican fag-queen, out in the streets. How the hell was humanity going to repopulate the earth if faggots like them were allowed to survive?

Louie didn't get it; of all the people who had bought the farm, or had been turned into monsters in the past few days, why had those two queers survived? In his own twisted way,

Louie was right-wing religious. When the alien invasion had begun, Louie had been sure it was the coming of "the end time" as predicted in the Bible and depicted in the novels of Hal Lindsey, and Jerry Jenkins and Tim LeHay, which were the only books he had read as an adult. But seeing fags like the two Latinos survive didn't make any sense.

What the fuck is God thinking?

Of course, Louie never placed himself in the category of those whom God was purging from the earth in preparation for the Second Coming of Christ, despite the fact that he was a bookie, a drug dealer, and a smuggler and dealer in stolen goods and weapons through his import-export business. Like any true sociopath, Louie saw nothing wrong in the way he made money.

Louie grimaced and spat as though thoughts of Rico and Juan left a bad taste in his mouth. Movement on the street caught his eye. The foursome was on the go again, still coming toward 27th Street, and only a couple stores away. The guy in the lead suddenly looked up and directly at Louie, who ducked. When he peeked again, the guy's eyes were back on the street, looking forward and backward as he led the two women and the boy to the next store, where they all slipped into the entrance alcove and out of Louie's sight.

Louie cursed himself. *I hope he didn't see me.* He looked back at the roof door. It was still closed. He looked over to the loose pile of red bricks and gray concrete blocks and made a decision: If the group down on the street kept on as they were and went past his import store and the restaurant, he'd let them be. But, if the guy had seen him, and they came to the store or the restaurant looking for a way in, he'd scare them away with a couple of well-placed bricks.

"No harm, no foul," he muttered.

The biggest problem with his plan would be the professor and Murphy and their "It's the right thing to do" bullshit. Those two would know if he didn't signal the foursome to come to the store if they didn't scare right away and banged on the doors or the restaurant and store windows. If that happened, the professor didn't worry Louie, but Murphy would have to be taken care of. If Murphy gave him any shit, or got rough with him, he had a .45-caliber pistol with Officer Murphy's name on one of its bullets.

5:18 a.m.

"I think I saw someone on the roof of the building at the corner across Twenty-seventh Street," Joe said.

"Do you think he saw us?" Sara spoke up. "Did he have a gun?"

"I didn't see one."

"Was it a policeman?" Corey asked hopefully, unable to give up the idea that his dad was still alive and hiding out somewhere.

Joe shrugged. "I didn't see him that good."

Sara looked at Corey and sadly shook her head. "I don't think so, hon." Seeing Corey's face sag with disappointment, she added, "Don't give up hope, yet."

Corey smiled weakly and Joe and Sara looked away, neither of them believing Corey had any realistic chance of re-uniting with his father.

"So what should we do?" Sara asked Joe.

Joe sighed and thought for a moment. "I only saw *one* guy and he didn't look armed. If he was, at least he didn't shoot at us. What's got me more worried is the fact that we haven't seen *any* 'Vaders since we came out. For the past three days we couldn't go more than a few yards on the street without being attacked by monsters or the flying things. And, in case you didn't notice, there were none of them sleeping on the street. I don't like it."

"Don't look a gift horse in the mouth," Sara said. "Having no monsters around is just fine by me."

"Me, too," Corey added.

"Do you think the guy on the roof is a lookout? Maybe there are more people there and we can join them. You know, strength in numbers?" Sara said.

Joe shrugged. "Yeah, that's what I thought back at the Sixth Precinct, and remember what happened there."

Silently, Corey started to cry. Not knowing what to say,

Sara crouched next to him, put her arms around him, and held him. After a few minutes, Corey's tears subsided.

"You know," Sara said, "I refuse to believe that there aren't any good people left and that everyone is out for themselves."

"Hah!" Cindy grunted. "People were like that *before* all this shit started; what makes you think they'll be any different now?"

"Not everyone was like that," Sara retorted. "I knew a *lot* of really great people, people who would give you the shirt off their backs if you needed it."

"How nice for you," Cindy muttered.

Sara ignored the comment. "Sooner or later, we've got to hook up with other people like us, or with some official government group like the National Guard, that will be able to help us and protect us."

"There's only one way to find out," Joe said, straightening and taking a last look up and down 6th Avenue and still seeing no sign of 'Vaders. "We were headed for Cho's Chinese, so that's where we're going. If there are people there who don't want us around . . . we'll figure out what to do then, *if* that happens."

"Yeah? And what if they have guns?" Cindy asked. "I think we should just find a car with the keys in it and a full tank of gas and head uptown for the Washington Bridge and get out of here while the 'Vaders are quiet. Maybe now is the *best* time to do that."

"If we get turned away from Cho's, then I guess that's what we'll do. I don't know about you, but I am really hungry, and I'm sore as hell. Sara's beat up, and so are you," Joe said. "Wouldn't you like something to eat and some clean bandages and *painkillers*?" He emphasized the last word and gave Cindy a look as if asking how could she pass that up?

When she didn't reply, Joe said, "Okay, let's go."

5:22 a.m.

Louie had just risen to his knees to look straight down from the roof just in case the foursome he'd been watching had gone by. He had been distracted the last couple of minutes or so with watching a swarm of sparkling alien eggs fly by high overhead. At first he had been terrified and had covered himself with a large sheet of black plastic roofing material they kept close just for that purpose. He had expected the things to start dive-bombing him, but they hadn't. It seemed they didn't even take notice of him. They just kept going, and more swarms followed, flying much higher than Louie had seen them do since the jet attack. Now, with the last swarm gone, Louie realized he had been lax in keeping an eye on the newcomers and checked to see if they were on the street directly below or had gone by.

They weren't below, but he saw them at the opposite corner of the intersection. And they definitely saw him. Louie immediately ducked back out of sight, silently cursing himself. Scrambling on his stomach, he crawled over to the pile of bricks and got ready to drop some bombs.

5:23 a.m.

Officer Murphy passed by the storage room as he left Louie's office and glanced inside. He was surprised to see Rico on his bed of pillows, curled up with his lover, Juan.

"Hey, aren't you supposed to be on watch?" he asked Rico.

"I went up, but Louie wanted to stay there and do a double. Who am I to argue with that?" Rico answered.

Murphy frowned. That didn't sound like Louie at all. He *hated* pulling his regular watch on the roof, never mind someone else's.

"What is that little prick up to?" he wondered out loud.

5:24 a.m.

Louie wasn't the only one who had seen the flying orbs passing over the city in great swarms. Just as he was about to lead the others across the intersection, Joe had looked up and seen them, also. He had immediately pushed the others out of sight.

"Where are they going?" Corey asked, peeking up from under Sara's protective arm.

"I don't know," Joe said slowly. "But I wish I hadn't forgotten the fire extinguisher in the tow truck. I doubt that what they're up to is a good thing for us."

"You know," Cindy spoke up, giving it one more try, "with those things heading away from us and with no monsters around, maybe now is the best time to grab a car and get the hell out of here."

"What's your hurry?" Joe asked, getting irritated.

"I'm not in any hurry," Cindy replied defensively. "I just want to get out of this city alive."

"I think they're gone," Corey said.

The three adults leaned out and looked up. The dawn sky was clear. Joe led the way again, and they reached the corner of the intersection.

"There's our friend again," Joe said.

"I see him," Sara replied.

"And there he goes," Cindy added. "If you ask me he doesn't look all that friendly."

Joe said, "Maybe you guys should let me check this out."

"No," Sara said immediately. "We stick together."

Corey nodded.

Cindy just shrugged.

"At least let me go over and try the front door. You stay here." He didn't wait for an answer.

Sara sidled up to the building, pulling Corey along with her.

Cindy looked around at vehicles in the street and went to the nearest one, a dark blue Lincoln Continental.

Sara started to call her back, then let it go. With things so quiet, she didn't think Cindy was in immediate danger now.

"This is weird," Sara said, looking around. "This quiet makes me nervous."

"Yeah, me, too," Corey murmured.

Across the street, Joe walked slowly past the front of Shangri-La Imports, keeping his eyes toward the roof.

Sara and Corey watched the roof, also. Just as Joe reached the entrance to the Chinese restaurant, Sara saw the top of a man's head, and a second later a brick dropped on Joe.

At that moment, Joe was bent over to peer through the window of the restaurant and never saw the brick coming. It struck him on the back of his head, and he went down where he stood.

5:27 a.m.

"Oops!" Louie whispered after hitting the guy; he hadn't been trying to, but *what the hell*.

From the street came a shriek from one of the women, and the boy with them called out, "Joe!"

Louie saw them dash across the intersection and grabbed another brick. Just as he was going to lean over the edge to drop it, he saw the shadow of someone behind him. A moment later, everything went black.

When he came to, he was lying on the floor of Shangri-La Imports' aisle for vases and lamps. He could hear muffled voices but couldn't tell where they were coming from. He tried to get up, but dizziness and nausea sent him back to the floor. He heard laughter followed by a voice he was unfamiliar with—a woman's voice.

Louie slowly raised himself up on one arm. His head was pounding and he felt sick to his stomach. He tried to remember what had happened, how he had ended up on the floor. The last thing that came to him was dropping a brick on the guy nosing around the front of the restaurant. He smiled, picturing the bull's-eye he'd made, bouncing the brick off the guy's head. Then . . . he remembered nothing after that.

No, wait a minute. I saw a shadow fall over me . . . then nothing!

Moving cautiously, afraid of passing out, Louie sat up and remained sitting, his head resting in both hands, face-down, elbows on his bent knees. Again he heard the strange woman's voice. Excited, he tried to stand again and did so after grabbing the edge of a table displaying huge Chinese vases. He staggered down the aisle to the rear of the store where there were three doors—one on the back wall leading to his office; next to it another leading to the storage room where most of the survivors slept; and the third on the right-hand wall that led next door to the kitchen of Cho's Chinese Restaurant. The latter door was open and from within it came the sounds of people talking. Taking a moment to brush himself off and smooth his comb-over, he went to the door.

"Well, well, well," Officer Murphy said, noticing Louie in the doorway. "If it ain't the welcoming committee himself!"

Murphy was standing behind the guy Louie had dropped the brick on. The guy was seated on a stack of egg noodle boxes and was being ministered to by a good-looking broad. Louie sized her up, taking in her long brown hair and pretty face over a rack that strained for release from the elastic tank top she wore. The rest of her body was just as nice—a tight ass and good-looking legs. There was another new broad—a blonde—in the kitchen, also, sitting on the metal countertop to the left of Murphy. Though not dressed as provocatively as the brunette, nor as pretty or well stacked as the broad holding the cold compress to the new guy's head, Louie thought the blonde looked like a party girl—someone willing to have a good time, especially if that good time came with lots of booze and dope. Louie smiled at her and she looked away.

Murphy stepped around the guy sitting and walked over to Louie. The rest of the survivors, the professor, Juan and Rico, Bill and Donna, all stood around the injured guy who, to Louie, didn't look that injured—when the broad with the rack pulled the compress from his head there was no blood on it. How hurt could he be?

I'm probably hurting more than he is, Louie thought, putting a hand to his own throbbing head. He wondered whose shadow it had been behind him; *that* was the prick who had knocked him out.

"Joe," Murphy said to the new guy while putting an arm around Louie's shoulder, "this is the guy who bounced a brick off your noggin. If you want to punch his lights out and work him over a bit, I'd be more than happy to hold him for you." He grinned at Louie and hugged him tighter.

So that's who coldcocked me, Louie thought, looking up at Murphy. *I should have known—the fucking coward.*

Murphy's hand gripped Louie's shoulder like a steel vice, pulling him closer in a crushing embrace. Louie could barely breathe, never mind move. He tried to play it light, grinning as if his arm weren't being crushed to pulp and chuckling as though Murphy were just horsing around, even though the cop's face was dead serious. Thankfully, for Louie, the new guy didn't look pissed, just dazed. He shook his head and declined Murphy's offer.

The hot-looking chick, though, carefully placed the cold compress on the guy's head again, turned, and faced Louie. He smiled at her, one eyebrow raised, unable to look her in the eye when her full breasts were so close, straining against the tight tank top. So fixated on her chest was Louie that he didn't anticipate the shot to the side of his face that she gave him with her closed fist—no wimpy girly slaps from her. She hit like a man, and though it hurt, Louie had to admit it also turned him on a little. He grinned at her and licked his lips.

She hauled off and punched him in the throat.

Louie's smile instantly disappeared. The pain in his head was immediately outdistanced by the incredible pain in his throat. Suddenly, he couldn't breathe; his throat was on fire. Though he tried, he could not inhale or exhale. He couldn't cough or make any noise at all, not even a whimper. His eyes bulged and watered and his ears rang with a high, irritating tone that pierced his skull. Behind his eyes an explosion of bright, white-hot pain rocked him where he stood. Back and forth on the balls and heels of his feet he swayed. Like a priest about to pray, Louie fell to his knees. He opened his mouth like a fish suffocating on dry land. His vision blurred and darkened at the edges. His heart pounded so fiercely it was all he could hear, booming in his ears, each beat renewing the pain in his head and throat.

He fell forward and put out his hands, but there was no strength left in his arms. His hands hit the floor under the weight of his body. His arms buckled as both wrists bent backward, sending knives of pain up his arms.

He hit the floor facefirst.

I'm going to die, was all he could think as the stabbing pain in his sprained wrists competed with the searing pain in his throat. For the second time in less than a half hour, Louie lost consciousness. The last thing he heard before going under was Murphy's exuberant voice:

"Damn, girl! I think you killed him. Way to go!"

5:55 a.m.

Sara's anger left her quickly after her fist connected with the grubby, balding little man's Adam's apple. Remorse and guilt rushed in to fill the void left by her dissipating anger. Both emotions grew stronger by the second as she watched the guy gasp for air and collapse at her feet. The look of even more pain on his face when he put out his hands to stop his fall and his wrists buckled affected her like a physical slap in the face; her head jerked, and she stumbled backward.

The huge cop voiced her fear that she had killed the guy. Then, remarkably, the cop started to laugh. Sara looked at him in horror as the guy she'd punched fell facefirst on the floor. She couldn't believe the cop sounded so happy that she might have killed the man who had dropped a brick on Joe.

"Don't worry about it, honey," he added. "Ain't no big loss." He laughed a big hearty belly laugh, and his face crinkled with laugh lines.

The oldest guy in the room—short with white hair and a kind face sporting a short, neatly trimmed white beard—knelt next to the one she had hit and checked his pulse before he leaned over and put his head close to the man's face. After a few moments he rose and smiled at Sara.

"It's okay," he said and winked at her. "He's all right."

As if to prove what the old man said was true, the guy on the floor began coughing and wheezing.

"Shoot! He's going to make it," the big cop said, still smiling.

"I'm . . . I'm sorry," Sara stammered.

"Don't worry about it," the cop said. "He deserved it. Believe me, if Louie here had killed your boyfriend he wouldn't show any remorse over it." The big cop looked down at the guy, who was now breathing much better. He was lying on his back, holding his sprained wrists to his chest and moaning.

The cop looked at Joe and said, "You're lucky he didn't kill you, man."

Sara looked around at the others. They all smiled and nodded at her. Corey came over and took her hand. Still sitting, Joe looked pale and in pain, but he, too, smiled at her.

"Thanks," he said, and grimaced as if just the act of speaking hurt his head. "I couldn't have done it better myself," he added, more softly.

The old man felt the downed man's wrists; the guy yelped and pulled his hands away.

"His wrists are badly sprained," the old man said. "Both of them. He'll be all right, though." He stood and looked at the cop. "I should give Louie and our new guest some of the painkillers you got from the CVS next door." He looked at the state of Sara, Cindy, and Corey. "They could *all* probably use some painkillers, from the looks of their injuries."

Sara noticed that Cindy perked up at the mention of the CVS and painkillers.

The cop grinned. "Sure," he said. He nodded at Sara, Joe, Corey, and Cindy. "Are you folks hungry?" he asked, then laughed loudly. "What am I saying? Of course you're hungry, right?"

"I'm starving," Corey spoke up, and everyone laughed.

"What?" Corey asked, blushing and pulling closer to Sara.

"Of course you are, little man," the cop said. "Juan!" he spoke to one of the Latin-looking men sitting near Cindy. "How about you cook up some of your delicious grub for our new friends?"

Juan smiled. He was almost as tall as the cop, and very thin. He wore his black hair in cornrows. He had sleepy brown eyes and a small, feminine nose and lips. When he smiled, dimples appeared in both cheeks.

"Si! Pronto!" Juan said, and hopped off the counter and went to the front part of the kitchen.

"That's Juan," the cop said. "And this is his . . ." The cop paused and looked at Corey as if unsure how to go on.

"I'm his life partner. I'm Rico," the other Hispanic-looking man said with a pronounced lisp and a heavy accent. He waved. Not as pretty as Juan, Rico was a little heavier and wore his long hair slicked back into a short ponytail. He had rough features—close-set brown eyes, a flat nose that looked as though it had been broken and not set properly, and a small mouth with thin lips and crooked teeth.

"This is the professor," the cop said, indicating the old man still squatting next to the guy with the sprained wrists. He smiled and nodded.

"Where's the Skipper and Gilligan?" Sara heard Cindy mutter.

The pregnant woman giggled.

"What's that, sugar?" the cop asked, still smiling, but Sara noted an edge to his voice. She thought he was a man who didn't take lightly to being made fun of.

Cindy was undaunted and looked openly hostile at the cop. "I *said*, 'Where's the Skipper and Gilligan?'" she answered in a tone that said, *fuck you*!

"The Skipper? Gilligan?" the big cop said, still smiling, but the edge behind the smile became keener. "Oh!" he added, laughing but with no laugh lines this time. His eyes bored into Cindy's. "I get it! It's a joke, right? That's what you're doing, isn't it? Making a joke? I said this is the *professor*, and you say: 'Where's the Skipper and Gilligan?'" He laughed without mirth, not even trying to fake being amused. "Like that TV show, right? *Gilligan's Island*?"

Cindy smiled viciously and nodded.

"Yeah," the cop said, drawing the word out. "Oh yeah, now *that's* funny. You're quite the comedienne." He looked at Cindy through narrowed eyelids. "You look familiar. Don't I know you?"

For the first time in the conversation, Cindy looked uncomfortable.

"I doubt it," she muttered.

"Hmmm," the cop said, fixing her with a squinty-eyed

stare a moment longer before turning to the pregnant woman. "This is Donna Volk, and her husband, Bill." Donna had short, dark hair and a tan complexion that were offset by light golden, almost yellow, pupils in her large almond-shaped eyes. Despite the heaviness in her face from being pregnant, it was easy to see that she was a beautiful woman. She had high cheekbones and a full, sensuous mouth. Her husband, Bill, was a little shorter than the cop and had short-cropped blond hair and a face full of freckles. His eyes were small and dark blue over a long pointed nose and small mouth filled with bad teeth.

The couple smiled and waved.

Looking down, the cop, not too lightly, nudged the guy on the floor with his foot.

"And this guy here is Louie Lafayette. Louie owns this building, both the restaurant and the store next door; *supposedly* an imported-goods store." The cop grinned and nodded as if at some unspoken joke. "And my name is Duane Murphy. Obviously, I'm a cop," he said, indicating the badge on his short-sleeve dark blue shirt. He also wore a police belt—replete with a holstered pistol, nightstick, and handcuffs—holding up his blue shorts.

"Do you know my daddy?" Corey asked hopefully. "He's a policeman, too."

"I don't know," Officer Murphy said. He leaned over with his hands on his knees. "What's his name?"

"Tom Aaron; I mean *Officer* Tom Aaron."

Murphy thought for a moment and shook his head. "Sorry, kid, but it doesn't ring a bell. What precinct was he with?"

"The Sixth."

"Ah, no. I don't know anyone from the Sixth. I've been working with a special task force under the Office for Homeland Security."

Corey looked downcast.

"What about you, buddy?" Officer Murphy asked him. "Can you introduce yourself and your friends?"

Corey smiled sheepishly and nodded. "I'm Corey Aaron."

"Nice to meet you, Corey," Murphy said, and shook Corey's hand.

"And this is Sara," Corey said, touching Sara's hand.

"Sara Hailey," Sara said, leaning over and shaking Murphy's hand, then shaking the professor's, Donna's, Bill's, and Rico's hands.

"Sara's an artist," Corey said as proud as if she had been his sister or mother.

"This is Joe," Corey continued. He stepped next to the sitting Joe and put a hand on his shoulder. "Joe's an actor, and he saved my life. He saved all of us."

Joe smiled at Corey and tousled his hair then nodded a hello at the other people in the room.

"That's Cindy," Corey said, pointing at her where she sat still on the metal counter. She gave a brief smile and a short wave.

"She was sick, but she got fixed and now she's okay," Corey explained.

Sara noticed Officer Murphy give a knowing nod toward Cindy at that bit of information.

5:57 a.m.

Cindy had recognized Officer Murphy the moment she laid eyes on him. He might be with the New York City Office of Homeland Security now, but years ago, right after she had gone to work for Z-Jay, he had been working with Vice in Harlem and had busted her and Linda outside the Apollo Theater. That was the first time Cindy had been busted. That alone would have been enough to explain her remembering Murphy so well, but he had also been a real prick to her and Linda, roughing them both up and slapping them around, trying to scare them into giving up their pimp and drug dealer. Neither she nor Linda did, and Z-Jay had taken care of them. Because it was her first arrest, Cindy got one year, suspended sentence, and had to do a year's probation and random drug tests. But Z-Jay had fixed it so that she never had to submit to any tests; all she had to do was visit her probation officer once a week and give the guy a blow job. Linda, who had priors, only did eighteen months in jail, where she was able to get high just as much, and as often, as when she was on the outside.

Cindy never forgot Officer Duane Murphy. As soon as Corey had made the innocent comment about her getting fixed, she had seen the glint of recognition in his eyes and knew that now he remembered her, also. As she sat on the metal counter she caught Murphy looking at her with contempt. She wanted to scratch his eyes out.

"Why don't we all go and have a seat at the tables out front so we can eat," Murphy suggested. "The restaurant has a decent bathroom with a shower stall that y'all can use to clean up after you get some grub."

Cindy understood that Murphy was in charge. With his knowing her past, she realized that her plan to get some prescription drugs from the CVS next door was probably futile. As everyone moved out to a table in the restaurant, she excused herself and went to the women's room, where she was able to cook up some dope and shoot up. She figured she had just enough left for one more high.

6:20 a.m.

Joe ate ravenously, despite his still-throbbing head. He was amazed at how good everything tasted. He couldn't remember ever having food so delicious. And the funny thing was that the food was very simple fare: egg noodles and rice mixed with snow pea pods. That was it. Seeing how Corey and Sara were also digging in with gusto equal to his own, Joe knew it wasn't just him. Only Cindy picked at her food, after she came out of the bathroom. She ate slowly and looked as though she'd rather be anywhere else but there.

While he ate, Joe sized up the new survivors they had befriended. With the exception of the asshole who had dropped the brick on him, they all seemed to be good people, and happy that Joe, Sara, Corey, and Cindy had joined them. Now, they each took turns telling how they had come to be there on the day the world ended.

6:25 a.m.

Juan and Rico, easily the friendliest and most boisterous of the group, went first. They took turns telling their story but never stepped on each other's words. Their dialogue was seamless and more like a monologue spoken by two people.

"We have a really cute place in the Village over near Union Square," Juan started.

"We just moved in together," Rico said.

"We've been seeing each other for almost a year," explained Juan.

"Our one-year anniversary will be on August fifth," Rico added. "We met at the Club Avalon in the Village." They both looked expectantly for confirmation. Though he had never heard of the place, Joe nodded.

"We've been slowly furnishing our new apartment," said Juan.

Rico said, "We want everything to be just right, you know?"

"We made a rule right off that *nothing* entered our home unless we both absolutely loved it, right, Rico? So we heard that Shangri-La Imports had *the* cutest golden Buddha lamps. Like to die for."

Louie cut in. "Yeah, I do a lot of business with the Village people." Louie laughed. "Village people? Get it?"

No one laughed and Louie slumped in his chair, cradled his wrists—which the professor had bandaged—and looked pissed off.

Juan went on. "Well, as we were saying before we got so rudely interrupted, we came over Sunday morning because our friend, Lamont, told us that Shangri-La was open on Sundays."

"Yes, and those Buddha lamps were just what we needed for our boudoir."

"What's a boudoir?" Corey asked.

Rico answered, "Why, honey, it means bedroom."

"You guys share the same bedroom?"

Rico and Juan looked at each other and giggled. "Yeah," Juan said, winking at the other adults, "we're best friends."

"That's cool," Corey exclaimed.

"So anyways," Rico went on, "we have Indian teakwood tables. Absolutely gorgeous. The Buddhas would have been perfect."

"It's funny," said Juan. "We slept in on Sunday, something we almost never do. If Lamont hadn't called to tell us the Shangri-La was only open until one on Sundays, we would have been home when . . ." He faltered a moment looking for the right word, but not finding it, he shrugged and said, "Well, you know. Anyway, we came over around eleven forty-five, and no sooner had we climbed out of the subway than all hell broke loose."

Rico started crying and there were several moments of awkward silence while Juan comforted him, whispering in his lover's ear and rubbing his back.

"We barely made it inside the store, and that's when we met Mr. Louie," Juan said.

"Actually, my last name is Lafayette," Louie corrected.

"Who gives a shit?" Murphy snarled at him.

In defense of Louie, Rico added, "He was very nice to us, especially when he saw what was going on outside."

"See?" Louie said to Murphy, smirking.

"And we have been here ever since. I know it's been only a few days, but it feels like months," Juan explained.

Everyone in the room knew what he was talking about and nodded.

"I wanted to try and go back to our new apartment," Rico said.

Juan quickly added, "But I said no!"

Rico looked at Juan and his face became sad. "But we have pets—our *babies*." He said the last word with emphasis as if imploring Juan. "What are Ju-Ju and Sparky going to do without us?"

"They're our toy poodles," Juan explained. Though he was in better control of his emotions than Rico, his eyes were filling with tears, also.

"And what about Mr. Wobble, and Wee Willy Whiskers?"

"They're our cats," Juan said.

Louie interrupted again. "The way I see it, they're either

monster meat, already chewed and digested by those things out there, or they *are* those things out there. And in that case, I'm sure they would love for you two fairies to fly back home to check on them," he said, a malicious grin on his face as he spoke. His words were the final straw for both Juan and Rico. They broke down sobbing and embraced.

"Could you be any more of an asshole?" Murphy said to Louie.

Louie looked around, surprised, as if to say, "What did I do?"

Trying to defuse the situation, Professor Ligget spoke up. "I teach . . . or rather, I *used* to teach Biology at NYU before the invasion. My wife, Ethel, and I live on Staten Island, but we had come into the city early Sunday to do some shopping before going to her sister's house for dinner. Her sister, Dorothy, lives on the Upper East Side overlooking Central Park. At least . . . she used to. Her husband is a stockbroker—*was* a stockbroker. Dorothy called my wife about the Sunday sale at Louie's store, so Ethel wanted to stop here on the way to her sister's.

"We were in a taxi when the invasion started. It was humid and overcast." The professor had a faraway look in his eye as he spoke. "It was so humid, remember?" He asked the question of no one in particular. "I asked the cab driver, a nice enough man from Pakistan, to turn on the A.C., but he said it was broken. So Ethel rolled down her window, and that's when we saw the first invader. It flew right inside the cab and just hovered in front of us for a moment. It was a truly remarkable thing to see, the way it spun and glowed, like a tiny planet. I remember thinking it reminded me of a spinning globule of liquid mercury.

"Ethel and I were stunned at the sight of it." He shuddered as he remembered and recounted what had happened next. "I was quite fascinated by the thing and tried to touch it, pluck it from the air, but Ethel said, 'Don't touch it.' That's when the thing flew in her mouth. She swallowed it and coughed and gagged like she was choking." The professor's eyes filled with tears and his voice grew tremulous with emotion. "I tried to slap her on the back, but it didn't work. I knew I was going to have to do the Heimlich maneuver, but I couldn't get in the right position for it quickly enough." He paused and wiped at the silent tears now streaming down his face.

"It didn't matter. In the next half a minute, or less, she changed from my loving wife of forty-five years to some kind of alien monstrosity. It happened so fast it's like a blur in my memory now. One minute she was the woman I loved, the woman I had shared so many good and bad times with, and the next thing I know she's a fifteen-foot monster. As I sat in the backseat of the taxi, she grew so large she tore the roof off the car. Then she leaned over and bit our Pakistani driver's head off." He paused and smiled wanly. "You know, it was so strange, but the man's hands stayed on the wheel. He kept driving for another ten yards without his head." The professor stared at his hands, his mind faraway. "I wonder just how far he could have driven without it if Ethel hadn't eaten the rest of him."

He chuckled softly, strangely, then looked up, seemingly startled and embarrassed by what he had said, as if he had forgotten there were other people in the room. "I was in shock," he started again, slowly. "I couldn't move. I was dinner sitting next to Ethel, yet, she didn't eat me. *She didn't eat me!*" he repeated slowly, as if disbelieving it himself.

"Even though Ethel was gone, I think enough of her was still alive inside that thing that she *couldn't* bring herself to eat me." He shook his head slowly in wonder and sadness.

The pregnant woman, Donna, reached across the table and took his hand gently. The old professor smiled at her.

"Luckily, we were less than a block from Louie's store. So, having nowhere else to go that I could think of—I was pretty panic-stricken by then, you understand—I came here, where we were headed in the first place. It was the only place I could think of."

The table grew silent. Joe sat next to the professor, and Juan and Rico sat next to him with arms around each other comfortingly. On the other side of the professor, Louie sat staring at his bandaged wrists with a glum look on his face. At the end of the table, Officer Murphy sat with his arms folded across his chest, looking stoic. Opposite the professor sat the married couple—Bill and Donna Volk. Next to them were Sara, Corey, and Cindy.

Bill broke the silence, clearing his throat and drawing all eyes. "We were leaving the city that morning, Donna and me. We don't live here; we're from Vermont. Burlington actually. Donna's brother has a huge apartment down on Canal Street here. We had been visiting him for a week, before the baby comes."

"I'm due in July, but my mother says it'll be earlier because I'm so big," Donna interjected. She patted her swollen belly proudly.

"Yeah," Bill went on. "So, we were heading for the Empire State Building—it's the one place we didn't get to visit during our stay."

His wife cut in again: "We went to the Statue of Liberty, Ellis Island, and we saw the memorial for the Twin Towers. Let's see, we went to the Met and Central Park. We wanted to go to the Empire State Building last week but the line was really long, and it was so hot I couldn't stand it. My brother, Jason, said Sunday morning is the best time to go because it's not so crowded."

"Yeah," Bill agreed again, casting a sidelong glance at his talkative wife. "So we were driving up Sixth Avenue, right behind the professor's taxi, when those little flying balls starting coming out of the sky. I thought it was a hailstorm at first, but these things were different than any hail I've ever seen. One of them hit the windshield of our Celica and cracked it. Thank God for safety glass, but I was so distracted by it that I almost rear-ended the professor's taxi. I had to turn onto Twenty-seventh Street to avoid it."

"It was like a bad dream that feels totally real, you know?" Donna interjected. Nearly everyone at the table nodded knowingly.

"I pulled the car over to the curb, right next to the side door to the import store, and got out of the car to look at the windshield. But as soon as I got out of the car, I saw this. . . ." He looked around the room as if he might find the word he was looking for posted somewhere. "I saw . . . this *thing* growing through the roof of the taxi. At first, I had no idea what it was. Then it started to take shape and . . . I could have sworn it was a friggin' giant gargoyle. I freaked out. And then I looked around and those things were *everywhere*. When I looked back, the thing in the taxi was *eating* the taxi driver."

"That's when I got out of the taxi and made a run for it," the professor said.

"The blood and gore was unbelievable. I've seen a lot of really violent, bloody movies, but nothing like this. I couldn't believe it. It was insane," Bill said quietly.

Again, everyone in the room nodded in commiseration.

"There was a police car down Twenty-seventh Street that I tried to wave to for help, but the cop driving it suddenly turned into one of those gargoyles and grew right through the roof of his cruiser. Before I could even think what to do, three or four of those things started toward us. I pulled Donna out of the car and we ran into Louie's store through the side entrance. I mean, I panicked big time." Bill looked ashamed to admit it.

"Can you picture *me* running?" Donna said with a shrug of her shoulders and a wan smile. "It was like getting a penguin to run. Actually, I waddled really fast." She laughed self-consciously.

Bill took his wife's hand and squeezed it. "That's about it," Bill concluded.

Silence followed while Joe, Sara, and Corey finished eating.

"I'm full," Cindy said, pushing her plate full of food away.

"Do you mind?" Donna asked, reaching for the plate and looking around at each of them. "I'm eating for two."

"No, go ahead," the professor said, and everyone agreed.

Corey had about half a dish of rice and noodles left and offered them to Donna.

"You can have mine, too," he said, and added softly, sadly,

"my mom's pregnant, too, and she always eats—she always *ate* whatever I couldn't finish."

Donna looked at Corey with sympathy, then at Sara, who shook her head to discourage Donna from asking about Corey's mom. She ruffled his hair and leaned over and kissed his cheek. "No, darling, that's okay. You still look hungry; you eat it. A growing boy needs as much food as me, maybe more. Thank you, though. You're a sweetheart."

Corey blushed and blinked tears from his eyes.

"So, Louie, what brought you here on a Sunday morning?" Murphy asked, clapping Louie on the back and startling him.

"What? Oh, well, you know, the sale," he said, awkward at being the focus of everyone's attention. "It's my store, why the fu—! Pardon my French," he said, glancing at Corey. "I mean why the heck wouldn't I be here?" Louie looked nervous as he spoke, as if he thought they wouldn't believe him.

"Don't you have staff that runs the store for you?" Murphy asked. "Seems kind of strange that you would be here just for a little sale, especially on a Sunday morning."

"Uh, yeah . . . sure, but it was Sunday, you know? They all wanted the day off," Louie said, squirming as if he were being interrogated for his part in a crime.

"And you, out of the goodness of your great big heart, gave them the day off and came in yourself?" Murphy said, his tone mocking.

"Yeah, that's right." Louie looked embarrassed.

"Lucky for us he was here," the professor said. "We're all lucky. If he wasn't here we would have had a hard time getting food."

"What about you, Officer Murphy?" Louie asked, emphasizing the word *officer* with the same tone of mockery Murphy had used toward him. "I don't think you've ever told any of us how you came to be here. As I remember, you were the last one to come in, looking for a place to *hide*."

Murphy smiled at Louie, but it was not a smile of warmth or camaraderie.

"Yeah, I was," Murphy agreed slowly and looked around

the table. "I was supposed to be on traffic duty at the corner of Sixth and Twenty-seventh, where the city was fixing a broken water line. But just as I got there, well, you all know what happened then. So, I came in here."

7:00 a.m.

Louie Lafayette looked at Officer Murphy and listened to his all-too-short story of how he had come to be there, and knew he was lying. Louie had been suspicious of Murphy from day one, but now he had proof. It wasn't until the kid, Corey, had asked Murphy if he knew the kid's father who was a cop that Murphy, thinking Louie was too hurt to hear, had let it slip that he was working with the Office of Homeland Security. Then, just now, he said he was on traffic detail.

It didn't add up. As his uncle Vito used to say: "There's something rotten in the state of Denmark, and it ain't the cheese."

As the newcomers shared their stories of how they came to survive the alien holocaust, Louie nodded his head, laughed, smiled, and looked sympathetic when everyone else did, but all the while he was wondering what Murphy had really been up to on the morning of the invasion.

9:00 a.m.

The group talk lasted until midmorning as Joe, Sara, Corey, and Cindy, to a lesser extent, told their stories. The day was another humid one, and they all went into the storage room in the import store, where three fans blew but brought little relief. Sara, Joe, Corey, and then Cindy each took turns showering in the restaurant's bathroom, then the professor dressed their wounds. Sara took a Vicodin the professor offered, but Joe declined and the professor gave Corey children's aspirin. Cindy took two Vicodin. After the four of them were clean, refreshed, and settled, they sat with the others—except Juan, who was on lookout on the roof—in the storeroom of Shangri-La Imports. There was only one window in the room and it had been boarded over, allowing them to use lights at night without fear of attracting monsters. The talk soon turned to speculation about the invasion and the aliens.

Professor Ligget, as the most educated member of the group, did most of the talking, expounding on the same theory most of them had reached individually, namely, that the flying glowing orbs and the monsters they turned people into were alien beings from outer space. The professor was a bit more specific in describing the orbs as seeds, or eggs, of the species, that needed to plant themselves in other living things, but not just *any* living things, like plants and vegetation, but *moving* living things like animals and people.

Eventually, the talk got around to speculation about what would happen next.

"The way I see it," Louie spoke up quickly after having been quiet for some time, "sooner or later the government is going to get the military mobilized again and we're going to go to war against these bastards. Or, if they don't," he added with a sly look at the two new women, "We'll have to repopulate the earth, like Adam and Eve."

"But don't you remember what the alien eggs did to the jets?" Donna asked, ignoring his Adam and Eve comment.

Louie shrugged. "Yeah, but there ain't that many of the eggs still around. And if they are eggs, won't they like croak sooner or later if they can't find anything to plant in and grow in?" He directed the latter question to the professor.

"Hmm, yes, you make a good point, Louie," the professor replied. "There is good reason to think that the alien eggs will either die or move on if they run out of living fauna in which to plant themselves. And, if that *does* happen, we certainly can make war against the remaining monster-aliens. They have no obvious technology and do not seem capable of making use of human technology even though they infect and transform us. Nothing human seems to remain in the people who are transformed. It's as though they remember nothing of their once-human selves, with certain exceptions, like what happened with my Ethel." The professor became suddenly somber and quiet.

"See?" Louie said. "They got no technology, so as soon

as those egg things aren't around, we can kick some alien butt."

Everyone was happy to agree with Louie's speculation, and all but the professor and Murphy seemed cheered and reassured by it.

1:00 p.m.

After a light lunch of rice and bread, when nearly everyone was napping due to the heat and for want of something to do, Joe, Murphy, and the professor met in Louie's office next to the storage room.

"Tell me," Joe said quietly, "why do I get the feeling that neither of you think Louie's scenario is something we can expect to see?"

Murphy sighed and squinted at Joe.

The professor just stared at the floor.

Murphy spoke up. "For starters, I think the military has already taken its best shot and it's been defeated. I mean, seriously, you saw those fighter jets go down, didn't you? Well, they represent the *best* of our military. You can be sure they were flying in support of ground troops . . . and the fact that we haven't seen or heard of any ground troops makes me think our military has been thoroughly defeated."

Joe nodded. He had thought that himself during Louie's ranting, but hadn't wanted to say anything to kill the hope he saw in the others' faces.

"Maybe I'm wrong," Murphy said. "I hope to God I am wrong, but I don't think so."

"So, what happens next?" Joe asked. "Is humanity relegated to living in hiding, always the prey and never the predator?"

"Hey, don't get me wrong. We can and will fight these things, but whether small bands of folks like us can do much, well, we'll have to wait and see. If the eggs don't die or go away, that's going to make any resistance on our part much more difficult."

Joe nodded. "Yeah, that's for sure." He thought a moment before asking, "So, Professor, what do you think they want?

Is it just food? Are we just food to them? Or are these monsters just the first wave—like storm troopers sent in to wipe us out before the *real* aliens move in to take over?"

"If they *are* the invading army, so to speak, come to pave the way for more intelligent beings, I'd think they'd have some type of weaponry. I mean, if they are making a way for another invading species, they could do it much more effectively with weapons rather than these . . . *monsters*," the professor answered.

"Corey calls them *'Vaders*, you know," Joe told them, "short for *in*vaders?"

"Very apropos," the professor said.

Murphy smiled. "Yeah, that's catchy."

"The real question is, how intelligent are these flying eggs and monsters?" the professor went on. "Murphy thinks they have little or no intelligence, but I think they *are* intelligent, they just have a different kind. From what I've seen of them, they remind me of the type of intelligence we see with social insects that have communal hives or nests, like bees and ants. The monster form of the species are *eating* machines. They remind me of caterpillars. The flying form seem to be the brains behind the brawn, so to speak. If there is no invading force coming in behind this one—and I don't think there is—I can't help but think there is something else going on here." The professor paused and seemed to consider whether or not to go on.

"That makes sense," Murphy agreed, but the professor shrugged.

"I don't know," he said, "but there's something else about these creatures that bothers me. Have you noticed that none of them have genitalia? They have no sexual organs at all—at least by their outward appearance they don't."

"Yeah," Joe said, thinking and remembering all the gargoyle-ish beasts he had seen since the invasion started. "Now that you mention it, why is that? What does it mean?"

"It could be that their genitalia has been internalized; that might be the norm for the species. Or it could support what Officer Murphy and you think—that these gargoyles, as you call them, could be the storm troopers sent in to wipe us out and make the planet ready for whatever *higher* life-form employs them. If theirs is a *hive* intelligence, the gargoyles could be the equivalent of drones, worker bees, and if that's true then they would have no need to reproduce, or . . ." His voice trailed off.

"What?" Joe implored.

"I didn't want to bring this up in front of the others, especially Donna, but I've told Murphy about it. I saw something very strange on Sunday, the first day of the invasion. Every person who swallowed one of the flying eggs was transformed into one of the giant eating machines, except for a pregnant woman I saw. When one of the orbs flew down her throat, she just froze where she was, like she was dazed by it. The next moment, one of the newly formed monsters, not as large as the others, scooped her up. I was sure he was going to eat her, but instead he carried her into the nearest subway station. It may have been that the creature did that so it could eat her without being bothered by the larger monsters, but . . ."

"The same thing happened to Corey's mother," Joe interrupted. "He told us she was pregnant and was carried off by one of the monster 'Vaders. I just assumed the thing had eaten her; he didn't see where the thing took her; he was too busy running from the other monsters."

"Hmm," the professor said, nodding.

"So what do you think that means?" Murphy asked him.

"I'm not sure," the professor said. "I think the monsters may be stockpiling food by carrying off pregnant women and not eating them. When the woman has the baby, they get two meals instead of one. Most people are in hiding now, or dead, so it will be interesting to see what the monsters and their flying overlords will do now that food is getting scarce. It wouldn't surprise me, once they've reached a saturation point here, if the monster forms of the aliens go into cocoons and gestate into orbs that would then leave the planet. If they've eaten or transformed a majority of us, it would no longer make sense to stay just to hunt down and eat or transform *every* last human. I think they may be like locusts and move on to another living planet after they've devoured everything they can here. I'm sure Earth is not the first world they've invaded, and it won't be the last."

1:30 p.m.

While Joe, Murphy, and the professor were in the office and nearly everyone else was napping, Cindy quietly left the storage room and headed for the women's room in the restaurant.

"Looking for a place to smoke?"

The voice startled her. It was the guy, Louie, who had almost taken Joe out with a brick. He was sitting on a covered trash can just inside the door to the kitchen.

She had been planning on shooting up, but asked, "How do you know I smoke?"

"I know a smoker when I see one. I smoke, too. I bet you're out of butts. Am I right?"

Cindy nodded.

"Then you came to the right place. I got a dozen cartons of Dunhills—you know, British smokes—and other European brands. They're one of the things I import. Come on. I'll show you a better place for a butt than the can. It's too fucking hot in there. Pardon my French," he said in a conspiratorial whisper. With a beckoning nod of his head, he led her farther into the kitchen.

"I'm glad to finally get someone in here who smokes," Louie whispered over his shoulder. "I own this building, but I can't even smoke in the place. God forbid any of them should *die* from my secondhand smoke. What a fucking joke! Pardon my French."

He led Cindy to a door and opened it. A light went on automatically and frigid air washed over her. Compared to the stuffy heat of the storage room this felt like Heaven.

"This is the cold-storage room for the restaurant," Louie said, stepping aside and letting her precede him in. "You know, Death is waiting just outside the second any of them step out and they're worried about secondhand smoke. What bullshit!"

"Tell me about it," Cindy said, grinning and loosening up a little. "The chick I came in with was bustin' my chops about smokin' around the kid."

"No shit," Louie said, letting the door close automatically behind him. He took a large flat pack of the foreign cigarettes and his Zippo lighter with a NASCAR logo decal on it from his pocket. He gave a cigarette to Cindy and then lit his own. "So, you said before you're a dancer in the Bronx?" he asked after sucking deeply on his butt.

"I was," Cindy said, letting smoke out slowly.

"Where?"

"Rabini's." She had a hunch what was coming next.

"I fucking *knew* it! Pardon my French," Louie said. "I knew I seen you before." He looked her up and down, unabashedly appraising her. "You were good."

"Yeah, thanks," Cindy answered, sucking on her butt and staring at her feet.

"That was, like, quite a while ago. You looked barely legal."

"I wasn't," Cindy admitted.

"I didn't think so," Louie added, almost apologetically. "I go there a lot. My buddies all hang out there."

Cindy regarded him anew. "You in the mob?"

Louie shrugged. "I ain't a wiseguy or anything like that. I'm only half Italian, on my mother's side, you know? But I got connections; we do business together. Why?"

"No reason. It's just that when I danced there it was a mob hangout."

"Yeah, well, things haven't changed much." Louie smiled. "So, what happened? Why'd you stop? They find out your real age?"

Cindy nodded.

Louie took a drag and squinted at her. "How long've you had a habit?"

"What?" Cindy was startled by the question.

"Come on, sugar. You're wearing a long-sleeve sweatshirt when it's ninety fucking degrees, pardon my French, and you were scratching your arms when you first came in like you was trying to dig your fucking veins out. You also been ducking in the john a lot but you ain't got no butts," Louie said. "You got the look, too. I know. I been around. And you can bet that bastard Murphy knows it, too, the rotten son of a bitch."

Cindy automatically scratched her left forearm, then caught herself and stopped.

"Hey! It's okay by me," Louie said quickly, and gave her a pat on the shoulder that was meant to be reassuring but with his wrists bandaged it was awkward. "But I wouldn't trust that black bastard as far as I could throw him. Even though all the rules and laws have gone out the fucking window, he's still fucking playing it by the book—once a fucking cop—pardon my French—always a fucking cop."

"Yeah, I recognized him the minute I saw him."

"He bust you before?"

Cindy nodded.

Louie paused and smiled lecherously. "He bust you turning tricks, or for dope?"

"Me for tricks, my girlfriend for dope," Cindy muttered.

"I knew it!" Louie said with a laugh. "I knew you was a hooker."

Cindy glared at him.

"Hey! Don't worry. I'm cool; I don't fucking care, pardon my French. I ain't going to say nothing."

Cindy crushed her cigarette out on the edge of a wooden shelf that was empty except for a half-full bag of white rice.

"It don't matter to me," Louie said, "but watch out for Murphy, the prick is still taking names like he thinks things are gonna go back to normal and he'll have the goods on everyone."

"Fuck him," Cindy said, and added with a smirk, "Pardon *my* French." She started toward the door.

Louie laughed. "Nah, you don't want to fuck *him*, sugar," Louie said, and laughed. "Now, *me* on the other hand . . ." He laughed again and held his arms out as though he were center stage in a spotlight.

"Yeah?" Cindy regarded him with a cold eye. "I don't do

it for nothing, *sugar.* And, pardon my French again, since fuck-ing money's no good anymore . . . what've *you* got to offer?"

"How bad is your habit?" Louie asked.

Cindy shrugged and didn't answer.

"I'll bet it's bad enough that you're worrying about scor-ing some more, right?"

Cindy shrugged again and said, "Maybe." Trying not to sound too eager, she added, "You got some?"

Louie hesitated, letting her hang for an extra moment be-fore answering. "I ain't got any smack, but I got something just as good. Ever do OxyContin?"

Cindy nodded. Though it wasn't her favorite cup of tea, it would do for a while. "You got liquid oxy?"

"Just pills, but strong doses—two hundred milligrams. Plenty of weed, too," Louie replied, smiling.

"How come you have that?"

"Hey, I'm in the import business; that don't mean just vases and rugs and shit." He smiled. "So what do you say we make a trade."

Cindy looked him up and down. She'd had worse johns than him. "Let me think about it, and I'll let you know."

"Sure, babe, sure," Louie said, his mouth grinning, but his eyes hard as he headed for the door. "Just don't think about it too long, or I might lose interest."

2:00 p.m.

Now that she was in a safe haven with plenty of food, water, and medicine at hand, Sara found, upon waking from her nap, that she felt less tense, less stressed. For the most part, she liked the group of survivors she'd met at Shangri-La Importers. She figured even the guy who had dropped a brick on Joe wouldn't be that bad once she got to know him. He had already apologized when they all were going from the restaurant to the storage room. He told her he hadn't meant to hurt Joe, he had just panicked and was trying to scare him away so he wouldn't attract any 'Vaders to their hideout. He had seemed sincere.

After her nap, Sara immediately hit it off with Donna, who was starved for the companionship of another woman. She reminded Sara of her sister. At Christmas when Sara had gone home, her sister, Melissa, had announced she was newly pregnant; the baby was due in August. Looking at Donna's swollen belly, Sara figured that must be close to what her sister looked like. Seeing Donna made her ask the question that she hated to think about but couldn't help: was Melissa still alive? To get her mind off it, and, perhaps to feel a little closer to her sister, she instinctively became Donna's surrogate sister.

She learned Donna was using the Lamaze method of natural childbirth and had taken classes before the invasion. Sara didn't say it, but she knew Donna was also thinking that the Lamaze method of natural childbirth was going to be extremely important now. Thinking about that brought on many other thoughts for both of them of how things had changed since Sunday, and how they would change even more in the future. It boggled Sara's mind that humankind, within the space of less than a week, had been thrust centuries into the past, practically back to the Stone Age, especially when it came to things like childbirth.

It was a frightening realization that staying alive was the only priority that mattered now. She imagined it would remain so for quite some time.

2:15 p.m.

Corey woke from a nap and sat, looking around at the other people in the room. He decided he liked his new home. He also liked the people—most of them anyway. He knew he would never forgive Louie for dropping a brick on Joe, but the rest of them seemed really nice.

Sara and Donna sat across the room, talking quietly. Corey especially liked Donna. Her being pregnant reminded him of his mom, and not in a sad way, but a good one. He could never have explained it, but he felt better about his mom since meeting Donna. Though he liked Donna best next to Sara, Joe, and Cindy, Juan and Rico, who were playing cards as they sat cross-legged in a corner of the room, were close behind. Corey thought they were funny and liked their accents when they spoke. Murphy and the professor were okay, too; not as funny as Juan and Rico or as cool as Joe, but nice.

Corey got up and wandered around. He saw Joe, the professor, and Murphy in the import store's office and overheard them talking about how it was interesting that the city still had power. The professor seemed worried that it wouldn't stay on for much longer. Corey went into the office to have a look around and was ignored by the men. He found a TV, but when he turned it on it on he got nothing but snow on every channel.

He continued exploring. Though the building was small in height by New York standards—only one floor—it was large, with plenty for a curious boy to discover. He started with the restaurant, avoiding Louie and Cindy who passed by him on their way back to the storage room, and looked into every nook and cranny in the kitchen. He liked the walk-in refrigerator, even though it smelled like cigarettes, and stayed in there for a long time.

He explored the rest of the kitchen, looking in, around, and under the cabinets and stove and counters. Under the stove, he saw a rat eat a cockroach. He ran back to the office to tell Joe, but Sara and Donna in the storage room next door overheard him and seemed very upset by that fact. The men, except for Juan, who gagged, seemed to take it in stride.

Murphy called out to them: "You'd be hard-pressed to find *any* restaurant in this city that *didn't* have either rats or roaches. Most have both."

Cindy seemed especially distraught by that information. Corey remembered how she had reacted to the rats and bugs under the UPS warehouse, and he wished he hadn't brought it up. He tried to make it better by telling her there weren't *that* many roaches in the restaurant, but she didn't want to hear about it at all.

Corey went back to his exploration of the kitchen and found something curious that intrigued him—a door behind a tall cabinet in the rear of the kitchen that had a small padlock on it. Corey thought the door at the back of the restaurant was an emergency exit to get outside, and wondered why it had a cabinet in front of it and a lock on it. Even though he didn't like Louie, his curiosity was too great; he asked the owner of the building about it.

"Listen, kid," Louie said, when Corey found him in the front of the import store looking out at 6th Avenue. He bent over to Corey's level and leaned so close to him that Corey could smell the tobacco on his breath and stale perspiration under his arms. "You ever heard about the curious cat?"

"No," Corey said, and took a step back.

Louie took a step forward, remaining in Corey's face. "You never heard the expression, 'Curiosity killed the cat'?"

"No," Corey answered again. Louie was starting to scare him.

"Well, it did," Louie said. "And if you know what's good for you, you won't be like that cat. You get my drift? 'Cause if I find out about you telling anyone, you *and* your friends will be sorry. Got it?"

Corey nodded, frightened by the menace in Louie's voice. He realized if Louie could drop a brick on Joe, he could do worse. Corey couldn't stand the thought of anything happening to Sara, or Joe, or Cindy for that matter. They had become his surrogate family—one that he didn't want to lose and would do anything to protect.

3:00 p.m.

In the office, Joe and the professor were continuing their talk while Murphy had gone up to the roof to check on things, explaining that with the arrival of Joe and his group their regular schedule of keeping watch up there for other survivors had gone out the window. When he came back, he didn't seem happy.

"There is definitely something going on," he said. "There are *no* monsters or flying' Vaders around, but outside you can hear this constant rumble, far away, but getting closer. I don't know what the hell they're up to, but it can't be good."

Joe said, "There were no monsters sleeping in the streets

last night. And, on our way here, I didn't see any either. Only once did I see the orbs, right around dawn, and they were moving far overhead and seemed to be going somewhere with a purpose."

"Yeah," Murphy said. "We noticed the lack of sleeping beasts last night, too. I think the scarcity of the aliens has something to do with that constant rumbling outside."

"What do you think we should do, Murph?" Joe asked. In the few short hours he had been around Murphy, Joe had become very impressed with the man. Part of it was the fact that Murphy was a cop. Because of that, Joe found it easy, and agreeable, to defer leadership to him. It felt good *not* to be the one making the decisions all the time. It was more than that, too; it was the way Murphy conducted himself, the way he spoke. He oozed confidence and charisma that Joe guessed was the stuff leaders possess. Joe had never met anyone like him before; he'd heard of natural-born leaders—guys like JFK, Patton, Lincoln, even Christ—but hadn't really known what the term meant until he met Duane Murphy. Joe could honestly say that he would follow Murphy anywhere, and he had never felt that way before about anyone.

"We need some recon to see what they're up to. We need to get to a higher vantage point," Murphy said. "We're surrounded by buildings taller than this one. If we want to know what's going on all over the city, we've got to climb, but we'll need tools to get in any of the buildings around here. I'm glad I've got my gun to protect us against the monster 'Vaders—"

"But not the flying ones," the professor interrupted.

"Actually," Joe said, smiling, "I know something that works *amazingly* well against the orbs. Are there any portable, dry chemical fire extinguishers around here?"

3:15 p.m.

Cindy and Louie were in the walk-in refrigerator again, smoking and talking in low voices, when Murphy barged in on them.

"Louie," Murphy said loudly, "I need your toolbox and any chemical fire extinguishers you got."

"I got no tools," Louie stammered.

Murphy slapped him on the back while giving Cindy one of his X-ray looks of intimidation. She looked right back at him, doing a good job of not showing her fear.

"Aw, come on, Louie, don't be like that," Murphy said, squeezing Louie's shoulder. "All I need is a crowbar or something like it to break into the building next door."

"I got a fire axe," Louie told Murphy.

"That'll do," Murphy said. He released Louie's shoulder. "Go get it." He followed Louie out of the refrigerator room after pointing a finger gun at Cindy. "Check you later," he said, grinning.

Cindy gave him her middle finger, but not until his back was turned.

Outside the walk-in fridge, Louie went to the front of the kitchen and opened the sliding door cabinet under the checkout counter. Behind several boxes of cash register receipt rolls was a fire axe.

Murphy hefted the axe, feeling its weight and running his thumb along the edge of the blade, testing its sharpness. "Okay, this'll do. What about the extinguishers?"

"Yeah, yeah," Louis said quickly. "I got three, two in here and one in the storage-room closet in the import store."

3:25 p.m.

The sun was fierce and the air was clammy with humidity. It immediately made Joe's clothing cling to his skin. It was so oppressive it felt like a physical weight on Joe's shoulders, and made the camera with the telescopic lens around his neck, and the portable extinguisher he carried, feel even heavier than they were. Getting to the tall building next door on 27th Street was easy for Joe and Murphy. They saw no sign of the 'Vaders, but they could hear a constant rumbling in the distance that reminded Joe of when he was a kid in Portsmouth. The New Hampshire highway department had torn down a neighborhood of about a dozen houses not far from Joe's neighborhood to make way for a new interstate highway. Those houses being razed sounded just like what he was hearing now.

At the building, getting inside proved to be difficult. Apparently, it was an office building—Joe peered through the upper glass part of the door and read a directory on the wall indicating the place was filled with offices for doctors, lawyers, and accountants, and an upscale hairdressing shop called *Curly's*.

The entrance to the building was recessed, allowing some cover while they worked on breaking in. Joe stood at the corner edge of the recess, the fire extinguisher held up in front of him with both hands. Every few moments he leaned toward the street and stuck his head out to glance quickly up and down 27th Street and up at the sky.

Murphy was cursing, muttering a litany of swears. The door wouldn't budge. It was a metal door, and its edge was flush against the stone of the building; Murphy could not find a spot in which to insert the axe blade and get some leverage.

"I knew a damn crowbar would have been better," Murphy muttered. "Shit! This axe is a piece of shit!"

Joe was getting nervous as Murphy's string of expletives got increasingly louder. Joe stuck his head out again, looked left then right, and finally up. There was a glint of reflected sunlight.

Joe grabbed Murphy's arm. "Shh. 'Vaders," he whispered.

They flattened themselves against the recessed walls, but when Joe looked again, there was nothing; the sky was clear in all directions.

"Sorry," Joe said. "False alarm."

"Maybe," Murphy said. "Maybe not. But this is taking way too long." He took a deep breath. "There's only one thing to do." Before Joe could ask what he meant, Murphy swung the axe with both hands against the glass, cracking it.

Joe reeled as if the blow had been against him. He staggered onto the sidewalk and looked at the sky, sure that he would soon see a swarm of 'Vaders descending on them. He looked east and west, certain a horde of beasts would soon be charging upon them.

He saw nothing.

"Damn! This shit is safety glass," Murphy said, and hammered the glass two more times before it crumpled.

An alarm went off in the building. It hurt Joe's ears and filled him with panic. If the sound of the axe on the glass hadn't got the 'Vaders' attention, this surely would. He wanted to run back to the import store and safety, but he didn't want to appear cowardly to Murphy.

For his part, Murphy seemed no more nervous than before. Murphy pulled the glass out of the door and stuck his head and right arm inside.

"Son of a bitch!" he cursed. He pulled back and turned to Joe. "I can't unlock it from the inside, either. We're going to have to climb through."

He threw the axe inside, then grabbed the bottom of the window frame in the door and hauled himself up. He leaned in until the upper part of his body was far enough inside that his waist was resting on the bottom of the frame. He rocked his body in a seesaw motion a couple of times and tumbled inside head over heels.

Joe's rising panic, due to the alarm, which sounded to him as loud as a sonic boom, had him so jittery he couldn't stand still. He kept looking at the sky and the street in both directions and was amazed there was still no sign of 'Vaders, the flying kind or the monster kind.

A moment after tumbling inside, Murphy calmly went over to a narrow area, set back a few feet to the right of the elevators, which held a locked glass-faced cabinet containing a series of buttons, an array of lights, and a map of the building's alarm system. Murphy went to it and shattered the cabinet with one blow of the axe. He pressed a few buttons and the alarm went silent.

Joe let out a sigh of relief but still kept an eye on the outside for any sign of 'Vaders.

"Now if that didn't bring them down on us, you *know*

there's got to be *something* going on," Murphy said, coming back to the door. "Give me the extinguisher," he told Joe.

Joe handed it over and tried to climb through as Murphy had done. He got stuck halfway and Murphy had to pull him through.

They were in a lobby with a black-and-gray tiled floor. Directly opposite the entrance were two elevators. Murphy went over to the elevators and punched both CALL buttons. "You know, come to think of it, there have probably been alarms going off all over the city from those things trying to get at people inside buildings. Maybe they've become accustomed to them by now and don't bother to investigate."

Both elevators arrived at the same time, their bells ringing as they settled into the lobby.

"Let's go," Murphy called as the right elevator door opened first. He stepped inside, followed by Joe. According to the elevator's panel there were thirty-five floors in the building, not counting the basement. Since there was no button for the roof, Murphy pressed the button numbered 35 and the doors closed.

Joe couldn't believe it. Muzak accompanied them as they rode; a schmaltzy string version of Nirvana's "Smells Like Teen Spirit." The surrealism of it brought laughter to his lips, especially when Murphy remarked:

"I hate this fucking song."

The doors opened on the thirty-fifth floor with a pleasant *ding*. The square ceiling lights in the corridor were on, as was the air-conditioning.

"Ahh!" Murphy said, stepping into the hallway and opening his arms wide to let the coolness infiltrate his clothing. "A little piece of Heaven. If that asshole, Louie, weren't such a . . . well, *asshole*, he'd have put AC in his store and the restaurant."

"What is it with you two?" Joe asked.

Murphy holstered his pistol, leaned the axe against the wall, and unbuttoned his shirt. "What do you mean?"

"You know . . . it's obvious you guys don't like each other

and . . . honestly, it seems to me at least that there's something going on."

Murphy scrutinized Joe for a moment. "It's that obvious, huh? Okay. I'll tell you, but you've got to keep it under your hat."

"But I don't have a hat," Joe said, grinning.

"Then keep it in your shorts," Murphy said, smirking. "We've been staking out Louie and his import store for a couple of months."

"We?" Joe interrupted.

"Agents of the Department of Homeland Security. About a year ago, they asked the police commissioner to assign half a dozen patrolmen to help with stakeouts at different locations. I volunteered and got assigned to the Shangri-La and dipshit dirtbag Louie. The FBI had identified him as a go-between with the Colombo Mafia family and several street gangs in the city and across the water in Jersey. Louie deals almost exclusively with the street gangs, mostly providing stolen prescription drugs. Lately, though, the FBI thinks he's expanded into weapons. And since a couple of the African American gangs on both sides of the river have identified themselves more and more with the fringe radical faction in Nation of Islam, and have got mixed up with a fundamentalist Muslim group called American Jihad, Homeland Security got involved.

"The day of the invasion, I was working a phony Public Works setup at the corner of Sixth and East Twenty-seventh, opposite Shangri-La. We had got a tip that Louie was either going to receive some weapons, or would be delivering some to Harlem and Jersey. The tip we got wasn't sure. Then the 'Vaders, as the kid calls them, showed up and just to save my skin I ended up hiding out in his store."

Murphy walked down the hall, heading for the EXIT sign at the end. Joe followed him into the stairwell and up the last flight of stairs to a door marked ROOF. AUTHORIZED PERSONNEL ONLY.

Murphy tried the door, but it was locked. He used the axe

on it with success. After half a dozen blows, Murphy finally got the door open, mangled though it was.

Murphy flattened himself against the wall and motioned for Joe to do the same next to him, then handed him the axe. Retrieving his pistol, Murphy stepped cautiously through the door onto the roof. Looking left and around the staircase housing, he then stepped cautiously to the open swinging door. Using it like a shield, he peered around it, checking the rest of the roof.

"It looks clear," he told Joe. "Stay low."

The two of them ran hunched over across the roof to the front of the building. Murphy looked over the edge and left and right over 27th Street.

"Give me the telescopic lens," he told Joe. Joe took it off the camera around his neck and handed it to Murphy, who began to scan the city with it. After ten minutes, he let out a low whistle.

"I'll be a son of a bitch!"

"What? What is it?"

"Wait until the professor hears about this! It looks like he was right!"

"What?" Joe asked, more adamantly.

"Here. Look for yourself."

Joe took the lens and looked in the direction Murphy was pointing.

"This definitely proves those things are more than just mindless eating machines, or simple eggs. They can communicate with each other, and it looks like they have a plan," Murphy said.

3:25:30 p.m.

As Joe and Murphy got ready to go out, Sara saw Cindy sitting by herself on her makeshift bed of rugs in the storeroom. She went over and sat next to her.

"How are you doing?"

Cindy regarded her through narrowed eyelids. "Okay."

Sara waited for more, but nothing came. "I'm good, too," she said.

Cindy didn't look at her, just kept staring vacantly ahead.

"Are you sure you're okay?" Sara asked softly. She reached over and squeezed Cindy's arm.

Cindy immediately pulled her arm away. "I said I was," she snapped.

"Sorry," Sara replied immediately. "It's just that you don't look so good. I don't mean to pry."

"Then don't!"

"Okay, sorry," Sara said, putting her hands up in surrender. She got up and walked over to where Donna lay propped up on her bed of throw pillows, reading a book. Donna lowered the book when Sara sat cross-legged on the floor next to her.

"You know, I've been trying to finish this book since Bill and I started our vacation. I should have finished it a week ago, but now I just can't seem to understand or remember what I'm reading. I keep having to go back and read the same sentence or paragraph over and over again." She seemed about to cry over it. "You know, I'm glad you're here, Sara," she added, tears welling in her eyes. "I've been really close to totally losing it a lot. It's nice to have another woman around." She glanced over at Cindy and added, "Especially one as nice as you that I can talk to."

Sara smiled and patted her hand.

"What's the matter with her?" Donna asked in a shaky whisper, looking from Sara to Cindy.

"Beats me."

"Have you known her long?" Donna asked.

Sara almost replied, "Long enough," but realized that wasn't true; she didn't know Cindy at all. She shook her head, no.

"I didn't think so," Donna remarked. "I mean, you two are very different. I wouldn't think you would have much in common."

"Only what we all have in common," Sara stated.

Donna looked puzzled.

"We're all survivors," Sara answered.

3:30 p.m.

As soon as Murphy and Joe left, Cindy went into the women's room, locked herself in a stall, and shot up the last of her heroin.

It wasn't enough; she barely felt it—she craved more. She felt panic awaken in her stomach and start to crawl into her chest.

She needed something, *anything*.

With Joe and Murphy gone, she decided it was the best time to get what she needed from Louie. She found him going into the walk-in refrigerator to finish the cigarette Murphy had interrupted.

"So, you've made up your mind?" Louie asked after lighting her cigarette.

"Yeah. But there's two things we got to straighten out first," she said. "I get paid up front."

"Okay," Louie said. "No biggie. And what's the other thing?"

"Where, exactly, are you planning on us doing this? If you're thinking of in here, think again. It's got to be somewhere that there's no chance of anyone walking in on us, especially the kid."

"I've got just the place," Louie said with a lecherous grin and a wink. "Follow me."

Everyone else was in the storage room. He led Cindy to the back wall of the empty kitchen. He pushed a freestanding tall wooden cabinet that was against the wall to the left, revealing a door behind it with a padlock. A key was taped to the back of the cabinet. Louie took it down, unlocked the door, and ushered Cindy through into a dark, nicely cool room. He pulled the cabinet back in place behind him before closing the door, and turned on a light.

"Whoa!" Cindy said. They were in a small garage, standing next to a brand-new black-and-yellow Humvee. Cindy couldn't believe her eyes.

"Like it? This is a one-of-a-kind, specially customized military model of the Humvee," Louie said. "It can be mounted with machine guns on the roof, and it's got all the state-of-the-art technology inside—GPS, radar, radio-jamming equipment, onboard computer—all kinds of cool shit."

Cindy nodded, wide eyed. "Where the hell did you get it?"

Louie looked smug. "I told you, there's more to the import business than vases, rugs, and lamps."

Cindy regarded him with newfound respect. "You *are* in the mob."

Louie shrugged.

"You'd have to be to have something like this." There was just enough space in the small garage for her to walk around the Hummer and admire it. "Who did you get this for?"

Louie shook his head and wagged his finger at her. "You should know better than to ask questions like that."

"What?" Cindy asked. "You don't trust me?" She laughed. "Maybe you think I'm wearing a wire."

Louie laughed, also. "Yeah," he said, "I guess it don't fucking matter now, pardon my French. This was ordered by the leader of a wacko group in Jersey called American Jihad, who were supposed to take delivery last Sunday, the day the fucking world came to an end, so I don't know if they backed out or just got fucked by circumstances, pardon my French. If things were different, I wouldn't have cared if they bailed on me; I know of a couple of Harlem gangs that would have loved to get their hands on this baby. They probably still would, if they're still around, especially now that all law and order has gone the way of the dinosaurs."

Cindy felt something she hadn't felt in a long time, a feeling she had started to think she might never feel again— *hope!* "Which Harlem gangs do you know about?" she asked.

"There's only two," Louie replied, "the Latin Kings and Family Way. Family Way is made up of the former Bloods and Crips. After they got broken up by the FBI, those two gangs joined forces and created Family Way. Nice name, huh? Who'd think it was a gang of bloodthirsty, drug-taking, pimping bastards with a name like that?"

"You know, the Family Way *has* survived," Cindy told him.

"How do you know that?"

"Because I work for Family Way. I know their leader, Z-Jay, and if he knew you had this here and were willing to deal it, he'd come and get it." She was standing behind the Hummer, facing Louie, her arms crossed with attitude that was all bluff. It took a monumental effort for her to keep her panicky need to get high in check; especially if there was a way Louie could get her to Z-Jay.

Louie regarded her thoughtfully for a few moments. "You can get in touch with him?"

"Of course; Z-Jay loves my ass," Cindy said with even more bluff attitude than her posture presented.

"So . . . why haven't you? Been in touch with him, I mean. You know, if he *loves* your ass so much, why ain't he come and got you if he's still alive?"

"Uh . . ." Cindy's bluff faltered. "I been having trouble with my cell."

It didn't fool Louis. "You are so full of shit, you stink."

Cindy got angry. "I am *not* full of shit, asshole!" She turned to leave.

Louie grabbed her arm. "Okay, okay. No need to get your undies all in a bunch about it. Here." He pulled a folded packet of paper, about the size of a dollar bill folded in half, out of his pocket and opened it. Inside were a dozen large white pills and three fat joints.

"Don't get upset, sugar," he said, snuggling up to her and putting the pills in her hand. "I never doubted you, doll, I was just playing."

"I *am* Z-Jay's number-one girl, and I *can* get in touch with him."

Louie took her in his arms, kissing her deeply. "Yeah," he said when their lips and tongues separated. "We can talk about that *after*." He grinned as he squeezed both her breasts. "I'm so horny I was starting to consider getting it on with Juan or Rico."

"Eww!" Cindy said, and nibbled on his ear while he kissed her neck.

"Hey, if you've ever done a long stretch in the can, you wouldn't be so quick to judge."

"I ain't judging, Louie, just commenting. Why plow the Hershey Highway when you can have me?"

"Oh, yeah!" Louie agreed, pulling up her sweatshirt and burying his face in her bare breasts.

"But let's not do it *right* here." She pushed him away lightly so as not to offend.

"Sure, sure," Louie said, unable to take his eyes or his hands off her breasts. "Let's get in the Hummer." He chuckled. "Then you can give me a *Hummer*!"

"Mmm!" Cindy moaned as if she thought that was a delicious idea. "But can I crush and snort a couple of these first? And let's smoke a joint. It always helps get me really horny, you know?"

"Sure, baby. I've got everything you need right in the Humvee."

True to his word, Louie pulled a small tool case out from under the backseat once they were in the Hummer. Cindy used the round end of the handle of a screwdriver as a pestle. The inside of the toolbox cover made a more than adequate mortar. They shared a joint while Cindy crushed the pills into powder. Louie rolled up a fifty-dollar bill for her to use as a straw.

As soon as Cindy finished snorting four of the ground-up tablets, Louie stubbed the joint out in the ashtray and started pulling her clothes off. She pushed his hands away and went to work. Louie was satisfied less than three minutes later, still dressed with only his zipper undone.

"God! I needed that," he said with a sigh. "How about you?"

"Oh, yeah," Cindy said, meaning the OxyContin high and not the oral sex. She snuggled up to Louie and put her head on his chest. "You know," she said, caressing Louie's flaccid phallus with her right hand, "we should take this thing and get the hell out of Dodge and leave Murphy and these other assholes behind before they get wise to it being here. I know where Z-Jay's crib is and it's a fucking fortress! We'd be safe there and you'd have access to just about anything you need or want, whether it be drugs or pussy."

"Yeah, well, that's easier said than done. I've seen what those things out there can do to *any* vehicle they get their paws on. There's no way I'm going up against those monsters, even with this baby. I ain't in a hurry to get killed."

Cindy continued her hand play, slowly arousing Louie again. "But I thought you said this is customized with weapons and shit that'll protect us?"

Louie moaned and pushed Cindy's head toward his renewed erection and said, "Yeah. The only problem is that I don't know how to trick this ride out with all its accessories. The buyers were going to do all that shit; I was just delivering it with the weapons separate. Most of the military gear for this bad boy is still hidden in a storage bin under the floor in my office in the import store. The trapdoor is right under my desk where fucking Murphy—pardon my French—and the professor always are. The only thing out here is a case of grenades." He pointed his thumb over his shoulder at the cargo area behind the rear seats.

Cindy disengaged her face from his lap. "Why can't you get that shit at night?"

"That asshole Murphy sleeps in there. Besides, there's too much stuff and most of it is too large to handle in secret and quiet."

"What's in there?" Cindy asked, getting an idea.

"Enough stuff to fight a small war," Louie said. "There's a machine gun that can be mounted on the top of the Humvee and can fire in a full circle. And look at these." He turned and pulled a large square cardboard box, about three inches thick, from the cargo area behind the backseat and pulled off the lid. "These are *grenades*! Pardon my French, but are these the coolest fucking things you've ever seen? I've also got half a dozen M-16 rifles in there, some plastic explosives, Uzi automatic pistols—lethal shit—and a few small handguns. All of it was ordered by the Jersey gang. They paid half up front, but, what good is money now, you know?"

"I just got an idea," Cindy said. "If I tell Z-Jay about all this shit, I think I can get *him* to come *here*."

"Yeah . . . maybe," Louie said, pushing her head down. "But we don't want to be missing too long and arouse suspicions. Finish me off so's we can get back."

4:00 p.m.

Murphy called for a meeting as soon as he and Joe returned. Everyone gathered in the import store's storage room.

"People," Murphy began, "it looks like we're going to have to relocate, and preferably out of the city." Murphy held his hand up against the barrage of "whys" and, "What are you talking about?"

"The reason we have been seeing fewer 'Vaders is because they are all congregating at the edges of the city, along the Hudson River and the East River."

"Isn't that good?" Bill promptly asked.

"It would be if they were planning on staying there," Murphy answered. "But, unfortunately for us, they seem to have other plans."

Louie spoke up. "What do you mean, *plans*? Those things don't make *plans*, they just eat everything in sight."

"Yeah," Bill added. "If they could plan that would mean they're intelligent, and I don't think any of us have seen any evidence of that."

"Well, think again," Murphy told him. "*I* didn't think they were intelligent, either, but I've just seen proof of it. The reason they are congregating at the rivers on both sides of us is because they're planning to ferret out any survivors like us by going from building to building, street by street. They're wrecking the smaller buildings—they've already destroyed a good part of the small apartment and residential buildings along the edges of the city. Any buildings too big for them to bring down, they're sending in the orbs and smaller monsters to flush people out. The flying 'Vaders are going two to three streets ahead of the destruction to spy and catch anyone who tries to get out before the monsters reach their

building. This is a well-planned, coordinated attack that the
flying 'Vaders are directing."

"Are you saying *those flying eggs* are intelligent, too?
That's bull!" Louie challenged.

"You don't have to believe me, smart guy. Get some balls
and go up to the roof of the building we just came from and
see for yourself." Murphy paused while he stared Louie
down, which didn't take long. Louie sat grumbling to himself.

"Look, I don't really give a rat's ass if y'all believe me.
Oops, sorry, Corey."

"It's okay, Murph," Corey said, smiling.

"Thanks. Like I was saying, I don't care if y'all believe
me or not. If you want to stay here and take your chances, go
right ahead. But know that if you do, I think you're going to
become dinner."

4:10 p.m.

While Murphy talked and then argued with the others,
Cindy's mind was racing and planning. She leaned close to
Louie and whispered in his ear, "This would be a good time
for me to call Z-Jay and get him over here to rescue us, don't
you think?"

Louie shook his head. "I ain't going nowhere. This is perfect for you and me. Murphy's nuts. Let these dickheads
leave; we can stay right here and have everything we need—
weapons to protect us, plenty of food, and drugs from the
CVS."

Cindy expected Louie to cop out, and she was ready with
Plan B. While the others talked over their options, Cindy
told him she was going to the can and slipped out of the
room. She went to the women's room in the restaurant and
took out her cell phone. Praying that the phone had enough
charge left, and that Z-Jay would answer this time, she dialed his cell number and waited. The Jam Man answered
again.

"Jam Man, don't hang up, please. You *have* to let me talk
to Z-Jay."

"Really? That's where you wrong, bee-atch. I don't have to let you do nothin'. Now unless you got somethin' Z-Jay *really* needs, which ain't your scrawny white ass, then you should know better than to bother the brother."

"I do! I do," Cindy said quickly before Jam Man could hang up on her.

"Yeah? Like what?" The Jam Man asked doubtfully.

"I got to tell Z-Jay, no one else," she said.

"Where the fuck do you get the idea that *you* got to do *anything*? Either you tell me, or you don't tell *no one*. You got *that,* bitch?"

"Okay, okay." Cindy gave in immediately. "Tell him I've got something he can really use, especially now." She went on to tell him about the military model Humvee and the munitions Louie had told her were stashed in the import store. When she finished, she held her breath for several moments until Jam Man said, "Hold on. I'll get Z-Jay."

Cindy nearly wept with relief.

She had broken out in a cold sweat, partly from nervousness, partly from the need for another fix. She waited for what seemed like forever before Z-Jay finally came on the line.

"Hey, baby! What's this Jam Man be tellin' me that you got a fuckin' tank and other army weapons and shit for me. You jivin' me, right? You just need your pony ride so bad you say anythin', right?"

"No, no, no, Z-Jay. I ain't bullshitting you. I know where the shit is—it's right here, where I'm hiding out. All you got to do is come get it and me."

"Oh yeah? It's like that, is it? What do you take me for? White? You think I'm stupid? You think I'm goin' to come over there only to find out you been lyin' 'cause you too hard up for smack?"

"I ain't lying, Z-Jay. Honest. The stuff's here; it's right here!" Cindy had to think fast and come up with something to prove to Z-Jay that she wasn't lying or he was going to hang up and write her off.

"Z-Jay, you . . . you know I could never lie to you, baby.

If you just send one of the guys over here with a car or a motorcycle, I'll bring you proof."

"Yeah? What proof?"

Cindy thought fast. "How about a couple of grenades?"

"Grenades, huh?"

She could tell from his voice that she finally had Z-Jay's agreement.

4:17 p.m.

The group meeting in the rear room of the import store had degenerated into a free-for-all argument. Bill thought they should stay but move to the basement of the building, which Louie claimed was a fallout shelter. Murphy and the professor had already checked it out on Monday and had found that Louie was either lying or had been misinformed.

"I'm telling you," said the professor, "I've looked at the basement and it is not a fallout shelter. This building is small enough for the aliens to destroy. When they do, the entire structure will collapse on you if you hide in the basement. If it had been built as a bomb shelter that would not be the case. To hide out there would be to sign your own death warrant. The place is a death trap."

"How do you know that?" Bill challenged. "I'm a real estate agent and I know something about architecture."

"Then go look for yourself," Murphy told him. "If you and your wife want to stay down there, go ahead; no one will stop you."

Bill glowered at Murphy but said no more.

Juan and Rico put forth the idea of hiding out in the subways.

"Maybe the trains are still running," Juan said.

Rico joined in. "Yeah. We haven't lost power, so they might be. Don't they run automatically, like on computers?"

"No, they don't," Murphy answered. "Some of the track switches are automatic, but not the trains. They need people to run them."

Rico looked dejected, but Juan countered with, "Still, wouldn't underground be the best place to hide? Those things . . . those monsters are too big to get into the subways, aren't they?"

Murphy looked at Joe and Joe answered. "There's something going on in the subways with these things. We saw a lot of the smaller ones going in and out of the subway entrances. The flying ones do the same. We're not sure what it means, but I don't think it's a good place to hide out. If the subways haven't been already cleared of people who were hiding out there, doing that seems to be part of the 'Vaders' plan now."

A despairing silence descended on the meeting. Donna wept silently and took Bill's hand. She held it so tightly her knuckles turned white. Juan and Rico did the same with eachother.

"So, what do we do?" Sara asked.

Joe shrugged. The professor kept his eyes down, intently studying his fingernails. Only Murphy seemed prepared to answer the question.

"I don't think we have a choice. Without any sort of government authority to help us out or tell us where to go, we're on our own. You know, during a normal disaster or emergency, the government would have rescue centers where we could go. But I don't think that's going to happen. We need to decide where we're going to go and figure out the quickest and safest way to get out of the city. We need to get off Manhattan Island. Unfortunately, that means either going through a tunnel or over a bridge."

"What about leaving by boat?" Sara asked. "Actually, couldn't we sail anywhere we want?"

"Yeah!" Juan joined in. "Maybe we could sail to an island where there are no aliens and monsters. You know, like some deserted place, like on *Survivor*."

"I've always wanted to live in Hawaii," Rico added, brightening a bit.

"Yeah," Murphy said, "and I'd like to grow roses out of my ass, but that ain't happening. We have to be very logical and cautious, folks. Do you really want to be on a boat with a very limited escape or hiding capacity when the alien eggs come flying after us? Because they will. And what if the orbs have transformed sea creatures? Do you really want to be attacked by a giant monster guppy, or worse? Besides, we'd have to get past the line of monsters to get to a boat. We're better off in cars."

Professor Ligget spoke up. "Officer Murphy is correct; the best chance for our survival is to get out of the city and go somewhere that is less densely populated. It's obvious the aliens are focusing their attention on the city, and it's safe to assume they are doing this in every city in the world." He looked at Juan and Rico, who were still pouting over their island idea being shot down.

"Remember, boys, Manhattan *is* an island, roughly twenty-three square miles, with over seven million people living in that space. I figure the 'Vaders have transformed roughly a third of that number, maybe half, and the transformed have eaten at least another third of the population. I think that may be a low estimate, but I can't be sure. That leaves approximately two and a half million or less who, like us, are still hiding out somewhere in the city.

"The fact that the aliens know this, which is exhibited by their recent behavior in their methodical way of going street by street and flushing out hiding survivors proves they are much more intelligent than any of us thought. At first, their attack was similar to, say, a situation where a large number of dangerous zoo animals got free—like man-eating tigers and lions. The animals would kill and consume whoever they caught outside. So if everyone just stayed inside, the animals would eventually starve, or be forced to look for food somewhere else. They would not think of going inside to hunt. We made the mistake of assuming the aliens are nothing more than animals with limited intelligence ruled by instinct. I see now that was wrong. They are a very calculating enemy, an intelligent enemy, but not intelligent in the way that we are; it's more like insect intelligence—collective intelligence, like bees or army ants."

The room was silent. Each person was lost in thought and the mental challenge of figuring out how to get away from the city, which had become a death trap.

"We're going to need transportation," Sara said, speaking up after several minutes of pensive silence. "And it's got to be something that can also protect us. We don't have a lot of weapons."

Murphy smiled and nodded. "My thoughts exactly."

Joe spoke next. "Since the 'Vaders are all at the edges of the city, working their way to the middle, we should be able to go out and find transportation if we're careful. Like Murphy said, we saw the flying eggs a couple streets ahead of the line of monsters looking for people trying to make a run for it, but they're still many blocks away; we should be able to stay out of sight of them, but we need to get ready and go now, *tonight*! And it'll be easier if we can find some weapons." Joe looked at Murphy, who looked pointedly at Louie.

"We can get our vehicles off the street, but we might not have to go too far for weapons." Murphy spoke to all, but looked at Louie as he said it. Louie was starting to appear uncomfortable.

"What about it, Louie?"

Louie looked at Murphy and did his best to act confused. "What about what?" he asked.

"You know what I'm talking about."

Louie became agitated. He stood and looked around the room. "I don't. I don't know what you mean."

"Really?" Murphy said.

"Yeah, really." Louie started for the door. "I don't have to take any shit from you, Murphy. You're not a fuckin' cop anymore."

With lightning speed, Murphy grabbed Louie by the arm and flung him to the floor. Except for Joe, the others in the room gasped and looked shocked. They regarded Murphy with new eyes filled with fear and intimidation.

"What are you doing?" the professor asked, confronting Murphy.

"Take it easy," Murphy replied to him and to all the questioning faces in the room. "I told you all that I'm a cop who was assigned to the New York Office of the Department of Homeland Security, and that is true. But what I didn't tell you is that on day one of the invasion my working traffic at the intersection outside was a fake. It was a cover for me to keep an eye on this store, Shangri-La Imports, and its owner, Louie Lafayette. Homeland Security had been keeping tabs on little Louie here for months."

The shocked and outraged faces changed to consternation and interest.

"Louie here is a dealer. He's not picky about what he deals, or who he deals it to. He started out with drugs, but has moved on to weapons. Ain't that right, Louie?"

Louie didn't answer and didn't look at anyone in the room.

"About three months ago, Homeland Security got a tip that Louie was doing a major weapons deal with a group of fundamentalist Muslims in Jersey who call themselves American Jihad. These guys are all U.S. citizens and none of them are linked to any Middle Eastern countries, which makes them hard to find and twice as dangerous. And lovable little Louie"—Murphy's voice dripped with sarcasm—"was going to provide them with weapons so they could pull off an attack à la nine-eleven."

"Is that true, Louie?" Juan asked.

"Fuck you, faggot," Louie spat out at Juan, but his eyes remained on Murphy.

"Fuck me?" Juan shouted, standing. "Fuck *me*? My brother was *killed* on nine-eleven and you want to help those scumbags do it again? No! I say *fuck you*!" Juan tried to kick Louie in the head but Rico restrained him. "You're a piece of shit!" Juan screamed at Louie. "A piece of filthy shit!" Juan began crying and Rico embraced him.

4:30 p.m.

Cindy closed her cell phone. Z-Jay had told her exactly what to do. While the others went on arguing in the storeroom, Cindy snuck through the kitchen, moved the cabinet out just enough to squeeze behind it and get the key taped to its back, and let herself into the shed. She climbed into the Hummer and stuffed a couple of hand grenades into her purse, then left by way of the shed's side door into the alley behind the import store and the restaurant. She was more scared than she had ever been in her entire life, but she was also in need of a fix more than she had ever needed one. She had sunk into the pit of drug addiction when the world had been normal; now that it was insane, she needed more of the drug than ever before. She hungered for the escape a strong shot of heroin would bring.

The first thing Cindy noticed as she slipped around the corner of the building and ran to the intersection was a distant rumbling sound. Since she had been too busy plotting to get to Z-Jay, or get him to come to her, she hadn't paid attention when Murphy and Joe were talking about what they had seen; she had no idea what the rumbling sound meant. She just presumed it was thunder. On hot humid days like today, New York often dealt with thunderstorms. She ran into the street and hid behind a white stretch limousine that had rammed the back of a tour bus. The wrecked vehicles were just long enough for her to get past the front of Shangri-La Imports and the Chinese restaurant. Once past, she continued to use wrecks and abandoned cars in the street to hide behind as she made her way up 6th Avenue. She had to get to 34th and 5th, the Empire State Building. Z-Jay had wanted her to come farther, but she was too scared and had pleaded with him. Only the enticement of the grenades with the promise of more, and the other powerful weapons, got him to agree. However, he did make sure she knew that if she was lying, the Jam Man, who was coming to get her on a motorcycle, had instructions to kill her on the spot.

4:35 p.m.

Corey didn't like all the shouting and crying and angry faces. The way Officer Murphy and Louie had fought and were now looking at each other made Corey nervous. He had rarely before seen such expressions of hate and anger.

It scared him.

While the grown-ups continued to argue and shout, Corey left the storeroom and wandered up and down the aisles of Shangri-La Imports, looking for something to play with. In aisle three, near the large display window at the front of the store, he found a wooden bin filled with large, square white tablecloths made of lace that were incredibly soft and silky. They were also smooth and sheer enough to see through.

Corey pulled one out of the bin, which was almost as high as his chin, and put it over his head, letting it fall to cover his face and entire body. He liked the way everything looked hazy through the material. He caught his reflection in the glass entrance door; he looked like a ghost. He raised his arms and moaned, "Boo-ooo!" Thoughts of ghosts brought thoughts of dying, which reminded him of his mom and all the people he had seen killed in the last few days.

He pulled the sheet off his head and stared at it, wondering if his mom was in Heaven now, watching him. Corey's mother had been Catholic, his father Jewish. His father wasn't religious, and his mother had insisted that Corey be raised Catholic and receive all the sacraments that religion bestowed. He had been baptized and had attended regular catechism classes, making his First Holy Communion last year when he was in second grade. He went to church every Saturday night with his mom.

Corey remembered a conversation he'd had with his mom when he was four or five. It had been a warm day during the seasonal January thaw. His mother had taken him shopping uptown with her and then for a walk in Central Park. There he had found a dead squirrel. His mother told him not to touch it, and he hadn't, but he had been unable to take his eyes off it and his mother had to pull him away. The image of the dead squirrel had remained with him the rest of the day until they were riding the subway home, and he had asked, "What happens when you die?"

His mother had looked at him with sad eyes and was

silent for several moments, thinking of how to answer. When she, at last, did answer, she said, "When you die, your soul leaves your body and—"

He had interrupted: "What's a soul?"

"It's like . . ." She paused for several moments before continuing. "It's the part of you that never dies. It's the thing that makes you human. It's the thing that makes you, *you!*"

He thought he had understood then. Sometime before that he had heard his mother talking about a friend's personality, and he had asked what a *personality* was. She had given him much the same answer as she had about the soul; *personality* was the way we thought and talked and laughed—in other words, all the things that made him Corey Aaron. It was all the things that made him a unique person. So, when his mother defined *soul* for him he had asked, "Is it my personality?"

"Yes." She had replied, "I think it is. It must be." She had smiled then and kissed his forehead.

Next question he asked, "Does your soul become a ghost after you die? Do you get to go around scaring people?"

She had laughed at that. "Maybe. Maybe that happens to some, but most souls go to Heaven, if the person was good, or to Hell if the person was bad. If you try to be a good person and live without hurting other people, but helping them, Heaven is your reward. It's a place where nothing bad ever happens and you are happy all the time."

"Like Disney World?"

She had laughed again. "I guess you could say that." She had tousled his hair and hugged him, whispering "I love you" in his ear.

"So what happens if you're a bad person like Andy Revelle?" he had asked.

"Who's that?"

"He's a mean kid at day care. He's always pushing kids off the swings and stuff," Corey had answered.

"Oh, I see. He's a bully."

"So what will happen to him when he dies?"

"Like I said, if he's a bad person, he'll go to Hell. That's a

place that is the opposite of Heaven. It's a place of punishment and he will never ever feel happy again."

"Like jail, where Daddy sends criminals?"

"Yes, Sweetie, like jail."

Corey wiped away the tears that came with remembering.
He hoped that his mother and Aunt Helen were in Heaven,
but he was worried that his aunt might not be since she had
been turned into a monster and tried to eat him. She might
be in Hell instead. Movement outside caught his attention,
and he looked up just in time to see someone duck behind a
long white limousine across the street. The limo had run into
the back of a big red bus.

Corey climbed into the display window and pressed his
face against the front glass, trying to see if it was one person
out there, or more than one, and if they were being chased by
'Vaders. He desperately wanted to open the front door and
yell for them to come inside, but he wanted to make sure
first. He looked down 6th Avenue as far as he could from his
position but didn't see anyone else. He looked up 6th Avenue,
and a moment later the person ran from behind the bus to
duck behind a van farther away.

Corey couldn't believe it; it was *Cindy*. Without a thought
for his own personal safety, he ran to the door and pushed it
open.

"Cindy! Cindy!" he yelled. With the rumbling of what
sounded like thunder in the distance, he didn't think she
heard him. If she did, she didn't show it. She kept going
without a glance back. Slowly, he closed the door.

"What's all the shouting for, Corey?" Joe asked. He and
the other survivors were coming out of the storeroom.

"Oh, my God!" Sara cried, and ran down the center aisle
to him. "Were you outside? You know better than that! What
were you doing?"

Corey looked at her, his lower lip trembling, his eyes
brimming with tears.

"Cindy's out there. She's running away." The tears rolled
down his cheeks, and he threw himself into Sara's arms.

Joe quickly went to the front display window and looked out.

"That bitch!" Louie muttered.

Murphy, who was close enough to hear him, laughed. "What's the matter, Louie? Did your girlfriend leave you hanging and horny?" He laughed again.

"Shouldn't we go after her?" Rico asked. Juan nodded in agreement.

"Why?" Murphy asked loudly. "Why should any of us risk our necks if she decided to leave? No one here made her go, right?"

Everyone looked at Louie. He put his hands up in surrender. "I sure as hell didn't make her leave."

"No," Murphy said pensively, his hand on his chin. "But you seemed pretty upset just now, Louie. Why is that?" Murphy could tell by the look on Louie's face that he had hit a bull's-eye. "Aw, did she break your little heart? Were you planning on her playing Eve to your Adam?"

"Fuck you!" Louie spat the words out and blushed a deep red.

"Hey!" Murphy warned. "Watch your mouth in front of the kid and the ladies." He walked over to Louie until he was standing right in front of him. At six-foot-two, he towered over Louie's five-foot-five.

"Now listen to me, Louie, and listen to me good, because I'm not going to repeat myself. We need *any* weapons you've got stashed, and we need them now. You're not going to be arrested, or punished, or anything like that for having these things. Those days are over, and I no longer give a shit *why* you have the weapons, or what you were going to do with them, or *who* you were going to sell them to. Even if it was Osama bin Laden himself, *I . . . don't . . . care*! But, if you don't tell me, I will beat you to a bloody pulp and no one here will stop me. Got it?"

The blush of embarrassment on Louie's face turned to the pale of fear. His nod was barely perceptible.

"So, are you going to tell us *where* you've got the goods hid?"

Louie looked around at the others, and all the fight seemed to suddenly go out of him. His shoulders sagged, and he looked down at his feet. "Yeah," he said softly.

"That's more like it," Murphy said, grinning broadly.

6:25 p.m.

Cindy was exhausted by the time she reached the Empire State Building at 5th Avenue and 34th Street. It had taken her close to two hours to travel the distance; she had gone slowly, stopping often to rest, running from hiding spot to hiding spot behind cars, trucks, demolished buildings, and recessed storefronts in her effort to go unnoticed by the 'Vaders.

At first, her fear had been overwhelming. So overwhelming, in fact, that for the first time in her life she thought of getting clean and kicking her heroin habit.

All I have to do is go back to Joe and Sara and the others; they'd help me go cold turkey, she had thought as she hid, crouching behind an overturned police car in the middle of 6th Avenue two blocks from the import store. *Is getting high worth this? Is it worth my life?* She might have turned back then, but even as she thought of doing it, the itch for the drug grew stronger. She literally ached for it, and the itch became real, spreading over her skin the way the bugs had in the tunnel.

She shivered at the memory. She dug her fingernails into the flesh of her arms and legs, trying to relieve the itch, but it was no good. The itch came from too deep within her. There was only one way to scratch it. Louie's OxyContin had helped stave off her need for a short time but not well enough to replace her beloved horse. She was a junk girl at heart and always would be. She despised herself for it, but she was a prisoner of her addiction. Deep down she knew that nothing but death would free her from her heroin prison.

Halfway to 34th Street she began to realize just how empty the city had become. Except for the strange, faraway rumbling sound—which she continued to tell herself was thunder, when she managed to think about it at *all* with everything else racing through her mind at breakneck speed—

it was quiet, too. She heard no sounds of screaming or monsters roaring. She had been expecting swarms of flying 'Vaders harassing her, followed by the people-eating giants, but the only thing bothering her had been flies, drawn by the blood smears and random bits and pieces of flesh left behind by the 'Vaders. A hope started to form, hope that the invasion was over. She dared to entertain the thought that the 'Vaders, both types, had somehow packed up and returned to wherever they had come from, or that they had been defeated and killed by the military. If she had paid attention back in the storeroom, and not run out so quickly, she would have known that to hope the invasion was over was stupid . . . and dangerous.

By the time she reached 34th Street, she was convinced that the worst was over, that the 'Vaders were indeed gone. That, combined with finally reaching her destination, quieted the thoughts and fears she'd had while being on the run alone. New fears crept in—like, "What the hell *is* that constant rumbling sound?" The eerie noise finally started to worry her. If this was thunder, it was the weirdest thunder she had ever heard. As she waited for Jam Man, feeling exposed, the clatter got on her nerves and made her as jittery as her need for her drug of choice. The tallest building in the city, looming behind her, felt like impending doom.

Her nervousness grew and her mind tortured her. *What if Z-Jay changed his mind? What if he's decided to leave me stranded out here? What if he chickened out and decided the weapons and the Humvee aren't worth the risk?*

At that moment, those thoughts scared her more than the threat of the 'Vaders and she spoke out loud, trying to drown the thoughts in her head by repeating, "Z-Jay wouldn't do that to me. Z-Jay will protect me and keep me in horse forever."

The question of what she was going to do when even Z-Jay ran out of smack, as he would if the horror continued, tried to worm its way into her mind, but she wouldn't let it. She didn't even want to consider that possibility—didn't want to face that truth. Secretly, she hoped she would die of an overdose before her supply was exhausted. Since first getting hooked on the drug, she had thought that overdosing would be the perfect death, the best way to go, like dying in your sleep. Peaceful. No pain.

But she had to have the horse to be able to ride it into oblivion.

Where the hell is Jam Man?

The sky had been overcast all day, and the humidity had been oppressive. Now it began to rain, and the shower made Cindy shiver, but the rumbling thunder still did not stop, nor did any lightning crackle across the sky. She moved closer to the building, seeking shelter under its enormous height. Something moved in the corner of her vision, startling her. She let out a short scream and was ready to bolt until she saw it was no threat—three rats were at the corner curb feeding on something. Not wanting to know what the meal was, but inexorably drawn to it, she slowly walked to the curb. A soft sob came from her lips, and her stomach did a nauseating turn when she saw a woman's left foot, severed at the ankle. She knew it was a woman's foot because it still wore a blue, plastic thong identical to the ones Cindy herself owned, and the foot's toenails were painted hot pink.

Cindy turned away from the gnawing rats and their feast. The rain came harder. Down the sidewalk a short way lay a folded newspaper. She ran to it, picked it up, and opened it to put it over her head against the rain. She was frozen by the front page. It was the Sunday *New York Times*, and the date was Sunday, June 23.

The first day of the invasion.

What day is it now? she wondered. She had no clue, and it bothered her. Before the 'Vaders, she had often been so wasted that she hadn't known the day or the time, and it hadn't mattered. Now it frightened her deeply, and she didn't know why. She felt as though she were at the edge of a dark chasm whose bottom was out of sight and she was about to fall into it.

Her shivers increased as she placed the thick newspaper over her head. The rain felt icy against her skin and made her teeth chatter. She was growing more nervous by the minute. She had already been out in the open far too long for comfort.

"Come on, Jam Man," she whispered. "Don't do this to me."

Twenty minutes passed and she was still standing in the rain. She looked around for some place inside to hide and wait and decided to try McManus's Empire State Restaurant across the street on 5th Avenue. There was a sign in its window advertising a Sunday brunch, so she figured it would be open.

She stayed close to the building until she reached the corner. Then, after a quick look north and south on 5th Avenue, she ran out to the street. The rats in the gutter at the corner were undisturbed by her presence, and that was fine with her as long as they kept their distance. There were more rats, a slew of them, in the middle of 5th Avenue, snouts to the asphalt feeding on a five-foot-long dark smear of goo on the road.

She did *not* want to know the source and went down 5th Avenue ten yards before crossing to avoid having to look at the goo too closely. She crossed the street at a run, feeling dizzy with fear at being so exposed. Despite the lack of any sign of 'Vaders—and her hope that they were gone—she still feared that, at any moment, one of the nightmare creatures would come thundering around a corner ready to snatch her up. Or worse, one of the glowing flying globes would chase her down and transform her.

Cindy reached the restaurant and tried the front door. It was locked. She cupped her hands over her eyes against the glass and peered inside. The place was dark. She took a daring chance and banged on the window. No answer. She looked at the sign advertising the place as open for Sunday brunch, but there was a handwritten addition below the large blocked letters. It read CLOSED FOR VACATION JUNE 23 TO JULY 7.

She turned her back to the door and leaned against it. This is bad, she thought. Why did I ever trust Z-Jay? I was better off with that slimeball Louie. At least he had the

OxyContin, and sooner or later she would have been able to get into the CVS next door and raid the pharmacy.

I've been really stupid. And for what? The good old brown horse, which is bound to dry up sooner or later with the world under the control of the 'Vaders. Why, why, why did I believe Z-Jay?

In the distance, mingled with the low-roaring rumble Cindy had heard constantly since leaving Louie's, there was a faint hum, gradually becoming louder and stronger than the thundering sound. She went out to the curb, trying to look everywhere at once in her paranoia, and listened. The sound was definitely getting louder and coming closer. It was no longer a humming sound but more of a buzz. She thought she recognized the sound but didn't want to get her hopes up and do something stupid that would get her killed. Still glancing furtively about, she retreated to the recessed entrance of the restaurant and looked up 5th Avenue where the sound was coming from, growing louder by the second.

Cindy crossed her fingers and did a jiggling little dance in place, like a kid who has to go to the bathroom. A manic whispered prayer passed her lips:

"Please God! Please God! Please God!"

When she finally saw the motorcycle coming down 5th Avenue, weaving in and out and around abandoned vehicles, she nearly shrieked with joy. She recognized Jam Man, Z-Jay's right-hand homey, immediately. He was barefoot and dressed in shorts with no shirt or helmet and wearing the sunglasses he almost never took off. He was also the only member of the gang who had a black Harley.

The rats in the street and at the corner scattered as the motorcycle neared. The bike was so loud it terrified Cindy; a sound as loud as that was sure to bring the 'Vaders down on them if they were still around. She hoped the rats had scattered because of the noise and approach of the bike and not the 'Vaders.

Cindy froze, too scared to step out and flag Jam Man down. He reached the corner of 34th and 5th and sat at the opposite curb revving his engine. She was positive the roar of his bike was going to bring 'Vader death as surely as the night brings darkness.

He continued revving the motorcycle and looking around. Cindy knew she had to step out and wave him over or he would leave without her, then she'd be truly screwed. Mustering all her courage, she dashed out to the street, waving her left arm at him. With a screech of tires, he spun the bike in a wide U-turn and pulled up in front of her.

The Jam Man regarded Cindy with contempt, which was his normal, every-day-and-every-situation expression.

"Thank God, Jam. I didn't think you were coming. I thought they got you."

The Jam Man hawked up a wad of saliva and spat it out. He ran a hand over his clean-shaven, dark brown head. Cindy noticed he had the beginnings of a beard decorating the sharp angles of his normally smooth-skinned face. "Nobody catches me when I'm riding," he said laconically.

"Yeah, yeah," Cindy replied. She was a bundle of nervous excitement tempered with fear. She reached for the helmet strapped to the back of the seat, but he slapped her hand away.

"Z-Jay says I gots to see the goods first. No pineapples, no rescue."

At first, Cindy was confused when he said "pineapples."

"What?" she asked.

Jam Man's look of contempt grew even more contemptuous. "The things that go boom, you know?"

Then she understood. "Oh! Yeah, right. The grenades." She opened her small purse, which was bulging from the two hand grenades in it, and showed the Jam Man.

He took one out, hefted it, getting a feel for its weight as he looked it over carefully.

"See? I got them just like I told Z-Jay." She looked around warily, and up at the sky. "Don't you think we should get going before the sound of your bike attracts the 'Vaders?"

Jam Man looked at her strangely. "The what?"

"The *in*vaders? You know, the things that have been turning people into monsters that eat everyone?"

"*'Vaders,*" Jam Man said slowly. "Shit! Sounds like a video game."

"Well, it isn't," Cindy said, going back to nervously jiggling like a kid with a full bladder. "Can we go now?"

"In a minute. I didn't see no *'Vaders* on the way here. They busy, so stifle yo'self," Jam Man replied, still looking the grenade over. "How many of these did you say is in the place you was jus' at?"

"A case full. Twenty or thirty, I guess. Plus there's machine guns and ammo and a Humvee that's all tricked out for carrying weapons, like for the army, you know?" she explained.

"No shit," Jam Man said slowly. Gripping the grenade tightly, holding its clip intact with the grenade the way he had seen it done in movies, Jam Man pulled the ring that removed the pin and armed the grenade.

"What are you doing?" Cindy cried. A new fear—the fear of being blown up—grabbed hold of her.

"Z-Jay says I gots to test the merchandise to make sure you ain't fuckin' us over." He looked around and threw the grenade with excellent aim through the open window of a silver BMW sedan that had been left sideways in the street about fifteen yards behind them. A second later the explosion blew the roof off the car, shattered all its windows, and set off its alarm as the entire car rose from the road a few inches and crashed back down. Almost simultaneously, the car's gas tank exploded with a more subdued *whump!* sound. Flames spread out in a widening pool behind the Beamer as the ignited gasoline poured from the ruptured gas tank.

"Holy shit!" Cindy cried. "That'll bring the 'Vaders down on us for sure."

Jam Man grinned, turned around, and removed the spare helmet strapped to the back of the bike and handed it to Cindy. "Then I guess we'll just have to outrun them, won't we?"

Cindy took the helmet, put it on, and climbed on the back of the bike as quickly as possible.

"Ready for a game of 'Vaders?" Jam Man asked with a laugh. "Then let's go!"

6:26 p.m.

Sara knelt next to the open trapdoor in Louie's office. Joe and Murphy were in the secret basement room below the trapdoor. From her position, Sara could see a cardboard box full of cellophane packages. Some of the packages held yellow bricks that looked like clay, the rest a green leafy substance she recognized as pot. Next to it was another box full of small cardboard packages of ammunition. In the last hour, Joe and Murphy had handed up six M-16 rifles and several crates of ammunition for those rifles to Bill and the professor. They were now searching through the rest of the contraband.

"What are those yellow bricks of clay for?" Sara asked Murphy.

"That ain't clay, darling, that is PBX—plastic bonded explosives. This particular formula is C4: cyclotrimethylenetrinitramine, also known as RDX. There's primer cord and remote electrical detonators down here, too. This stuff is very safe to handle, but once it's primed and detonated, look out! With four bricks, I'd say Louie's got enough here to blow up a good-size building—like the Stock Exchange, or the Statue of Liberty." He looked at Louie. "Is that what your buyers were planning with this stuff?"

"I-I don't know. I was just the middleman; I didn't even know what that shit was till you just explained it," Louie said nervously.

Sara moved back as Joe, then Murphy, emerged from the subterranean ammo dump with the bricks of explosives, leaving the marijuana below. Murphy brought a large leather overnight bag up with him and put it on the desk, which had been pushed against the back wall. He opened it and whistled at the contents.

"Woo-hoo! Looky here! We got micro Uzis—two of them." He pulled out a surprisingly small, funny-shaped gun. "I believe these are nine by nineteen millimeter." He pulled a long, narrow black magazine from the bag and clipped it into the Uzi. "These bad boys can fire twelve hundred fifty rounds per minute!" Next he took out several small handguns. One of them was a snub-nosed revolver. He handed it to Sara.

"Here. This should be perfect for you."

Sara gingerly took the weapon, noticing it was similar to the gun she had taken from the pizza parlor. That seemed so long ago now that it was difficult to accept that it had been only three days ago.

"Let me show you how to handle that," Murphy said, reaching for the pistol as she turned it over in her hands, examining it carefully. He thumbed a lever and the pistol opened between the cylinder and the handle.

"See?" he said. "This is how you load it." He looked through the box of cartridges Joe had brought up and picked one out.

"These are the ones," he told Sara, handing her the box. She held it up in her hands like an offering as he took the bullets out one by one and slid them into the open cartridge cylinder on the gun. It took six bullets. He spun the cylinder when it was fully loaded and snapped the pistol back together. It gave out a loud metallic *click!*

"This one is pretty light and doesn't have a lot of recoil. You should be able to handle it and fire it easily. Have you ever shot a gun before?"

She nodded.

"Good. It doesn't have a safety, so be careful."

Sara emptied the box of bullets for her pistol onto the desk and put them, one by one, into the front and back left pockets of her denim miniskirt. She counted eighteen bullets—twenty-four with the six in the gun's chamber. They made her pockets bulge. She didn't know where to put the pistol; her denim skirt was a little too loose at the waist to stick it there the way Joe and the other men were carrying theirs. She was afraid it would fall through. She wished she had a holster like Murphy had on his belt for his police-issue firearm.

Murphy noticed her trying to figure out where to put her gun. "Try this," he said, and took out a small leather holster with long thin rawhide straps from the overnight bag. He got on one knee in front of her and tied the holster to the calf of her right leg.

"Good old Louie's got a little of everything in his secret room of goodies—guns, ammo, plastic explosives, reefer, and leg holsters. Lucky for us, huh?"

Sara nodded and slid the pistol into the leather pocket. She walked around, testing it out. It felt awkward, like walking with one shoe on and one off.

"You'll get used to it," Murphy told her.

Sara continued, trying to get accustomed to the weight of the gun against her leg.

Murphy doled out the remaining weapons. He gave the M-16 rifles to Joe, Bill, Juan, Rico, and the professor, keeping one for himself. Louie got a small .22-caliber handgun that he didn't look too happy about, but he didn't complain. Donna declined a weapon and snuggled close to her husband as if to say, "He'll protect me."

Murphy went back through the trap door and handed up a box holding a brand-new Dell laptop computer.

"That's legit!" Louie said loudly. "It's mine. I only put it down there until I could bring it back to Staples; the fucking thing wouldn't work right. Every time I tried to go online, the thing crashed. I called Dell and got some guy in fucking India—pardon my French. They told me it had to be my Internet service, which is bullshit! I got broadband."

"Maybe I can fix it," the professor said. "It would be nice to see if the Internet is still up and if it can tell us about what kind of response the government and the military are taking, and whether this is worldwide as I suspect."

"Be my guest," Louie said, and shrugged. "I guess I ain't taking it back now, anyway."

Sara walked back and forth in the aisle nearest the office door until she felt used to the gun strapped to her leg. She stood still and practiced lifting her leg and drawing the pistol as quickly as possible from its holster, feeling a bit like a Western gunslinger. It wasn't an easy thing to do with the holster so low on her leg. She knew she would never get the drop on anyone, but that was okay.

A thought occurred to her that she hadn't ever considered before, even when she'd had the gun from the pizzeria. Back then, at the start of the invasion, she'd had a strong will to live and survive. Then she had seen her pistol as a means of protection. Now, after all that had happened, and contemplating a future where life was going to get much harder and more dangerous before it got better, she saw her new pistol as a means of escape.

For the first time in her life, she entertained the thought, and possibility, of suicide. She silently pledged to herself that if she ever got infected by one of the flying alien eggs, or grabbed by a monster, she would use the pistol on herself—if she was fast enough on the draw—rather than turn into a man-eating monster or get eaten alive. To that end, she practiced drawing the gun over and over, working on getting it out as fast as possible.

"Do you really know how to use that?" Donna asked her.

Sara shrugged. "Probably not well enough to hit a fast-moving target. But, if I find myself in a hopeless situation . . ."

Donna didn't understand at first what she meant, but caught on quickly and gasped in shock.

"No! Would you do that?"

Sara shrugged again. "Tell me, what would *you* rather be, one of those monsters turning on your own husband and friends, maybe even your own *baby* and *eating* it as easily as we used to eat junk food without a second's thought? Or would you rather be dead?"

Donna shuddered. "I don't like either of those choices."

"Yeah, too bad we have such a limited selection."

"I think me and Bill will be safe if we stay here, don't you?" Donna tried to project an air of confidence, but it was a poor attempt. To Sara she sounded like she was pleading for confirmation of something she really didn't believe herself.

Sara did not think it mattered whether any of them stayed or went and wanted to say, "No, you're not safe anywhere; none of us are," but she didn't. She had become fatalistic and had given up all hope of any of them seeing this thing through to any end other than death to all and the world they had once known.

The human race is already extinct, she thought. We just don't know it yet.

7:10 p.m.

Once Murphy had handed out all the weapons, he jumped into the secret storage room again. He gave out a loud whistle. "There's another secret compartment down here that was buried under all that other stuff," he called to the others. A moment later, he reappeared and handed up a large canvas bundle to Joe.

"What the hell is this?" Joe wondered aloud. He opened it. "This looks like the kind of machine gun you'd mount on a tripod."

"Give that man a see-gar!" Murphy said before ducking down again and coming up with another large round bundle. "That is an M-sixty, seven-point-sixty-two-millimeter, belt-fed machine gun." Still standing in the basement, he placed the round bundle on the floor of the room, which was at his chest level, and opened it to reveal a large circular piece of metal with gears and four bolting stations around it. There were three packages of bolts, rods with small wheels attached to them, and wrenches taped to the metal ring. "And this is a vehicular ring-mount for that machine gun, to allow it a three-hundred-sixty-degree arc of fire." He ducked down a third time and brought up several more boxes of belted ammunition for the machine gun and placed them on the floor next to the ring-mount before climbing out.

"Louie! You've been a naughty boy!" Murphy said.

Louie looked nervous, but then, Corey thought, he always looked nervous, as though he had just done something bad and knew he was going to get caught.

Murphy stood over the seated Louie. "You've got an M-sixty, seven-point-six-two, machine gun with a full arc ring-mount that is used *only* by the military on jeeps, tanks, or Humvees. Now, Louie, why would you have this? I *know* you got something else up your sleeve, so don't be holding out on me."

Louie looked even more nervous and scared than usual as he looked around the room from person to person. He lingered on Corey a bit longer than the others, and Corey immediately got the feeling that what Murphy was talking about could be found behind the locked door hidden behind the cabinet in the restaurant kitchen. He felt Louie's glance at him was a warning.

"I don't know what the customer wanted those for," Louie stammered.

"Really," Murphy replied sarcastically. It was obvious, even to Corey, that he didn't believe anything Louie said. "I'm sorry, Louie, but it doesn't make sense to have a machine gun like this that can only be mounted on a *military* vehicle, and not have said military vehicle to mount it on."

"Hey, maybe they had their own jeep or tank to put it on," Louie said, licking his lips and wiping nervous sweat from his forehead with the back of his hand. "Like I told you. I was just the middleman. You know? Like I rented out the hidden storage place here to the real players until the deal went down. Then they were supposed to come here, pick the stuff up, and pay me. That's all."

Again, Louie glanced around, his eyes narrowing slightly when he looked at Corey.

Corey mustered his courage and spoke up: "He's lying,"

Louie visibly paled at his accusation.

"See, Louie? You can't even fool a kid," Murphy said with a laugh.

"No," Corey went on. "I *know* he's lying. I can prove it. Come on."

Louie gave Corey such a threatening and murderous look that Murphy rapped his knuckles hard on the top of Louie's head as though he were knocking on a door. "Don't be looking at the boy like that, Louie, or I'll hit you so hard I'll send you into the middle of next week."

"What do you mean?" Joe asked Corey.

"There's another secret door in the kitchen of the restaurant."

"Aha! Now I see, said the blind man," Murphy said, and chuckled. He wagged a finger in front of Louie's face. "Show us, kid," Murphy said to Corey. "Bill, Juan, and Rico, bring this cockroach, and don't let him out of your sight."

7:20 p.m.

Cindy loved thrills. She had always been a daredevil and a danger seeker; the first kid to get on the roller coaster at Coney Island—sitting in the first seat of course—and the last one to reluctantly leave. She had always been willing to swallow or shoot up the newest drug and had always loved riding in fast cars. But after riding on the back of the Jam Man's Harley, through the deserted city from the Empire State Building to West 125th Street, where Z-Jay had his headquarters near the legendary Apollo Theater, she had the thrill-seeker knocked right out of her.

Never had she felt her life so endangered as she did riding with Jam Man. Maybe if she had been suitably messed up she would have enjoyed the outing. Maybe the events of the past few days, since the 'Vaders showed up, had changed her. Maybe she had been in enough danger and seen enough death to make her different from who she had been.

Most of the ride was quiet, as far as danger from the 'Vaders was concerned. That had been her first fear when she mounted Jam Man's bike. But that anxiety was quickly replaced with the fear that she was going to end up dead on the pavement if Jam Man crashed them. He drove like the proverbial madman. When he had asked her if she was ready for a game of 'Vaders, she hadn't realized that meant he was going to push the bike at top speed all the way up 5th Avenue, weaving in and out of the abandoned cars and around the rubble from two destroyed buildings. The first building was at East 57th Street and the other was the former Mt. Sinai Medical Center across from Central Park. Both had been destroyed when U.S. Air Force jets had crashed into them.

Cindy couldn't remember how long ago it had been since

the planes had attacked the 'Vaders—it felt like months— but the buildings they had hit were still burning, still pouring dense black smoke into the sky.

After passing the first crash site, she noticed other black plumes rising over the dead city. She counted fifteen of them before they reached the shambles of Mt. Sinai. With the destroyed hospital blocking 5th Avenue, Jam Man had turned into Central Park, popping a wheelie and almost knocking Cindy off the back as they went over the curb and sidewalk. He had driven just as fast through the East Meadow as he had on the street.

It was in Central Park where they picked up their first flying orb. It came flitting through the trees, buzzing directly in front of the bike, and Jam Man's face, but he handled the bike expertly and successfully veered away from the pod.

Jam Man was undaunted by the orb. He just revved the bike higher and went faster. Cindy thought they had left the orb in the bike's wake until she saw three orbs behind them now chasing the bike. The funny thing was, she knew, from the way the orbs had attacked the jet fighters, that they had more than enough speed to catch the motorcycle and easily infect them both, or they could have attached to the bike and melted right through its engine or gas tank and caused them to crash.

But they didn't.

The orbs just followed, like they were trailing the bike, waiting to see where it would go. That worried Cindy more than if they had attacked and made them crash. It also worried her that during the entire ride, not once did she see any evidence of the gargoyle-like 'Vaders. She had thought that a blessing at first, but after the way the orbs acted, she wasn't so sure.

Cindy felt better when they reached the paved pathway for pedestrians and followed it out onto West 110th Street. From there, Jam Man took St. Nicholas Avenue to Frederick Douglass Boulevard, turning off at West 126th Street.

As Jam Man turned the bike into the alley that led to a small garage with a rear entrance to Z-Jay's crib, the orbs slowed and hovered as if watching until one of Z-Jay's homeys rolled up the garage door and let the bike inside. As she and Jam Man went from the shed to the back door, she saw the orbs flit away, all traveling in the same direction.

Z-Jay met them in the back hallway of the first-floor apartment. Cindy had never been so glad to see her short, slightly paunchy pimp with his crooked nose, '60s-style Afro, heavy gold chains around his neck, and gold teeth gleaming from within his mouth. Like Jam Man, he wore shades most of the time, day or night, inside or out.

"Any trouble?" Z-Jay asked Jam Man.

"Piece-a-cake," Jam Man answered.

"So since ya brung her, I guess she wasn't lyin'."

"Nope. She had two live pineapples. I tested one. That sucka made a big boom!"

Cindy quickly opened her purse and handed Z-Jay the other grenade. "There's a case of these where I was, baby. Just like I told you," she said.

Z-Jay tossed the grenade in the air a couple of times and grinned. With a nod of his head, he turned and walked down the short hall to the kitchen and through it to the living room.

Cindy was surprised at the number of people present. In the kitchen, two women, Leticia and Cherry, two of Z-Jay's "ho's," were cooking a huge pot of rice and refried beans in tomato sauce.

The living room was full of people. The smell of reefer was so strong Cindy got a buzz just from breathing. All the windows had been boarded over, and the only light was from a huge TV screen and many candles situated throughout the room. Because Z-Jay owned the building, the living room was big, much bigger than in the original floor plan. Long before the 'Vaders, Z-Jay's boys had taken out a wall between the two apartments on the first floor, turning it into one big apartment.

The enlarged first floor was where Z-Jay and his closest friends—the crew he called his *niggas*—lived and partied. The second floor was called the "store." All business was conducted there—it was where people off the street could buy dope. The third floor was Z-Jay's crib and his alone. It was garishly decorated with thick shag rugs of orange and neon-blue on every floor, leather furniture everywhere, and a home entertainment center that rivaled a theater's with its massive TV screen taking up most of one wall, and speakers everywhere. Cindy had been on the third floor a lot when Z-Jay had still fancied her, but over the years she had been invited less and less. The last time she had been invited upstairs had been over a year ago.

There were at least thirty people in the large living room. Most were members of Z-Jay's inner circle. They were doing everything from watching DVD movies on the big-screen TV to cleaning guns and snorting coke. Near one of the boarded-up front windows, Cindy recognized Muhammad Jones, second only to Jam Man in being close to Z-Jay, dancing with Shenika Grainer, another of Z-Jay's prostitutes. Z-Jay called his girls his "ho's," his close friends and gang members were his "nig*gas*," and his enemies were "nig*gers*."

There were at least a dozen children of various ages running around the place playing tag or watching the movie. A few of them lay on the floor drawing and coloring. In a lounge chair just inside the door to the kitchen a big white kid whom Z-Jay used as a reinforcer due to his size and strength, and whom he called "Wigger Jim," because of his black affectations, was enjoying a blow job from Linda, Cindy's best friend, whom she had been most worried about after they become separated the night before the 'Vader invasion.

"Hey, Wigger Jim! What the fuck are you doing?" Z-Jay yelled. "Ya can't do that shit out here in front of my kids. Take it somewhere private or I'll throw yo' nigga-lovin' ass out on the street and let the boogeymen eat yo' sorry ass."

Wigger Jim got up fast, grabbed Linda by the hand, and dragged her into a nearby room, slamming the door before Cindy had a chance to say hi to Linda or for Linda to see Cindy was there.

Jam Man laughed and tapped Z-Jay on the shoulder. "Yo,

Z, check it out. You know what this crazy bitch calls the boogeymen? You tell 'em, girl." He nudged Cindy none too lightly.

"It's not what *I* call them really . . . it was this kid I was with. He called them 'Vader*s*."

Z-Jay picked up on the meaning immediately. "Like short for *in*vaders?"

"Yeah!" Jam Man said. "Sounds like a sick video game, right?"

Z-Jay chuckled. "Ya'll think everythin's a fuckin' game, nigga." To Cindy, he spoke seriously. "Okay, tell me about the rest of it. Ya said this Mafioso honky had a shitload of weapons?"

Cindy scratched her arms and spoke pleadingly. "Can I get a fix first, Z-Jay? I'm fuckin' dying, man. I ain't had nothing in two days," she lied.

Z-Jay raised his eyebrows in doubt. "Two days? Shee-it! If ya'll ain't had nothin' in two days you'd be climbin' the fuckin' walls, bitch. Don't be givin' me that shit."

"Okay, yeah, I mean, I did have *something*. I-I shot the last of my stash this morning, but it wasn't much. The Mafia guy, Louie, gave me some OxyContin that I crushed and snorted, but it ain't as good as the H, you know? He had a shitload of Oxy. You can take that, too. I think he also had some weed."

"OxyContin?" Z-Jay said, his voice in falsetto. "He had Oxy and ya'll risked yo' ass to come here for some scag? *Damn*! I knew ya weren't all that bright, girl, but I didn't think ya was *that* stupid. What is it with smack and bitches?" he asked Jam Man, who just shrugged. "All ya bitches just love the junk. Ya gots to ride that pony, don'cha?"

Cindy agreed. At that moment, so close to getting her dope, she would have agreed to anything he said.

"Please, Z-Jay?" she whimpered.

Z-Jay frowned at her and then looked at the grenade in his hand. "Okay. Jam Man, take her upstairs and tell Busta to give her a dose 'a the China White."

Cindy's eyes widened. *China White* was the purest and

strongest heroin Z-Jay dealt. Usually, she only got what he called *Mexican Brown,* which was a lower grade and took more to satisfy her habit.

"China White? Did you say China White?" Jam Man asked incredulously.

"Did I fuckin' stutter? Do it, nigga!" To Cindy, Z-Jay said, "I'm goin' to go out and blow some shit up." He held up the grenade and smiled, showing his gleaming gold front teeth, all three of them. "You done good, baby."

"Thanks, Z-Jay," Cindy said, nearly bawling at his generosity.

"Go on now, feed ya monkey. Then we'll talk."

7:30 p.m.

"Louie, Louie, Louie! You know, all during our surveillance of you I thought Homeland Security and the Feds had you pegged all wrong. I thought for sure they were giving you way too much credit. I was sure they were overestimating your status as a major player in weapons dealing, but I was wrong." Murphy slapped Louie hard on the back, nearly knocking him off his feet. They were in the garage/shed with Joe, Juan and Rico, and Sara, gathered around the Humvee.

Louis was visibly angry, but, surprisingly, not at Murphy. His anger had erupted when he'd found the cabinet in the restaurant kitchen moved and the secret door to the shed unlocked and open. His anger had dimmed only slightly when he found the Humvee still inside.

Corey stood in the no-longer-secret doorway from the kitchen. Donna wasn't feeling well and Bill had taken her back to the storeroom. The professor was in Louie's office trying to get Louie's computer to work.

"Do you believe this guy?" Murphy asked Joe.

Joe wasn't sure if it was a rhetorical question, but shook his head anyway. Like the others, he was amazed at the military model Humvee they found in the garage behind the Chinese restaurant. Joe had always liked cars and had grown up with a special fondness for American muscle cars and all-terrain vehicles, like jeeps and trucks. His father had owned a 1967 Camaro Z-28 and his uncle had had an army surplus jeep that had seen action in Vietnam. But the Humvee in-front of him now surpassed both of those. It was a magnificent, customized vehicle, painted bright yellow with black trim, and darkly tinted windows. The front of the Hummer was protected by wraparound metal bars resembling a cage. The roof was open between the driver's and passenger's seat to allow a man to stand there and fire the machine gun, the ring-mount for which Murphy was installing on the roof around the hole as he spoke. Joe couldn't believe how big and wide, yet compact, the Hummer was—about fifteen feet long and eight feet wide, but only the same height as Joe, who was five-foot-ten.

Murphy looked over the Humvee, appraising it, as he screwed bolts in and assembled the 360-degree ring-mount on the roof.

Joe thought he looked like a proud father staring at his offspring.

"The High Mobility Multipurpose Wheeled Vehicle, also known as the M ten twenty-five. I was assigned to one of these in the Gulf War—Desert Storm. Pound for pound, this is the best all-purpose military vehicle around. I'm impressed, Louie. I thought you could only get these military models *used*, and then only if they were stripped of their armament capabilities, but you have obviously managed to snag a new one that is fully armored and combat-ready customized, *with* a custom paint job and tinted windows to boot. I've never seen one quite like this."

Murphy finished the mount installation. "Joe, get me the machine gun for this baby, would you?"

Joe went to Lowie's office, grabbed the heavy weapon, and brought it back to the garage. He handed the huge gun to Murphy, who deftly mounted it on the circular ring-mount. He then swung the machine gun around on its mount. The gun moved fluidly and easily completed a full circle. He ducked down inside the vehicle for a moment and saw something he hadn't noticed before. He let out a loud, "Well, I'll be damned!" He opened the driver's door and came out with a box. "A case of grenades!" he said happily. "This just keeps getting better and better. You are naughty, Louie, naughty-naughty."

He looked at Joe. "Can you imagine, Joe, what the bastards who ordered this stuff were going to do with it? *Grenades,* the heavy-duty machine gun, and four blocks of C-four plastic explosives!" Murphy looked at the contents of the box again and fixed Louie with threatening eyes.

"There are two grenades missing, Louie. What happened to them?"

Louie looked genuinely shocked. "There are?" He quickly went over to where Murphy was. "Son of a bitch!" he swore. "I *knew* that little whore took *something.*"

"By little whore, I assume you mean Cindy?"

"You know it!" Louie answered.

"What the hell would she want with grenades?" Joe asked.

"I suppose she needed some kind of protection to get her to wherever she went," Murphy said.

Louie shrugged but looked uncomfortable.

7:40 p.m.

The grown-ups' oohing and aahing over the Humvee in the garage quickly bored Corey. And with everyone so excited about the weapons and the new car in the secret garage, no one was bothering to make supper. He went into the kitchen and had a stale roll with butter and a glass of tap water before heading over to Louie's office to see how the professor was doing. The professor was the only adult, besides Bill and Donna, who wasn't in the garage. He was bent over the computer, tapping on the keys and talking to himself softly while he worked.

Corey said hello to the professor, who barely acknowledged his presence. He looked under the professor's arms at the laptop screen. It was white with large black words on it that read *The page cannot be found.* There were instructions in smaller print below the words that Corey didn't bother to read. He picked up the remote for the small thirteen-inch television instead and turned it on. He started flipping through the channels, not expecting to find anything. He went right past a clear picture with printed words on the screen, like those on the computer, before he realized he had seen it.

"Professor! Look!" Corey said excitedly when he flipped back to the channel with the words.

"Hmm?" the professor said.

"Professor, I got something!"

"Yes? That's nice."

It was obvious to Corey that Professor Ligget wasn't really listening to him. "It says something on the TV," Corey said.

"Uh-huh."

"I can read, you know. You want me to read it to you?"

"Sure. You do that," the professor mumbled.

"Okay. At the top it says, 'This is the Emergency Broadcast System coming to you from Madison Square Garden on the Madison Square Garden Network. This is not a test. This message is authorized by the Office of Homeland Security,'" Corey read slowly, pronouncing each word carefully.

Suddenly, the professor was by Corey's side, reading the rest of the message aloud much faster than Corey could have. It made Corey angry; he thought the professor was showing off.

"The National Guard," the professor read quickly, "under the auspices of the Department of Homeland Security, has set up an emergency center at Madison Square Garden. Survivors of the present emergency are instructed to come to Madison Square Garden by any means possible for food, medical attention, and protection. This has been a message from the Emergency Broadcast System. This is not a test. Repeat: This is not a test."

The professor began whooping at the top of his voice and shouting for the others to come see.

7:45 p.m.

Sara had just left the garage to start cooking dinner when she heard the professor let out several loud whoops and a "Thank God," followed by the urgent command, "Everyone come here! Quickly! We're saved!" Sara ran to the import store office. She was the first to reach it, with Bill and a queasy-looking Donna right behind her. The professor caught her completely off guard when he wrapped his arms around her and hugged her.

"We're saved!" he shouted in her ear. He disengaged from her and pointed to the message on the TV screen. Sara read it over several times before its meaning sunk in. When it did, she knelt on the floor in front of the television set and started to cry.

"Don't cry, Sara," Corey beseeched, coming over to her and putting his arms around her. Tears streamed down his face, also. "You should be happy," he said. "We're saved."

"I know," Sara said, and hugged him. "I just can't believe it."

"I think my dad must be there at Madison Square Garden," Corey said. "He'd be there, right?"

"Yeah, yeah. He will," Sara said, smiling through her tears.

One by one the group answered the professor's call and entered the office to see the message that an emergency shelter had been established at Madison Square Garden. Many of the reactions were similar to Sara's. Donna, Juan, and Rico each cried and reached out to their loved ones to hug. Murphy and Joe exchanged high fives and hugged briefly. Louie was the last to enter the office, and the only one who did not seem happy about the news. He remained in the background, smiling when any of the others looked at him or spoke to him. He looked morose when no one paid him attention.

After exchanging kudos with Murphy and the others, Joe hugged Sara and Corey at the same time. All three sat on the floor and stared at the words on the screen, as did everyone else.

"We made it, didn't we?" Sara asked softly of Joe. He smiled, nodded, and kissed her.

She kissed him back.

11:00 p.m.

Under a cloud-free sky lit by a full moon, Cindy looked at the line of vehicles—seven motorcycles and two pickup trucks—that made up Z-Jay's caravan to retrieve the weapons and the Humvee from Louie. The bikes held two riders apiece. The first bike was Z-Jay's Yamaha with Cindy riding on the back. She hadn't wanted to go, and tried to talk Z-Jay out of taking her, but after he gave her another dose of the primo China White, she would have jumped off a building if he'd told her to; she was flying so high she didn't think she'd ever touch the ground again. The rest of the bikes each had a rider and a homey riding shotgun. Two of Z-Jay's niggas rode armed in the cab of each pickup truck, which would travel in the middle of the caravan, with three more heavily armed gang members riding in the beds of the trucks. In all, twenty-four of Z-Jays toughest, craziest, and most trusted homies were in the caravan.

Besides being armed, all wore wool caps pulled over their ears and bandannas over their noses and mouths. Even though it was night, the humidity had not let up at all and the wool caps and bandannas made everyone hot, sweaty, and ir-ritable.

After she'd had her first, long-awaited, much-anticipated fix, Cindy had told Z-Jay everything she knew about Louie and the Humvee and the weapons that were hidden at Shangri-La Imports and behind Cho's Chinese Restaurant. For over two and a half hours, Z-Jay had questioned her thoroughly about the weapons, and though she hadn't been able to answer all of his questions she answered enough to convince him it was worthwhile. When she told him Officer Murphy was there, Z-Jay had slammed his fist down on the table and grinned fiercely.

Z-Jay had run afoul of Murphy a year before Cindy had, back when Murphy had been a vice cop in Harlem. During a raid on one of Z-Jay's first crack houses in East Harlem, by the river, Z-Jay had nearly escaped out a window, only to be caught by Murphy outside. Z-Jay had called Murphy, "brother," in an attempt to invoke some racial sympathy and offered Murphy a fat roll of fifty-dollar bills—fifteen hundred dollars in all—to let him go.

It had been the wrong thing to do.

Murphy just laughed and then used some kind of kung fu pressure point hold on Z-Jay's neck that paralyzed him and forced his mouth to drop open. As he had tried to move and gasp for air, Murphy had taken the wad of bills and stuffed it in Z-Jay's mouth, commanding him to "Eat it!" Z-Jay was sure the crazy fucker would have choked him to death with the money if one of Murphy's superiors hadn't come along and stopped him. Murphy had taken him in cuffs to the paddy wagon while the superior officer had pocketed the fifteen hundred dollars. Due to a good lawyer and the fact that it was only Z-Jay's second offense and the DA couldn't prove the crack house had been his, Z-Jay got a CWAF—Continued Without A Finding—and one year's probation with random drug testing.

Shortly after Cindy's bust, adding to Z-Jay's ire with, and desire for, revenge against Murphy, the cop had been transferred out of Harlem and Z-Jay never saw him again. But he never forgot Murphy and had made a vow to get even with him, some day, somehow. So it was with homicidal anticipation that Z-Jay planned to head south. He was prepared to kill everyone—men, women, even children—to achieve his vendetta against Murphy. For Z-Jay it was as much a reason for the trip as the need to get the weapons and the Humvee.

Though Z-Jay made light of the 'Vaders while the caravan was getting ready to leave, Cindy could tell he was worried and afraid. Like Joe and Murphy, Z-Jay had discovered the 'Vaders' plan to raze the city and flush out any hiding humans. She now realized why she'd seen so few monsters or orbs on her way to the Empire State Building. Like the survivors in Louie's building, Z-Jay and his gang had also been planning to break out of the city and into Jersey to escape the oncoming methodical search by the aliens. The one thing holding him up had been a lack of weapons and ammunition sufficient to fight their way out of Manhattan if it came to that. Most of the gang's ammo had been used up during the first two days of the invasion. Z-Jay had been planning to raid the closest police precinct house, to grab some weapons and bullets, but was worried about having to fight not only the 'Vaders but any police that might be holed up there. He had sent out a couple of gang members to recon the closest police station, but they never returned.

Z-Jay didn't tell Cindy, but she was the answer to his prayers. With a combat-ready Humvee decked out with a heavy-duty machine gun, and a case of grenades and the other weapons, he figured he could gain the upper hand against the 'Vaders. As soon as Cindy had explained about the name 'Vaders, Z-Jay and his homies had started using it exclusively when referring to the aliens. Before her arrival they had all called the aliens *boogeymen*.

Day Five: Thursday

12:00 midnight

The group of survivors living in the Shangri-La Import Store and Cho's Chinese Restaurant had spent the evening getting ready to venture into the open and make a run for Madison Square Garden, only one block west and four blocks north. Officer Murphy had gone over the loading and firing of each of the weapons they were to carry. Though he planned on manning the machine gun mounted on the roof of the Humvee, he taught each of them how to load and fire it.

"The M-sixty machine gun is air-cooled and belt-fed, and it has a closed bolt. It has a short recoil, but it still packs a wallop. It can fire five hundred fifty rounds per minute with a maximum effective range of one-point-two miles, but a total range of four-point-two miles. The M-sixty *cannot* be fired continuously for a full minute or you will shoot the barrel out. It has a spade handle with handle grips for both hands. The trigger is V-shaped and in the middle of the handle grips. The bolt release is right above it. Putting the bolt release in the upper position allows for single-shot firing, which can come in handy if the weapon gets too hot." He then showed them how to load the ammunition belt into the bolt for continuous feed.

In the same vein—not expecting them to have to use it

but just in case—he showed each of them how to prime the four yellow blocks of C4 plastic explosives with the primer cord and how to set and use the remote electrical detonator, adding, "If worse comes to worse, a well-placed bullet will detonate this stuff, but I wouldn't recommend it; you'll want to be *far* away from it when it does so you'll need to be a very good shot."

Murphy's lifelong credo had always been: "It's better to be safe than sorry."

After the weapons lessons, everyone had helped load the Humvee with the overnight bag containing the explosives, the two micro Uzis with ammunition and two high-powered emergency flashlights from the import store, ten plastic gallon jugs of water, two twenty-pound bags of uncooked white rice plus a ten-pound box of lo mein noodles, and a box of one hundred fortune cookies. After some debate, the group agreed the M-16 rifles were too unwieldy to be used by the passengers in the Hummer, and the other vehicle, Bill's car, that they would be taking. The six rifles with two boxes of ammunition for them were loaded into the cargo area also. One of the three fire extinguishers completed the Humvee's cargo load. The other two extinguishers were to be ready-at-hand in the Hummer and Bill's car. Finally, Murphy distributed an extra handgun to everyone except Corey.

Despite the short distance to Madison Square Garden, Murphy, Joe, and the professor worried about getting there. When they had opened the shed door, around 7:00 p.m., the sound of the 'Vaders' approaching line of destruction had seemed much closer than earlier. The aliens' flushing-out tactic was proceeding much faster than they had anticipated. The professor pointed out that there were only six blocks to the east of 6th Avenue, and seven or eight to the west. He estimated that even if the 'Vaders stopped to sleep at night, they'd be at 6th Avenue within two days, maybe less.

At 10:45, Juan went up to the roof to see if the immediate vicinity around the intersection of 27th Street and 6th Avenue was clear. He came back with good and bad news—the constant sound of the 'Vaders' methodical destruction of the city had stopped, but there was an orb hovering around the intersection. Murphy wasn't surprised and told everyone that he and Joe had seen orbs scouting ahead and watching every street and intersection within a few blocks of the advancing monsters.

An hour before midnight, Murphy had called everyone into the storeroom to go over the plan for departure and to discuss the new threat. Joe was to drive the Humvee while Murphy manned the machine gun on the roof, or sat in the passenger seat in the unlikely event they were able to travel without harassment. With the Hummer armed with its full-radius machine gun, there was room for Sara, Corey, and the professor to ride in the backseat with the weapons and food in the cargo area behind them.

Bill still had wanted to stay, but Donna, feeling she was very close to delivery, was scared and convinced him to go. The plan was for them to take their own car, a Buick Century, which was parked outside on West 27th Street. Louie, Juan, and Rico would ride with them.

"We're going to need a distraction for the flying egg Juan saw spying on the intersection," Murphy said when everyone was certain of their seating arrangements in the escape vehicles. "We need something that will give us enough time to get a head start. It's got to be something that will confuse the egg and keep it from calling in the monsters until after we've left." He didn't wait for suggestions. "I think the grenades will work nicely. One of you traveling with Bill is going to have to toss a couple of grenades to distract the egg watching this place. We'll move out of the garage with the Humvee and go first since it can be used as a battering ram to get through blocked streets. Bill's car will follow us down West Twenty-seventh Street. If needed, I can give full cover with the machine gun and easily fire over Bill's car at any threat behind us. Since Bill's car is already facing that way on Twenty-seventh Street, the person throwing the grenades should have plenty of time to get into the car before it leaves.

Rico, I think you should be the one to throw the grenades, since you played baseball in college and were a pitcher, right?"

"Si," Rico said.

"Since it's his car, Bill's going to drive, and Juan can help him get Donna to the car and inside. Louie, you just worry about getting yourself into the backseat as quickly as possible. Yesterday, Joe and I reconned Twenty-seventh Street to Seventh, and it's open enough for us to get through easily. We may have some problems on Seventh Avenue, but I don't think they'll be major. With the protective armor on the front of the Humvee and with its power we should be able to plow through anything in the way, except for a large truck. I'm hoping there won't be any since this thing all started on Sunday morning—a time when few large delivery trucks are out on the city streets." He paused and looked at the others expectantly.

"What if the big 'Vaders—you know, the ones who want to eat us—show up?" Rico asked timidly.

"That's why I want you to distract the orb watching this place. I want us to be well onto Seventh Avenue by the time it realizes we're making a run for it and flies off to get reinforcements. Once we hit Seventh Avenue, it's only four blocks to Madison Square Garden."

"I don't like this," Bill quarreled. "Too much can go wrong. What if Seventh Avenue is blocked farther up? What if the monsters are hiding right around the corner and aren't at the edge of the city like you think?"

Murphy opened his mouth to answer, but Bill went on.

"What if my wife goes into labor while we're riding around out there?" He sounded angry and scared, more the latter than the former. "Even if we make it to the Garden, how are we going to get inside? We don't know if that emergency bulletin on the TV is for real. It could be just an automated signal that goes off by itself under certain circumstances. *And*"—he went on again before Murphy could reply—"once we're in the Garden, won't we still be in the same pickle? If the 'Vaders are going building by building and street by street, they'll sure as hell get to the Garden, too. In fact, if that's an emergency shelter, they'll probably target it right away. How do we know they *haven't* attacked it already?"

Murphy looked irritated, but he forced a smile and patiently nodded. "You done?" he said, but it was more of a command than a question.

"Most of what you are asking, Bill, is up to fate and chance. Yes, the man-eating 'Vaders could be waiting around the corner, but I don't think so. The orb is watching this place because the 'Vaders don't know how many of us are hiding out here. They only saw Juan. If they knew there were a lot of us, and it was worth their while, they would have already called the monsters down on us. I'm figuring they won't waste time interrupting the street-by-street operation for one lousy survivor. So I think there's a good chance that there won't be any monster 'Vaders waiting around the corner. They might come running when the orb calls them, and probably will, but I'm hoping we'll be able to get a good head start if the distraction works well enough."

Murphy took a deep breath and went on. "As to your wife's condition, that's just something we'll have to chance. But I do have some good news. Using my police radio, I was able to raise another officer at the Garden earlier tonight and told him we were coming. He told me they have a few doctors there. They have *not* been attacked yet. They also told me how to get in; we can drive right in via the delivery entrance. I don't know if Seventh Avenue will be blocked farther up, but we won't know until we try. At any rate, we've got to go that way to get into the Garden's delivery entrance. It seems they have some weapons there and are prepared to provide cover fire for us once we get there. Though we didn't discuss it, it makes sense that, if they know about the 'Vaders' approach, they'll have an evacuation plan. Being from out of town, you may not know that Penn Station is under the Garden. Now they *might* have the trains running, and we'll be able to evacuate the city on them. Even if the trains aren't running, we can get out of the city, or at least beyond the 'Vaders' attacking line, through the train tunnels if we have to."

12:30 a.m.

Like the import-store survivors had done, Z-Jay had posted lookouts on the roofs of several tenements and tall buildings in his neighborhood. It was how he knew the aliens were congregating along the rivers on both sides of Manhattan and working their way in. But, due to the fact that every one of his lookouts was high on one drug or another, they had not noticed the several flying eggs that had remained day and night, hovering just under the roof façades, or awnings, or in narrow alleyways around Z-Jay's apartment house, watching. As soon as Z-Jay's caravan started lining up on West 126th Street, the orbs flitted off to the east and west at high speed.

None of Z-Jay's crew in the caravan noticed.

With a raised fist from Z-Jay, the line of motorcycles and two trucks moved forward, heading east on 126th Street. Z-Jay had plotted the shortest and, by his reckoning, the straightest route, which was based on what his grandfather had always said about the best way to travel between two points being "as the crow flies." He planned on going two blocks east on 126th and turning right onto 5th Avenue. They would travel south on 5th, skirting Garvey Park, and keeping Central Park on their right just in case they needed to take cover. At 27th Street, they would hang a right and go one block west and they would be at the import store.

The evening was quiet, leading Z-Jay to assume the 'Vaders had bedded down for the night, and would renew their attack on the city in the morning. He also thought it meant he and his homeys would have a safe, attack-free ride. They had no trouble for a short time after they set out and the caravan traveled south. They had just skirted Marcus Garvey Park using East 124th Street to Madison Avenue south, then West 120th Street back to Fifth Avenue, when Cindy was the first to see a sparkling reflection of something in the sky to her left. Within seconds a lone flying 'Vader descended on them. It came down fast and zipped over the caravan, looking for the easiest target. With everyone wearing protective gear covering their mouths, ears, and noses, Z-Jay figured they didn't have much to fear from *one* orb if they kept it from getting too close, and if they didn't panic.

Unfortunately, one of Z-Jay's homies riding in the back of the first pickup truck couldn't do that. Three gang members rode in the rear of the truck—two were armed with small-caliber pistols, the third carried a sawed-off shotgun. The shotgun wielder's name was Melvin Brown. He was six-foot-two, two hundred and ninety pounds, twenty-two years old, and a methamphetamine freak who loved Western movies. Copying his favorite Western, *Pat Garrett and Billy the Kid,* by his favorite director, Sam Peckinpah, Melvin had emptied his shotgun shells of buckshot and repacked them with dimes.

Before leaving with the caravan, Melvin had snorted enough meth to kill any other person, but Melvin had a unique ability to tolerate large doses of the drug on a regular basis. Even when he was straight, which was rare, Melvin was wound a bit too tightly; when high, he was certifiable.

When the orb picked Melvin and his two pistol-packing companions to descend on, Melvin panicked. He tried swatting at the thing with his shotgun and was unsuccessful. Suddenly, the glowing orb hovered right in front of his shotgun barrel. Grinning maniacally at the opportunity to blast the thing to smithereens, Melvin pulled the trigger.

The only problem was that right behind the orb sat the other two men in the back of the truck.

The orb rocketed past one of the guys' ears so close he heard it splitting the air as it went by a half second before the coins reached him. The dimes erupted from the shotgun in a fiery cloud and seemed to hang in the moonlight for a moment—just long enough that the guy opposite, and to the right of Melvin, could see that one of the coins was a Liberty-head dime. The cloud of change ripped into him and the fellow beside him with such force that the man to Melvin's left flipped backward, heels over head, out of the truck. Dimes shredded the face and head of the other man until all that was left was the bottom of his jaw and the jagged end of his spine sticking out of the bloody mush that was the man's neck.

Seeing what he had done to his friends, Melvin stared in shock at the carnage, his mouth open under his bandanna, worn Western-outlaw style over the bottom half of his face. Before he could utter a sound or react in any way, the orb he had shot came back at him, unharmed, and heated up just enough to easily burn right through Melvin's bandanna and immediately cool as it flew into his mouth and down his throat.

Melvin's slaughter of his friends took less than a minute. His transformation took even less time than that.

The orb took hold of Melvin, and he started to shake. He dropped the sawed-off shotgun and let out a strangled cry of pain as his body started to grow and stretch. Bones crackled, ligaments snapped, and tendons ripped as they grew. Each injury to bone, muscles, ligament, and tendon was immediately followed by repair starting at the cellular level and working up from there at an incredible speed of healing that allowed him to grow so quickly.

His head jerked violently back and forth, causing and re-causing whiplash injury to his neck, which healed as quickly as it was damaged. Ten seconds into the transformation, Melvin's torso inflated with a series of squishy, popping sounds. His chest, stomach, and hips expanded so rapidly his T-shirt and jean shorts split apart and flew from his body. His arms and legs immediately grew in proportion to the rest of his body until he was twenty-five feet tall and naked. His genitals shriveled and disappeared as he reached his full height.

Melvin's pretransformation face could have been best described as one that only a mother could love—small close-set eyes, a large crooked nose, a small, cruel-lipped mouth, no chin, bad teeth, and a complexion cratered from acne and a teenage bout with chicken pox. Melvin's transformed face wasn't an improvement. Three short spikes of bone erupted from his forehead. His small beady eyes grew large and crossed; his nose remained crooked, only larger. His teeth benefited most from the change. Yellow and black and caked with food and plaque from rarely being cleaned, they were replaced with long, sharp, gleaming white daggers.

As Melvin shot up, his weight increased dramatically so that by transformation's end he was too heavy for the truck to support him. The rear tires exploded in a rush of escaped air, and the front end rose into the air like an empty seesaw seat with a fat kid sitting at the other end.

The new and improved Melvin's first order of business was to snatch up the headless remains of his former friend and gobble him down in a few quick bites, barely chewing him before he swallowed.

The driver of the second pickup truck directly behind Melvin was so startled by what he saw that he stepped on the gas when he meant to step on the brake. The truck rammed the back of Melvin's truck, toppling him from the truck bed. He fell heavily onto the second truck's hood. The truck see-sawed forward with such force the guy riding shotgun was thrown through the windshield and onto the hood, his bloody face mere inches from Melvin's hungry maw, as though he were manna from Heaven. Melvin the monster made quick work of the body, burping loudly after and spitting out the guy's sneakers with the feet still in them.

The three homies riding in the back of the second truck were thrown into the street, suffering a variety of injuries. One of them landed on his head and received a cracked skull and broken neck. The other two were luckier; one landed on his side, suffering road burn and bruised muscles, while the other landed on his knees, crushing both kneecaps and breaking both shinbones before falling forward to hit the pavement facefirst, breaking his nose on impact.

The driver of the second truck had a bloody gash across the bridge of his nose caused when it slammed into the steering wheel. It bled profusely onto the scarf over his mouth and chin and went into his throat when he tried to breathe. Choking and nauseous from the taste and quantity of the blood he was swallowing, he staggered out of the truck, his hands over his face.

With so much food at hand, Melvin the monster hesitated for a moment, unsure of whom to eat first. The actions of the driver with the bloody nose helped him decide. Like a child whose attention can always be captured by a moving object as opposed to a stationary one, Melvin focused on the driver.

Melvin ate him; headfirst, feet last—but Melvin did not know it was to be his last meal.

Z-Jay reacted first and was quickly joined by the shooters on the other bikes. They circled the two stalled trucks and unleashed a barrage of bullets into Melvin, making him do a herky-jerky dance of death before he wound up sprawled on the pavement in a pool of his own monster-blood.

2:00 a.m.

At 27th Street and 6th Avenue, the dash to Madison Square Garden hit a glitch before it had even got started; just before they were supposed to leave at 1:30 a.m., Louie announced he couldn't find the key to the padlock on the shed's double outside doors.

Murphy didn't believe him and was ready to beat Louie into coughing up the key, but the professor and Joe stopped him. Joe realized that if Louie *was* lying, he was doing a pretty good job of it; he was trembling with fear and a small dark wet spot had appeared on the front of his trousers when Murphy had him in his grip.

After a half hour of shouting, shoving, and accusations tossed back and forth, Murphy calmed enough to help search for the key.

It was fruitless. They searched everywhere in the import store and the restaurant, with everyone taking part. Though they turned up no key, Sara found a box of flares and an army flare gun under a cabinet in the Chinese restaurant and added them to the Hummer's cargo. Louie claimed he had forgotten he had those, but no one believed him this time.

Murphy's ire was rekindled by that, but Louie saved himself by suggesting the Hummer could just crash through the doors with little problem.

Murphy had to laugh—surprised he hadn't thought of that himself. "Okay . . . we're finally ready to roll!" Murphy announced. "Everyone get in position."

2:30 a.m.

Without the two pickup trucks to slow it, the line of motorcycles moved faster, weaving in and out of abandoned traffic, traveling on the sidewalk and on both sides of 5th Avenue for long stretches. Immediately after killing Melvin, three more orbs arrived and caused an accident resulting in the loss of two of the eight bikes. The two gang members riding shotgun were killed, and the two drivers were too badly injured to go on. As he had done with the injured survivors of Melvin's attack, Z-Jay left them behind, armed but with little hope of surviving if the monsters showed up. As he rode away, fearful of hanging around and letting the orbs get him, Z-Jay shouted that he would come back and get them after they got the Humvee. It was a lie; he had no intention of doing so. He figured fewer people would make the flight from the city easier. Except for himself, the Jam Man, and several of Z-Jay's cousins, not to mention his girlfriend Mariana and a few of his truly fine ho's—Cindy *not* being considered one of them—all others were expendable.

Pushing the motorcycles as hard as they could, the remaining riders soon outdistanced the orbs.

Or so it seemed.

What the riders didn't see, or understand, was that they didn't outrun the flyers, the flyers chose not to pursue. Instead, they veered off toward the East River, traveling much faster than any of the bikes were capable of doing. Within ten minutes, two monster 'Vaders arrived on the scene and made a quick meal of the injured survivors Z-Jay had left behind. After they had consumed everything edible, including the bullet-ridden corpse of monster Melvin, the two deformed giants set off at an easy loping pace, running surprisingly fast for their size and awkwardness, following the smell of motorcycle exhaust.

2:37:30 a.m.

Wearing imported Indian silk scarves over their noses and mouths, and nylons from the CVS on their heads like snow hats pulled down over their ears to protect them as much as possible, Juan, Rico, Louie, Bill, and Donna were ready at the side door of Shangri-La Imports, which opened on West 27th Street. Rico clutched two grenades in his hand and Bill carried a portable fire extinguisher in his left hand and held Donna's hand with his right. He had a .45 tucked into his waistband, as did Rico and Juan. Louis held his small .22-caliber pistol at the ready. Bill and Donna's car was two parking spots from the door, on the same side of the street. The five of them were waiting for Murphy's signal via Juan's walkie-talkie cell phone.

In the secret shed in the alley behind the restaurant where the Humvee was running, everything was loaded and ready to go. Joe was behind the wheel. Corey, Sara, and the professor were in the backseat. Murphy was standing behind the machine gun, ready to give Rico the signal to toss the grenades.

Murphy spoke quietly into the cell phone. "Are you guys ready?"

The crackling reply came almost instantly. "*Si*. We're ready."

"Okay. You know what to do. As soon as we hear the first grenade explode, we're heading out. Get to Bill's car as fast as possible."

"Okay," Juan replied. He looked at the others, and all but Louie nodded.

After the way Murphy had been humiliating him in front of everyone, Louie had other plans.

Murphy looked at Joe and nodded. He spoke into the walkie-talkie, "Throw the diversion *now!*" he shouted into the phone.

2:47 a.m.

Ten feet to the left of the alley, Rico opened the side door of Shangri-La Imports. He took a deep breath and stepped onto the sidewalk. He pulled the pin from the grenade in his hand and threw it in the direction of the front of the store and the 6th Avenue intersection.

He got pretty good distance on the toss. The grenade arced through the air and landed on the roof of a beat-up brown-and-black Ford wagon sporting an independent taxi emblem on the front door. The grenade bounced off the roof and landed in the intersection, where it rolled at least eight feet, ending under a Jeep Cherokee before exploding. The Jeep's gas tank followed less than a second after the grenade. The dual explosions lit up the night and made the vehicle jump two feet off the ground before flames erupted from it with a windy puffing sound. Rico looked about for the orb, but couldn't see it yet; he hoped the first distraction had worked and would cover their exit from the store.

Bill ran out first, his keys clutched in one hand, almost dragging his wife along with his other in his panic to get to the car as fast as possible. Juan carried the fire extinguisher and ran slightly ahead of them to open the front passenger door for Donna.

As per Murphy's instructions, which he gave only to Rico to keep Louie from objecting, when Rico got to the driver's side of the car, just before he was to get in the backseat, he pulled the pin on his second grenade and got ready to toss it onto the roof of Shangri-La Imports. He looked to make sure everyone was clear and in the car before throwing it, but Louie was standing at the corner of the alley the Hummer was going to come out of.

"Louie! Get in the car!" Rico yelled. "We got to go!"

2:48 a.m.

Louie ignored Rico's command and held up his pistol, waiting for the Hummer with Murphy exposed in the roof hatch for the machine gun to go by him.

"You think you're such a badass, Murphy," Louie whispered to himself. "Let's see how you like a bullet in the side of the head, motherfucker."

2:48:20 a.m.

Rico realized what Louie was going to do and reached for the .45 caliber pistol he had stuck in the waistband of his shorts. As he tried to pull it out it got snagged and he dropped the grenade.

It landed at his feet and rolled under Bill's car.

Rico had just enough time to utter a tearful, "Oh fuck!" before the bomb exploded.

The rear end of the car leaped into the air and crashed down.

Shrapnel from the grenade and the car's chassis ripped Rico's shins to shreds, throwing him into the street on his back, shrieking in pain.

In the backseat, Juan was launched up into the roof. He fractured his neck and was knocked unconscious.

Bill slammed his nose on the steering wheel, and blood poured from his ears. Donna was thrown forward, cracking the windshield with her forehead. Just before the second explosion—the car's gas tank—Bill still had enough presence of mind to shove Donna out the passenger's door, which had been ripped open by the blast, and try to follow her.

She landed heavily on the sidewalk, but Bill didn't make it. Before he could get free of the car, he, and the unconscious Juan, inhaled the flames that suddenly shot through the car's interior. They died instantly.

2:48:35 a.m.

Murphy stood in the space between the driver's seat and the passenger's, with his head, chest, and arms protruding through the middle of the hole in the roof and the ringmount around it. He grabbed the machine gun's handles and yelled, "Let's go!"

Joe put his foot to the gas pedal and the Humvee roared forward. The immediate power and speed of the engine caught him off guard. The Hummer blasted through the shed doors, ripping them into splinters as it forced them open, and sped down the alley.

At the alley corner, Louie put up a hand against the flash of heat and flames rushing out at him from Bill's car and stumbled away from it, right into the path of the Humvee as it came roaring out of the alley.

Before Joe could react, Louie was suddenly in the Hummer's headlights. The combat vehicle slammed into his back, causing him to go airborne. He soared across 27th Street and hit the building on the other side headfirst.

Striking Louie and seeing Bill's car in flames, Joe was too distracted to make the right turn onto 27th Street, and the left front end of the Hummer crashed into a car parked at the curb on the opposite side of the street. Damage to the Hummer was negligible, but Murphy paid a price as he was thrown back and forth.

Joe sat stunned. Everything was going wrong—Louie was dead; Bill's car was in flames, its occupants dead.

In the backseat, Corey and Sara screamed and started to cry. The professor was stunned into silence.

In shock and feeling displaced from himself, Joe put the vehicle in reverse. He heard Rico's screams of pain. He turned and saw him bleeding to death in the street. As the Humvee started to back up, it was suddenly peppered with bullets.

2:50 a.m.

The five remaining motorcycles in the caravan had made good time.

Near West 29th Street, Cindy had looked back to see two monster 'Vaders chasing after them. The creatures were running far faster than she ever thought they would be capable of; she realized that if they kept up their pace they would soon catch up.

As the bikes had reached the intersection of 5th Avenue and West 27th Street, the faster of the two monsters caught the slowest bike in the caravan—a home-built dirt bike made from scavenged parts and ridden by a small half-Asian, half-African-American kid, barely eighteen, that everyone in the gang called "Little Tiger Woods" or "Little Tiger" for short. His rider—his sixteen-year-old brother, nicknamed "Tigger" by Z-Jay—carried a Colt .45.

The 'Vader never broke stride as it reached out with its right hand and plucked Tigger from the back of the bike so smoothly that Little Tiger had known his brother was gone only because the bike felt lighter and sped up with the sudden weight loss. Little Tiger looked back just in time to see the 'Vader wolf down the human fruit it had plucked from the bike. He cried out to his brother and lost control of his bike, dumping it, and falling with it on top of him. The exhaust pipe burned into the inside part of his right calf while the road burned off the outside part as both bike and rider slid along the hot asphalt. Seeing Little Tiger down, the second 'Vader scooped him up before the bike, or Little Tiger, stopped sliding. The 'Vader tossed the dirt bike aside and gobbled Little Tiger down.

Finished with its small snack, the first 'Vader had set its sights on the next bike in the procession, a Suzuki. Wigger Jim, carrying a Walther P99 semiautomatic pistol, rode on the back of the motorcycle. He saw the 'Vader in the extended round mirrors on the bike's handlebars. Turning as best he could, he fired a wild burst at the chasing beast and missed. The driver of the bike, a kid Z-Jay called Alvin because he had a high-pitched voice like the cartoon chipmunk of that name, swerved hard right, trying to give Jim a better angle to fire from.

It worked. Wigger Jim's next spray of bullets from the semiautomatic had ripped across the first 'Vaders' kneecaps. The creature let out a bellow of pain and rage and lunged at the bike as it fell. The outstretched claws of its right hand just caught the rear of the Suzuki enough to cause it to crash into a Mercedes convertible parked at the curb.

Alvin's right leg was caught and crushed between the Suzuki and the Mercedes.

Wigger Jim catapulted over the Mercedes and hit the rear windshield of a yellow taxi that had crashed diagonally into the front of the Columbia Coffeehouse and Bakery twenty yards down the street. His hip cracked the windshield and the windshield shattered his hip. He spun over the roof of the taxi like a contortionist doing a cartwheel and crashed through the display window of the bakery. His body came to rest inside, against the end of the coffee bar. He had wound up covered in moldy bits of cake and frosting and stale wads of pie from the pastries that had been on display in the window.

When the smaller, faster 'Vader had finished the remains of Little Tiger, it hurried to take advantage of the fresh meat offered by the trapped Alvin, who came to screaming in pain. The wounded 'Vader lay on its side in the road, moaning. Beside its shattered kneecaps, its chest was scraped raw, as was the left side of its face. Still the monster tried to crawl over to Alvin before the other 'Vader could steal its treat. The smaller 'Vader got to Alvin and pulled him from between the motorcycle and the Mercedes. Alvin's crushed leg tore free at the thigh and the monster wolfed him down, cutting off his screams as it bit him in two. Despite the wounded monster's inability to get far, the smaller 'Vader quickly gulped down Alvin's remains and hurried over to get the sugarcoated Wigger Jim as if it were afraid the other one might get there and rob it of the pastry-covered goodie. Instead of wolfing Jim down, though, it took its time licking the frosting and pastries from his broken body before eating him.

While it enjoyed its sugary treat, two more 'Vaders—huge hulking beasts—arrived on the scene from the East River. Both leaped on the moaning 'Vader with the shattered kneecaps and cannibalized it while it was still alive and trying to crawl away. It screamed until its throat was torn out. Four more monsters, larger and more gruesome looking, emerged from the night shadows and loped by the two feasting on the fallen comrade.

After finishing Wigger Jim off, the smaller 'Vader had run after the larger ones like a little brother wanting to be included in the older boys' fun.

Cindy had looked back at that point to see the light of the full moon emerging from behind a cloud a glimpse of the carnage behind her. Soaring so high on the China White Z-Jay had given her, she watched the carnage behind her with the same sense of detachment she had watched violence in movies and didn't discern any threat to herself.

As the remains of the motorcycle caravan reached West 27th Street, Z-Jay raised his right arm to signal the other two remaining bikes to turn right. Ahead, the block between 5th Avenue and 6th was clear. All the cars were parked neatly at the curbs on both sides of the street.

Ahead, over Z-Jay's shoulder, Cindy could see the 6th Avenue intersection. Suddenly, a Jeep Cherokee at the left corner closest to her and Z-Jay exploded and jumped in the air. Z-Jay veered away from it. A moment later, the Jeep's gas tank exploded and it was engulfed in flames. By the firelight, Cindy saw a group of people pour out of the side of the import store. She recognized Bill, Donna, Louie, Juan, and Rico. All but Louie ran to a car parked at the curb. Louie ran to the end of his building and stopped. The next moment, the car Bill, Donna, and Juan had got into exploded. Standing next to it, Rico was thrown onto his back into the street, where he lay screaming.

The Humvee that Z-Jay was there to steal came flying out of the alley behind the import store and plowed into Louie, catapulting him across 27th Street and into the building on the opposite side.

As he drove across the intersection, Z-Jay steered with one hand and pulled a mini Uzi machine pistol from the shoulder holster he wore strapped to his naked upper torso. Both he and Cindy recognized Officer Duane Murphy, whose head and shoulders were visible behind a machine gun mounted on the Hummer's roof. Cindy also saw that Donna had been thrown clear of the exploding car and lay next to it on the sidewalk, her maternity dress smoldering.

Z-Jay didn't slow down. He saw the Hummer stopping and reversing toward the guy lying in the road. Z-Jay opened the bike full throttle and fired the Uzi but missed Murphy. The bullets sprayed harmlessly across the Hummer's rear armor.

Cindy saw Z-Jay aim again for the hated Murphy. She realized that in his fervor to kill the cop he wasn't watching the road; they were headed right for Rico lying in the street, screaming in pain and anguish. Cindy could see an impending crash, but her drug-induced high seemed to slow down time, and she thought she had *hours* to warn Z-Jay when she really had only seconds.

Z-Jay leaned forward and used the motorcycle handlebars to steady his shooting hand. Just as Cindy opened her mouth to warn him, the front wheel of his motorcycle hit Rico.

Rico was just about bled out and barely reacted to the hot rubber tire plowing into his midsection. The collision forced the last breath from his lungs in one loud sighing exhalation.

He never inhaled.

Z-Jay's motorcycle flipped over, sending him and Cindy sailing toward the Hummer. Z-Jay hit the protective rear-armored cage and snapped his neck, instantly paralyzing his entire body. He crumpled to the street, facedown behind the Hummer.

Cindy missed the rear of the Hummer by mere inches but didn't miss the pavement. She hit it hard on her left side and slid a short distance before tumbling and flopping over the street surface for several yards. By the time she came to a stop nearly every bone in her frail body was broken or fractured.

She was unconscious, but she wasn't dead.

In the Humvee, Murphy recovered from the effects of Joe's driving as soon as Z-Jay's fire sprayed the vehicle, but Z-Jay was lying dead behind the Hummer before Murphy could fire on him.

Seeing Rico being run over by Z-Jay's motorcycle, Joe slammed on the brakes and watched in horror and awe as Cindy sailed by.

The Jam Man popped a wheelie over the curb and started down the sidewalk next to Shangri-La Imports in an attempt to outflank the Hummer and prevent it from getting away. He missed running over Donna's head by less than six inches. Busta, his shooter, took aim at Murphy with a .45-caliber revolver that he called Dirty Honky, fired, and missed.

Murphy felt the bullet whiz past his ear. He instinctively ducked and spun the machine gun around to fire a burst that trailed just behind Jam Man's bike. The bullets tore up the side of the import store and sent chunks of brick and concrete in all directions. Some of it rained down on the unconscious Donna lying on the sidewalk.

The last motorcycle through the intersection was the one ridden by Z-Jay's number-three homey, Muhammad Jones. He copied Jam Man's maneuver on the opposite side of the street, though the curb was lower on the left side and he did not have to pop a wheelie to climb over it. Z-Jay's cousin, nicknamed Blunt-Boy, rode behind Jones and carried a sawed-off shotgun. He had used it before in drive-by shootings in Philly and Jersey and was quite accurate with it from a moving car. However, he had never fired it from the back of a moving motorcycle.

As soon as they were on the sidewalk, he brought up the shotgun to fire but was distracted by the sight of Z-Jay dumping his bike and being thrown into the Hummer. Muhammad saw it, too, and cried out, "No!" He hit the brake and skidded to a stop at an angle on the sidewalk with the front wheel pointed toward the Humvee. Blunt-Boy fell off the bike and hit the sidewalk hard. He dislocated his left shoulder upon impact, but being high on reefer laced with copious amounts of angel dust, he felt no pain. He staggered to his feet and raised the sawed-off shotgun with his good arm and fired both barrels. A blast of buckshot harmlessly peppered the side of the Hummer.

The injury to his left arm became a problem as he tried to crack the breech of the shotgun and load two more shells. While he worked at opening the breech, Muhammad Jones pulled a Browning 9-mm semiautomatic machine pistol from the rear waistband of his cutoff jeans. He had stolen the gun during a break-in of a gun store in Brooklyn and it was his prize possession. Still straddling his motorcycle, his feet braced on the sidewalk to either side of the bike, he brought the pistol up with two hands, aimed, and fired two short bursts that went wide. He adjusted and fired three more. Two of the bullets ripped through Murphy's shoulder, one right next to the other, while another tore through the bicep of his right arm.

2:51 a.m.

Murphy cried out, "I'm hit," and slumped to the side, his grip on the machine gun the only thing holding him up.

Joe was frozen with indecision. Everything seemed to be happening in herky-jerky fast motion, like an old-fashioned silent film. It seemed to him as if motorcycles and gunfire were coming out of the night from every direction. The shock was paralyzing and the noise of gunfire nearly ear-shattering.

In the backseat, Corey screamed and cried and clapped his hands over his ears. Sara did the same. The professor turned this way and that, trying to see in all directions at once.

Get out of here! Get out of here! Joe thought frantically, but his body wouldn't respond. It wasn't until he realized that Murphy was shot that Joe's reflexes finally kicked in. His movements felt slow and sluggish, as if weights were attached to his arms and legs.

The professor shouted, "They're coming! They're coming!"

Joe looked in the large side mirror, and by the light of the burning fires saw several 'Vaders coming from the other side of 6th Avenue. Donna was lying on the sidewalk with her husband's flaming car between her and the Hummer, and Joe couldn't see that she was still alive. With great difficulty, he put the shift in gear and floored the gas pedal. The tires spun and burned rubber while a belch of gray exhaust spit out of the dual tailpipes. The Hummer shot forward, but Joe's attention was slow in returning to the road ahead of him.

There was a loud crash from the front of the Humvee, and

he stepped on the brake reflexively. A motorcycle had bounced off the front end's armored cage and lay broken on the road in the pool of the Hummer's headlights. Its rider was thrown onto the front hood, bloody but still alive. He looked at Joe with such hatred Joe felt afraid. The biker reached around his back to retrieve his pistol, and fired it point-blank at Joe. The round ricocheted off the bulletproof windshield, leaving only a very faint pockmark.

Joe didn't want to give the guy a second shot. He shifted the vehicle into reverse once more and backed up so fast the biker slid off the hood before he could squeeze the trigger again.

"What are you doing?" the professor cried, his voice high-pitched with fear and panic.

Joe took a quick glimpse in the mirror. By the light of Bill's burning car, he could see the 'Vaders less than fifteen feet behind them. He heard a loud gunshot followed by a sound like a flurry of hailstones striking the side of the Humvee. Joe looked left and back; there was a kid, not more than sixteen or seventeen years old, pointing a sawed-off shotgun at the Hummer. A blast of fire erupted from the shotgun again, but its buckshot hit the road next to the vehicle as its shooter, who was holding the sawed-off shotgun with one hand, was thrown onto his back by the recoil. Another teenager sat astride a motorcycle next to the one with the shotgun. He had a large pistol in both hands and was taking careful aim at Murphy, who was slumped against the machine gun.

"Murph! Look out! On your left!" Joe cried, but Murphy only groaned and did not move. Joe shifted into drive again and trounced the gas pedal. The Humvee took off with such force it reminded Joe of a roller coaster as he was pushed back into his seat.

2:52 a.m.

Jam Man realized too late that he'd made a mistake in cutting in front of the Hummer. His much-loved Harley lay behind him, dented and leaking gas from its cracked fuel tank. Busta, his shooter, lay unconscious in the gutter to his left. Jam Man spit out several broken teeth and slowly got to his knees in front of the Humvee. He brought up his gun to fire again but didn't make it before the headlights rushed at him, and he kissed the Hummer's protective armored cage over the front grill. His neck and spine snapped as he was bent backward from the force of the large vehicle running over him.

Lying in the gutter, Busta regained consciousness in time to see the Hummer roar past him. As he stood to fire at the retreating vehicle, a large shadow fell over him. Before he could fire a shot or turn around, a 'Vader snatched him up and shoved him in its mouth with two quick bites. It chewed a couple of times, spit out Busta's pistol and some of his tattered clothing, and swallowed.

Across the street, Muhammad Jones fired twice more as the Humvee pulled away. He shoved his pistol in his waistband, and was about to give chase, but a giant hand came down heavily upon his head, shoving his spine up into the back of his skull. Death was instantaneous. A moment later, he was gone, down the gullet of an obese 'Vader. His shooter, Blunt-Boy, having managed to reload his sawed-off shotgun, struggled up from the sidewalk and fired both barrels at Jones's cannibalizer. The blast ripped through the grotesquely fat 'Vader's gut just as chunks of Muhammad's body reached its stomach. The shot tore through monster flesh and human flesh at the same time. The thing grabbed its bloody stomach and exposed intestines and toppled forward, landing on Blunt-Boy and knocking his shotgun from his hands. Pinned to the sidewalk, Blunt-Boy could only lie there until more 'Vaders came and dined on him and the 'Vader he had killed.

2:53 a.m.

The fastest of the 'Vaders lunged and snapped at the back of the Humvee as Joe hit the gas. There was a slight jolt that shook the vehicle and its inhabitants, but the Hummer pulled away. Joe steered with one hand and reached over to grab Murphy by the waistband of his pants and pull him back inside. As he did, he yelled to the professor to find the first-aid kit. Murphy's body responded to Joe's tug; his legs spun around and he collapsed onto his butt inside the Humvee. But that was all that remained of the former police officer. The top half of his torso, from the waist up, had been bitten off. Joe could see the ragged edge of the bite and could clearly see the triangular teeth impressions in the raw, bloody flesh.

Sara and Corey screamed simultaneously at the sight of Murphy's remains. Corey hid his face in Sara's side, and his screams quickly turned to sobs. Sara turned away and closed her eyes. The professor sat sobbing with his head down, his face in his hands.

Joe felt he might vomit. In spite of all the horrible gory deaths he had witnessed since the first day of the invasion, he was more sickened by the sight of Murphy's half-eaten corpse. The smell of the policeman's exposed lower intestines and bowels—never mind the sight—contributed to his nausea. Holding his breath and steering with his left hand, Joe reached over Murphy's bloody lower torso—trying not to touch it but failing—and opened the passenger door. He pushed Murphy's remains out into the night, where they spilled into the street.

The door swung shut with a loud clap.

Tears streaming down his face, Joe drove on. In the backseat, Sara, Corey, and Professor Liggett sobbed uncontrollably.

"Stop it! Stop it! *Shut up!*" Joe screamed.

In the backseat, Sara and Corey abruptly stopped their wailing. Professor Ligget, however, did not stop rocking back and forth and emitting a low, keening sound. The interior of the Humvee was splattered with Murphy's blood. In the humidity of the night, the stench was sickening; the smell of his exposed intestines and bowels still lingered in the vehicle.

Joe, too, fought back the urge to scream and cry and give himself over to panic and hysteria. It was a difficult battle, but staying alive was even more difficult. By the light of the moon and the two burning cars behind, Joe looked back through teary eyes and saw several 'Vaders taking advantage of the cadavers left behind. Two of them, standing side by side in the road, were trying to get the roasted bodies out of Bill's still-burning car; while one of them blew on the flames like a kid blowing out birthday candles, the other kept trying to pry off the car's roof. But it kept burning its fingers. A third monster sat in the street with legs splayed to either side of Rico's body. Instead of gobbling him down as quickly as possible, which every other 'Vader Joe had seen had done, this one pulled Rico apart slowly, as though he was a well-done chicken. It appeared to be dunking each part of Rico in the pool of blood that remained on the street before eating it. When it finished with Rico, it went over to the sidewalk and scooped up Louie's brainless remains and made quick work of him.

Three 'Vaders on the other side of the street—two on the sidewalk and one at the curb—were eating the kid with the shotgun and the gut-shot 'Vader that had fallen on top of him. A smaller 'Vader suddenly charged across the intersection and around Bill's burning car.

At that moment Joe spotted Donna lying on the sidewalk next to her husband's inferno of a car. He cursed himself for not having seen her before. He thought of going back for her but realized it was too late. The smaller 'Vader stood over Donna, and Joe could have sworn he saw the thing nod its head as if to some disembodied voice, then reached down and gently picked Donna up and carried her around the corner, out of sight.

Another small 'Vader pounced on Z-Jay's crumpled corpse. Picking the former gang leader up with both hands, the small cannibal took quick bites, barely chewing each one before swallowing. It looked around, furtively as if expecting one of the larger 'Vaders to try and take its meal away.

A few feet away, the monster trying to get at the cooked meat inside Bill's roasted car burned its fingers one time too many and gave up. Spying Cindy's bundle of broken bones and flesh, it lumbered over and plopped itself down next to her.

2:55 a.m.

Cindy regained consciousness but was paralyzed from the neck down, so couldn't feel anything as the 'Vader bit her legs off and sucked the juicy blood squirting from her femoral arteries, but she could *see* the 'Vader doing it. She heard someone screaming but couldn't tell who it was. Still floating in the best heroin high she'd ever had, she could watch, with indifference, the horror eating her alive as if it were a boring TV program. As the thing sucked the blood, and life, out of her, Cindy suddenly realized the screams she was hearing were her own.

The 'Vader who had been trying to blow out the flames also gave up on the gas-fed inferno and looked about for something else to eat. It spied Jam Man lying in the road. At the same moment, the smaller 'Vader that had just finished making a meal of Z-Jay saw Jam Man, too. Both 'Vaders made a dash for the body. The smaller of the two got hold of Jam Man's head and right arm, while the larger one grabbed both his legs in one of its large hands. The two faced off over the body and yanked on their parts. The shorter 'Vader fell back hard on its rump, with Jam Man's head and one arm torn from his shoulder socket. The larger 'Vader came away with the rest. The smaller 'Vader growled angrily but didn't hesitate to pop Jam Man's head and arm into its mouth like a bonbon. The larger 'Vader was content to sit in the road and eat its meal in peace.

2:55:30 a.m.

Joe took it all in, looking from the side mirror to the rearview mirror and back again, over and over as he drove. The sight of what he saw did nothing to help him battle the lump of hysteria rising in his chest. The only good thing was none of the 'Vaders were chasing the Hummer. As it reached the intersection of 27th and 7th Avenue, Joe saw why, and realized Bill had been right to voice fears that the monsters would be lying in wait for them around the corner.

Because they were.

Just around the corner of 7th Avenue, the dark hulking forms of three 'Vaders crouched in wait for them. Above them hovered the orb that had been keeping an eye on the import store and the intersection. It was obvious now to Joe that Murphy's distraction with the hand grenades hadn't worked. The orb had obviously flown west to awaken and bring back these monsters to ambush them. The only thing Murphy's distraction had accomplished was the deaths of five of their group, including himself.

The waiting monsters were ten yards from the corner. Joe started to make the turn, but when they suddenly appeared in the headlights he quickly spun the wheel back to the left. He floored the gas pedal, and the Hummer shot through the 7th Avenue intersection and continued on West 27th Street. In the block between 7th and 8th Avenues, Joe had to think quick and deftly maneuver the Humvee past several abandoned cars. There were only five vehicles, but their position on the road made for a lot of weaving. Joe managed to pass by all the cars with only two minor crashes where the Humvee clipped a peach-colored Cadillac's rear end and caught the front fender of a black Lincoln Continental. The Hummer smashed both cars out of the way without sustaining any damage.

The three 'Vaders and their guiding pod chased the Humvee down 27th Street. Joe was about to shout to Sara to climb in front and take over the wheel while he manned the machine gun, but he hesitated, afraid that trying to do so would cause them to crash or slow down too much so that the 'Vaders would catch them. He was surprised when the professor, tears streaming down his face and his white hair in wild disarray, put his pistol in his waistband, crawled into the front, and stood up. Putting his head and shoulders through the roof portal, he grabbed the machine gun. Letting out a primal scream, Professor Ligget opened fire on the 'Vaders chasing them.

Initially, the power of the machine gun was too much for him. His first spray of bullets went far over the monsters' heads. The professor compensated, bracing himself against the roof and using every ounce of strength he had to bring the rapid-firing gun on target. His second burst of fire was too far down and succeeded in only tearing up the asphalt a few yards in front of the three 'Vaders. It did slow them down a half a step, though, as the bullets kicked up chunks of blacktop and the cobblestone beneath it. The third time the professor got it right. He brought the barrel of the machine gun up by pulling down on the trigger handle, then fired. Empty shells clattered against the roof and rolled off both sides and the rear of the Humvee. Many of the spent shell casings fell into the vehicle where they bounced around on the floor.

The middle 'Vader caught a burst of fire in midchest. The power and force of the bullets threw the monster backward with its arms and legs extended as though it had been tied to a tether that had reached its limit.

The professor kept the trigger depressed and swung the barrel to the right, but the machine gun went suddenly silent. He pressed the trigger again and again but nothing happened. To make matters worse, the two 'Vaders flanking the one that had been hit didn't stop to feast on their fallen comrade as the professor had expected. As though spurred on by the orbs flashing rapidly around them, the beastly 'Vaders continued the chase.

The professor ducked his head back into the Hummer. "I think I'm out of ammunition," he shouted at Joe. From the backseat, Sara handed him a full ammunition belt. Though Murphy had taught all but Corey how to load the machine gun, the professor struggled to do so with the Humvee swerving left and right. The vehicle reached the corner of 8th Avenue. In the moonlight, Joe could see ahead to where the 'Vaders appeared to have reached 9th Avenue, two blocks away. He cut a hard right, not touching the brake and not letting up on the gas.

The professor dropped the belt as he jostled back and

forth. The ammunition belt clattered off the roof and fell into the road.

"Give me another one!" he shouted and Sara did.

There was a nerve-irritating screech and sparks flew up on both sides of the Hummer as Joe propelled it between two cars with little room to spare. The professor was thrown forward and backward by the squeeze, but he managed to hold on to the ammo belt this time.

"Sara!" Joe shouted over his right shoulder as he put his window down. "Hand one of the grenades to me."

Sara scooted around onto her knees and reached over the backseat into the cargo bed. The grenades were behind her seat in an open wooden box, the inside of which was divided into rows of square cardboard compartments just large enough to hold each grenade as snugly as if in an egg carton.

Using just her thumb and forefinger, she plucked one of the grenades from the box as though it were smelly and gross. The truth was she hated touching the grenades; they scared the hell out of her. She was afraid that the slightest mishandling would cause them to explode despite what Murphy had explained about them.

The Hummer made a sharp left, and she had to grab the grenade with both hands to keep it from falling. She held her breath, her heart pounding so hard she could feel its pulse in the temples on both sides of her head and in the jugular vein in her neck. Slowly, holding the explosive clasped in both hands, she tried to place it in Joe's hand as he reached back, palm up. He steered with his other hand and kept his eyes on the road.

"Don't drop it," she said.

"What?" Joe shouted, not looking at her.

"Don't drop it!" she shouted just as Joe cut the wheel hard right, driving the Hummer over the curb and onto the sidewalk. Sara dropped the grenade. It bounced on the floor between her feet. She let out a hysterical shriek, grabbed Corey with both arms, and hugged him in a protective embrace.

Startled by her screams, Joe involuntarily jerked the steering wheel to the left, and the front fender of the combat vehicle clipped a mailbox, separating it from its narrow metal legs and sending it spinning into a blue Volkswagen Jetta.

"What happened?" Joe shouted.

"I'm sorry! I dropped the bomb!" Sara shouted back.

"The what?" Joe yelled, confused.

"I . . . I mean the grenade-thingy."

"Well, pick it up and give it to me!"

Sara reached for it but withdrew her hand. "Will it blow up on me?" she leaned forward and asked loudly.

"No! Remember what Murphy said? Not as long as the pin is still in!" Joe yelled back.

While she cautiously leaned over and felt on the floor for the grenade, Joe reached over and tapped the professor's leg.

"Hey, professor? Kind of quiet up there. You doing okay?"

"Yes . . . yes."

Joe could hardly hear him. The professor was panting as though out of breath.

"Here!" Sara shouted, and shoved the hand grenade over Joe's shoulder. He grabbed it, looked in the mirror at the 'Vaders still chasing them, and put the grenade in his left hand. Looking between the road and the mirrored reflection of the pursuing monsters, Joe put the grenade pin between his teeth and pulled it out. He slowed the vehicle just enough for the monsters to gain a few feet. With a little flick of his wrist, he tossed the grenade out the window and back toward the creatures. He sped away and in the large side mirror watched the deadly pineapple bounce a couple of times before exploding about five feet in front of the 'Vaders.

Sara and Corey shrieked and covered their ears. Joe was surprised at how loud the explosion sounded and how much smoke it created. For several moments, he couldn't tell if the grenade had done any damage. Then he saw the 'Vader on the right come through the smoke, still running though it was clutching its left shoulder. It was hard to tell with the Humvee moving so fast, but Joe thought he saw blood seeping between the creature's fingers as it held its shoulder. Its left arm was hanging loose as if injured.

When the smoke cleared completely, Joe let out a whoop. One of the other 'Vaders was lying in the road, facedown, unmoving. Joe's joy was short-lived, though. At least half a dozen more monsters and orbs had joined the chase and were coming on fast from behind.

3:00 a.m.

By the light of the half moon, Professor Ligget saw the new group of 'Vaders and orbs following. A stabbing pain ran through his left shoulder and down his left arm. He grunted and closed his eyes. He tried to take a deep breath, but when he did his chest felt as if it were on fire. With a supreme effort, he grabbed the ammunition belt and put it into the open breech on the machine gun. Moving by sheer willpower alone, he reached up with his right hand and snapped the breech closed. The effort left him exhausted and weak. Another pain shot down his left arm, and his chest burned worse than ever, but he knew he couldn't give up now. The 'Vader that was closest to the Humvee appeared to be wounded and slowing down. The professor could see blood seeping through the clawed fingers that clutched its left shoulder.

While he rested a moment, trying to will away the pain in his chest and arm, and get some air into his squeezed lungs, the professor watched intently as the group of 'Vaders raced toward the Hummer. They appeared to be moving quite fast— faster than he had ever seen them move. He scrutinized them and saw that they were the smaller variety of 'Vaders—the ones that had been children before being transformed. This group was only ten to twelve feet tall depending on the child's height before it had morphed into a nightmare. Being smaller, and presumably lighter, they were able to move much faster than their adult counterparts.

They were moving so fast, in fact, that they were nearly abreast of the wounded 'Vader within seconds of his first having seen them. The professor waited for the smaller group to pounce on the wounded, bloody one, but to his surprise they kept coming and didn't even look at the slowing bloodied creature. The professor looked farther back and saw that the gray form of the 'Vader Joe had killed with the grenade was still lying in the street uneaten.

This was new behavior for the 'Vaders, and the professor realized it had something to do with the flashing orbs that were zipping around the heads of the younger 'Vaders as if spurring them on, commanding them to continue the chase. Under different circumstances, Professor Ligget would have been fascinated with this behavior.

Since he was concentrating on the rear of the vehicle, and couldn't see the obstacles ahead, every move the Hummer made as Joe steered through the labyrinth of abandoned and crashed cars was an unexpected one to the professor. Just as the professor reached for the machine gun's trigger again, Joe cut a hard left, sending the professor hard right and hammering his shoulder into the side of the round portal cut into the roof. The front right end of the Hummer clipped the rear left of a street cleaner. Unlike in its encounters with other, smaller vehicles, the Humvee lost this matchup with the mammoth city maintenance machine. The Hummer bounced off the street cleaner. The right headlight went out and a piece of the Hummer's front bumper armor was ripped off. The professor jostled back and forth and side to side painfully, like a pinball in play.

With each slamming jolt, the pain increased in the professor's left arm and his chest. Despite the discomfort, he struggled valiantly and grabbed the handles of the machine gun. He brought the gun to bear on the herd of young 'Vaders and suppressed the trigger with both thumbs. The machine gun came to life, punishing his arms with its rapid short recoil. It brought so much more pain to him that he had to let go after a short burst of firing. He hugged his left arm with his right and squinted to see if he had done any damage. He was pleased to see the larger, wounded 'Vader was facedown in the street. One of the smaller creatures appeared to have been hit also; it had separated from the rest of the pack and was limping.

The professor reached for the dual handles on the weapon again, but a brutally sharp stab of pain pierced his chest and kept on going through his shoulder and down his left arm to his hand and back again. He cried out and his vision went fuzzy. For a moment he felt as though he were floating. His vision cleared, but the pain remained and he found himself sitting on the floor next to Joe, with his legs folded beneath him and his head resting against the passenger seat.

3:10 a.m.

Harry Wynks, the mayor of New York City, sat in a plush leather chair and sipped a Scotch and soda water with a twist of lemon from a plastic cup. He looked around the conference room where other men like him—men of power in city or state politics and men of fame from movies, music, and television—sat in identical chairs with identical opaque plastic cups in their hands or in front of them. Despite the time, most of them were drinking hard liquor.

Fred Roux, the head of Madison Square Garden security, sat at the head of the table, just to the mayor's left. He nodded at the mayor, looked around at the other men seated at the table, and cleared his throat.

"I called this early meeting to let you know about a new turn of events that will greatly affect all of us here in this room. Late last night, we were contacted by nine survivors outside that have been hiding in a store and adjacent restaurant at the intersection of West Twenty-seventh Street and Sixth Avenue."

"I know the place," the mayor spoke up. He looked around at the others. "My wife loves the restaurant; it's a Chinese place. Best *dim sum* in the city. It's called Cho's Chinese Restaurant."

"That's the place," the security head affirmed.

The faces of several men in the room lit up at the mention of the restaurant.

"Are they bringing food?" asked an obese, red-faced balding man with eyebrows so light they were invisible. He was the director of the Garden's food and vending operations.

The head of security shrugged. "A little. We've asked them to bring whatever they can. It looks like they will be able to contribute twenty pounds of uncooked white rice and ten pounds of lo mein noodles, and a box of fortune cookies."

Some of the men chuckled at the latter.

The director of vending operations, though, was not happy. He shook his head. "That will keep *us* for a while, but it does nothing to alleviate our very serious situation with the fans in the arena."

The police commissioner, Aldo Sierra, spoke up. "How did these people come to contact *us here*?"

"One of the police officers who had been working the game last Sunday, and who has continued working for us and the Garden's security force to keep things in hand, received a transmission on his handheld police radio from a Patrolman Duane Murphy." He paused and looked at Commissioner Sierra, who had been sitting in a luxury box to watch the basketball game on the day of the invasion. The commissioner shrugged and shook his head to indicate he did not recognize the name.

Murmurs rolled around the table.

Commissioner Sierra shook his head. "How can we take them in when we can't feed the people that are here?"

"What should I have done, Aldo?" Roux said, palms open. "Turn them away? One of your *own* officers? Besides, we've got worse things to worry about than the food shortage. I may have a fairly simple solution to that problem, if we need it. I doubt it will matter, though. The aliens' recent movements and organized plan of attack will soon make the food shortage a moot point. We need to plan for what we're going to do about the greater threat."

Star of the screen and Academy Award winner Jack Nickelback spoke for the first time. "If you're talking about evacuating this place, I don't see *how* we're going to get all these people out of here without getting most of them, and maybe us, too, *killed*. And *now* we got *more* people to worry about coming in? For what? Their food? As far as I can see *that's* a moot point for us as well as the fans in the stands."

"No," Roux said. "I'm not interested in the food they're bringing." Roux smiled. "Remember that we put the emergency broadcast out on the MSG network to see if there was any help out there. Well, our new friends claim to be coming in a combat-ready military armed transport Humvee."

Commissioner Sierra smiled. "Really! Where'd they get such a thing?"

"Who cares?" Roux said, matter-of-factly. "If it's true, it may be just the thing *we* need."

The murmurs in the room became an excited buzz.

3:12 a.m.

When Sara saw the professor suddenly slump to his knees in the front seat, his breath wheezing in and out of him and a look of intense pain on his face, she knew she should take over the machine gun mounted on the roof, but she couldn't see any way to do that with the professor in the way. She was secretly glad. She doubted she could handle the big gun anyway, or stand its noise.

"Sara!" Joe shouted over his shoulder.

Sara tensed, certain that he was going to command her to climb up front and take over for the professor. She was ready to shout back, "There's not enough room," even though she could perhaps straddle the professor and stand with her crotch in his face. Joe surprised her, though.

"Give me another grenade!"

Gladly this time—figuring it was better than having to fire the awful gun on the roof—Sara grabbed another grenade from the box in the rear cargo area and placed it in Joe's outstretched hand. She put her fingers in her ears, mimicking Corey, who'd had his that way from the moment the professor had started firing the machine gun. Nervous about the grenade bouncing under the vehicle and exploding, she watched as Joe dropped the grenade out his window.

Her fears were not unfounded.

The grenade took a weird bounce back at the Hummer and ricocheted off her backseat window. She shrieked at the impact and pulled back expecting the thing to explode in her face, but it bounced away and rolled under a parked black Lexus. The car exploded just as the middle of the pack of mini-'Vaders passed by. Those in the lead and those bringing up the rear were virtually unhurt, but the three or four in the middle of the group were knocked sideways and torn up badly.

Two of the small monsters at the rear of the group stopped when they came to the pile of their dead comrades. They started feeding despite the orbs zipping around their heads. Too hungry, and the lure of fresh meat too much for them to pass up, they ignored the orbs. It was a deadly decision. The burning Lexus's gas tank exploded, dousing them with flames.

Sara gave a mental cheer and noticed, with relief, that several of the small 'Vaders in the front of the pack were dropping out and going back to eat their newly cooked fellows. The allure of fresh meat appeared to be stronger than the frenetic orbs around them.

"Give me another!" Joe again shouted.

Sara had another one ready and immediately gave it to him. This time Joe didn't just drop it, but tossed it backward so it had no chance of bouncing into the Hummer. The grenade hit the road about seven yards in front of the four 'Vaders still in pursuit and took a high bounce with enough arc that the lead 'Vader was able to catch it on the fly. The next moment, the creature's hand blew off and its chest turned into raw hamburger. The remaining three monsters appeared to be mortally wounded.

3:15 a.m.

"Yes! That's the ticket!" Joe cried as the last of the small 'Vaders gave up the chase in favor of food. The road ahead was lit by a fire burning on the right side of 8th Avenue where a jet had crashed. The entire two blocks between 28th and 30th Streets, and part of the block starting at 31st, had been all but destroyed by the fire. Joe could see the orbs zipping around the 'Vaders who had paused to feed, but the beasts paid no attention. Joe figured, as he had seen with the feast at the site of the Zion Gourmet Deli massacre, the smaller 'Vaders usually had to fight larger ones for food, or wait until the big ones were done before they could take whatever was left over, which usually wasn't much. Now, with no big brother around, they couldn't pass up the chance to gorge themselves. Joe understood clearly now that the professor was right: the monster 'Vaders were like caterpillars—pure eating machines ruled by their desire to eat.

There was enough light now that Joe could see the Garden a block away, but there was a problem. Eighth Avenue, starting at West 31st Street, was impassable all the way up to and beyond West 33rd Street. Joe saw there was no way through all the cars—mostly taxis and police cars—that filled the street in front of the Garden. The cars were not in normal straight lines of traffic, but were haphazardly pointing in all directions, filling the street from sidewalk to sidewalk, creating a giant maze.

At first Joe wondered if it was a barricade such as they had seen at the Sixth Precinct. Then he saw the marquee advertising the seventh and championship game of the NBA playoffs between the Lakers and the Knicks and remembered that the 'Vaders had arrived about an hour before the game was to begin last Sunday, day one of the invasion, which now seemed like years ago. He remembered how traffic was always tied up around the Garden whenever there was a huge event taking place there. Now the jumble of cars made sense; he could imagine their drivers all frantically trying to turn their vehicles around, or in any direction, to get away from the 'Vaders.

"I think we've got to make a run for it from here, folks!" Joe said, bringing the Humvee to a stop at the edge of the massive traffic jam. Joe looked back and was relieved to see the group of small 'Vaders still feasting. The orbs, however, had ceased buzzing like angry wasps around the heads of the small monsters and were flying toward the stopped Hummer.

Joe pressed the button on his door console to put up all the electric-powered windows.

He did a quick scan in all directions. It appeared that the orbs were the only danger in sight. He looked over at the professor and saw that the gray-haired teacher's face was dark red, almost purple, and his breathing was weak and wheezing. His eyes were closed and his jaw clenched so tight Joe could see the muscles standing out along his jawline.

Joe reached over and slowly shook the professor's leg. "Time to go, Professor. We've got to make a run for it from here," Joe said loudly.

The professor's eyelids fluttered and opened. He stared at Joe with eyes dazed and unfocused until Joe gently shook him again.

"Professor Ligget, can you make it?" Joe asked.

The professor barely nodded his head; it was an unconvincing yes.

"I'll help you," Joe said. "Give me the bag," he told Sara. She turned in her seat and onto her knees to lift, with some difficulty, the heavy leather valise out of the cargo area and handed it to Joe.

Joe checked weapons and ammo in the bag: under the two high-powered emergency flashlights were the two 9-by-19-millimeter micro Uzis with neck straps. Besides several small boxes of bullets for other pistols, there were six magazines in the bag for the Uzis and, at the bottom, four bricks of the C4 explosive. Joe took one out, loaded a magazine clip into it, and hung it around his neck.

"We'll have to leave the M-16s here; I can't carry the bag *and* one of those and the professor doesn't look like he can carry anything. We'll have to leave the food, too; it's too heavy to carry that far and be able to move fast if we need to. Sara, be ready to take out your pistol and use it if any of the monsters show up," Joe instructed. He removed two of the four blocks of C4 plastic and put them under his seat to make room for the flare gun, flare cartridges, and grenades. He handed the bag back to Sara and said. "Fill this with as many grenades as you can, and throw in the flare gun and cartridges. If we're going to be evacuating from the Garden soon, which looks likely, we're going to need all the fire-power we can bring, even if we do go by Penn Station."

While Sara did as she was told, Joe pulled his silk scarf up over his face, and his nylon cap over his ears, making sure both were tight. He reached over and did the same for the professor.

"Can you run, Professor?" he asked the old man. "Do you think you can make it about fifty yards to the entrance over there?" Joe pointed with his left index finger.

The professor squinted and nodded, a little stronger this time.

"Good," Joe said, and turned back to see how Sara was making out.

3:22 a.m.

Even though his mouth and ears were covered, Corey didn't like the idea of getting out of the Humvee and running to the entrance of Madison Square Garden. For one thing, he knew he couldn't keep up with Joe and Sara if they had to run fast and he didn't want either of them to slow down to help him and put themselves in danger. For another, there didn't ap-pear to be any easy, straight path through the traffic jam. Even the sidewalks were blocked by cars that had gone off the street when the first wave of 'Vaders had arrived.

Corey was reminded of a time, a couple of years before, when his parents had taken him to visit his cousins in Con-necticut. Just down the country road they lived on, a farmer had created a maze in his cornfield and charged two bucks to wander around in it. The traffic jam was like that—a maze of narrow paths between cars, zigzagging all over the place. It had taken Corey and his parents over an hour to maneuver the cornfield maze, and it hadn't been much larger than the jam of abandoned vehicles in front of him. In addition to all the above, Corey didn't think the professor was going to make it; there was something obviously wrong with him. He was sick and even Corey could tell that it was serious. He looked the way Corey's Grampa Butch, who had lived with him and his parents until three years ago, had the morning his heart had attacked him. He had died before the ambulance could arrive.

Even though there were no giant 'Vaders around, Corey was afraid of being out in the open. Corey found himself wishing they had stuck to Cindy's plan—which had also been Murphy's original plan before the message on the TV from the Garden—and had taken the Hummer and left the city. Perhaps they would now be safely out of the city with everyone still alive.

"Okay," Joe said, breaking Corey's train of thought. He picked up the portable fire extinguisher from the floor next to him. "Sara, grab the other one out of the back," Joe said, looking at her in the rearview mirror. "See the pin? Pull it out." She did. "Now it's ready to fire. Just squeeze the lever and aim it at the orbs—you've seen how much they hate it, so we should be well-protected against them at least. So . . . is everybody ready?" Joe asked.

Sara adjusted Corey's protective scarf and nylon cap, took his hand with a reassuring smile, and said to Joe, "Yes. We're ready."

Joe adjusted the rearview mirror to look at Corey. He reached back and patted Corey's knee. "Don't look so glum, kid. We're going to make it. Look around . . . all the monsters are busy and these extinguishers will keep the orbs away. Just keep a keen eye out for them and help tell Sara where to point that thing, okay?"

Corey nodded weakly.

"All right," Joe said, and put the leather valise's strap over his left shoulder. "Let's get to safety before any hungry 'Vaders show up looking for a snack."

3:26 a.m.

The night air was humid and hot, made hotter by heated winds from the huge fire a block away. As soon as they left the Humvee, they all immediately became aware of the sound of approaching destruction as the 'Vaders appeared to have renewed their methodical search-and-destroy tactics.

Smoke from the blaze blew over the foursome, making their eyes water. The steamy humidity, combined with the heat from the fire, made it several degrees hotter than the Hummer's interior. Their clothes stuck to them uncomfortably.

Professor Ligget struggled with every step. His feet seemed to stick to the pavement, and it took every ounce of his strength to lift them and move forward He kept his head down as he walked and every time he looked up, the entrance to Madison Square Garden seemed no closer. The sea of automobiles stretched on forever. With the hot winds from the fire, the air over the massive abandoned traffic jam wavered and appeared liquid.

With his nose, ears, and mouth covered, the professor felt claustrophobic. Though the scarf and cap were light, airy materials, they were suffocating, and he breathed laboriously through teeth clenched behind his silk scarf. Joe kept the professor in front of him, one hand on the old teacher's shoulder, steering him, and kept leaning over to ask him if he was okay. Professor Ligget nodded each time, and each time he did his head felt heavier. Thankfully, Joe and the others stopped often, ducking down between the cars—pulling Professor Ligget down with him where he could slump against a car and rest—to stay out of sight as much as possible.

Despite their efforts, four orbs that had been angrily buzzing around the monsters that had given up the chase to eat now came searching for them. They soon discovered the group and attacked like angry bees. Joe saw them and nailed two with his fire extinguisher. Sara got a third as it dived toward her and Corey. The last one backed off and hovered well above them, out of extinguisher distance.

The pain in the professor's chest dulled to a constant constriction, but despite this reduction in pain, he wasn't fooling himself; he'd had a heart attack once before and knew that without medical attention, he would soon be unable to go on. His lungs still felt squeezed so that every breath was a chore, and his left arm, from the shoulder to the tips of the fingers on his left hand, was tingling and numb. The arm hung limply at his side. Whenever Joe pulled him down to a crouch, or he accidentally bumped it against one of the cars—usually the side-view mirrors—the shooting pains were so intense he wanted to cry like a child. He had to bite his lip to remain quiet.

He bumped the arm hard, again, against the side mirror of a Cadillac and blacked out. He woke on his knees, propped up by Joe, whose hands were under the professor's armpits, keeping him from falling all the way to the ground. He tried to tell Joe to leave him and go on, but his words were cut off by the most excruciating pain yet coursing through his chest and arm. As he lost consciousness, he heard a sound that the cotton stuffed in his ears made sound far away. It was a rhythmic, thundering sound, too regular to be thunder, or the approach of the destroying 'Vaders.

3:45 a.m.

Sara and Corey crouched behind Joe and the professor. Sara, like Joe with the professor, had Corey in front of her. She put a reassuring hand on Corey's shoulder and felt him trembling.

"It's okay," she whispered at the back of his head. "Don't be scared; we're going to make it."

Corey nodded and Sara wished she could believe her own reassurances.

Joe turned while propping the professor against his knees and handed Corey his fire extinguisher. "Hold this for a sec, would you, buddy?" Using the fireman's carry, he hefted the professor onto his shoulders. Already laden with the bag of weapons and his Uzi, the move was awkward and greatly re-stricted his use of the fire extinguisher when he took it back from Corey.

As they started walking again, Sara squinted at the sky, looking for the rogue orb that had been dogging them, stay-ing just out of reach of the extinguishers, and then back the way they'd come, fearful that the thing might have gone to summon the monsters. She hoped the resumption of the sounds of destruction blocks away meant that the monster 'Vaders were too occupied. She sweated profusely from the humidity and waves of heat that blew over them, and from fear.

She, too, noticed a difference in the rumbling noise coming from the east and west—the addition of another sound, growing louder than the 'Vaders' sounds of destruction . . . and coming from the north.

It worried her.

When Corey turned to look at her, she saw that he was scared and worried about the noise, too. A twinkling above and to the right caught her eye. She saw the orb she'd been searching for and five more. Pointing her extinguisher, Sara sprayed the chemical in their direction, but the orbs were out of range. Fortunately, the threat of the fire-killing foam alone kept the flying 'Vaders from getting too close to her or Corey.

Ahead, she could see Madison Square Garden getting closer; her eyes could trace the winding path amid the cars that led to the entrance. In a straight line it was no more than twenty yards, but with the twists and turns in and around and over the crazy angles of the bumper-to-bumper abandoned vehicles, it was more like fifty.

The new rumbling sound grew louder and louder.

She looked skyward again, hoping that thunderclouds would account for the noise. There were none. She put her hands on Corey's shoulders, hurrying him along behind Joe, whose pace had slowed with the professor on his back.

It suddenly occurred to Sara that she had heard this sound before, only not so loudly. At age fourteen she had spent a lot of time at her best friend Stacy's family farm. There she had heard the noise often. She also had heard the sound a lot in Western movies.

"It can't be that," she muttered, looking around. The sound had grown so loud it was deafening even with her ears blocked. She saw that Joe heard it, too, and was looking around for its source. The noise was slowing from a fast hammering to a slow *clop-clop*. She noticed the line of cars leading away to the right from the curb in front of the Garden all had crushed roofs. She stood on her tiptoes to look at a small BMW and saw the giant, yet still distinctive, mark of a horse's hoof in the dented silver metal. From the direction of 34th Street, north of the Garden, came a loud blustering sound not unlike the "raspberry" sound of ridicule.

Distracted, Sara didn't see the orbs were harassing Joe. He tried to spray them but couldn't aim accurately with the professor on his back. He swung the now-unconscious professor's legs at them as he carried him and stumbled as he did so. He nearly fell but managed to catch and right himself. Sara saw what was happening and sprayed the orbs from behind. Two that were hit spiraled off into the sky; the others retreated.

4:00 a.m.

Moving slowly with the weight of the professor on his shoulders, Joe turned and looked up 8th Avenue toward the sound of horse's hooves louder than any he'd ever heard before.

Out of 34th Street a massive creature appeared, chestnut brown and three times the size of a bull elephant. It was a horse the likes of which Joe had never seen nor could have ever imagined. It had grotesquely enlarged features and attributes of a horse with ears that were batlike, curling inward. Four small horns protruded from the spaces between and under its ears. The thing's eyes bulged from the sides of its head like those of a fish. Its nostrils were the size of manhole covers. As with every other creature that had been infected by an orb and transformed, the biggest change had occurred to the horse's mouth. Gone were its large flat teeth perfect for chewing grass and grinding grain. Now it sported a mouthful of ivory daggers that interlocked when it closed its mouth, the two front eyeteeth protruding from the closed mouth like giant fangs.

Behind him, Joe heard Corey ask, "What is it?" The boy was unable to see over an SUV he was standing next to. Sara didn't answer; she was mesmerized by the giant equine. Joe, likewise, said nothing. He just stared as if hypnotized.

The mammoth horse whinnied as loud as a gale-force

wind. It pawed the road, pulverizing the asphalt and digging it up in large fractured clumps.

4:01 a.m.

Corey took a couple of steps forward and used the SUV's side mirror for leverage to climb on the front tire and see what was going on.

"Holy *shit*!" Corey cried.

"Watch your language," Sara said without thinking.

The mega-horse caught sight of them and reared at the corner of 34th Street and broke into a run, coming toward them.

"Come on!" Joe cried, and hefted the professor onto his shoulders again.

"Go! Go! Go!" Sara shouted at Corey.

He ran.

The horse came on and reached the edge of the traffic jam. It skidded to a stop and pawed the street again, looking nervously back and forth for a clear way. It reared again and suddenly leaped, its massive hooves crushing the car roofs it landed on. The horse paused and let out another blustery neigh. Its eyes were panicky and its legs wobbly on the uneven surface of different-size cars. Uncertain where to go next, the creature awkwardly took a couple of steps toward them. With nostrils flared and eyes bulging red with broken blood vessels and fear, the monster horse gnashed its teeth as if on a bit and churned out a great wad of bloody foam.

Despite being scared, Corey couldn't help but feel bad for the animal.

4:01:30 a.m.

Sara could barely tear her gaze away from the menacing horse as it unsteadily made its way closer. When she did look forward, she saw that Joe had shifted the professor's weight higher onto his shoulders and the silk scarf covering Professor Ligget's nose and mouth had slid down around his neck. His mouth was slack and open to the orbs, but Joe couldn't see it.

She shouted to Joe, but at that moment the great horse lunged forward again, taking a few more quick steps atop the automobile roofs. The crunch and crash of metal and glass drowned out her voice. She shouted again just as the horse whinnied loudly and nervously, but, again, Joe couldn't hear her.

An orb whizzed past Sara's head and went straight for the professor. She attempted to spray it, but the thing was too fast and flew straight up the professor's nose. Sara opened her mouth to scream a warning and stretched out her hand to try to pull the professor from Joe's back before the old teacher started transforming, but two seconds after going in, the orb came out of the professor's mouth and flew at her. She jerked the extinguisher spout up just in time to catch the orb with a full, head-on blast of monoammonium phosphate. The orb whirled away, doing crazy loops and spins to try to get the stuff off. Foam drifted down like snow onto Corey's head and shoulders. Sara quickly brushed it off and looked closely at the professor, wondering why the orb had not stayed in him. It suddenly dawned on her: there could be only one reason for the orb to leave the professor. She could see the proof of it in his half-open, glazed eyes and the discoloration seeping slowly into his face.

Unaware, Joe continued on, lugging the professor through the narrow maze. Sara could do nothing about it; the racket from the car-crushing horse was too loud. The massive equine was still gingerly making its way across the automobile stepping-stones. Its hesitant, awkward steps reminded Sara of a foal she had seen on her friend's farm walking on its shaky legs within minutes of being born.

Corey turned as he ran and looked up at Sara, nearly colliding with a police car. She grabbed and steered him out of harm's way, but she could tell by his eyes and the look on his face that he knew something was wrong with the professor. Tears brimmed over his lower eyelids and slid down his face.

Sara's heart ached for him and tears sprang from her eyes, also. She realized Corey had seen too much death of late not to be able to recognize it. Sara felt angry; it wasn't fair—a boy his age should be blissfully unaware of such things. Though she had experienced as much horror as he since the arrival of the 'Vaders, his suffering was much more poignant than her own. After all, he was all alone now in the world, and he wasn't a child anymore, despite his age.

A shrill scream of panic and pain suddenly came from the horse. Its right rear hoof was caught in the top of an SUV. It neighed and whinnied—both loud and frightening sounds— and struggled to pull its hoof free. The harder the monster tried, though, the more stuck it became. The hell-horse began to thrash about madly, kicking cars with its hind legs and crushing several more with its right front hoof in its frenzy to get free. The latter hoof quickly became jammed in a Chevy van and it wasn't long before its rear left hoof became wedged in a brand-new Lexus. It pawed at the cars around it with its one good, left front hoof, trying to escape. The terrified cries grew louder and more pathetic.

Joe reached the end of the stalled traffic jam. He stumbled through the pass between the last few cars that had jumped the curb and fell heavily on the sidewalk twenty feet foot from the Garden doors. He twisted as he fell, trying to keep the professor's weight off himself as much as possible while still letting the old man down without injury.

Sara picked Corey up and hurried the few remaining steps to where Joe lay.

As soon as he hit the sidewalk, Joe rolled the professor gently off his shoulders and sat up, rubbing the back of his neck and checking to see that no orbs were nearby, threatening. He turned and looked at the professor and noticed, as Sara and Corey already had, that the white-haired man's scarf was down around his neck, exposing his nose and mouth. Joe leaned closer and slapped the professor's face lightly, trying to revive him.

"Joe, he's dead," Sara said.

Corey squeezed her hand and let out a soft whimper.

Joe looked at her uncomprehendingly, as if she were

speaking another language, and shook his head. He got to his knees, bent over Professor Ligget, and started to perform CPR.

Sara cast a nervous look toward the monster horse as it gave out a horrible whinny of fright. The creature lost its balance and toppled over onto one side with a loud echoing *crack* as two of its legs broke in the fall. A loud *crunch* followed as the cars beneath it were flattened. The thing screamed in pain so loud it hurt Sara's ears and Corey covered his and cried louder.

Sara had to turn away, sickened by the sight of the bloody, jagged end of the horse's front right legbone sticking through its flesh. She gagged, pulled the linen from over her mouth, and bent over, retching. Nothing came up. As she straightened, her mouth still open, she realized something; the orbs were *gone*. They appeared to have had enough of the foam they found so poisonous and were nowhere in sight. Still, she thought they needed to get inside and *fast*.

On the sidewalk, Joe still knelt over the professor, trying to revive him with CPR, but it wasn't working; the old man didn't respond.

Sara crouched next to Joe and tugged on his arm. "He's gone, Joe," she shouted close to his ear so that he could hear her over the fearful racket from the trapped horse. "I saw it just a minute ago and tried to tell you, but you were moving too fast and couldn't hear me over the horse."

Joe looked at the professor, and his shoulders sagged. Putting his left hand to his face, Joe broke down.

Sara was taken completely by surprise and didn't know how to react. Since meeting Joe in the kitchen of the pizza parlor, he had been a rock that she, and everyone else, had been able to depend on. He had been the glue that had kept them together. He had been their hope that they would make it through this alive. He had been the leader—someone to believe in and follow when she'd had no idea what to do next. If it hadn't been for Joe, she knew she would not now be alive. She knew Corey felt the same way.

Corey's tears, which had started for the professor, now in-

creased with empathy for Joe. His tears were the catalyst to
her own and she began sobbing as well.

"Joe," she said tearfully, her mouth close to his ear,
"please, we've got to get inside. Please, please, let's go."

Joe wouldn't move. He only sobbed louder and shook his
head.

Sara was suddenly terrified; *Joe is giving up!*

Corey stood to the other side of Joe, crying softly. He
kept glancing back the way they had come, nervously looking for approaching monsters. The great horse's scream became intermittent as it tired from its struggle and loss of
blood. Corey still felt bad for the creature, even though he
knew the thing would have eaten him if it had got the chance.
The mewling, moaning cries now tore at Corey's innocent
heart. Even worse and more heart-wrenching than the poor
animal's cries was the sight of his hero, Joe, sobbing and
giving up.

The sound of footsteps caught Corey's attention. He looked
up to see three policemen running toward them from the
Garden entrance. The last cop had his gun out and covered
the other two as they knelt by Joe and the dead professor. Joe
stood, and the two cops picked up Professor Ligget's body.

"You've got to come inside, *now*, sir," one of them said to
Joe.

Joe let Sara take his left arm and Corey his right. Together, the three followed the cops carrying the professor inside. The policeman with the gun followed, covering them
all the way to the Garden's doors.

4:15 a.m.

Security people were waiting inside the front doors of the
Garden for Joe, Sara, and Corey. One of them, a tall, dark,
Italian-looking man, asked, "Which one of you is Officer
Murphy?"

Joe shook his head and more tears spilled from his eyes.
"He didn't make it."

"You're the only ones?" the same security guy asked.

Sara nodded.

"Where's the Humvee? Why didn't you come in the service entrance on Seventh Avenue? Where are the weapons and food Officer Murphy told us he had?"

Joe thought it was a strange question, but answered, "Seventh Avenue was blocked. We had to leave the Hummer back on Eighth Avenue; there were too many abandoned cars in the way. The food is in it; it was too heavy to carry. I brought some weapons, though." He took the leather valise from around his neck.

The security guard took the bag but didn't look in it. "What're the fire extinguishers for?"

When Joe didn't answer Sara spoke up. "They repel the flying orbs. They hate the foam in these things."

The security guard raised one eyebrow and took the extinguisher from Sara and looked at it. He took out his radio as he did, and spoke into it. "Sir, the survivors you've been waiting for are here. They came in the Eighth Avenue side and they didn't bring the Humvee."

The crackling voice that replied over the radio sounded angry. "What? What do you mean they didn't bring the Humvee?"

"They said they had to ditch it down between Thirtieth and Thirty-first Streets and come on foot. They did bring some ordnance with them, and one dead body."

"How many are there?" the radio voice asked.

"Guns or people?"

"People, you idiot!"

"Just three, sir. Officer Murphy, I've been told, didn't make it. We have a man, a woman, a child, and, like I said, one dead guy."

"Bring the man to my office, take care of the other two, and dispose of the corpse, understand?"

"Yes, sir." The security guard clicked off and spoke to the other guards and the three policemen who had escorted Joe, Sara, and Corey inside. "Sir, for safety we'll need to take all of your weapons."

"Uh, yeah, sure," Joe said, and handed his Uzi to the

guard, who gave it to the policeman who had covered them out on the Garden steps.

Sara gave him her snub-nosed revolver.

"That's it," Joe said. "The rest are in the bag or back in the Hummer."

Corey looked at the cop and thought he looked familiar. He was young, with no hat. His sandy, blond hair was a little long over his ears and collar. He had an open, pleasant face with large brown eyes, a narrow, long nose, and small mouth. His face and hands were peppered with freckles.

"Do you know my dad?" Corey asked. "His name is Officer Tom Aaron."

The cop looked at him and shook his head. "Sorry, kid, never heard of him."

The head guard spoke to the other security guards with him. "Take care of the boy and his mother," he said to the first two. "You," he said to the remaining two, "take care of the body."

They bent and picked up the professor's corpse, one taking his arms, the other his legs.

"Sir, please come with me," the head guard said to Joe.

Exhausted and emotionally spent, Joe wearily nodded.

"Where are you taking us?" Sara asked, concerned. She didn't like being split up.

"It's all right, ma'am," the guard said to her. He smiled, but Sara thought it looked false. "The director just wants to talk to him about how you all got here and what the situation is like out there. It's kind of a debriefing."

"I can tell you in less than ten words," Sara said. "It's hell out there."

The guard nodded and his smile became more false and patronizing. "Thank you, ma'am. That's very helpful, very descriptive, but you'll have your chance to impress the director with such compelling details later. Right now, go with these two gentlemen. They'll get you something to eat and drink and find you a place to rest. You must be tired."

Sara didn't like his sarcastic tone and opened her mouth

to tell him so, but Joe reached out and squeezed her upper arm.

"It's okay, Sara. Just go with them. We're safe now."

4:18 a.m.

Mayor Wynks and Bob Jones, the head of food and vending services, were drinking martinis in the Club Bar & Grill, when the director of security, Fred Roux, walked in. The mayor could tell he was angry just by the way he was walking.

"Our new *friends* have arrived," Roux said, speaking the word *friends* as if it were something disgusting and diseased.

"Let me guess," the mayor said. "There are more of them than we were led to believe?"

Roux shook his head.

"They didn't bring the food," the mayor guessed next.

Roux nodded.

Bob Jones cursed loudly.

"Who gives a shit about the food?" Fred Roux said. "They didn't bring the Humvee they said they had, either. They brought some weapons, but no Humvee mounted with a machine gun and plated with armor. They also brought an old dead guy."

Bob Jones drained his glass before pouring another from the shiny metal shaker on the bar. "That's something, at least," he said sarcastically.

Fred Roux slammed his fist on the bar. "Do you have *any* clue what we're facing here?" Roux asked the two men as he went around to the other side of the bar to help himself to a tumbler of Scotch, neat. "That Humvee was our ticket out of here; away from the aliens, who, I shouldn't have to remind you, are getting closer every day."

The mayor looked at Roux. "So, they lied to us about having a Hummer?"

"The guy says they had to abandon it because Eighth Avenue was blocked, which is bullshit. The cop who contacted us was *told* to come in by the Seventh-Avenue delivery entrance. They *lied* to us about the Humvee. If they had truly been in a combat Hummer with a mounted machine gun they should have *easily* been able to come in that way."

"Really?" the mayor said, a growing smirk on his lips. His normally florid face and bulbous, vein-ridden nose became more so when he drank and every expression became exaggerated. "And you know this because . . . *you've* been out there yourself?"

"I know it the same way *you* do. Don't pull that shit on me, Harry. I don't see *you* volunteering to go out and do any reconnaissance, but you are quick enough to order others to do it."

The mayor's expression turned somber. He took another drink. "You're right, Fred. You're absolutely right. I'm a goddamned coward, and so are you; so are all of us in the so-called Survivor Council." He shouted the last words and finished his drink.

"Please," the security director said. "Spare me your melo-dramatics, and your guilty conscience."

The mayor lifted the martini shaker to pour another drink. Fred Roux slapped it from his hand.

"You need to get off the sauce! We need you to do your job, and you need to do it sober. The people trust you, and, God knows why, they actually like you. And *we* need them to keep on liking you and believing you, no matter what crap you tell them. So quit your 'I'm so pitiful' act and do what you're told to do, and maybe *we'll* get out of this *alive!*"

Mayor Wynks stood, swayed slightly, and gave a mock salute. *"Jawohl! Mein Fuhrer!"*

The mayor turned away to leave with Bob Jones, but stopped and asked Roux, "Just how many new people came in?"

"A man, a woman, and a child, plus a dead guy," Roux muttered

The mayor looked at him uneasily. "What will you . . . we . . . do with them?"

Roux smiled and the smile scared the mayor. "After I talk to the man, if it turns out he was lying and can't produce the Hummer, he goes out with either tonight's or tomorrow night's lottery winners." He looked at the director of food and vending. "Bob? Stick around. With no Humvee, we need to talk about going ahead with our . . . new *system* until we can figure out the best way to evacuate this death trap."

Bob Jones looked queasy, as though the gin and vermouth in his stomach was sickening him.

"What new system?" the mayor asked, looking from Roux to Jones.

"Doesn't concern you, Harry," Roux said dismissively.

"Trust me," Bob Jones whispered as the Mayor turned to leave, "you don't want to know."

4:25 a.m.

The security guard and Joe sat in the waiting room of an office. A plaque on the door read DIRECTOR OF SECURITY. The inner door suddenly opened automatically and the guard and Joe stood. The guard motioned for Joe to go in first. He followed and placed the valise of weapons on the floor by the director's desk, then stood behind Joe.

The man behind the desk appeared to be tall and wore his gray hair in a crew cut. His suit and tie gave the appearance of just another workday. But closer examination revealed a wrinkled outfit that looked like it had been worn for a week without changing, which Joe guessed was about right. The director was broad-shouldered and looked to be in good shape. His face was long and angular with high cheekbones and a narrow nose set between small, close-set eyes. His mouth was small, his lips thin. The nameplate on his desk read FRED ROUX, DIRECTOR OF SECURITY.

The air conditioner was on in the office though Joe had not felt it in other parts of the building he had just come through. Compared to the sweltering humidity outside, the cool air of the office actually gave Joe a chill. As he approached the desk, the man looked up from some paperwork in front of him and stood, offering his right hand.

"Hello," Fred Roux said, smiling. His voice was rough and raspy. "Welcome to Madison Square Garden. My name is Fred Roux."

"I gathered as much," Joe said, shaking his hand and nodding at the nameplate on the desk. "I'm Joe Burton."

The director of security motioned toward a chair in front of his desk, then sat again behind the desk. Joe noticed that his chair was conspicuously lower than Mr. Roux's desk and chair.

"I heard that you've had some problems getting here," Roux said. He clasped his hands together on the desktop and smiled again at Joe. It was one of the phoniest smiles Joe had ever seen, immediately putting him on his guard.

"Yes," Joe said. "We did."

The phony smiled disappeared for a moment, then returned more fake than before. The man looked as though genuine smiling was something he was unaccustomed to, and was a strain for him. "How, *exactly*, did you get here?" Roux asked.

It seemed to Joe that the man was carefully choosing his words. He wondered why. "We managed to drive until we hit the traffic jam out front, then we hoofed it as fast as we could from there."

"What happened to the Humvee Officer Murphy told us you'd be coming in?" Mr. Roux leaned forward, anxiously.

Joe thought it was an odd question, but answered, "Like I said, we couldn't get through the stalled cars out front and had to leave it." He added, "Why?"

Roux sat back suddenly. "Well, um . . . we like to know how all our survivors get here . . . so we can find out what way is the safest way to travel. Surely you know that the aliens are on the move?"

Joe nodded.

"We were contacted by Officer Murphy, who informed us that you had a combat-ready, military model Humvee, mounted with a machine gun and carrying a cache of weapons and explosives. He also told us you would be bringing food; twenty pounds of rice and ten pounds of noodles."

"So if you know that, why are you asking me?" Joe asked.

Roux's face reddened with anger. "Since you arrived on foot, Mr. Burton, I'm wondering if Officer Murphy was telling the truth."

"He was telling the truth," Joe said, growing angry. "He's not here because he didn't make it; just like the other seven people who started out with us but didn't make it. And I told you, the food is in the Humvee, which is out on Eighth Avenue."

Roux looked flustered, as though he were unused to people using that tone with him. He looked pensive for a moment, as if thinking how to best phrase what he said next. "Officer Murphy was told how to get here so that he could drive the Humvee directly into the delivery area on Seventh Avenue. Why didn't you do that?"

Joe didn't answer.

Now it was Mr. Roux's turn to show anger. "Mr. Burton, I don't think you understand what's going on here. Those weapons, the food, and especially that vehicle are very much needed here." He stood and opened a curtain behind him, revealing a large glass window with horizontal sliding panes.

"Look, Mr. Burton," Roux said.

Joe stood and looked out the widow. It overlooked the basketball arena. The stands were filled with people who looked like they had been there too long.

"We have close to nineteen thousand people living here whom we are trying to protect and keep alive as best we can considering the circumstances. We are trying to come up with a viable evacuation plan and we need weapons to do so. We also have a growing shortage of food. Now, if you expect to become part of this community, it is your duty to cooperate."

Joe felt a pang of guilt at Roux's reprimand. "You're right," he said. "I'm sorry. We didn't come in the way we we're supposed to because Seventh Avenue was teeming with monsters. As it is we were chased by them the entire way. We would have carried the food if we had known you needed it so badly. It's really not much, though; certainly not enough to feed nineteen thousand people. But everything Murphy told you is true: the Hummer is armored and has an M-sixty machine gun mounted on its roof. But, it doesn't carry many people, six or so, I guess, maybe a couple more if you cram them in.

The food and six M-sixteen rifles are still in the Hummer. I'd be willing to get the rest with some help," Joe offered sincerely, but also to see how Roux would react. Something about the man did not sit well with Joe. For one thing, he seemed far more interested in the Hummer and the weapons than the food.

"No, no," Roux said quickly. "If it's where you say it is, we can send out a detail to get it."

Joe wondered why Roux was so anxious to get the Hummer. It couldn't carry many people. Even with the rear cargo section configured to carry troops it wouldn't carry more than ten, twelve people. True, it had a powerful weapon and armor, but the machine gun wasn't enough to cover 19,000 people trying to evacuate the city.

Another thought occurred to Joe: Roux wanted the Hummer for himself, to save his own ass.

Roux looked at the security guard standing behind Joe and said, "We're finished here, Frank."

Joe stood and asked, "I'm curious, but where did the horse from Hell on Eighth Avenue come from?"

"As you say," Roux answered, "from *Hell* just like all the other abominations out there."

"Uh, yeah," Joe said slowly, unsure if Roux was making a joke or not. "But really, where did it come from?"

Fred Roux sighed and looked at Joe the way a bothered parent looks at an annoying child. "Haven't you ever seen the New York City Police's Mounted Division?" he asked condescendingly.

"Oh, yeah," Joe said. "I didn't think of that."

Roux nodded and stood.

The security guard came forward and stood by Joe.

"Frank," Roux said. "Put Mr. Burton with tonight's volunteers. Then come back and see me. I have a very important job for you and your men."

"What?" Joe asked. "What volunteers?"

Roux heaved a tired sigh, obviously tired of Joe's presence. "They're men who have volunteered to help keep our little community going. Each night it's a different group.

They'll tell you what you need to do, that is, if you *are* planning on helping us out?"

"Um, sure," Joe said.

"Fine," Roux said, looking down at papers on his desk. "Frank will take you to them."

4:26 a.m.

"Aw, cool!" Corey cried. After the two security guards with them had had a lengthy private discussion off to the side, which Sara had sensed was about who was going to get stuck with taking her and Corey to get food, the taller of the two led them through the mezzanine, where large display cases contained the history of the Garden in pictures, plus sports memorabilia with photos of famous athletes who had played for New York teams.

"This is the first time I've ever been here," Corey told Sara and the security guard with them. "I've always wanted to come. My mom said we'd go to the Ice Capades this year, after the baby . . ." His voice trailed off and tears filled his eyes.

"I've never been here before, either," Sara said, trying to keep Corey from dwelling on the loss of his mother. "Are you a sports fan, Corey?"

"Yeah," Corey said, and a little grin lit up his face. "I like baseball."

"So you must be a Yankee fan," Sara asked, glad to see the boy smiling again.

"Nope. My dad is." Corey gave her a devious smile. "I'm a Red Sox fan."

Sara had to laugh at the way he said it, with such pride.

The security guard, an imposing, muscular man with an acne-scarred face, turned and gave Corey a stern look. "We don't let Red Sox fans stay around here."

At first Corey thought he was serious and was afraid. Then the guard winked at him and smiled.

"Just kidding," the guard said.

Corey and Sara laughed.

After the mezzanine, the guard led Corey and Sara along

a back hallway, to a left turn down another hallway that went by the kitchen. The warm smell of food cooking drifted out to them. Corey's stomach gurgled with hunger. He and Sara were disappointed when the guard led them past the open kitchen door and kept going.

"Um, I thought we were going to get something to eat," Sara said to the guard.

"You will in a little bit," he answered. Sara noticed that he avoided looking at her when he spoke.

"Where, exactly, are you taking us?" she asked. She had a sudden wary feeling about the guard.

"Right here," he said, stopping outside a door marked A-STORAGE. He pulled a key ring from his belt and unlocked the door. "Someone will be along with food shortly," the guard said, again avoiding a direct look into Sara's eyes. "You need to be debriefed, also, to help us understand what's happening on the outside."

He opened the door and stepped into the room, holding out his left hand to motion Corey and Sara to enter.

Corey went willingly, but Sara entered slowly. She had a strong feeling that something was wrong. The storeroom wasn't large—only ten by twenty feet or so—and cardboard boxes filled half the room. They were marked PLASTIC CUPS and CUTLERY. Sara couldn't see how they were going to eat comfortably in there. She turned to tell the guard that, but he abruptly stepped out of the room and pulled the door shut and locked it behind him. Sara immediately went over and tried the knob. She banged on the door with her open right hand.

"Hey! Hey, mister! Open up! Why'd you lock us in? Hello-o?"

No answer, no response.

"What the hell is going on?" Sara muttered.

"Why did he lock us in here?" Corey asked, his voice nervous and strained.

Sara didn't want to scare Corey any more than he already was, so she smiled and sat on one of the boxes that held plastic forks. "I guess they just want to make sure we don't wander off and get lost before they can feed us and talk to us. This is a pretty big place, you know. I bet it's easy to get lost in here."

Corey relaxed a little at that and sat down next to Sara. She put her arm around him and tried to contain her own growing sense of fear at being locked in the room.

5:15 a.m.

After his meeting with Roux, Joe had been led by the security guard to a room near the freight elevator. The guard unlocked the door and pushed it open. Joe looked in and saw that it was a stark, white room. A group of twenty or so men sat on the floor against the walls.

Joe stepped in and looked at the sitting men. Only a few of them took notice of him; the rest were morose and indifferent to his presence.

"What's this?" Joe asked the guard.

The guard answered by slamming the door and locking Joe in.

Joe surveyed the men in the room. They ranged in age from old to young, and from fat to slim—the youngest ones looked to be in their late teens, the oldest in their sixties; and the weight spread ran from skinny to obese.

"Can anyone tell me what the hell is going on here?" he asked. "Why are you locked in here?"

The men sat silent, as if entranced, staring at the floor in front of them or at the opposite wall. When no one answered, Joe slumped against the door. He was exhausted and almost beyond caring.

After a while, a guy about Joe's age, with red hair and a ruddy complexion, sitting closest to the door asked, "You a new arrival?"

"Yeah," Joe said.

The guy held out his hand. "My name's Terry Costello."

Joe shook it. "Joe Burton."

"Welcome, Joe. There's a bathroom through that door if you need to go," Terry said, a wry smile on his lips. He beckoned Joe closer.

Joe slid over and sat next to Terry. "What's going on? I was told you guys are volunteers, helping out; why are you locked in here? Why is everyone looking so bummed."

"Is that what they told you, that we're *volunteers*?" Terry asked.

"Yeah. That guy, Roux, told me I'd have to join you volunteers and learn what I need to do to lend a hand."

"Volunteers!" Terry said, and laughed sarcastically. "We're not volunteers, we're lottery winners! Right, guys?" There were grunts, dirty looks, and a couple of middle fingers from the other men in the room.

He went on at Joe's puzzled look. "All of us were here for the seventh game between the Lakers and the Knicks when the invasion started. None of us knew what was going on outside until the game was over and they made an announcement on the PA that everyone should stay in their seats, that it was dangerous to go outside." Terry paused and shook his head.

"Of course, tell people they can't do something and right away most of them do it. My friends and I were pretty drunk and up for celebrating the Knicks beating the Lakers and winning the championship—"

"The Knicks won?" Joe interrupted excitedly.

"Yeah," Terry answered.

Joe let out a loud, "Yes!" None of the other men in the room shared his moment of triumph or even looked at him.

"As I was saying," Terry went on, "me and my friends didn't want to stay in the Garden no matter what was going on outside. Actually we figured it had to be some kind of terrorist attack, you know? Osama fucking-bin Laden, right? So we headed out. A lot of other people felt the same way . . . until we got outside and saw what was happening." Terry shook his head. "It was unbelievable. We were blown away, you know?"

"Yeah," Joe said with complete understanding.

"Most of the people leaving were just paralyzed by what they saw. Those monster things had a fucking feast. I was with three other guys and they all were either killed or turned into monsters before I was jolted enough to recover from shock and disbelief at what was happening. Most of us who were outside and saw what was going on managed to get back inside safely.

"At first it was okay. Mayor Wynks is here and he assured us that the military was going to counterattack and that we were all lucky since we were safe and sound in here. They opened up all the concession stands and let people eat and drink for free. It turns out that was a big mistake. I guess they thought we wouldn't be here that long and the military would . . . well, now we all know the army, air force, and the fucking marines couldn't do jack-shit against those things. Who knew, right? Go fucking figure. . . .

"On Monday we watched the coverage of what was happening on the big screens in the arena and saw how those little glowing bastards destroyed the air attack and turned most of the land force into those man-eating monsters. It was a fucking massacre. The big screens went dead soon after that; someone shut the signal down 'cause it was too depressing." Terry looked at his feet and Joe could see tears in his eyes; he looked like he was fighting against just breaking down and bawling.

"That's when the mayor and a bunch of suits realized that they had made a mistake letting people eat and drink as much as they wanted. They formed the Survival Council on Tuesday with all the important city bigwigs that were here and the celebrities that always come to the Lakers games— you know, guys like Jack Nickelback, the actor, and Nails McGee, the director, the rapper Dollar-Dollar—and they started rationing food. Still . . . it was obvious that sooner or later the food was going to run out; there were just too many people, you know?" Terry looked around at the other men in the room. Joe followed his gaze and saw that just a few of them were listening—they all knew the story only too well.

"So, they made an announcement that anyone who wanted to leave, you know, like to check on family and loved ones, could. Quite a lot of people did. *Those* were the volunteers.

Some of us went up to the doors to see how they did, 'cause, you know, we were thinking of going, too, but didn't have the balls after what happened the first time. Personally, I got a wife and kid in Queens. . . ." His voice cracked and he had to pause to regain control.

"The volunteers were massacred outside. So, suddenly, nobody wants to volunteer to leave anymore, but there's still too many people here and not enough food, you know?"

"Then, yesterday, Wednesday, one of the suits got the bright idea of having a lottery." Terry looked at Joe. "You ever read "The Lottery" by Shirley Jackson?"

Joe thought a moment and nodded.

"We got a lottery like in that story," Terry said, and stared at the floor.

Joe waited patiently for him to go on. After several moments of continued silence, Joe cleared his throat, which brought Terry out of his stupor. He looked questioningly at Joe.

"You were telling me about the lottery?" Joe prompted.

"Yeah, yeah. . . . It's kind of like the numbers game. This is only the second day we've had it, but they base it on the stadium's seat numbers. Every day they put all the seat numbers in a big spinning barrel and pick out twenty seat numbers. The men sitting in those seats have to leave. That's it. We have to leave that night, but we're given no food or weapons. They make us wait in here until it's time so that none of us will try to hide and get out of going. They take us out of here one by one—I guess it gives us a better chance that way. If a woman or a kid is in the seat and they came with a man, he goes; if a woman or a kid came alone or with other women, the man in the closest seat to the one picked has to go.

"That seemed fair. But just after they pulled the first seat numbers and called them out, they told us they were going to start running two lotteries starting today. So tonight, we'll be going out with *another* group of twenty guys."

Joe couldn't believe it.

"I guess it won't be that bad," Terry shrugged. "They got to do something, right? It just irks me that I ain't seen any of the Survival Council winning the fucking lottery."

"That's incredible," Joe said. "I can't believe it."

"Believe it," Terry emphasized.

"But if there are too many people here already and they're making people leave, then why are they sending an emergency broadcast signal out and telling people to come here?"

"They did that?" Terry asked.

"Yeah, why do you think we came?" Joe answered.

"Shit, I just thought you came here by chance to escape the fucking aliens out there. With all the fucking problems we got here, why would they send out that signal?" Terry wondered aloud.

"An even bigger question is why are you guys putting up with this lottery bullshit? Why don't you refuse to do it?" Joe wanted to know.

Terry shrugged. "Ah, it ain't that bad, really. What else are we going to do? We're all up Shit Creek without a paddle anyway. Besides, this ain't going to last forever. The Survival Council announced earlier that the aliens are getting scarce. They think they're either leaving or dying off somehow. Our chances of surviving outside are pretty good now, I hear. I probably would have volunteered to go in a couple days anyhoo; there's a rumor going around that the military released a nerve gas that is killing the fucking E.T.s left and right, but it's harmless to humans. Whatever it is, we're all going to get out of here soon and be able to go home and try to go back to our lives," Terry looked wistful. "It's going to be a different fucking world, though, I bet."

"Listen to me," Joe said, gripping both of Terry's arms. "The Survival Council is lying to you." He noticed this statement finally caught the attention of the other men in the room. "The aliens aren't leaving. They've been amassing at the edges of the city and they're conducting a street-by-street, building-by-building search for human survivors. The monsters are tearing down *every* building they can to flush out people hiding inside; it's a planned, methodical process of extermination. The buildings that are too big to destroy, they send in the glowing orbs, or the smaller monsters, to find people hiding." He now had the attention of everyone in the room.

A look of astonishment passed over every face. The men became animated and spoke to each other in subdued voices until the room was filled with a low rumbling murmur.

One of them—a balding, overweight middle-aged man—raised his hand as if he were in school and asked, "How far away are the aliens from here?"

"Not far. Last night they were just to the other side of Ninth Avenue. That's just a block away. I got to figure they're going to make it here by tomorrow," Joe answered. "The thing is, the mayor and Fred Roux and the rest of the so-called Survival Council know about this. I was questioned by that asshole Roux and he told me he knew and gave me the idea there would be some sort of evacuation. Now I think he and the other members of the Council are making plans to get the hell out of Dodge and leave you poor suckers behind to feed and distract the monsters while they make their get-away."

Terry and the other men displayed a sudden unity of emotion, and that emotion was *anger*.

12:00 noon

After seven hours in the storage room, Sara feared they had been forgotten and no one was going to bring food and water. The room was stifling. Both she and Corey were soaked with perspiration. Sara had ripped the flap off one of the cardboard boxes and was using it intermittently as a fan, but her hand tired quickly in the energy-sapping heat.

"Where do you think Joe is?" Corey asked after a while.

"I don't know, but I'm sure he's okay." She patted Corey's knee. "I bet he'll come get us soon."

Corey smiled and nodded, but she could tell he believed her about as much as she believed herself.

A noise from behind the stack of boxes against the back

wall startled them both. Sara immediately thought of rats and backed away.

Corey was braver and went closer.

"Don't be afraid," came a voice from behind the boxes, startling them again.

"Who's there?" Corey whispered.

"I'm a friend," came the answer. "If you want to get out of there, move the boxes."

Corey looked at Sara; Sara looked at the door, then back at the boxes. She nodded, and both began moving the boxes away from the wall. They uncovered a wire mesh grate covering an air vent. Behind it crouched a gray-haired black man, who turned around in the shaft with some difficulty, placed his feet against the inside of the grate, and pushed on it until it popped out.

The black man crawled out of the air duct feetfirst and stood. He was tall and wiry. He looked to Sara to be between fifty-five and sixty. He had an open, gentle face. He stretched with his hands on his lower back. There were several popping sounds and the man grunted. "I'm too damn old for this," he said, smiling. He held out his hand to Corey, who was closest.

"I'm Robert Jefferson," he said.

Corey shook his hand. "My name is Corey Aaron, and this is my friend, Sara." He pointed at her.

"Sara Hailey," she said, stepping forward and shaking Robert's hand. "What is going on here?" Sara asked.

"Nothing good, young lady. Nothing good," Robert said, shaking his head sadly.

"They're treating us like prisoners, locking us in here," Sara told him.

"I know. You're lucky I found you. We need to get out of here, pronto."

"Why?" Sara asked, eyeing the square air duct. It was no larger than four feet high by three feet wide. "What is going on *here*?"

"It'll take too long to tell you here. We need to get to a safer spot and then I'll reveal all." He bowed like a showman and Corey smiled. Robert saw the look of apprehension on Sara's face as she regarded the air duct.

"Are you claustrophobic?" he asked.

She shook her head. "No, not really . . . it's just that . . . um, there aren't any rats in there, are there?"

"Not that I've seen," Robert said, and smiled. "If there are, I'm sure we have nothing to fear from them. They're probably more afraid of us than we are of them."

Corey was already crouched in front of the open air duct, looking in with anticipation.

"Go on in, son," Robert told him. He motioned for Sara to follow Corey. "Don't worry, I'll be right behind you. I need to pull those boxes back in place to cover our escape, for a little while at least."

1:00 p.m.

In the air-conditioned conference room, the Survivor Council sat looking at Fred Roux, who stood at the head of the table again, leaning over it, both hands on its surface.

"Gentlemen, there has been a turn of events and we have to make some tough decisions. You know we are going to have to tell the fans that we must evacuate because of the advancing aliens. I know we've misled them on that of late, but it was only to keep their hopes up and to keep them calm. But now we, and they, face some hard truths. We don't have the capability to evacuate and protect the fans. Everyone we've sent down to Penn Station to explore the trains and tunnels as an avenue of escape has failed to return, so . . . we can assume the worse.

"When the fans leave here, it's going to be a bloodbath—that's inevitable—but *some* will survive, and some of those survivors can be *us*!"

Anxious faces peered at Roux, hanging on his every word.

"The new arrivals *did* bring the military vehicle—an armored Humvee mounted with a machine gun! They also brought the food they promised. The problem is that they had to leave it all out on Eighth Avenue."

The men around the table nodded, but the anxiety remained in their faces.

"I sent Frank Leary and four of my best men to retrieve the vehicle and bring it into the delivery entrance."

More approving buzz went around the table. Some of the men smiled, thinking they saw what Fred Roux was leading to.

"But . . . there is one small problem." He paused to look at each of the fifteen men around the table squarely in the eye. "Frank Leary, my senior guard, drove a Hummer in Iraq in Desert Storm. From what he says, the Humvee can only carry eight men when it's fully armed and loaded with cargo, and three of those men will be either uncomfortable or exposed to danger since one will be crammed into the cargo space with the supplies and the other two will have to stand on the side runners."

The room grew somber and quiet.

Roux let the information sink in before proceeding.

"So, my friends, it seems the old saying, 'What goes around comes around,' is true. I hope you all appreciate the irony of the situation. It looks as though we shall have to conduct our *own* little lottery. . . ."

Each of the men on the Survivor Council silently wrote their names on slips of paper and placed them in an empty Dunkin' Donuts box. Fred Roux stood at the head of the table, hands on hips, watching the proceedings. The two-way radio on the table in front of him suddenly squawked to life.

"Chief! Chief!" The crackling voice was urgent.

Roux picked up the radio and spoke into it. "What is it?"

"We've got a problem, Chief. The squad I sent out to get the Hummer still hasn't come back."

Roux's face turned red with anger. "What do you mean they haven't come back? Did they take off with it?"

"No, sir, they're either dead or they're monsters now," came the reply. "The aliens are much closer than we thought. They're less than a block away."

"Damn it!" Roux muttered. All eyes at the table were on him.

"Send out another squad," Roux spoke into the radio, trying to keep his voice calm.

"Um . . . I think we're going to have a problem doing that."

"What? Why?"

"Well, sir, everyone's worried about ending up as food for those things, or becoming one."

Roux glared at the other men at the table and each looked away. "You listen to me," Roux barked into the radio. "I don't give a damn what they're worried about. You send another squad out *now*, or *you* go out and do it, or you *and* your men will be *turned out* without any weapons."

There was no reply for several moments—only static.

"With all respect, *sir*," came the voice, "you're forgetting *what* we've *done* for you in the last couple of days. Without me and my men, you can't carry out those threats. I'm not risking my life or anyone else's anymore for you. If you want the Hummer so bad, you go out and get it."

Roux's face was livid with anger. His rage was so intense it took away his voice; he could only make grunting sounds.

"What does he mean by that?" Mayor Wynks asked. "What have him and his men done for you?"

Roux ignored him and stormed out of the room.

3:00 p.m.

After a day full of grumbling and talk, the men in the room with Joe had reached a decision and had started to plan.

"We need to fight these bastards," Terry Mahoney said. "And we need to tell the people in the stands. We need to let them know that we're being set up so the fat cats on the Council can escape at the cost of all our lives."

"Yes, but we need to get out of here first," Joe said. Before he could say any more there was the sound of a key in the door's lock and the door opened. The head security guard and two of his men entered the room carrying guns. Just outside, four police officers waited with their pistols in hand.

Terry looked at Joe, squinted, and gave a slight nod of the head toward the guards, as if to say, "Let's jump them now."

The guard caught the look. "Don't do it, pal," the guard said, and leveled his gun at Terry.

"Looks like you guys aren't even going to pretend anymore that we're all in this together, huh?" Terry said, his face red with anger.

The guard didn't reply. He just grabbed Joe by the arm and pulled him to the door. Another guard covered their exit, keeping his gun pointed at Terry and the rest until Joe and the first guard left. The guard pulled the door closed and locked it.

3:15 p.m.

"Mr. Burton, I have an offer for you."

Joe was again standing in Fred Roux's office. Roux was seated behind his massive oak desk. The arena window behind him was hidden behind its curtains.

"Yeah?" What's that?" Joe asked.

"Just this," the director of security answered. He put his hands together and made a steeple with his fingertips. "I want you to go outside and get the Humvee you came in, and bring it here."

Joe shook his head and laughed. "You're kidding, right?"

"No, Mr. Burton. I'm not the type of man who kids. In fact, I've been told I have no sense of humor at all."

Joe looked at the man and chuckled. "You ever hear the old saying 'You can fool some of the people some of the time, but you can't fool all of the people all of the time'?"

Roux gave him a dour look.

"'Cause that's the situation here now. You're through fooling the people. You know the group of guys who are supposed to leave tonight? They're on to you, and soon, everyone else will be, too."

"Really," Roux replied with no apparent shock at the news. "That doesn't change anything. In fact, it makes it easier. If you don't go out and retrieve the Humvee and bring it around to our delivery entrance, I will have your woman, your boy, and your new friends killed."

Joe's eyes narrowed and his face reddened. His upper lip curled into a scowl. "You're sick, you bastard!" Joe growled, and made a lunge for Roux. The next moment he was convulsing on the floor as Roux zapped him with a Taser he pulled from under his desk. Joe was helpless. After a few seconds, the current subsided, leaving Joe on the floor, twitching slightly.

"Get up," Roux ordered. Joe stayed on the floor. "If you don't get up now, Mr. Burton, I shall give you another dose of electricity."

Slowly, Joe regained his feet and stood, less defiant, in front of Roux again.

"Now," Roux said. "I'll even make it easier for *you*. You don't have to go until it gets dark. You can wait here, under guard, of course, but if you're not back before dawn, your wife and kid and all the men in the room you just came from will die. Of course, I can't let you have any weapons, but Frank Leary tells me you brought fire extinguishers that can keep the flying aliens at bay. I'll let you take one of those. Do we have a deal?"

Joe nodded slowly, but he had other plans in mind.

3:45 p.m.

Sara lay in a small, round metal room only four feet high, under one of the Garden's circulating roof fans. Next to her, Corey lay sleeping, and across from her, Robert Jefferson's haunted eyes reflected her own as he paused from his story.

Sara wanted to sleep. She was so exhausted her body and mind cried out for sleep, but it wouldn't come—not after what she'd seen and learned. Over and over the events of the past few hours kept playing in her head.

It had been as hot as an oven in the air duct when Sara and Corey had first climbed in, and it had gotten steadily hotter. With the closeness of the metal shaft all around her, Sara had begun to feel as if she were in an actual oven. Only Robert Jefferson's promise that it would get cooler had kept her going.

True to his word, in five minutes he had led them to a shaft that was an air-conditioning duct. It had been deliciously cool in there and Sara and Corey had savored it.

They had been crawling through the duct, on their way to the room she was in now, until Corey had complained, "I'm hungry."

"Yeah," she had agreed. "Can we get something to eat? On our way in we passed the kitchen. Whatever they were cooking smelled wonderful. Do you think we could get some of that?"

Robert Jefferson had hesitated for a moment, seemingly considering something, then nodded. "Take your next left. That will take us to food storage."

Sara had done as instructed, crawling into a shaft that led off to the left. The rich smell of something good cooking had wafted to her, making her mouth water.

Behind her, Corey's stomach had growled loudly and was answered by a gurgling in Sara's own. A puff of icier air had washed over her; it felt heavenly. It had come from a wire mesh grate about twelve feet ahead.

"Shhh," Robert had whispered at her and Corey. There were distant voices and the clang of pots followed by the faint whir of some kitchen appliance.

Sara and Corey had nodded; they understood. Being as quiet as possible, Sara had crawled to the grate from which the frigid air was coming. Carefully, lying flat on her stomach and using her elbows to pull herself along the last few inches to the opening, she had reached the wire mesh and peered through.

It was dark beyond the grate and it had taken a minute for Sara's eyes to adjust. When they did, she had stopped breathing as though she'd just received a kick in the stomach, knocking the wind out of her.

The room was an abomination.

It was a meat locker, full of meat, but not the kind Sara had expected. From hooks on a metal runner that went around the room hung human corpses.

Hands over her mouth, wanting both to scream and vomit, Sara had stared in disbelief. The urge to scream and be sick had become strongest when she recognized the cadaver nearest the meat locker door.

Professor Ligget.

Sara had pulled back then, unable to look anymore. She put her head down and wept.

"What's wrong?" Corey had whispered, straining forward to see.

Sara had quickly wiped away her tears and pushed him back. She embraced him to keep him from seeing what she had seen. Over the top of his head, Robert had nodded, affirming that she had, indeed, just seen what she had.

For the first time she had noticed that his eyes, too, were hollow with the shock of what she had just witnessed.

"Soylent Green is people," Robert had said sadly.

"What's that mean?" Corey had asked.

Now, after the shock of what she had seen in the meat locker, Sara didn't want to be hungry anymore, but her body would not comply. Though the thought of what had been hanging in the freezer sickened her, the smell from the kitchen as they had crawled away had made her mouth water and her stomach gurgle just the same. She had been thankful when Robert took her and Corey to the round room under the large circular roof fan where he had a stash of food—a trash bag filled with stale popcorn. To drink, he had a half case of warm cans of Coke.

Sara hadn't been able to eat anything, and thought she might never be able to eat again.

"Why can't we have burgers?" Corey had complained.

"It's too dangerous," Sara had quickly replied.

When they had finished eating, Robert had coaxed Sara to tell him how they had survived and ended up at the Garden thinking it was a place of safety. Halfway through, Corey had curled up next to her and gone to sleep. When she was done Robert told his story.

"I work here—at least I used to—as a custodian. I know

this building inside and out. I knew when they started the lottery that things weren't as they seemed, so I started to stash stuff up here."

"What lottery?" Sara asked.

Robert explained the lottery for cutting back on the number of mouths to feed. "Right from the start, though, Fred Roux, the head of the Survival Council, had no intention of letting people leave. It's *his* plan to use 'em up like you saw in the freezer. I eavesdropped on their meeting after they started the lottery and heard them worrying that there wasn't enough food left to last more than a week. Fred Roux told them not to worry about it. I just discovered his solution to the food shortage myself. The dead men you saw in the meat locker were the losers of the first lottery. Your dead friend has been added to the total."

"He's really using them for food?"

"No, he ain't done it yet, but why else would he have the men who lost the lottery killed and their bodies hung from hooks in the meat locker? The worst that was supposed to happen to the losers was that they'd get turned out to fend for themselves." Robert paused and smiled ruefully. "You can look at it like there's not much difference—if they got turned out they'd be killed and eaten by the monsters out there; if they stay, they get killed and eaten by the monsters in here."

"Are the other Council members going along with this?" Sara asked.

Robert chuckled, but it was a mirthless sound. "I don't think they know about it. The chief cook and bottle washer, Bob Jones, must know, and some of his chefs obviously, and Roux's men must be doing the dirty work of murder. Roux must be bribing them with something. I think Bob Jones is pulling a Pontius Pilate; you know, he's washed his hands of responsibility, thinks he's just following orders. Like with the Nazis, I think Jones tells himself he's just carrying out orders. I don't even think the mayor knows what Roux has planned, and the others definitely don't. Roux couldn't get away with it if all the Council members knew. There are some decent men on the Council, after all."

"Oh, my God!" Sara said in disbelief. "Is that what they were going to do with us? Is that what they're going to do with Joe, the guy we came with?"

Robert said, "Yes, probably tonight, but don't worry, I ain't letting that happen. You all would have ended up in the meat locker tonight. They would have knocked you on the head with a hammer when you weren't looking and put you in there."

Corey stirred and gave out a weak cry in his sleep. Sara put a comforting hand on his back and rubbed it.

"That's why I got you two out of the room you were locked in," Robert explained.

"Can you find Joe and help him escape, too?" Sara asked.

Robert nodded and looked at his watch. "They'll be giving out rations in an hour. Security will be too busy keeping the food lines orderly. I was watching when you came in; I know what this Joe fella you came with looks like. Let me go check it out. I'm pretty sure I know where he is. I'll bring him back here, if I can. I'll try to set the fellas he's with free, too, and tell 'em what Mr. Fred Roux's been up to. I don't think they'll let him get away with it."

Sara smiled at him and said, "Thank you."

5:12 p.m.

Robert came back and didn't look happy.

"He wasn't there, *and* the lottery winners for tonight aren't being turned out. There's extra-heavy guards on their room. There's something going on and it scares me. I don't like it."

"Do you think he's . . ." Sara couldn't finish the question.

"No. I checked the freezer; he's not there. Look, you get some rest and let me do some scouting and spying and see if I can find where he is. I can go faster and quieter by myself, so you stay with the boy, okay?"

"As soon as you find him, or hear anything about him, you come back and get me," Sara said, and reluctantly agreed.

9:00 p.m.

From the 8th-Avenue entrance to Madison Square Garden, Joe set out to retrieve the Humvee. Joe could smell rain, and by the puddles on the sidewalk and water droplets on the cars, he assumed it had rained just before sunset. It had not relieved the heat and humidity, but it had doused the fire. The block glowed with dying embers now, which poured black smoke into the sky. Almost immediately, he noticed the absence of the rumbling sound from the 'Vaders' destruction of the city. The reason for that became obvious when he looked around; the massive U.S. Post Office across the street from the Garden was partially destroyed. Its roof was gone and one of its walls had collapsed, revealing an interior in ruins. The 'Vaders had done their worst to it, even though Joe was pretty sure it had been empty when the invasion started last Sunday. It was a chilling testament to the monsters' thoroughness.

The 'Vaders had reached the Garden. Everywhere he looked it was the same—the city had completely changed. Every small building Joe could see within view of the Garden had been completely or partially razed. Larger buildings had gaping holes in their sides and broken windows. Against the cloudy sky, he could still see skyscrapers standing, but wondered how much damage the light of day would reveal.

In and around the ruins, on the sidewalks and in the streets, the 'Vader monsters slept.

The city was dead silent, which bothered Joe more than normal, though he couldn't say why. He chalked it up to the fact that he felt, as he had every night since the invasion, so *strange* being out in the city with it so quiet. It was unnatural.

As he reached the beginning of the maze of abandoned cars, the moon appeared from behind the clouds. Joe could clearly make out the giant horse's skeleton picked clean where it lay, gleaming in the lunar-reflected light, on the cars it had crushed and flattened. By the number of sleeping creatures in the immediate vicinity of the Garden, and by the level of damage all around the famous building, it looked to

Joe as if the 'Vaders had deliberately directed their path of destruction to converge on the arena. By the moon, Joe had several clear lines of sight for blocks where smaller structures had been demolished amid the skyscrapers.

Joe moved as quietly as possible so as not to wake any of the nearby 'Vaders. As if in collusion, the moon disappeared again, helping to hide his passing. As soon as the sun rose, Joe knew the monsters would begin the final assault on Madison Square Garden, which *had* to have the most people still alive within its confines. It appeared the 'Vaders knew it, too. Joe no longer doubted their intelligence; it was obvious they knew the Garden was *the* last stronghold of humanity in the city. They surely knew it held a jackpot of food and, like many a gourmand is wont to do, had saved the best for last.

But that was okay with Joe; in fact he was counting on it. His only hope of getting Sara and Corey safely out of there was to bide his time and wait for the dawn, when Roux and his goons were distracted by the attacking aliens. If his plan was successful, he figured the best and safest escape route out of the city—maybe the *only* escape route—would be under the Garden, through Penn Station and the train tunnels. He didn't know why Roux and the people running things in the Garden weren't evacuating the arena through there. As soon as he got Sara and Corey back, he would take anyone who wanted to come with them through the tunnels. Based on his prior underground experience, he wasn't exactly thrilled about going that way, but he saw no alternative.

He reached the Hummer around 10:00 after walking slowly and cautiously. Surprisingly, the snail's pace left him exhausted. Joe knew he had plenty of time to prepare, and he had to do it right. He opened the front door of the Humvee and took the two blocks of C4 plastic explosives from under the seat and put them on the passenger's seat. Though the rest of the explosive and the detonator caps, primer cord, and the remote transmitter to detonate the caps were in the bag in the Garden, Murphy had told him the stuff could be detonated by a bullet.

He sat behind the wheel and went over his plan carefully. Since Roux wanted the Hummer so badly, Joe planned to use it to trade for Sara and Corey. Before dawn, he was going to rig the Hummer with the C4 and if Roux refused to deal with him, Joe was going to use one of the M-16s to kill Roux before he could hurt Sara or Corey and then shoot the C4 and blow the Hummer sky-high. If he timed it right, the attack of the 'Vaders would be diversion enough to allow him, Sara, and Corey to get back inside the Garden and head underground to the train tunnels in Penn Station. If Roux kept his word and turned Corey, Sara, and the "volunteers" over, Joe still planned on killing him if he could. Maybe life with the 'Vaders had hardened him, but there were enough monsters in the world without letting that particular ghoul live any longer.

Of course, all that depended on him being able to get the Hummer over to 7th Avenue and the Garden's delivery entrance. It would be difficult, but there was nothing else he could do. He'd either make it and save Sara and Corey, or die trying. Joe decided his best chance of making it would be around 3:00 the next morning. That would give him just enough time before dawn *if* he made it through the gauntlet of 'Vaders. Feeling exhausted from everything he'd been through in the past five days, Joe crawled into the backseat of the Humvee to get some much-needed shut-eye so that he would be as sharp as he needed to be come tomorrow.

Despite worrying about Sara, and the knowledge that he was surrounded by hundreds, maybe thousands of sleeping monsters, and that the next day might be his last on earth, he fell asleep surprisingly fast.

Day Six: Friday

5:00 a.m.

Joe woke and sat up quickly, saw the dawn light creeping over the city around him, and was horrified.

"I can't believe I overslept!"

Quickly, he grabbed a loaded M-16 out of the backseat of the Hummer. He didn't have enough time to drive around to 7th Avenue. He'd have to improvise.

That's when he saw something that made him step away from the vehicle.

It was a 'Vader monster, about twenty yards away, lying half on the sidewalk and half on the street. When Joe had crept by the hulk earlier, he had assumed it was sleeping, but now he thought otherwise. He realized that last night, other than when the 'Vaders had all headed for the edges of the city, was the only time when things had been *completely* and utterly silent. He'd been too preoccupied to dwell on it. Other nights since the invasion had started had been quiet, but not *silent*; he had always *heard* the 'Vaders sleeping— some of them snoring and all of them *breathing*. The 'Vader he beheld now was doing neither. Its chest was not rising and falling with the rhythm of its breathing.

He went closer. The creature was bloated and discolored.

Its skin was grayish and a mottled purple color had collected along its underside, which lay against the sidewalk.

The thing was dead.

Joe couldn't believe it. He had seen 'Vaders die before, but he had *never* seen a *dead* one just laying out in the open. Their ravenous appetites made them cannibals; they never left their dead uneaten.

Dazed, Joe started back the way he had come through the maze of cars on 8th Avenue. The 'Vaders that he had seen lying as dark shadows and had thought were sleeping, he now saw were dead. Their bloated, lumpy and discolored carcasses were strewn everywhere—amid rubble and ruin and all over the street and sidewalks.

Joe ran through the maze as fast as he could, shouting at the top of his lungs. By the time he reached the sidewalk outside the Garden doors, he wasn't the only one who had become aware of the phenomenon. All of the Garden's doors burst open and throngs of people spilled out onto the sidewalk. They looked as dazed as Joe felt, and they walked like sleepwalkers suddenly waking from a nightmare to find themselves in a strange place.

A woman he didn't know ran up and threw her arms around him. She planted a wet kiss on his surprised lips.

"It's over!" she said breathless with excitement. "It's finally over."

Joe nodded and the woman released him and ran on, hugging every person, man, or woman she encountered from the huge crowd that now poured from the Garden doors.

A young long-haired man, walking arm in arm with a beautiful redhead, went by Joe. He heard the man say, "It's just like *War of the Worlds*! All the germs and viruses—hell, maybe even the pollution—that we're immune to must have killed them." The woman readily agreed, not caring what the reason only that it had happened.

Joe pondered the theory. It wouldn't be the first time life had imitated art, but something bothered him; something that didn't fit the *War of the Worlds* scenario—namely, where were all the flying orb aliens? Why weren't they littering the streets, shriveled up like old raisins? If something inherent to our planet—whether natural disease or man-made pollution—had caused the death of the monster 'Vaders, wouldn't the orbs have been just as susceptible? Wouldn't there now be thousands of the things laying around? What had happened to them? Had they, as the professor had suggested they would, returned to outer space to seek out some planet less toxic? But . . . there was something about that scenario that bothered him, something the professor had said, but he couldn't remember it with the distraction of all the celebrating going on around him.

He pushed through the crowd coming out of the Garden like a fish swimming against the current. Every person he passed, every face he looked at, was imprinted with the stamp of dazed joy and happiness. People were sobbing with relief while others were whooping and hollering as loud as they could. Seeing the joyful people filing through the maze of cars in the street and climbing over them, Joe wanted to slough off his suspicions and share in those feelings, too. He mentally kicked himself for being such a pessimist. Whatever had happened to the orbs, the invasion was *over*! The nightmare 'Vaders were dead and gone! He tried to tell himself he would share in the celebration when he saw Sara and Corey again. With that thought, he saw how much they had come to mean to him. They had become family. With that realization came another revelation—one that made him smile and feel something of the elation and wonder he saw expressed by others.

He stopped.

Could what he was thinking—what he was *feeling*—really be true?

"I'm in love with her," he said quietly. *I'm in love with Sara!*

It had been a long time since he had felt like this—five years. Then, he had been engaged only to have it end when he tried to convince his fiancée, Gwen, to live in New York City after the wedding so that he could pursue his acting career. It had taken him a long time to get over Gwen and convince himself that he had made the right decision. If he had stayed with her in Portsmouth, New Hampshire, and gone to work in her father's real estate office, he would have regretted it for the rest of his life. And . . . he never would have met Sara.

His amorous suspicions were proven true—the final litmus test—when the last of the crowd had left the Garden and he laid eyes on Sara coming out with her arms around Corey's shoulders, and a tall, older black man with them. His heart beat faster, and he felt a jolt of adrenaline flood his system.

As soon as she and Corey saw him, they ran to him, nearly tripping in their haste. Sara reached him first and threw herself into his arms. He caught her and their lips met. Their mouths disengaged only when Corey tugged on Joe's shorts. He and Sara let Corey into their embrace.

"Is it really over?" Sara whispered, tears of joy running down her face.

Corey's cheeks were wet with similar tears and he nodded, looking to Joe for confirmation.

"I hope so," he said, and hugged them both again, tighter.

"I want you to meet someone," Sara said, and turned to the gray-haired black man. "This is Robert Jefferson. He saved our lives in there."

"Thanks," Joe said, and started to shake his hand, then embraced him.

"Oh, Joe," Sara said tearfully, "you wouldn't believe what they were going to do to people in there. They killed the losers of the first lottery and were going to start using them as meat to feed the rest of the people. I saw the professor's body in a meat locker! We've got to tell someone. We've got to expose the guy, Fred Roux, who was responsible it."

"Having met Roux, I'm not surprised to hear that," Joe said. "Don't worry, we'll go to the police or the papers, *somebody*, as soon as we can and make sure he doesn't get away with it."

A chorus of cheers from the street drew their attention. The four of them turned to see the mass of people who had spread throughout the maze of cars. They were staring across the street at a crowd gathered around a dead 'Vader lying amid rubble halfway up the stairs of the damaged U.S. Post Office. A bare-chested man stood atop the beast's bloated stomach, wielding a two-foot length of pipe. Urged on by cheers from the crowd, the man swung the pipe repeatedly, delivering blow after blow to the giant cadaver. The more the man hit the dead 'Vader the louder the cheers became and the larger the crowd grew.

As Joe watched, his arms around Sara and Corey and Robert close by, he finally remembered what Professor Ligget had said that still bothered him. The professor thought the monster 'Vaders were like caterpillars and might just be a stage of development; when they had eaten their fill, they would cocoon and perhaps gestate more *orbs* inside them.

"A *stage* of development," Joe whispered with a growing sense of horror. He looked at the dead 'Vader the man was wailing on with a pipe. "Come on," he said to Sara, Corey, and Robert. "I think we should go back inside." He led them quickly back toward the Garden entrance.

Puzzled, Sara didn't like the look of renewed fear she saw on Joe's face. "What is it?" she asked. The loudest cheer yet from the crowd drew their attention before Joe could answer.

A crack had appeared in the side of the bloated 'Vader's chest and a gush of slimy green fluid now poured out. The crowd cheered deliriously as several more lesions appeared. The cheering stopped suddenly when a long, pointed black rod suddenly sprouted from the crack beneath the bare-chested man and stabbed into his midsection.

The sudden, horrified, stunned silence of the crowd was absolute.

The man dropped the metal pipe and looked at the people as if he'd just realized he had been made the butt of a cruel joke. A loud buzzing and liquid sound followed. The man's body bulged and inflated like a balloon filling with helium. Just as fast as he inflated, though, he deflated as the liquid, buzzing noise became a *sucking* sound. As though his entire insides had been turned from solids to fluids and were now being sucked out of him through the black, strawlike rod, the man began to shrink. His skin became looser and looser; his stature shrunk smaller and smaller until all that was left of him was a pile of skin that quickly began to bubble and dissolve.

More cracks and lesions appeared in the dead 'Vader. To everyone's horror, the head of a giant insect—as large as a man's—the nose of which was the pointed black rod like a mosquito's feeding proboscis, emerged from the first crack in the dead 'Vader. Using its swordlike organ, it sucked up the bubbling soupy remains of the bare-chested man's skin. From the other cracks in the bloated alien cadaver, similar large insect heads, followed by bodies as large as Saint Bernards yet more akin to tarantulas than mosquitoes, poked through. Once free of the cocoon that had been feeding their developing bodies on human flesh and blood, the insects stretched their legs and began to vibrate. As they did, wings unfolded from their slick black bodies. Within seconds, they were airborne and began to attack.

The shocked and silent crowd suddenly erupted into screams and frantic motion as people tried to flee the new terror.

Joe, Sara, Corey, and Robert stood frozen by the spectacle. Joe counted at least six flying spiders that had emerged from the 'Vader's body. Everywhere he looked, wherever dead 'Vaders lay, the phenomenon was being repeated. Each alien monster's bloated corpse was splitting open. From each body cavity crawled between three and six giant flying spiders.

The air soon filled with a droning buzz as the arachnoids set upon the crowd of recently jubilant humans who thought they had been delivered from death only to find they had been delivered into it. Hundreds were trapped in the maze of cars that became a killing and feeding ground for the monstrous flying spiders.

Joe picked up Corey and grabbed Sara's hand. Together, they and Robert were among the first and few to head back to the safety of the Garden.

5:45 a.m.

"What are we going to do?" Sara sobbed as soon as they were inside. She was trembling and quickly approaching hysteria. Clinging to her right leg, Corey had the dazed look of a person in shock.

"What are we going to do?" Sara repeated, unleashing the words in a scream at Joe and Robert.

The two men looked at each other, saw the terror in each other's eyes, but had no immediate answer.

Outside, the killing and feeding frenzy continued. The crowd of people closest to the Garden doors had made an about-face and rushed to get back inside, but there were too many. The ones in the back of those closest to the doors surged forward before anyone in the front could pull open a door. They were pressed against the doors and crushed. Joe could see terror and pain on the faces pressed against the glass as slowly and steadily their lives were crushed.

"Come on!" Joe commanded, partly to get Sara and Corey away from the horrible scenes of people being crushed to death, and partly because he had an idea that was quickly blossoming into a plan.

"Get on my shoulders, Corey," Joe said, and lifted the boy into a sitting position on his shoulders. "Let's go!" he shouted, and started off into the Garden.

The small number of people who had retreated back inside, or who hadn't been able to get out before the flying spiders hatched, were all headed back to the safety of the basketball arena. When Joe turned off to the right and away from the arena, Robert asked where he was going.

"To Roux's office," Joe explained.

6:00 a.m.

At dawn, thinking Joe had been killed by the aliens, Fred Roux secretly had been making his final preparations for leaving. With no Humvee, he knew he'd have the best chance going alone, taking the bag of guns and ammo Joe had brought. Despite his threat to Joe, he wasn't about to waste his time, or risk his life, killing the girl and the others. He had known it was time to get out—now or never.

Fifteen minutes later, when the word had come over the radio from his second in command, Frank, that the giant man-eating aliens were all dead and the invasion was over, Roux had been staggered by the news. Suddenly all the terrible things he had done and planned to do in order to stay alive weighed heavily on him. In his mind's eye, he saw nothing but disgrace and humiliation ahead. With the invasion over and the aliens dead, he knew he would now have to pay the piper. It didn't matter that he hadn't acted alone; *he* had ordered the murder of innocent people and had planned the processing of their remains into food for the rest of the innocent people who had been living in the Garden.

His face had paled at the realization and a sharp pain shot through his chest, leaving him breathless. A moment later, a searing explosion of pain in the left side of his head knocked him off his feet. He had fallen against his desk, tried to grab it, but couldn't and slid to the floor. When he came to, Roux immediately knew something was wrong. He couldn't focus and couldn't think straight. He couldn't move his left arm, and the entire left side of his head and face felt numb. His head pounded with an excruciating migraine. He tried to get up and couldn't, flopping helplessly on the floor.

6:05 a.m.

With Corey still on his shoulders, Joe led Sara and Robert to the Director of Garden Security's office door.

"I've got to put you down now," Joe told Corey, and set him on his feet.

Sara immediately took Corey's hand and put a protective arm around his shoulders.

"What are we doing here?" Robert asked.

"Roux's got something we need," Joe said, and opened the door. He was surprised, but not sorry, to see Fred Roux incapacitated on the floor next to his desk. Joe crossed the room quickly to where Roux lay, ready to hurt the man until he stood over the director and saw the left side of his face.

From his eye to his mouth, his face was hanging slack as if it were melting from his skull.

Joe immediately recognized it as a stroke; when he was twelve, he had seen his Uncle Dave have one and had never forgotten the way half his uncle's face had sagged, just like Roux's did now.

"Hel . . . hel . . . m . . . m . . . meee," Roux slurred, pleading.

All the anger and desire for revenge Joe had felt toward the man suddenly drained away when he saw Roux's pitiful condition and realized nothing he could do to the man would be more punishing than what he was suffering now. Death was too good for the likes of him.

Next to Joe, Robert stood over Roux, a look of rage upon his face. "We should kill this bastard. He was the head of the Survival Council. He was responsible for murder and was planning to turn unsuspecting people into cannibals."

"No," Joe said. "Look at him. He's finished. I doubt he'll live more than a few hours. We've got more important things to do."

Behind Roux's desk, next to a duffel bag stuffed with canned and packaged nonperishable food, sat the leather valise holding the flashlight, the weapons, and the explosives Joe had brought in with him at their initial arrival.

"Grab the food," Joe instructed Sara, and took the two micro Uzis from the bag and handed one to Robert. "Do you think you can use this?"

Robert nodded and asked, "Is it loaded?"

"Yeah, here." Joe took two narrow magazines from the valise and handed them to Robert, who stuffed them in his pockets.

"We're not going outside, are we?" Sara asked, her voice shaking with fear. Corey looked terrified at the prospect.

"No," Joe said. "I've got another idea."

As Joe spoke, Robert stepped to the large window behind Roux's desk and pulled the curtains open. "Holy shit," he exclaimed.

Joe went over to him, followed by Sara and Corey.

"Fuck," was all Joe could say.

"They're inside!" Sara said as her voice rose in pitch and volume. "They're inside! They're going to get us!" she cried, her voice becoming shrill with panic.

Corey screamed and started crying loudly.

Joe grabbed Sara's shoulders and shook her. "They're not going to get us, Sara! They're not. I've got a plan to get us out of here." He pulled Sara close and wrapped his arms around her. "Trust me," he said softly. "I need you to trust me, and I need you to be strong. Don't flip out on me now. I need you. Corey needs you."

Sara sobbed into his chest and nodded her head against him.

Joe looked over her head and through the observation window that overlooked the basketball court and arena. The place was thick with the 'Vaders' new form of insect-like predators. The people who had not yet made it out of the Garden, and those who had returned to what they had thought was the safety of the arena, were now being preyed upon by the flying spiders.

It was a massacre and feeding frenzy.

But, Joe wondered, how the hell did those things get inside?

6:12 a.m.

With an extreme effort of will, Sara pulled herself together and stepped back from Joe. She avoided looking at the arena and knelt in front of Corey. She embraced him and whispered in his ear, telling him everything was going to be okay.

"We've got to trust Joe," she said, pulling back from him to look into his eyes. "Joe won't let anything happen to us, right? You know that, right? He's kept us safe so far and he'll keep on keeping us safe."

Corey stopped crying and nodded. He looked up at Joe who winked and smiled at him. Corey managed a wink but could not summon a smile.

"Okay," Joe said. "Sara, can you carry the food?" he asked, picking up Roux's bag of dried and canned goods.

Sara nodded and took the duffel bag. She slung it over her head and shoulders so that the strap crossed her chest and she could keep her hands free.

"Here," Joe said, and pulled the snub-nosed revolver Murphy had given her from the professor's leather briefcase.

Sara took it in her trembling hands, doubtful it would be much good against those horrid flying spiders.

"Let's go," Joe said. With the weapons bag in one hand and the Uzi in the other, he started for the door, followed by Sara carrying the gun in her right hand and holding Corey's hand with her left.

Robert stayed behind at the observation window until the others were leaving Roux's office. He slid the window all the way open and went over to Roux, who was still lying on the floor and mumbling incoherently. Robert slapped his face a couple of times until the director of security's good right eye focused on the former custodian.

"You're going to have some visitors soon," Robert told him, and smiled viciously. "Some really *nasty* visitors," he added, and stood. Robert quickly went to the door. As he stepped into the corridor, he heard a loud buzzing and looked back to see one of the flying spiders come through the window and light on Roux's body. As Robert closed the door, Roux gave out a weak scream that was immediately drowned out by the sound of buzzing and a loud sucking noise.

"What did you do?" Joe asked as Robert joined them in the hallway.

"Just making sure old Fred doesn't get lonely," Robert said, and smiled.

Joe nodded with grim understanding.

"What's the quickest and safest way to get down to Penn Station?" Joe asked Robert.

"The freight elevator," Robert said immediately. "This way."

6:21 a.m.

Corey held tightly on to Sara's hand as the freight elevator descended to Penn Central railroad station beneath Madison Square Garden. Though he hadn't been tall enough to look out the window in Fred Roux's office, he had been able to figure out what was happening in the arena: the flying spiders were in the building.

Corey wanted to cry again—could feel the sobs pushing up from his chest into his throat—but he swallowed, determined to act like Joe and be brave. But it was so hard.

He was more afraid now than ever. He couldn't believe that minutes ago he had been so happy. Like all the other survivors, Corey had thought the 'Vaders were dying, or dead, and the nightmare was over. But his joy spiraled into despair and fear again.

It wasn't fair.

He wanted to scream, "It's not fair!" so loud God Himself would hear him.

The elevator stopped. A bell rang. The doors slid open.

6:24 a.m.

"Stay here for a minute," Joe whispered to the others before stepping out of the elevator.

The rotunda of Penn Station, where passengers waited for and boarded trains, was well lit. He looked around, eyeing the gift shop, the ticket and baggage-check counters, and the Penn Tavern & Grill, and saw no one. He returned to the elevator.

"Okay," he said softly. "It looks clear down here, but let's keep quiet just in case."

Sara, Corey, and Robert nodded.

"We're going to do like Murphy said and get out of the city through one of the train tunnels. I'm not sure it will take us all the way out of the city before the tracks go above-ground, but I think it will take us pretty far safely."

Sara and Corey looked terrified.

"I'm sorry, guys," Joe said in response to their fear. "It's our best chance."

Sara bit her lip and nodded. Corey tried to hold back his frightened tears.

"Okay, let's go," Joe said, and led them out of the elevator into the empty rotunda.

"The northbound tracks to New England are on the right," Robert said. "I think they run underground the farthest."

Joe nodded and started for the boarding gate. Sara and Corey followed.

"Wait a second," Robert said, and ran into the Penn Tavern & Grill. He came out a minute later with two bottles of Jack Daniel's and a six-pack of mineral water. "Can you fit these in one of those bags?" he asked, holding up the bottles and grinning.

Joe grinned back. He stepped behind Sara and opened the duffel bag while it was still on her back. "Is this going to be too heavy?" he asked her after he'd put the bottles inside. She shook her head. Joe opened the weapons bag and took out the emergency flashlight before continuing down the loading ramp.

"It's going to be very dark in the tunnel," he said. "We've got to keep together. I'll lead with the flashlight." He turned the emergency lantern on and played its bright beam down the boarding ramp past the gate.

"Let's go."

6:30 a.m.

The darkness of the tunnel was more than they had expected, which made the going slow. Despite the round circle of light preceding them, Sara felt as though she were walking blind. Looking away from the flashlight beam into the surrounding darkness was like having her eyes up against a black wall. The darkness was so complete it appeared solid and without depth. When she looked back at the light, the darkness seemed to rush in around her as though alive and reaching for her.

She held Corey's hand and knew from his tight grip that the poor kid was just as frightened as she; probably more so. She wanted to reassure him with words, but found herself afraid to speak in the darkness—afraid of what might be lurking within earshot. She hoped her eyes would adjust, but the farther they went, the less it seemed she could see. She knew it was from looking at the light, but she couldn't bring herself to look away.

Suddenly, Joe stopped and turned the flashlight on Corey, Robert, and Sara.

"Shhh," he whispered. "Let me go ahead and check things out."

6:36 a.m.

Joe had seen something at the edge of the light that had made his entire body break out in a cold fear sweat. Just ahead lay a dead, bloated, and cracked-open body of a small monster 'Vader.

Now it was apparent how the flying spiders had gotten inside the Garden—the 'Vaders had been in the train tunnels below all along. As if that weren't bad enough, he could see something else, farther on—

Glowing lights!

Joe quickly pulled the light-beam off the 'Vader cadaver before Sara and Corey could see it. He walked forward to investigate the glow ahead. Suddenly, he heard a buzzing sound getting rapidly louder. Before he could react, one of the flying spiders flew past, paying him and his companions no mind as it continued on into the tunnel.

"It didn't see us," he heard Sara exclaim with relief.

It was a relief he didn't share—it was obvious to him now why Roux, or anyone else at the Garden, hadn't used the Penn Station train tunnels to escape the city.

Joe shut off the flashlight and looked ahead. Definitely, glowing lights were farther on in the tunnel. Like a moth to a flame, the flying spider was drawn to them. Instinct told Joe to turn back, but he didn't. A knot of apprehension formed in his chest.

The tunnel ahead was lit enough by the soft-glowing lights that Joe was soon able to see the tracks and the cement walls and ceiling of the tunnel. He turned off the flashlight.

He could see the silhouette of the flying spider crawling over the lights, which were made up of many smaller, *round* glowing lights.

A few feet later, he saw the source of the lights and couldn't believe his eyes.

6:42 a.m.

The palm of Sara's hand holding Corey's was clammy from fear. Hearing the buzzing of the huge flying spider coming toward them in the darkness had filled her with a terror so strong it threatened to push her over the edge of sanity. The only thing keeping her mind grounded and her body from fleeing as she screamed with insanity was Corey's small, sweaty hand in hers.

When the 'Vader insect flew by, paying no attention to her and the others, she had felt an elation that was as powerful as her terror had just been. Within the next few minutes, though, the terror returned stronger than before. It brought back the specter of madness trying to invade her mind again. Pulling Corey close to her, she ran with him to catch up to Joe.

He heard them coming and tried to prevent them from seeing what lay ahead in the train tunnel, but it was too late.

6:44 a.m.

Corey felt Sara's hand tighten on his so strong his fingers hurt, but he didn't cry out.

What he saw in the tunnel ahead stole his voice.

The glowing light, which he could perceive now was actually many smaller glowing lights, was the first thing that drew his attention. The lights appeared to be inside something, like a light seen through an almost transparent lampshade. The flying spider was crawling over the thing with the lights inside.

Slowly, that thing was revealed in the soft glow.

Huge and spread across half the width of the tunnel, its feet sat on the tracks and its head and shoulders rested against the tunnel wall. The anomaly was human in shape, a

woman—twice the size of a normal woman—but not deformed like the monster 'Vaders. Its legs and arms were
stubby atrophied appendages sticking out of the woman's
massive, bulging stomach. Inside her stomach could be seen
numerous globes of light.

"They're orbs," Corey said out loud without thinking.
"She's full of the flying 'Vader orbs!"

The flying spider crawled over the stomach like a fly on a
watermelon. Reaching the woman's face, it turned and placed
its own swollen, wasplike abdomen up to the woman's mouth
and she began to drink from it.

Corey saw the woman's face and pissed his pants.

6:48 a.m.

As Sara looked at the bloated carcass that had once been
a woman, but was now filled with glowing orbs, she wanted
to scream, but she shoved her fist into her mouth and bit
down hard on her knuckles to keep silent.

As horror took her breath away, she saw two more glowing bodies just a little farther down the tracks. The second
one was Donna Volk. Beyond her, the line of bloated pregnant women filled with glowing 'Vaders stretched out of
sight into the darkness of the tunnel.

6:49 a.m.

"Sara, take Corey and get out of here. Now!" Joe commanded.

Sara didn't move. She and Corey stood staring at the
monstrosities lying on the tracks ahead. Joe shook Sara and
forced her to look at him.

"Sara! Get Corey out of here, *now*!"

Sara obeyed but moved stiffly, like someone in shock and
dazed by a catastrophe.

"Help them," Joe whispered to Robert, who was staring
as wide-eyed and full of fear as Sara and Corey.

"What are they?" Robert mumbled.

"They're queens," Joe said, and took the weapons bag
from Robert. "The professor was right about them being like

insects but was wrong about this," Joe mumbled to himself. "*This* is why they wanted pregnant women."

He looked up from the bag. Corey and Sara were slowly walking backward, unable to pull their eyes away or turn and run from the scene in front of them.

"Get them the hell out of here!" Joe said as loudly as he dared. He handed Robert the flashlight.

Robert nodded and passed a hand over his eyes. He turned away. "We've got to get out of here," Robert whispered to Sara and Corey, and got them turned around.

The sound of buzzing came again and grew louder by the second. Another flying spider came buzzing through the tunnel with a swollen abdomen full of liquefied human to feed the queens.

Robert didn't have to urge Sara and Corey to run.

With the others running back the way they'd come, Joe went to work by the light of the closest glowing queen. Seeing the queens had reminded Joe of something else he knew about hive insects—they always try to protect their queens. Now, remembering what Murphy had taught him about priming the C4 explosives for remote detonation, he removed the cap and cord from the bag. He wrapped the primer cord around the claylike blocks of plastic explosive and stuck a detonator cap into it. He set the blocks against the tunnel wall as close to the queen as possible, then took the remote electrical detonator transmitter, the flare gun, a cartridge, and a grenade from the weapons bag. He followed the others, leaving the bag with the grenades still in it next to the explosives.

Joe stopped halfway to the bottom of the boarding ramp and crouched against the wall. He loaded the flare gun and, taking careful aim at the closest queen's swollen belly, fired.

7:00 a.m.

Sara looked at the blood-smeared doors of the 8th Avenue entrance to Madison Square Garden and didn't know how she had arrived there. The last thing she remembered was total darkness and hearing Joe say, "They're queens." She couldn't remember what he meant by that and had a strong feeling that she didn't *want* to remember.

She heard a faint bang that she thought came from outside and looked out the Garden doors. Suddenly, all the flying spiders outside that had been slaughtering and feeding on the multitudes were flying directly toward her.

"Look out!" Robert shouted. As hard as he could, he shoved Sara and Corey out of the way. A second later, the first wave of the approaching flying 'Vader insects sacrificed themselves and crashed through the glass doors. They fell, cut and bleeding, to the mezzanine floor.

They did not die in vain.

Behind them, the great swarm of freshly hatched flying spiders poured en masse through the smashed doors.

Sara, Corey, and even Robert screamed at the sight of them, but their screams were drowned out by the giant insects' ferocious buzzing.

7:01 a.m.

Joe looked at the flare burning brightly where he had shot it into the first queen's bloated stomach. It had stuck there. Screams of pain came from her still-human mouth, but they were the most inhuman sounds Joe had ever heard.

He pulled the pin on the grenade and tossed it over the first queen, toward the ones farther on, killing the queen that had been Donna Volk. Immediately following its explosion, which brought pieces of the ceiling and walls falling onto the other queens, Joe heard the crash of the doors and the approach of the angry swarm from above and from farther down in the tunnel. He ran as fast as he could and dove into the shadows below the loading platform. A moment later, he felt the wind from the hundreds, maybe thousands, of winged monsters that flew over him down the boarding ramp. He saw flying spiders winging through the tunnel behind him and from the opposite direction as well. Eager to save their queens, they were coming by all ways possible.

When the swarm thinned, Joe took his chance and ran up the boarding ramp, the micro Uzi in both hands, up and ready to fire. As he reached the rotunda, two flying spiders confronted him and attacked. He was happy to shoot them to pieces with the rapid-fire micro Uzi. He ran for the nearest exit and up the unmoving escalator.

7:07 a.m.

Sara looked around, dazed, and suddenly Joe was by her side. She smiled up at him.

"You okay?" he asked, looking at her strangely. She nodded vaguely.

"Corey, are you okay?" Joe asked the boy whose hand was still clasped in hers.

Corey just stared at the floor.

"He's fine," Sara said, and wondered who was talking. The voice sounded far away and strange, yet close and familiar at the same time.

"We're going to make a run for the Humvee now," Joe said.

"Fine," Sara replied, smiling vacantly as if Joe had said they were going for a stroll.

7:11 a.m.

The sidewalk leading to the Garden entrance was awash with blood and bubbling puddles of goo that had the color of human flesh. All the people who had been clamoring to get back into the Garden, and those who had been crushed against the doors, were gone. In the maze of cars, the survivors of the flying spider attacks took advantage of the reprieve and scattered in every direction, clambering out from under and inside the stalled vehicles and looking for safer places to hide like children in a deadly game of Olly Olly Oxen Free.

Corey ran along side Sara, his hand in hers, but couldn't feel his legs. He stared at the death and destruction through eyes numbed by shock. He watched Joe lead him and Sara and Robert into the maze of cars on 8th Avenue.

He thought nothing.

Even when Joe stopped running and pressed the button on a little box with an antenna that he pointed back at the

Garden and there was a muffled explosion that made the road vibrate beneath his feet, Corey's mind was empty and his emotions blank.

As they ran the rest of the way through the maze of cars, Corey put his head down and stared at the ground. He held on to Sara's hand and let her lead him. All around him, Corey could hear explosions and feel them in his feet. Parts of the streets themselves suddenly heaved up from explosions beneath them. A manhole cover not blocked by a stalled car flew into the air like a UFO. After what seemed like a week to Corey, Joe was lifting him and putting him in the big car with the machine gun on it that he had ridden in before.

He heard Joe say to Robert, "The explosives must have ruptured a gas line!" And, "You drive, I'll man the machine gun!"

Then Joe was leaning over him, saying, "It's going to be okay, Corey," but the words made no sense. "We're going to get out of the city now and find someplace safe. Are you okay, buddy? Huh?"

Corey looked at him and blinked. A large tear ran down his face.

"That was my mom," he said.

He saw Joe's face pale and heard him say, "Oh, my God," and that was the last thing Corey heard or saw for a long time. He pulled his legs up and curled into a fetal position on the backseat of the big car. He put his thumb in his mouth and closed his eyes.